Praise for *John Dies at the End*

"Sure to please the *Fangoria* set while appealing to a wider audience, the book's smart take on fear manages to tap into readers' existential dread on one page, then have them laughing the next."   —*Publishers Weekly*

"It is funny, sure, but it also contains more creep-out value than Stephen King."   —*The Daily Telegraph* (Australia)

"Reads as if Bill Murray's world-weary Ghostbuster and sassy Buffy the Vampire Slayer spawned a slacker child—like *Clerks* with monsters. . . . Surprising, disturbing, and inventive."   —*Herald Sun* (Australia)

"Strikes enough of a balance between hilarity, horror, and surrealism here to keep anyone glued to the story."   —*Booklist*

"You can (and will want to) read *John Dies at the End* in one sitting."
                                                            —*BookReporter.com*

"Wong blends horror and suspense with comedy—a tricky combination—and pulls it off effortlessly."   —*FashionAddict.com*

"It's interesting, compelling, engaging, arresting, and—yes—sometimes even horrifying. And when it's not being any of those things, it's funny. Very, very funny."   —*January Magazine*

"This is one of the most entertaining and addictive novels I've ever read."
                                    —Jacob Kier, publisher, Permuted Press

"A loopy buddy movie of a book with deadpan humor and great turns of phrase. . . . Just plain fun."   —*Library Journal*

"*John Dies at the End* is like an H. P. Lovecraft tale if Lovecraft were into poop and fart jokes."   —*Fangoria*

JOHN DIES AT THE END

DAVID WONG

Thomas Dunne Books ✿ New York St. Martin's Griffin

This is a work of fiction. All of the characters, organizations, and events portrayed in this novel are either products of the author's imagination or are used fictitiously.

THOMAS DUNNE BOOKS.
An imprint of St. Martin's Press.

www.thomasdunnebooks.com
www.stmartins.com

Book design by Rich Arnold

The Library of Congress has cataloged the hardcover edition as follows:

Wong, David, 1975–
    John dies at the end / David Wong. — 1st ed.
        p. cm.
    ISBN 978-0-312-55513-9
    1. Friends—Fiction.   I. Title.
    PS3623.O5975J64 2009
    813'.6—dc22
                                    2009016944

ISBN 978-0-312-65914-1 (trade paperback)

10 9 8

For my wife, who has been so tolerant and wonderful through all of this that I think she might be a product of my imagination. Also, my best friend, Mack Leighty, who gave birth to the "John" mentioned in the title, and who years ago convinced me to get into writing as a hobby instead of alcoholism.

Mack, I'll never forget that when things got really tough in my life, you stepped up and killed those dudes for me.

Prologue

SOLVING THE FOLLOWING riddle will reveal the awful secret behind the universe, assuming you do not go utterly mad in the attempt. If you already happen to know the awful secret behind the universe, feel free to skip ahead.

Let's say you have an ax. Just a cheap one, from Home Depot. On one bitter winter day, you use said ax to behead a man. Don't worry, the man was already dead. Or maybe you should worry, because you're the one who shot him.

He had been a big, twitchy guy with veiny skin stretched over swollen biceps, a tattoo of a swastika on his tongue. Teeth filed into razor-sharp fangs—you know the type. And you're chopping off his head because, even with eight bullet holes in him, you're pretty sure he's about to spring back to his feet and eat the look of terror right off your face.

On the follow-through of the last swing, though, the handle of the ax snaps in a spray of splinters. You now have a broken ax. So, after a long night of looking for a place to dump the man and his head, you take a trip into town with your ax. You go to the hardware store, explaining away the dark reddish stains on the broken handle as barbecue sauce. You walk out with a brand-new handle for your ax.

The repaired ax sits undisturbed in your garage until the spring when, on one rainy morning, you find in your kitchen a creature that appears to be a foot-long slug with a bulging egg sac on its tail. Its jaws bite one of your forks in half with what seems like very little effort. You grab your trusty ax and chop the thing into several pieces. On the last blow, however, the ax strikes a metal leg of the overturned kitchen table and chips out a notch right in the middle of the blade.

Of course, a chipped head means yet another trip to the hardware store. They sell you a brand-new head for your ax. As soon as you get home, you meet the reanimated body of the guy you beheaded earlier. He's also got a new head, stitched on with what looks like plastic weed-trimmer line, and it's wearing that unique expression of "you're the man who killed me last winter" resentment that one so rarely encounters in everyday life.

You brandish your ax. The guy takes a long look at the weapon with his squishy, rotting eyes and in a gargly voice he screams, "That's the same ax that beheaded me!"

IS HE RIGHT?

I WAS PONDERING that riddle as I reclined on my porch at 3:00 A.M., a chilled breeze numbing my cheeks and earlobes and flicking tickly hairs across my forehead. I had my feet up on the railing, leaning back in one of those cheap plastic lawn chairs, the kind that blow out onto the lawn during every thunderstorm. It would have been a good occasion to smoke a pipe had I owned one and had I been forty years older. It was one of those rare moments of mental peace I get these days, the kind you don't appreciate until they're ov—

My cell phone screeched, the sound like a sonic bee sting. I dug the slim little phone from my jacket pocket, glanced at the number and felt a sickening little twinge of fear. I disconnected the call without answering.

The world was silent again, save for the faint applause of trees rustling in the wind and crumbly dead leaves scraping lightly down the pavement. That, and the scuffle of a mentally challenged dog trying to climb onto the chair next to me. After two attempts to mount the thing, Molly managed to send the chair clattering onto its side. She stared at the toppled chair for several seconds and then started barking at it.

The phone again. Molly growled at the chair. I closed my eyes, said an angry five-word prayer and answered the call.

"Hello?"

"Dave? This is John. Your pimp says bring the heroin shipment tonight, or he'll be forced to stick you. Meet him where we buried the Korean whore. The one without the goatee."

That was code. It meant "Come to my place as soon as you can, it's important." Code, you know, in case the phone was bugged.

"John, it's three in the—"

"Oh, and don't forget, tomorrow is the day we kill the president."

Click.

He was gone. That last part was code for, "Stop and pick me up some cigarettes on the way."

Actually, the phone probably *was* bugged, but I was confident the people doing it could just as easily do some kind of remote intercept of our brain waves if they wanted, so it was moot. Two minutes and one very long sigh later, I was humming through the night in my truck, waiting for the heater to blow warm air and trying not to think of

3

Frank Campo. I clicked on the radio, hoping to keep the fear at bay via distraction. I got a local right-wing talk radio program.

"I'm here to tell ya, immigration, it's like rats on a ship. America is the ship and allllll these rats are comin' on board, y'all. And you know what happens when a ship gets too many rats on board? It sinks. That's what."

I wondered if a ship had ever really sunk that way. I wondered what was giving my truck that rotten-egg smell. I wondered if the gun was still under the driver's seat. I wondered. Was there something moving back there, in the darkness? I glanced in my rearview mirror. No, a trick of the shadows. I thought of Frank Campo.

Frank was an attorney, heading home from the office one evening in his black Lexus. The car's wax job gleaming in the night like a shell of black ice, Frank feeling weightless and invincible behind the greenish glow of his dashboard lights.

He senses a tingling on his legs. He flips on the dome light.

Spiders.

Thousands of them.

Each the size of a hand.

They're spilling over his knees, pushing up inside his pant legs. The things look like they're bred for war, jagged black bodies with yellow stripes, long spiny legs like needle points.

He freaks, cranks the wheel, flips down an embankment.

After they pried him out of the wreckage and after he stopped ranting, the cops assured him there wasn't a sign of even one spider inside the car.

If it had ended there, you could write it off as a bad night, a trick of the eyes, one of Scrooge's bad potatoes. But it didn't end there. Frank kept seeing things—awful things—and over the months all the king's doctors and all the king's pills couldn't make Frank's waking nightmares go away.

And yet, other than that, the guy was fine. Lucid. As sane as a sunset. He'd write a brilliant legal brief on Wednesday, and on Thursday he'd swear he saw tentacles writhing under the judge's robes.

So? Who do you go to in a situation like that?

I pulled up to John's building, felt the old dread coming back, churning like a sour stomach. The brisk wind chased me to the door, carrying a faint sulfur smell blown from a plant outside town that brewed drain cleaner. That and the pair of hills in the distance gave the impression of living downwind from a sleeping, farty giant.

John opened the door to his third-floor apartment and immediately gestured toward a very cute and very frightened-looking woman on his sofa. "Dave, this is Shelly. She needs our help."

Our help.

That dread, like a punch in the stomach. You see, people like Frank Campo, and this girl, they never came for "our help" when they needed a carburetor rebuilt.

We had a specialty.

Shelly was probably nineteen, with powder-blue eyes and the kind of crystal clear pale skin that gave her a china doll look, chestnut curls bundled behind her head in a ponytail. She wore a long, flowing skirt that her fingers kept messing with, an outfit that only emphasized how small she was. She had the kind of self-conscious, pleading helplessness some guys go crazy for. Girl in distress. Makes you want to rescue her, take her home, curl up with her, tell her everything is gonna be okay.

She had a white bandage on her temple.

John stepped into the corner of his tiny apartment that served as the kitchen and smoothly returned to place a cup of coffee in her hands. I struggled to keep my eyes from rolling; John's almost therapist-like professionalism was ridiculous in a room dominated by a huge plasmascreen TV with four video game systems wired to it. John had his hair pulled back into a neat job-interview ponytail and was wearing a button-up shirt. He could look like a grown-up from time to time.

I was about to warn the girl about John's coffee, which tasted like a cup of battery acid someone had pissed in and then cursed at for several hours, but John turned to her and in a lawyerly voice said, "Shelly, tell us your story."

She raised timid eyes to me. "It's my boyfriend. He . . . he won't leave me alone. He's been harassing me for about a week. My parents are gone, on vacation and I'm . . . I'm terrified to go home."

She shook her head, apparently out of words. She sipped the coffee, then grimaced as if it had bit her.

"Miss—"

"Morris," she said, barely audible.

"Ms. Morris, I strongly recommend a women's shelter. They can help you get a restraining order, keep you safe, whatever. There are three in this city, and I'll be happy to make the call—"

"He—my boyfriend, I mean—he's been dead for two months."

John cast a little gleeful glance my way, as if to say, "See how I deliver for you, Dave?" I hated that look. She went on.

"I—I didn't know where else to go. I heard, you know, through a friend of mine that you handle, um, unusual problems." She nudged aside a stack of DVD cases on an end table and sat the mug down, glancing at it distrustfully as if to remind herself not to accidentally drink from it again, lest it betray her anew. She turned back to me.

"They say you're the best."

I didn't inform her that whoever called us "the best" had pretty low standards. I guess we were the best in town at this, but who would you brag to about that? It's not like this shit has its own section of the phone book.

I walked over to a cushioned chair and scooped out its contents (four worn guitar magazines, a sketch pad, and a leather-bound King James Version of the Holy Bible). As I tried to settle in, a leg broke off and the whole chair slumped over at a thirty-degree angle. I leaned over nonchalantly, trying to look like that's exactly what I had expected to happen.

"Okay. When he comes, you can see him?"

"Yes. I can hear him, too. And he, uh . . ."

She brushed the bandage on the side of her skull. I looked at her in bewilderment. Was she serious?

"He hits you?"

"Yes."

"With his fist?"

"Yes."

John looked up from his coffee indignantly. "Man, what a dick!"

I did roll my eyes this time and glared at John once they stopped. I don't know if you've ever seen a ghost, but I'm guessing that if you did, the thing didn't run over and punch you in the face. I'm guessing that's never happened to any of your friends, either.

"When it first happened," Shelly said, "I thought I was going crazy. Up until now, I've never bel—"

"Believed in ghosts," I finished. "Right." That line was obligatory, everybody wanting to come off as the credible skeptic. "Look, Miss, I don't want to—"

"I told her we would look into it tonight," John said, heading me off before I accidentally introduced some rational thought into this thing. "He's haunting her house, out in [town name removed for privacy]. I thought you and I could head over there, get out of the city for a night, show this bastard what's what."

I felt a burst of irritation, mostly because John knew the story was bullshit. But then it suddenly clicked in my mind that, yes, John knew, and he had called me because he was trying to set me up with this girl. Button-cute, dead boyfriend, chance to be her hero. As usual, I didn't know whether to thank him or punch him in the balls.

Sixteen different objections rose up in my mind at once and somehow they all canceled each other out. Maybe if there had been an odd number . . .

WE HEADED OUT, in my Bronco. We had told Shelly not to drive herself, in case she had a concussion, but the reality was that, whether or not her story was true, we still had vivid memories of Mr. Campo and his unusually spidery car. You see, Frank found out the hard way that the dark things lurking in the night don't haunt old houses or abandoned ships. They haunt *minds*.

7

Shelly was in the passenger seat, hugging herself, looking blankly out the windshield. She said, "So, do you guys, like, do this a lot?"

"Off and on," said John. "Been doing it for a few years."

"How does somebody get into this?"

"There was an incident," he said. "A series of incidents, I guess. A dead guy, another dead guy. Some drugs. It's kind of a long story. Now we can see things. Sometimes. I have a dead cat that follows me around, wondering why I never feed it. Oh, and I had one hamburger that started mooing when I ate it." He glanced at me. "You remember that?"

I grunted, said nothing.

It wasn't mooing, John. It was screaming.

Shelly didn't look like she was listening anymore.

"I call it Dante's Syndrome," John said. I had never heard him call it any such thing. "Meaning, I think Dave and I gained the ability to peer into Hell. Only it turns out Hell is right here, it's all through us and around us and in us like the microbes that swarm through your lungs and guts and veins. Hey, look! An owl!"

We all looked. It was an owl, all right.

"Anyway," I broke in, "we just did a couple of favors for people, eventually word got around."

I felt like that was enough background and I wanted to stop John before he got to the part where he says he kept eating that screaming hamburger, down to the last bite.

I left the truck running as I jumped out at my place for supplies. I bypassed the house for the weatherworn toolshed in the backyard, opened the padlocked door and swept over the dark shelves with my flashlight:

A Winnie the Pooh toy with dried blood around its eyes;

A stuffed and mounted badgerconda (a cross between a badger and an anaconda);

A large Mason jar filled with cloudy formaldehyde, where inside floated a six-inch clump of cockroaches arranged roughly in the shape of a human hand.

I grabbed a medieval-style torch John had stolen from the wall of a theme restaurant. I picked up a clear squeeze bottle filled with a thick green liquid that immediately turned bloodred as soon as I touched it. I reconsidered, sat it back on the shelf and grabbed my vintage 1987 ghetto blaster instead.

I went into the house and called to Molly. I opened a small plastic tub in the kitchen cabinet filled with little pink, rubbery chunks, like erasers. I put a handful in my pocket and rushed back out the door, the dog following on my heels.

Shelly lived in a simple two-story farmhouse, black shutters on white siding. It sat on an island of turf in a sea of harvest-flattened cornfields. We walked past a mailbox shaped like a cow and saw a hand-painted sign on the front door that read THE MORRISON'S—ESTABLISHED 1962. John and I had a long debate at the door about whether or not that apostrophe belonged there.

I know, I know. If I had a brain, I would have walked away right then.

John stepped up, pushed open the front door and ducked aside. I dug in my pocket and pulled out one of the pink chunks. They were steak-shaped dog treats, complete with little brown grill lines. I realized at that moment that no dog would know what those grill lines were and that they were purely for my benefit.

"Molly!"

I shook the treat in front of her and then tossed it through the door. The dog ran in after it.

We waited for the sound of, say, dog flesh splattering across a wall, but heard only the padding of Molly's paws. Eventually she came back to the door, grinning stupidly. We decided it was safe to go in.

Shelly opened her mouth as if to express some kind of disapproval, but apparently decided against it. We stepped into the dark living room. Shelly moved to flip on a light, but I stopped her with a hand motion.

Instead, John hefted the torch and touched his lighter to it. A foot-tall flame erupted from the head and we slowly crept through the house by its flickering light. I noticed John had brought along a thermos of his coffee, this "favor" already qualifying as an all-nighter. I admit, the horrific burning sensation really did keep you awake.

I asked, "Where do you see him, mostly?"

Shelly's fingers started twisting at her skirt again. "The basement. And once I saw him in the bathroom. His hand, it, uh, came up through the toilet while I—"

"Okay. Show us the basement door."

"It's in the kitchen, but I—guys, I don't wanna go down there."

"It's cool," John said. "Stay here with the dog, we'll go down and check it out."

I glanced at John, figuring that should have been *my* line as her handsome new knightly protector. We clomped down the stairs, torchlight pooling down the stairwell. Shelly waited behind us, crouching next to Molly and stroking her back.

A nice, modern basement.

Washer and dryer.

A hot-water heater making a soft ticking sound.

One of those waist-deep floor freezers.

John said, "He's not here."

"Big surprise."

John used the torch to light a cigarette.

"She seems like a nice girl, doesn't she?" John said softly and with a kind of smarmy wink in his voice. "You know, she reminds me of Amber. Jennifer's friend. When she came to my door, for a second I actually thought it was her. By the way, I wanna thank you for comin' along, Dave, sort of being my wingman on this. I'm not saying I'm going to take advantage of her distress or anything, but . . ."

I had tuned John out. Something was off, I knew right then. Lingering in the back of my mind, like a kid in the last row of the classroom with his hand up. John was acting all detectivey now, leaning over a large sink with a bundle of white cloth draped over the side.

"Oh, yeah," said John, pulling up a length of cloth. "Take a look at this shit." The garment was white, a single piece with straps, like an apron. Well, it *had been* white. Once. Now it was mostly smudges of faded-blood pink at the center, like a kindergarten kid's rendering of the Japanese flag.

I turned to the large floor freezer. That freaking dread again, cold and hard and heavy. I strode over and opened the lid.

"Oh, geez."

It was a tongue. That's the first thing I saw, rubbery and purplish and not quite human. It was longer, animal-like, twisted inside a zip-lock bag and coated in frost. And it wasn't alone; the freezer was filled with hunks of flesh, some in clear bags, some bigger chunks in pink-stained white paper.

Butcher paper. White apron.

"Well, I think it's obvious," said John. "Those stories of UFOs that go around mutilating cows? I think we just solved it, my friend."

I sighed.

"It's a deer, you jackass. Her dad hunts, apparently. They keep the meat."

I nudged around and found a frozen turkey, some sausages. I closed the lid to the fridge, feeling stupid, though not for the reason I should have felt stupid. I wasn't thinking. Too late at night, too little sleep.

John started poking around in cabinets. I glanced around for the boom box, realizing now that we hadn't brought it down here. Why did that bother me? It was upstairs with Shelly, right?

"Hey, Dave. You remember that guy whose basement got flooded, then called us and swore he had a fifteen-foot great white shark swim-min' down there?"

I did remember but didn't answer, afraid of losing that thread of thought that kept floating just out of reach like a wayward balloon on a windy day. Besides, when we got there, it wasn't a great white at all. Just a garden-variety eight-foot tiger shark. We told the guy to wait until the basement dried out and call us back. When the water left, so did the shark, as if it evaporated or seeped out the tiny cracks in the concrete.

Think. Damned attention span. Something is wrong here.

I tried to pull myself back from my tangent, thinking of the boom box again. John had found it at a garage sale. There's a story in the Old Testament, a young David driving away an evil spirit by playing pretty music on his harp—

Wait a second.

"John, did I hear you say you thought she looked like Amber?"

"Yeah."

"John, Amber's almost as tall as me. Blond hair, kind of top-heavy, right?"

"Yeah, cute as hell. I mean—"

"And you think Shelly looks like her? The girl sitting upstairs?"

"Yeah." John turned to face me, already getting it.

"John, Shelly is short. Short with dark hair. Blue eyes."

—They haunt minds—

John sighed, plucked out his cigarette and flung it to the floor. "Fuck."

We turned toward the stairs, took a step up, and froze. Shelly was there, sitting halfway up the stairs, one arm curled around Molly's neck. Innocent, wary eyes. Playing the part.

I stepped slowly onto the third stair, said, "Tell me something, Miss, uh, I'm sorry, I've forgotten your last name—"

"Shelly is fine."

"Yeah, remind me anyway. I hate forgetting things."

"Morris."

I took another step toward her.

"That's what I thought."

Another step. I heard John step up behind me.

"So," I said, "whose house is this?"

"What?"

"The sign out front says Morrison. Morris-son. Not Morris. Now would you describe your own appearance for me?"

"I don't—"

"You see, because John and I have this thing where we're both seeing completely different versions of you. Now, John has eyesight problems because of his constant masturbation, but I don't think—"

She burst into snakes.

That's right. Her body sort of spilled out of itself, falling into a dark, writhing puddle on the ground. It was a tangle of long, black serpents, rolling over each other and down the steps. We kicked at them as they slithered past, John warding them off with the torch.

Some, I saw, had patches of color on their scales, like flesh or the flowered pattern of Shelly's dress. I caught a glimpse of one snake with a writhing human eyeball still embedded in its side, the iris powder blue.

Molly jumped back and barked—a little too late, I thought—and made a show of snapping at one of the snakes as it wound its way down the stairs. She bounded to the top of the stairs and disappeared through the doorway. We kicked through the slithering things and stomped up after the dog, just as the stairwell door banged shut on its own.

I reached for the knob. At the same moment it began to melt and transform, turning pink and finally taking the shape of a flaccid penis. It flopped softly against the door, like a man was cramming it through the knob hole from the other side.

I turned back to John and said, "That door cannot be opened."

We stumbled back down the stairs, John jumping the last five, shoes smacking on the concrete. The snakes fled from the firelight and disappeared under shelves and between cardboard boxes.

That's when the basement started filling with shit.

The brown sludge oozed up from the floor drain, an unmistakable stench rising above it. I looked around for a window we could crawl out of, found none. The sewage bloomed out from the center of the floor, swirling around the soles of my shoes.

John shouted, "There!"

I whipped my head in his direction, saw him grab a little plastic crate from a shelf and set it on the floor. He climbed up on it, then just stood there with the muck rising below. Finally he looked at me and said, "What are you doing? Go find us a way outta here!"

I was ankle-deep now in a pool that was disturbingly warm. I sloshed around, looking above me until I found the large, square duct feeding into the first floor from the furnace. The return air vent. I went to a

13

pegboard on the wall and grabbed a foot-long screwdriver. I jabbed it into the crease between the metal of the duct and the floor, prying down the apparatus with a squeal of pulled nails.

I finally got a hold on the edge of the metal duct and felt it cut into my fingers. I pulled it down to reveal the dark living room above me, blocked by a metal grid. I jumped and knocked the grate aside with my hands. I leapt again and grabbed floor with both hands, feeling carpet under my fingers. With a series of frantic, awkward movements I managed to pull my limbs up until I could roll over on the floor of the living room.

I looked back at the square hole and saw a flicker of flame emerge, followed by the torch and then John's hand. In a few seconds we were both standing in the living room, glancing around, breathing heavily.

Nothing.

A low, pulsing sound emerged from the air around us. A laugh. A dry, humorless cough of a noise, as if the house itself was expelling the air with giant lungs of wood and plaster.

John said, "Asshole."

"John, I'm changing my cell number tomorrow. And I'm not giving you the new one. Now let's get this over with."

We both knew the drill. We had to draw the thing out somehow. John handed me his lighter.

"You light some candles. I'll go stand in the shower naked."

Molly followed me as I went back to where we left the boom box and the other supplies. I lit a few candles around the house—just enough to make it spooky. John showered, I found another bathroom and washed the sludge off my shoes and feet.

"Oh, no!" I heard John shout over the running water. "It's dark in here and here I am in the shower! Alone! I'm so naked and vulnerable!"

Out of things to do, I walked around for a bit and eventually found a bedroom. I glanced at my watch, sighed, then lay down over the covers. It was almost four in the morning.

This could go on for hours, or days. Time. That's all they have. I heard Molly plop down on the floor below. I reached down to pet her and she licked my hand the way dogs do. I wondered why in the world they felt the need to do that. I've often thought about trying it the next time somebody got their fingers close to my mouth, like at the dentist.

John came back twenty minutes later, wearing what must have been the smallest towel he could find. He lowered his voice. "I think I saw a hatch for an attic earlier. I'm gonna see if there's room to crawl around up there, see if maybe there's a big scary-looking footlocker it can pop out of or somethin'."

I nodded. John raised his voice theatrically and said, "Oh, no. We are trapped here all alone. I will go see if I can find help."

"Yes," I answered, loudly. "Perhaps we should split up."

John left the room. I tried to relax, hoping even to doze off. Ghosts love to sneak up on you when you're sleeping. I scratched Molly's head and—

SLEEP. LICKING. A soft splashing sound from another room. I dreamed I saw a shadow peel itself off the far wall and float toward me. Most of my dreams are like that, always based on something that really happened.

My eyes snapped open, my right arm still hanging over the edge of the mattress, the rough tongue still flapping away at my ring finger. How long had I been out? Thirty seconds? Two hours?

I sat up, trying to adjust to the darkness. A faint glow pulsed from the hall where the nearest candle burned away in the bathroom.

I quietly stepped off the foot of the bed and headed across the room into the hallway. Down the hall now, toward the sound and the light. I ran my hand along the textured plaster of the wall until I reached the bathroom, the source of the gentle splashing. Not splashing. Slurping. I peered in.

Molly, drinking from the toilet. She turned to look at me with an almost catlike "can I help you?" stare. I thought absently that she was drinking the poowater with the same mouth she used to lick my hand. . . .

If she's in here, then that wasn't her by the bed.

I picked the candle off the counter and headed back to the bedroom. I stepped in, the candle casting an uneven halo of light around me, rustling the shadows aside. I moved toward the bed and saw . . .

Meat. Dozens of the wrapped and now partially unwrapped hunks from the freezer, laying neatly on the floor next to the bed in an almost ceremonial fashion, the objects arranged in the rough shape of a man.

I moved the light toward the head area, where I found a frozen turkey still in the Butterball wrapper. Under it, wedged between turkey and torso, was the disembodied deer tongue, flapping around of its own accord.

Hmmmm. That was different.

I jumped back as the turkey, the tongue, and a slab of ribs levitated off the floor.

The man-shaped arrangement of meat rose up, as if functioning as one body. It pushed itself up on two arms made of game hens and country bacon, planting two hands with sausage-link fingers on the floor. The phrase "sodomized by a bratwurst poltergeist" suddenly flew through my mind. Finally it stood fully upright, looking like the mascot for a butcher shop whose profits went entirely to support the owner's acid habit.

"John! We got, uh, something here."

It was about seven feet tall, its turkey head swiveling side to side to survey the room, the tongue swaying uselessly below. It extended a sausage to me.

"You."

It was an accusation. Had we dealt with this thing before? I didn't remember it, but I was bad with faces.

"You have tormented me six times. Now prepare to meat your doom!"

I have no way of knowing that it actually said "meat" instead of "meet" but I'll give it the benefit of the doubt. I ran.

"John! John! We got a Situation Fifty-three here!"

The thing gave chase, its shaved-ham feet slapping the floor behind

16

me. My candle went out. I tossed it aside. I saw a closed door to my right, so I skidded to a stop, threw it open, and flung myself in.

Linen shelves smacked me in the face and I fell back out of the closet, dazed. The meat man wrapped its cold links around my neck and lifted me up. It pinned me against the wall.

"You disappoint me. All those times we have dueled. In the desert. In the city. You thought you had vanquished me in Venice, didn't you?"

I was so impressed by this thing's ability to articulate words using that flapping deer tongue and a frozen turkey that I almost lost track of what it was saying.

Venice? Did he say Venice? What?

Molly came by just then, trotting along like everything was just A-OK in Dogland.

Then she noticed some meat standing nearby and started happily chewing on a six-inch-wide tube of bologna serving as the thing's ankle.

"AARRRRRGHHHH!!!!"

It dropped me to the floor. I scrambled to my feet and ran downstairs. The meat man followed.

At the foot of the stairs, John was waiting.

He was holding the stereo.

The monster stopped halfway down the staircase, its eyeless turkey head staring down the device in John's hands, as if recognizing the danger.

Oh, how that Old Testament demon must have howled and shrieked at the sight of young David's harp, seeing at work a form of ancient magic that can pierce any darkness. The walking meat horror knew what was coming, that the same power was about to be tapped.

John nodded, as if to say, "Checkmate."

He pushed the "play" button.

Sound filled the room, a crystal melody that could lift any human heart and turn away any devil.

It was "Here I Go Again" by Whitesnake.

The monster grabbed the spots on the turkey where its ears would

17

be and fell to its knees. John wielded the stereo before him like a holy talisman, stepping up the stairs, driving the sound closer to the beast. Every inch of its fat-marbled skin and gristle writhed in agony.

"Take it!" John screamed, suddenly emboldened. "It looks like you should have taken time to *beef* up your defenses!"

The beast grabbed its abdomen; in pain, I thought.

Instead it pried loose a canned ham and, before John could react, hurled it at the stereo, the can whizzing through the air like a Randy Johnson fastball.

Direct hit. Sparks and bits of plastic flew. The stereo tumbled out of John's hands and fell heavily to the stairs.

Disarmed, John hopped down to the floor as the beast rose to its feet and pursued. It grabbed John by the neck. It snatched at me, but I dodged and grabbed the coffee thermos from the table. I ran back with the thermos, spun off the top and dashed the contents at the meaty arm that held John.

The meatstrocity screamed. The arm smoked and bubbled, then burst into flame. The limb then blackened and peeled off from the socket, falling to the hardwood below. John was free, falling to his knees and gasping for air.

The beast howled, collapsing to the floor meatily. With its only remaining arm, it pointed at me.

"You'll never defeat me, Marconi! I have sealed this house with my powers. You cannot escape!"

I stopped, put my hands on my hips and strode up to it. "Marconi? As in, Doctor-slash-Father Albert Marconi? The guy who hosts *Magical Mysteries* on the Discovery Channel?"

John stepped over and glared at the wounded thing. "You dumbass. Marconi is fifty years old. He has white hair. Dave and I aren't that old combined. Your nemesis is probably off giving some seminar, standing waist-deep in a pile of his own money."

The thing turned its turkey at me.

"Tell ya what," I offered. "If I can get you in touch with Marconi so you two can work out your little differences, will you release us?"

"You lie!"

"Well, I can't get him down here, but surely a being as superhumanly powerful as you can destroy him at a distance, right? Here."

It watched me as I fished out my cell phone and dialed. After talking to a secretary, a press agent, a bodyguard, an operator, the secretary again and finally a personal assistant, I got through.

"This is Marconi. My secretary says you have some kind of a meat monster there?"

"Yeah. Hold on."

I offered the phone to Meaty. "Do we have a deal?"

The thing stood up, hesitated, then finally nodded its turkey up and down. I held out the phone, while giving John a dark look that I hoped conveyed the fact that Plan B involved me letting the monster beat the shit out of him while I tried to escape out of a window somewhere. Fucking girl and her "ghost boyfriend." Marconi would have seen this shit coming a mile away.

A bundle of sausage fingers took the phone from my hand.

"So!" it boomed into the receiver. "We meat again, Marconi. You thought you had vanquished me but I—"

The beast spontaneously combusted into a ball of unholy blue light. With a shriek that pierced my ears, it left our world. The lifeless meat slapped to the floor piece by piece, the cell phone clattering next to the pile.

Silence.

"Damn, he's good," said John. I walked over and picked up the cell phone. I put it to my ear to ask the doctor what he had done, but it was the secretary again. I switched it off. The doctor hadn't even hung around long enough to say hello.

John made a casual hand-dusting motion. "Well. That was pretty stupid."

I tried the front door and it opened easily. Who knows, maybe it had never been sealed. We took time to straighten up the place, not finding any Morrisons restrained or dismembered and figuring that "Shelly" was at least telling the truth when she said the real family was on vacation. The shit had vanished from the basement, but I couldn't fix the heating duct I had messed up earlier. We packed the meat back into the freezer as best we could, with one exception.

The sun was already dissolving the night sky by the time I got home. I opened up the toolshed and set the broken boom box inside. I found an empty jar, filled it from a square can of formaldehyde and dropped the deer tongue in. I placed it on the shelf next to a stuffed monkey paw, lying lifeless with two fingers extended. I locked up and went to bed.

—from the journal of David Wong

BOOK I

THEY CHINA FOOD!

CHAPTER 1
The Levitating "Jamaican"

THEY SAY LOS Angeles is like *The Wizard of Oz*. One minute it's small-town monochrome neighborhoods and then boom—all of a sudden you're in a sprawling Technicolor freak show, dense with midgets.

Unfortunately, this story does not take place in Los Angeles.

The place I was sitting was a small city in the Midwest which will remain undisclosed for reasons that will become obvious later. I was at a restaurant called "They China Food!" which was owned by a couple of brothers from the Czech Republic who, as far as I could tell, didn't know a whole lot about China or food. I had picked the place thinking it was still the Mexican bar and grill it had been the previous month; in fact, the change was so recent that one wall was still covered by an incompetent mural of a dusky woman riding a bull and proudly flying the flag of Mexico, carrying a cartoon burrito the size of a pig under her arm.

This is a small city, large enough to have four McDonald's but not so big that you see more than the occasional homeless person on the way. You can get a taxi here but they're not out roving around where you can jump off the sidewalk and hail one. You have to call them on the phone, and they're not yellow.

The weather varies explosively from day to day in this part of America, the jet stream undulating over us like an angry snake god. I've seen a day when the temperature hit one hundred and eight degrees, another when it dipped eighteen degrees below zero, another day when the temperature swung forty-three degrees in eight hours. We're also in Tornado Alley, so every spring swirling, howling charcoal demons materialize out of the air and shred mobile homes as if they were dropped in huge blenders.

But all that aside, it's not a bad town. Not really.

A lot of unemployment, though. We've got two closed factories and a rotting shopping mall that went bankrupt before it ever opened. We're not far from Kentucky, which marks the unofficial border to the South, so one sees more than enough pickup trucks decorated with stickers of Confederate flags and slogans proclaiming their brand of truck is superior to all others. Lots of country music stations, lots of jokes that contain the word "nigger." A sewer system that occasionally backs up into the streets for some unknown reason. Lots and lots of stray dogs around, many with grotesque deformities.

Okay, it's a shithole.

There are a lot of things about this undisclosed city that the chamber of commerce won't tell you, like the fact that we have more than quadruple the rate of mental illness per capita than any other city in the state, or that in the '80s the EPA did a very discreet study of the town's water supply in hope of finding a cause. The chief inspector on that case was found dead inside one of the water towers a week later, which was considered strange since the largest opening into the tank was a valve just ten inches wide. It was also considered strange that both of his eyes were fused shut, but that's another story.

My name is David, by the way. Um, hi. I once saw a man's kidney grow tentacles, tear itself out of a ragged hole in his back and go slapping across my kitchen floor.

I sighed and stared blankly out of the window of They China Food!, occasionally glancing at the clock sign that flashed 6:32 P.M. in the darkness from the credit union across the street. The reporter was late. I thought about leaving.

I didn't want to tell this story, the story of me and John and what's happening in Undisclosed (and everywhere else, I guess). I can't tell the story without sounding as nuts as a . . . a nut bush, or—whatever nuts grow from. I pictured myself pouring my heart out to this guy, ranting about the shadows, and the worms, and Korrok, and Fred Durst, babbling away under this wall-sized portrait of a badly drawn burrito. How was this going to turn into anything but a ridiculous clusterfuck?

Enough, I said to myself. *Just go. When you're on your deathbed you're gonna wish you could get back all the time you spent waiting for other people.*

I started to stand but stopped myself halfway up. My stomach flinched, as if cattle-prodded. I felt another dizzy spell coming on.

I fell hard back into the booth. More side effects. I was already light-headed, my body trembling from shoes to shoulders in random spells, like I swallowed a vibrator. It's always like this when I'm on the sauce. I dosed six hours ago.

I took slow, deep breaths, trying to cycle down, to level off, to chill out. I turned to watch a little Asian waitress deliver a plate of chicken fried rice to a bearded guy on the other side of the room.

I squinted. In half a second I counted 5,829 grains of rice on her plate. The rice was grown in Arkansas. The guy who ran the harvester was nicknamed "Cooter."

I'm not a genius, as my dad and all my old teachers at Undisclosed

Eastern High School will inform you with even the slightest provocation. I'm not psychic, either. Just side effects, that's all.

The shakes again. A quick, fluttery wave, like the adrenaline rush you get when you lean your chair too far past the tipping point. Might as well wait it out, I guess. I was still waiting on my "Flaming Shrimp Reunion," a dish I ordered just to see what it looked like. I wasn't hungry.

A flatware set was wrapped in a napkin on the table in front of me. A few inches away was my glass of iced tea; a few inches from that was another object, one I didn't feel like thinking about right then. I unwrapped my utensils. I closed my eyes and touched the fork, immediately knew it was manufactured in Pennsylvania six years ago, on a Thursday, and that a guy had once used it to scrape a piece of dog shit from his shoe.

You've just gotta make it through a couple of days of this, said my own voice again from inside my skull. *You'll open your eyes tomorrow or the next day and everything will be okay again. Well, mostly okay. You'll still be ugly and kind of stupid and you'll occasionally see things that make you—*

I did open my eyes, and jerked in shock. A man was sitting across from me in the booth. I hadn't heard or felt or smelled him when he slid into the seat. Was this the reporter I spoke to on the phone?

Or a ninja?

"Hey," I mumbled. "Are you Arnie?"

"Yeah. Did you doze off there?" He shook my hand.

"Uh, no. I was just tryin' to rub somethin' off the back of my eyelid. I'm David Wong. Good to meet ya."

"Sorry I'm late."

Arnie Blondestone looked just like I imagined him. He was older, uneven haircut and a bad mustache, a wide face made for a cigar. He wore a gray suit that looked older than I was, a tie with a fat Windsor knot.

He had told me he was a reporter for a national magazine and wanted to do a feature on me and my friend John. It wasn't the first request like this, but it was the first one I had agreed to. I looked the guy up on the Web, found out he did quirky little human-interest bits, Charles Kuralt stuff. One article about a guy who obsessively collects

26

old lightbulbs and paints landscapes on them, another about a lady with six hundred cats, that sort of thing. It's what polite people have instead of freak shows I guess, stories we can laugh at around the coffee machines in the office break room.

Arnie's gaze stayed on my face a little too long, taking in my beads of cold sweat, my pale skin, the thatch of overgrown hair. Instead of pointing out any of that, Arnie said, "You don't look Asian, Mr. Wong."

"I'm not. I was born in [Undisclosed]. I had the name changed. Thought it would make me harder to find."

Arnie gave me the first of what I assumed would be many, many skeptical looks. "How so?"

I half closed my eyes, my mind flooding with images of the 103 billion humans who have been born since the species appeared. A sea of people living, dying and multiplying like cells in a single organism. I squeezed my eyes shut, trying to clear my mind by focusing on a mental image of the waitress's boobs.

I said, "Wong is the most common surname in the world. You try to Google it, you've got a shitload of results to sift through before you get to me."

He said, "Okay. Your family live around here?"

Getting right to it, then.

"I was adopted. Never knew my real dad. You could be my dad, for all I know. Are you my dad?"

"Eh, I don't think so."

I tried to figure out if these were warm-up questions to prime the interview pump, or if he already knew. I suspected the latter.

Might as well go all-in. That's why we're here, right?

"My adopted family moved away, I won't tell you where they are. But get out your pen because you'll want to write this down. My biological mom? She was institutionalized."

"That must have been hard. What was the—"

"She was a strung-out, crank-addicted cannibal, dabbled in vampirism and shamanism. My mom, she worshipped some major devil when I was a toddler. Blew her welfare check every month on black candles.

27

Sure, Satan would do her favors now and then, but there's always a catch with the Devil. Always a catch."

A pause from Arnie, then, "Is that true?"

"No. This, this silliness, it's what I do when I'm nervous. She was bipolar, that's all. Couldn't keep a house. Isn't the other story better, though? You should use it."

Arnie gave me a practiced look of reporterly sincerity and said, "I thought you wanted to get the truth out, your side of it. If not, then why are we even here, Mr. Wong?"

Because I let women talk me into things.

"You're right. Sorry."

"Now, since we broached the subject, you spent your senior year in high school in an alternative program . . ."

"Yeah, that was just a misunderstanding," I lied. "They have this label, 'Emotionally Disturbed' that they put on you, but it was just a couple of fights. Kid stuff, no charges or anything. Craziness is not hereditary."

Arnie eyed me, both of us aware of the fact that juvenile records are sealed from public viewing and that he would have to take my word for it. I wondered how this would end up in his article, especially in light of the utter batshit insanity of the story I was about to share.

He moved his gaze to the other object on the table, from his perspective, a small, innocent-looking container. It was about the size and shape of a spool of thread, made of flat, brushed metal. I rested my fingers on it. The surface was icy to the touch, like it had spent all night in the freezer. If you set the thing out in the hot sun from morning to night it would still feel that way. You could mistake it for a stylish pill bottle, I suppose.

I could blow your world away, Arnie. If I showed you what was in this container, you'd never sleep another full night, never really lose yourself in a movie again, never feel at one with the human race until the day you die. But we're not ready for that, not yet. And you sure as hell won't be ready for what's in my truck. . . .

28

"Well," Arnie began again, "either way, mental illness is nothing to be ashamed of. We just get sick from time to time, part of being human, you know? For instance, I was just talking to a guy up north, a high-priced lawyer-type who spent two weeks in the psych ward himself a little while ago. Name of Frank Campo. You know that name?"

"Yeah, I knew him a little."

"Frank wouldn't talk to me, but his family said he was having hallucinations. Almost daily, right? Guy had this car wreck and from then on he just got worse and worse. He freaked out at Thanksgiving. Wife brought in the turkey, but to Frank, it wasn't a turkey. Frank saw a human baby, curled up on the platter, cooked to a golden brown. Stuffing jammed in its mouth. He went nuts, wouldn't eat for weeks after that. He got to where he was having incidents every few days. They figured it was brain damage, you know, from the accident. But the doctors couldn't do squat. Right?"

"Yeah. That's about it."

You skipped over the weirdest part, Arnie. What caused the accident in the first place. And what he saw in his car. . . .

"And now," said Arnie, "he's cured."

"Is that what they say? Good for him, then. Good for Frank."

"And they swear that it was you and your friend who cured him."

"Me and John, yeah. We did what we could. But good for Frank. I'm glad to hear he's okay."

A little smile played at Arnie's lips. Acidic. Look at the crazy man with his incompetent, crazy-man haircut and his crazy little pill bottle and his crazy fucking story.

How many decades of cynicism did it take to forge that smirk, Arnie? It makes me tired just looking at it.

"Tell me about John."

"Like what? In his midtwenties. We went to school together. John isn't his real name, either."

"Let me guess . . ."

The images start to rush in again, the mass of humanity spreading across the globe over centuries like a time-lapse video of mold taking over an orange. *Think of the boobs. Boobs. Boobs. Boobs.*

". . . John is the most common *first* name in the world."

"That's right," I said. "And yet there's not a single person named John Wong. I looked it up."

"You know, I work with a John Wong."

"Oh, really?"

"Let's move on," Arnie said, probably making a mental note that this David Wong guy isn't above just making shit up.

Holy crap, Arnie, just wait until you hear the rest of the story. If your bullshit meter is that finely tuned, in a few minutes it's liable to explode and take half a city block with it.

"You guys already got a little bit of a following, don't you?" he said, flipping back to a page in a little notebook already riddled with scribbles. "I found a couple of discussion boards on the Web devoted to you and your friend, your . . . hobby, I guess. So, you're, what, sort of spiritualists? Exorcists? Something like that?"

Okay, enough farting around.

"You have eighty-three cents in your front pocket, Arnie," I said quickly. "Three quarters, a nickel, three pennies. The three pennies are dated 1983, 1993 and 1999."

Arnie grinned the superior grin of the "I'm the smartest man in the room" skeptic, then scooped his coins out of his pocket. He examined the contents, confirmed I was right.

He coughed out a laugh and brought his fist down on the table, my utensils clinking with the impact. "Well I'll be damned! That's a neat trick, Mr. Wong."

"If you flip the nickel ten times," I continued, "you'll get heads, heads, tails, heads, tails, tails, tails, heads, tails, tails."

"I'm not sure I want to take the time to—"

For a brief moment, I considered taking it easy on Arnie. Then I remembered the grin. I unloaded.

"Last night you had a dream, Arnie. You were being chased through a forest by your mother. She was lashing you with a whip made of knotted penises."

Arnie's face fell, like an imploded building. As much as I hated the expression on his face a few minutes ago, I loved this one.

That's right, Arnie. Everything you know is wrong.

"You got my attention, Mr. Wong."

"Oh, it gets better. A lot better."

Bullshit. What it gets is worse. A lot worse.

"It started a few years ago," I began. "We were just a couple of years out of high school. Just kids. So that friend of mine, John, he was at a party . . ."

JOHN HAD A band back in those days. The party was happening Woodstock-style in a muddy field next to a lake in a town a few minutes outside of Undisclosed city limits. It was April of that year and the party was being put on by some guy, for his birthday or whatever. I don't remember.

John and I were there with his band, Three-Arm Sally. It was around nine o'clock when I strode out onto the stage with a guitar slung over my shoulder, greeted by a smattering of unenthusiastic applause from the hundred or so guests. The "stage" was just a grid of wooden pallets laid together on the grass, orange drop cords snaking underfoot from the amps to a nearby shed.

I glanced around, saw a set list taped to one of their crackly old Peavey amplifiers. It read:

Camel Holocaust
Gay Superman
Stairway to Heaven
Love My Sasquatch
Thirty Reasons Why I Dislike Chad Wellsburg
Love Me Tender

We took our places.

It was me, Head (the drummer), Wally Brown (bass), Kelly Small-wood (bass) and Munch Lombard (bass). John was lead guitar and vocals, but he wasn't on stage, not yet. I should let you know that I had no idea how to play the guitar or any other musical instrument, and that the sound of my singing voice could probably draw blood from a man's ears, and perhaps kill a dog outright.

I stepped up to the mic.

"I want to thank you all for coming. This is my band, Three-Arm Sally, and we're here to rock you like the proverbial hurricane."

The crowd muttered its indifference. Head hammered the drums for the intro to "Camel Holocaust." I slung the guitar around and got ready to rock.

Suddenly, my whole body wrenched in a display of unbearable pain, knees buckling. My hands shot to my head and I collapsed to the stage, screaming like a wounded animal. I scraped the guitar strings to throw out some painful, spastic feedback on my way down. The crowd gasped, watching as I flew into a series of exaggerated convulsions, then finally lay still.

Munch rushed over, studied me like a paramedic. I lay there like a dead man. He touched my neck, then stood and turned to the mic.

"He's dead, ladies and gentlemen."

A rustling, drunken panic in the crowd.

"Wait. Please, please. Everyone. Pay attention. Just calm down."

He waited for quiet.

"Now," he said. "We have a whole show to do. Is there anyone here who knows how to sing and play guitar?"

A tall man stepped out of the crowd, a head of curly long hair like a deflated afro. This was John. He wore an orange T-shirt with a black stenciled stamp bearing the logo of VISTA PINES FACILITY FOR THE CRIMI-NALLY INSANE. The last two words had been crossed out with a black Magic Marker and the words NOT INSAN were scrawled crazily over it. The whole shirt, logo and all, was John's handiwork.

"Well," John said, in a fake Southern accent, "I reckon I can play a little."

Kelly, according to script, invited him onto the stage. John pried the guitar out of my dead hands while Head and Wally dragged me carelessly off into the grass. John picked up the instrument and tore into the "Camel Holocaust" intro. Three-Arm Sally began every single show this way.

> *"I knew a man*
> *No, I made that part up*
> *Hair! Hair! Haaairrr!*
> *Camel Holocaust! Camel Holocaust!"*

That whole bit was something John had come up with, the man having a terrible habit of carrying out his drunken 3:00 A.M. ideas even after daylight and sobriety came. It was always 3:00 A.M. for John.

I turned onto my back and stared into the night sky. That's what I remember, from that last moment of real peace in my life. The rain had ended hours ago, the stars freshly cleaned and polished against their black velvet background. The music thrummed through the ground and the cool moisture of the grass soaked up through my sweatshirt as I gazed into the twinkling jewels of infinity, all spit-shined by God's shirtsleeve. And then the dog barked and everything turned to goat shit.

It was rusty red, maybe an Irish setter or a red Labrador or a . . . Scottish rustdog. I don't know my dogs. Ten feet of thin chain trailed off its collar. Bounding around the partygoers, a bundle of manic canine energy, drunk on the first freedom of its life.

It squatted and peed on the grass, ran over to another spot and peed there, too. Marking this whole new world as its territory. It came toward me at a trot, the chain hissing through the grass behind it. It sniffed around my shoes, decided I was dead, I guess, and began snuffling around my pockets to see if I had died with any beef jerky on me.

It recoiled when I reached up to pet it, a catty "don't touch the hair" look on its face.

A brass tag, on its collar.

Etched with a message.

I'M MOLLY.
PLEASE RETURN ME TO . . .

. . . with an address in Undisclosed listed below. At least seven miles from home. I wondered how long it had taken the animal to etch that tag.

The dog, having nothing else to gain from our relationship, trotted away. I followed it, deciding on the spot that I would load up the dog and return it to the owners, who were probably worried sick about it. Probably a family with a little girl, crying her eyes out waiting for it to come back.

Or, a couple of sorority girls dealing with their grief through a series of erotic massages . . .

It's hard to look cool chasing after a dog, especially since I sort of run like a girl anyway. The dog pitched annoyed glances back my way as I trotted after it, picking up speed each time. I wound up taking a circuitous path all the way to the other side of the field, where I heard something that turned my guts cold.

A shriek. High-pitched, almost a whistle. Only two creatures on God's Earth can make that sound: African Grey Parrots and fifteen-year-old female humans. I spun around, moved toward the commotion. The dog seemed to eye me carefully, then ran off in the other direction. I looked around—

Ah. Giggling now. There was a bundle of girls, away from the stage, huddled with their backs to the band. They were surrounding a black guy with dreadlocks, an overcoat. He had one of those Rastafarian berets on his head, definitely going for a look, wanting the attention. Two of the girls had their hands over their mouths, eyes bulging, screaming for the guy to do it again, do it again. From the reaction I figured I

34

had just encountered the most dreaded of all partygoers: the amateur magician.

"Oh my gawd!" said the nearest girl. "That guy just levitated!"

One girl looked pale, on the verge of tears. Another threw up her hands and walked away, head shaking.

Gullibility is a knife at the throat of civilization.

"How high?" I asked blandly.

The Jamaican turned his gaze on me, trying to pull off the piercing stare of the exotic voodoo priest. It was an expression that was supposed to make me hear theremin music in my head.

"You gotta love the skeptic, mon," the guy said in a rubber accent that was part Jamaican, part Irish and part pirate.

"Show him! Show him!" screeched a couple of the girls.

I'm not sure why I feel the need to rain on this kind of parade. I like to think I'm standing up for skepticism but in reality I was probably just pissed that this guy was going to have sex tonight and I wasn't.

"What, about six inches above the grass, right?" I asked him. "Balducci levitation? Made famous by magic hack David Blaine in his television special? All you need is some strong ankles and a little acting, right?"

And a stupid, drunken audience . . .

His gaze froze on me. I had a familiar, nervous sensation, one that goes all the way back to elementary school. It's the simultaneous realization that I may have talked my way into another fistfight, and that I had not spent any time learning to fight since the last one. In a town where Friday night bar brawls make the Undisclosed emergency room look like the aftermath of a Third World election, sometimes it's better for smart-asses like me to just keep walking.

Then, he broke out in a big, white, toothy smile. A charmer.

"Let's see . . . what can I do to impress Mr. Skeptic Mon? Ah, lookee there. You didn't wash behind your ears, did ya?"

I let out a loud, theatrical sigh as he reached out to the side of my head, presumably to pull out a shiny quarter from behind my ear. But when he pulled back his hand, he was holding, not a coin, but a long, wriggling black centipede. He let it dangle over his fist, turning his hand over as it crawled around and around. One of the girls squealed.

He pinched it between thumb and forefinger, held the wriggling thing up for everyone to see. I noticed for the first time he had a few layers of first-aid tape wrapped around his other hand. He passed this hand in front of the bug and in a blink, the centipede was gone. The girls gasped.

"Well, the bug was a nice touch," I said, glancing at my watch.

"You wanna know where it went, mon?"

"No." I wasn't feeling well all of a sudden. This guy was giving me an odd feeling in my gut. "But, you know, don't get me wrong. I am one entertained son of a bitch."

"I got other talents, you know."

"Yeah, but I bet all your really good tricks are back at your apartment, right? And you'd be happy to show them to me, if only I were sixteen and female?"

"Do you dream, mon? I interpret dreams for beer."

That's the town of Undisclosed in a nutshell. This run-down half city with more weirdos per capita than you'll find anywhere outside of San Francisco. We should have that printed on the green population sign coming into town: WELCOME TO [UNDISCLOSED]. DREAMS INTERPRETED FOR BEER.

I said, "Well, I don't have any beer so I guess I'm outta luck."

"I tell you what, Mr. Skeptic Mon. I'll do it just like Daniel in the Old Testament. I'll tell you the last dream you had, *then* I'll break down its meaning for you. But if I'm right, you gotta buy me a beer. Okay, mon?"

"Sure. I mean, you've obviously been blessed with supernatural gifts. What better way to use them than to fish for free beers at parties." I craned my head around, and thought I saw the dog trotting around a tent where somebody was selling corn dogs. I told my feet to turn and walk after it. I commanded my mouth to tell this guy "never mind." Neither responded.

I knew that absolutely nothing good could possibly come from this encounter and, somehow, that a whole lot of bad could come instead. But my feet were planted.

"You had a dream early this morning, in the middle of the thunderstorm."

I looked him in the eye.

Pfft. Lucky guess . . .

"In the dream, you were back with your girl Tina . . ."

Whoa, how'd he know—

"—and you come home, and she's there with a big honkin' pile of dynamite. One of those big cartoon plunger detonators, ready to blow. You ask her what she's doin' and she says 'this' and shoves down the handle and," he spread his hands in the air, "boom. Your eyes snapped open. The explosion in your dream became the clap of thunder outside your window. So tell me, mon. Am I close?"

Ho. Lee. She. It.

He smiled. All eyes were on me, the naked shock on my face. A girl whispered, "Oh my God . . ."

There is no feeling I hate as much as speechlessness in the face of another man. I mumbled something.

One of the girls muttered, "Was he right? He was right, wasn't he?"

A raven-haired girl next to her wearing raccoon eye shadow suddenly looked like she had been drained by a vampire. The group had unconsciously taken a step or two backward, as if there was some kind of safe distance at which the world would start making sense again.

"The look on his face tells me I was right," he said, through a grin. "Wouldn't you say, girls? But wait, there's more."

I wanted to walk away. Up on the pallet stage behind me John was tearing away the solo that marks the end of "Camel Holocaust," rapping some impromptu lyrics, all over the cacophonous drums of Head "the entire show is one big drum solo in my mind" Feingold, and the band's thunderous triple-threat bass. I've been to a lot of concerts, everything from garage bands to Pearl Jam. Maybe my opinion is biased, but I would have to say that Three-Arm Sally is the shittiest band I've ever heard.

"You can guess the meaning of the dream, mon. The girl layin' in wait for you, ready to wreck your world again. But the dream be tryin' to tell you somethin' else, too. The dream be tryin' to warn you, givin' you a demonstration."

"Okay, okay, okay," I said, holding up my hands. "You made a lucky guess, somebody probably told you about—"

"You see, you gotta be brave to ask yourself the scary questions. How did your mind, David, know the thunder was coming?"

Thunder? What? Get away from this guy, man. Get away get away—

"What? You're full of—"

"The thunder came right as she hit the detonator in your dream. Your mind started the dream thirty seconds before the thunderclap. How did it know the thunder would be coming at that moment, to coincide with the explosion at the end?"

Because it's a poor sort of memory that only works backward, I thought, crazily. *Holy shit I'm quoting* Alice in Wonderland. *This is the worst fucking party ever.*

"I don't know. I don't know. This, this is bullshit." I was looking everywhere but at the Jamaican, suddenly terrified that I'd see him floating a foot off the grass. The girls were tittering to each other in amazement, a story to tell in the hallway Monday. Screw them. Screw everybody. But the bastard just wouldn't stop talking.

"We've all had those dreams, mon. You dream you're on a game show, on TV wearin' nothing but a jockstrap. At the exact moment the game show buzzer goes off to tell you you've lost, the telephone buzzes in real life. A call your mind *couldn't have known was coming.* You see, time is an ocean, not a garden hose. Space is a puff of smoke, a wisp of cloud. Your mind is a—"

"—Whatever. Whatever."

I turned away, shaking my head, my mouth dry.

Walk away, walk away. This ain't right, you know it. You want no part of this guy.

Onstage, John was now crooning the slow, mournful dirge that was "Gay Superman."

"The camel of despair
soars, strapped to his jet pack
of haunted memories . . ."

"Want me to tell you where your daddy really was when you were in the hospital with that broken leg?" he said to my back. This stopped me, my guts turning to ice again. "Want me to tell you the name of your soul mate? Or how she'll die?"

"Stop, or I'll tell you how *you'll* die"—that's what I wanted to say but didn't.

I walked away, forcing the steps. It was that jarring sensation of unreality, like the first time you see the road go spinning around your windshield in the middle of a car crash. I was actually dizzy, unsteady on my feet.

"Do you want to know when the first nuclear bomb will go off on American soil? And which city?"

I almost launched myself at the guy. But, once again a probable trip to the hospital was avoided by physical cowardice. This guy could probably kick my ass even without magical powers. I was so wired at this point I had the insane urge to punch one of those girls instead. Probably lose that fight, too.

"You know what, *mon*, why don't you take your fake Jamaican accent and get back on the boat to Fake Jamaica," is another thing it would have been cool to say, had I thought of it. Instead I sort of mumbled and made a dismissive motion with my hand as I stumbled into the crowd, acting like the conversation failed to hold my interest.

"Hey!" he shouted after me. "You owe me a beer, mon! Hey!"

Gypsies and psychics and Tarot readers have a hundred generations of practice at their art. And practice is all it is. Cold reading, wishful thinking, deductive reasoning. Throw out some general statement that could apply to any person on this Earth—

"I'm sensing that something is troubling you."

"You're amazing! Yes, it's my husband . . ."

—and the mark tells you the rest. But the fake Jamaican had no way of knowing what he knew. No possible way. I watched my shoes mash through the weeds. This man had just ruptured the thin fabric of all I believed to be—

I walked right into a girl, broadsided her, felled her like a tree. I saw, to my horror, that it was Jennifer Lopez.

YOU KNOW HOW to tell if you've been single too long? When you help a girl to her feet and get a rush of excitement for the two seconds you hold her hand on the way up.

"Jeez, sorry," I said as Jennifer picked up her beer bottle. "I was walking away from, uh, you know, voodoo. Thing. Flying voodoo man."

She was in denim shorts and a tank top, hair in a ponytail. I guess I should point out that this was not the famous Jennifer Lopez, but rather a local girl I was fond of who happened to have that same name. I guess it would have made a better story if it turned out to be the singer/actress and if you want to picture J. Lo whenever I mention this girl, feel free, even though my Jennifer only looked like the famous one when she was walking away from you.

She worked as a cashier at Home Depot these days and I made it a point to show up in her lane buying the manliest items in the store. In my apartment I now had an ax, three bags of cement mix and three different crowbars. On the last visit I bought a ten-pound sledgehammer and, looking disappointed, asked her if they had a bigger one. She didn't answer, not even to count back my change.

As she brushed grass clippings off her butt I felt the intense urge to reach over and help her. I managed to restrain myself.

Holy crap, there is no mood-changing substance on Earth like testosterone.

"I'm really, really sorry. You okay?"

"Yeah. Spilled my Zima a little, but . . ."

"What are you doin' here?"

"Just, you know. Party." She gestured vaguely with her hand at the crowd and music. "Well, good seein' ya . . ."

She's walking away! Say something!

40

"I'm, uh, here with the band," I said, following her while using the most casual, non-following stride I had in my walking repertoire. She glanced up at the band, then back at me.

"You know they started playing without you, right?"

"No, I don't, like, play an instrument or anything. I'm just . . . well, you saw me at the beginning there. I was the guy that fell down and died."

"Well, I just got here." She walked a little faster.

She's getting away! Tackle her!

"Well," I said after her, "I'll see you around."

She didn't answer, and I watched her walk away. Intently.

She met up with some blond kid in droopy pants, a sideways ball cap and a band T-shirt. The whole sequence depressed me so much I didn't think about the floating Jamaican again until . . .

THREE HOURS LATER, John and the crew were packing their scratched equipment into a white van with the words FAT JACKSON'S FLAP WAGON spray-painted on the side. That was the name of the band before they changed it a few months ago.

"Dave!" said John. "Look! Can you believe how much sweat I have on this shirt?"

"That's . . . somethin'," I said.

"We're all meeting at the One Ball. You comin'?"

That's the One Ball Inn, a bar downtown. Don't ask.

"No," I said, "I gotta go to work in seven hours." John had work, too. We both worked the same shift at the same video store. John had been through six jobs in three years, by the way. Some girl came up behind John and put her arms around him. I didn't recognize her, but that was normal.

"Yeah, me, too," he admitted. "But I gotta buy Robert a beer first."

"Who?"

"Uh, the black guy."

John gestured toward a group of five people, three girls and two

41

dudes with their backs to me. One was a huge guy with red hair, next to him was the rainbow beret and dreadlocks of my voodoo priest.

"See him? He's the one in the white tennis shoes."

Not only did I see him, but he turned toward me. He made eye contact and shouted, "You owe me a beer, mon!"

"The man likes his beer," said John. "Hey, I heard there was somebody from a record company out there tonight."

"I don't like the guy, John. He's . . . there's something not right about him."

"You like so few people, Dave. He's cool. He bet me a beer he could guess my weight. Got it on the first try. Amazing stuff."

"Do you even know how much you weigh?"

"Not exactly. But he couldn't have been off by more than a few pounds."

"Okay, first of all—never mind. John, the guy does an accent. What kind of a person goes around like that? He's phony. Also, I think he might be, uh, into somethin'. Come on."

"'Into something'? You are so quick to judge. Have you thought that maybe he was raised by his father, who was a fugitive from the law? And that, to conceal his identity, his father had to fake an accent? And that maybe young Robert learned how to talk from his dad and thus adopted that same fake accent?"

"Is that what he told you?"

"No."

"Come on, John. My car is behind the trees back there. Come with me."

"Are you goin' to the One Ball?"

"No, obviously not."

"Then I'm ridin' with Head in the Flap Wagon. You're still welcome to come if you want."

I declined. They loaded up and left.

I felt a little abandoned. There wasn't anybody else I really knew there, so I wandered around for a bit, hoping to run into Jennifer Lopez or at least that dog. I did find Jennifer, where she was sitting in a cherry-red '65 Mustang making out with that blond kid. He looked barely old enough to drive. This made me furious for some reason and I sulked my way back to my underfed Japanese economy car, shoes kicking up little sprays of moisture from the tall grass as I went.

The dog was waiting for me.

Right there by my door, like it couldn't understand what had taken me so long. I unlocked the door and "Molly" leapt into the passenger seat. I gawked, half expecting the dog to reach around with her teeth and pull down the seat belt. She didn't. Just waited.

I flung myself down into the little Hyundai, feeling like a thousand questions were squirming around my gut. I dug into my pocket for my car keys. I pulled my hand out—and screamed.

Not a full-fledged female-victim-in-a-slasher-movie scream. Just a harsh, rasping "WHAH?!?" On the palm of my hand, etched into the skin, was the phrase, YOU OWE ME ONE BEER.

I sat there, in the dark, staring at my hand. I did this for several minutes, felt my stomach clench, then decided to lean out the door and vomit in the weeds. I spat and opened my eyes, saw movement in the puddle. Something long and black and wriggling.

So that's where the centipede went . . .

I squeezed my eyes shut and leaned back in my seat. In that moment I decided to go home and crawl into bed and pretend that none of this had ever, ever happened.

TELLING THE STORY now, I'm tempted to say something like, "Who would have thought that John would help bring about the end of the world?" I won't say that, though, because most of us who grew up with John thought he *would* help end the world somehow.

Once, in chemistry class, John "accidentally" made a Bunsen burner explode. I mean it actually shattered a window. He got suspended for ten days for that and if they could have proven it wasn't an accident he'd have been expelled, as I was a year later.

He was kicked out of art class for submitting very, very detailed

43

charcoal nudes of himself, only with about six inches added to his genitalia. He broke his wrist after a fall while trying to ride a friend's van like a surfboard. He has burn scars on the back of his thighs from what he told me was a mishap with homemade fireworks, but what I believe was the result of his and some friends' attempt to make a jet pack. He told me a year ago he wanted to go into politics some day, even though he didn't have even one minute of college. A month ago he told me he wanted to go into the adult film industry instead.

CHAPTER 2

The Thing in John's Apartment

DARKNESS AND WARMTH. And then, an all-beep rendition of "La Cucaracha."

My cell phone. I peeled my eyes open. Bedroom. Night-time. My floor looked like a Laundromat explosion. Magazines here and there, overflowing trash can. Just as I had left it.

Beepbeepbeep BEEP, BEEP. Beepbeepbeep BEEP, BEEP. BEEP-BEEPBEEPBEEPBEEP—

My hand managed to knock over every single object on

my nightstand before it found the cell phone. I squinted at my clock, now lying helpless on the floor. Quarter after 5 A.M. I had to be at work in less than two hours.

"Hello?"

"David? It's John. Where *are* you?"

Voice scratchy, breathing heavier than he should be. Like a man just after a fistfight.

"I'm in bed. Where am I supposed to be?"

Long pause.

"Is this the first time I've called tonight?"

I sat straight up, fully awake now.

"John? What's going on?"

"I can't get out of my apartment, Dave."

"What?"

"I'm scared, man. I mean it."

"What are you scared of?"

"It can't be real, Dave. It can't. The way it moves, the way it's made . . . this is not a product of any kind of evolution or anything. It's not real. No. But it still managed to bite me."

What?!?

"What?"

"Can you come over?"

One time, John wound up in the hospital after he blacked out behind the wheel of his car. He wasn't moving at the time, thank God, but was in line at a Wendy's drive-through. This was after five sleepless and foodless days of vodka and some combination of household chemicals he was using for speed. I didn't know about it until a week later because he didn't tell me, knowing I would have kicked his ass right there in the hospital.

But I told him if he ever got into that kind of trouble again *without* telling me I would not only kick his ass, but would in fact beat him until he died, then pursue him into the afterlife and beat his eternal soul. So John being spaced out on crank or crack or skank tonight wasn't reason to declare a national holiday, but at least he came to me this time.

I said, "I'll be there in twelve minutes."

I hung up, pulled on some clothes I found draped over a chair, almost killed myself tripping over Molly the dog curled up in the doorway. I went out the front door with the dog in tow. It was raining again now, fat drops of April ice water that tingled down the back of my shirt as I ducked into my car. I was halfway to his building when my phone sang again. John's number popped up on the glowing display.

"Yeah, John. You okay?"

"Dave, I'm sorry to wake you up. I got a problem and I need you to listen—"

"John, I'm on my way over. You called me five minutes ago, remember?"

"What? No, David. Stay away. There's somethin' in here with me. I can't explain it. I don't think it'll kill me, it seems to just want to keep me here. Now, I need you to go to Las Vegas. Contact a man named—"

"John, just calm down. You're not making sense. I want you to sit down somewhere, try to chill out. Nothin' you're seeing is real."

A pause, then John asked, "How do I know this is really you?"

"You'll know in just a few minutes. I'm comin' up on your block now. Just chill, like I said. John?"

Nobody there. I sped up, rain drumming the windshield and boiling up into puddles on the passing pavement.

I was pounding on the door to John's apartment seven minutes later, still pounding on it five minutes after that. I considered going down and waking up his landlord when I tried the knob and realized the door had been unlocked the whole time.

It was dark. No use looking for a switch—John's only light was a floor lamp across the room and far be it from John to do something as rational as putting the light source where you could reach it from the door. Memory told me at least two pieces of furniture and probably twenty empty beer bottles stood between me and the lamp.

"John?"

Nothing. I tried a tentative step into his apartment, my shoe kicking

47

over a stack of magazines. I tried to step over them, cracked something glass or porcelain on the other side.

"John? Can you hear me? I'm going to call the—*ooomfff!!!*"

I was hammered by either a flying body tackle or an unnecessarily aggressive hug. My assailant and I landed hard on the carpet, pounding the breath from my lungs.

"It almost killed you!" John screamed, inches from my face. "You're an idiot, you know that? You're an idiot for coming here. We're both gonna die now. You could have brought help but now we're both gonna die in this room."

He sat up off me and in the darkness I could detect his head whipping back and forth, as if searching for a sniper. He put one finger up to my face.

"Shhhhhh. I don't see it. When I say 'go,' we're goin' to the other side of the room as fast as physically possible. You can clear it in three steps, dive at the end. Move like the Devil himself were after you. Ready?"

"John, listen to me." I paused, forced air into my lungs and tried to think. "You can't miss any more days at work. If you let me take you to the hospital, we'll tell them you've been poisoned or something. I don't think they'll go to the cops. We can get a note from the doctor there. If we've got a note I could talk Jeff into keeping you on."

"Go!"

John pushed himself to his feet, sprinted across the room and flung himself over an overturned sofa next to the wall. He sailed over it, arms flopping about like a rag doll, smacking into the wall behind it with a heavy thud.

I calmly stood up, walked to my right and turned up the floor lamp. I looked over to see John peer over the overturned sofa. Next to it was an armchair, on the other side a capsized coffee table. The man had built a furniture fort on that side of the room.

"John . . ."

He stood up, eyes wide. He put his hands out to me, fingers splayed.

"Dave, do *not* move." He spoke flat, low and dead serious.

"What?"

"I'm begging you," he said, almost whispering now. "I know you don't believe me. But when you turn around, you will. But *do—not—scream*. If you do, you're dead. Now. Very slowly, turn around."

Very slowly, as asked, I turned.

For a split second I was sure I *would* see something. I felt the hairs stand up on the back of my neck, as if swept by a puff of warm breath.

There was nothing there. I sighed, pissed at myself for getting sucked into this.

I faced John again, my raised eyebrows telling him I saw nothing more threatening than a very large and very naked poster of what appeared to be a female professional wrestler.

"No, it moved," he said. "There." He pointed to the corner, near the ceiling.

Very slowly, I turned and craned my neck, eyes following his pointed finger to the spot on the wall he so desperately needed me to see.

Still nothing.

"John, you can either come with me to the hospital, or I'm calling an ambulance. But what I'm not going to do is—"

"The door! Go!"

John hurdled the sofa, then ran and threw himself through the open door. I stood watching as he tumbled onto the carpet and then smoothly unfolded into a dead run down the hall outside. I faintly heard him thump through the stairwell doors, shouting victoriously.

I sighed and looked around his apartment. I found and pocketed his keys, then poked around some more and found his jacket on his bed. I grabbed for it, then yanked my hand back in pain. Something jabbed my finger, left a dot of blood on it. I reached into the jacket's front pocket . . .

A syringe.

It was one of those cheap disposable ones they sell to diabetics. There was residue inside and it was fucking *black*. Like used motor oil. I broke off the needle in the trash and stuck the rest of the syringe in my pants pocket. I had never done this before and I didn't know if a doctor would need it or not, to examine the contents. If not, I was going to shove it up John's ass.

I rooted around in his pockets for vials or pipes or anything else that would indicate what he had in his system. All I found was an empty pack of Chesterfields and a wadded-up FedEx receipt for something he sent to a Nevada address.

I stopped myself before I drifted into the area of what could be called "snooping" and locked up the apartment behind me. I went down and found John pacing back and forth in the parking lot, rain pelting him, fists clenched, ready for the dark god Cthulhu himself to come flopping out of the first-level doors. I tossed him his jacket, told him to get in my car. He opened the door, and froze in fear.

"What?" I barked. "What is it now?"

John was staring at Molly like she was the fluffy devil incarnate.

"John?"

"Uh . . . nothing. When did the dog find you?"

"You know this dog? It's been following me around like a lost, uh, dog."

"I dunno. It doesn't matter. Let's go, before . . . something else follows us." He glanced up at the apartment building.

I ducked into the car but didn't start it.

John glanced up at the building once more, said, "Just tell me you could see it. At least that."

"I didn't see it. Tell me what this is."

I held up the syringe. John rubbed his eyes, a man exhausted.

"You don't wanna touch that. What time is it?"

"Just past five in the morning."

"What day?"

"Friday night. I mean, Saturday morning. It feels like Friday night because I've barely slept yet. And we got work today, remember?"

"You shouldn't have come here."

"You called me. You begged me."

John leaned back, closed his eyes. For a second I thought he had dozed off. Finally, he mumbled: "I did? When?"

"Tell me what this stuff is, John. They're gonna ask me, first thing. Tell me before you fall asleep."

"I remember now. Calling you. It's hard, everything's running together. I called and called and called. Like a shotgun, firing in every direction hoping to hit somethin'. I bet I called you twenty times."

"Twice. You called me twice. John, answer my question."

"Really? You kept getting weird on me. You know what I think? I think you'll be getting calls from me for the next eight or nine years. All from tonight. I couldn't help it, couldn't get oriented. Kept slipping out of the time . . . you've got a voice mail message three years from now that's freaking hilarious."

I jammed the syringe back into my pocket and started the car. John reached over, grabbed my wrist. His eyes were open and alarmed.

"Wait. Where are we gonna go? Where are we gonna be safe from this thing?"

"Emergency room, John. I'm not playing this game with you. I don't know what else to do and I don't know how we're gonna pay for it. You're on a bad trip, or whatever they call it. Maybe it's a big deal, maybe it's not. Maybe you can just sleep shit like this off. I don't know because I'm not a junkie and I'm not a doctor."

"No. The hospital's no good. We'll go to your place, or somewhere. Anywhere but here."

I can't make myself recount the rest of this conversation. I'm too ashamed of it. The long and the short of it is that I let John talk me out of taking him to get treatment, that I worried more about him liking me than about whether he lived or died, that on that night, at that moment, I was the lowest, most selfish, worthless coward who ever lived.

So where was there to go? We were both scared for different reasons. He needed safety and I needed some kind of familiar comfort.

I'm not sure how we decided on Denny's but that's where we wound up. Well-lit, familiar, full of people. We sat in a booth and downed cup after cup of coffee in silence, John smoking his cigarettes and sneaking furtive glances out the window, me counting the seconds that passed without any psychotic ravings. I convinced myself with every passing peaceful moment that things were getting better, that the worst was over. In that, I was pants-shittingly wrong.

"Well?" I asked. "How are you doin'? Any better?"

"I saw things. Tonight. Both before and after I . . ." He trailed off, sucked on his cigarette instead.

"Okay," I said. "Back up. You don't know the name of the drug?"

"Robert called it 'soy sauce.' But I'm thinking now that was just a nickname and that it wasn't, you know, actual soy sauce."

Robert? Oh, of course. Robert, the Fake Magical Jamaican from the party. I would be finding Robert, I decided. I would be having a word with him.

"Robert?" I asked. "What's his last name?"

"Marley."

Of course.

"That's the only name he gave you?"

"Yeah. I didn't want to pry."

"And he gave you the—"

My cell phone chirped. I ignored it. Who could possibly be calling at this hour? Tina, crying, wanting to get back together a sixth time because she's at home and lonely? Jennifer Lopez, deciding she was wrong to have brushed me off at the party and wanting to play a game of Hide the Cocktail Wiener?

"Yes. He did," answered John. "We were drunk, in the One Ball parking lot, after close. We were passing around a joint; Head and Nate Wilkes crushed up some kind of pills between spoons and snorted it. There was . . . other stuff. Anyway. We drank some more."

Beepbeepbeep BEEP, BEEP . . .

"And then the Jamaican guy pulls out the sauce. 'It be openin' doors to other worlds, mon,' he says. We made him do it first, saw that he didn't die. It seemed to make him pretty happy and then—Dave, the guy—I know I didn't really see this—but the guy *shrunk himself,* made himself three feet tall. We all laughed our asses off, then he was back to normal again."

"And you still tried that shit?"

52

"Are you kidding? How could I not?"

The phone sang its electronic ditty again.

"Did anybody else do it?"

"Are you gonna get that?"

"You avoid my question one more time and I will come over this table and punch you in the face. Look into my eyes. You know I mean it. I'm tired of your—"

"It's not that easy, Dave. Everything's mixed up, like if somebody made you watch ten movies at once and then made you write an essay on 'em. That stuff . . . Dave, I'm remembering things that haven't happened ye—I mean, that didn't happen. Even right now, all that stuff from Vegas. Did we go to Las Vegas? You and me?"

The phone chirped a third time. Or fourth, I lost count.

"No, John. We've never been in our lives, either one of us. Are you the only one who took the sauce?"

"I don't know, that's what I'm tryin' to say. We went to Robert's place, but Head and the guys didn't come. I think they got nervous when they saw a needle come out. There were some kids around, the party kind of landed there, at Robert's trailer. Now please, please, please get your phone or turn it off. That damned song you got in there is driving me up a wall."

"Wait, wait, wait. You took something that *scared Head?* The guy who did the stuff that killed River Phoenix just to prove he was the better man?"

"Dave . . ."

"All right, all right."

I pulled out the phone, flipped it open, slapped it to my head.

"Yeah."

"David? It's me."

Ah, that feeling again. That chill of unreality, my belly full of coffee turning to liquid nitrogen.

The voice was John's.

No question about it. The man who was sitting across from me, smoking quietly without a phone anywhere near his head, had called me.

I glanced at John, said into the phone, "Is this a recording?"

"What? No. I don't know if we've talked tonight, but we don't have much time. I think I called you and told you to come here. If so, don't do it. If I haven't called, then obviously you should still stay away regardless. Now, I need you to go to Las Vegas. There's a guy there—"

"Who is this?"

John, in the booth there with me, gave me a look. On the phone: "It's John. Can you hear me?"

"I can hear you and I can see you," I said, a tremble in my voice. "You're sitting right here next to me."

"Well, just talk to me in person, then. Oh, wait. Do I look like I'm injured in any way?"

"What?"

"Fuck! Someone's at the door."

Click. He was gone.

I sat there, the phone still pressed to my ear, suddenly very, very tired.

IF I HAD been sitting with anyone else, I would have assumed I was being set up for some drunken practical joke. But I knew this wasn't some elaborate prank of John's for two reasons: one, John knows how I get when I'm pissed off and wouldn't intentionally do it, and two, it wasn't funny.

I was scared. Truly scared, maybe for the first time since I was a little kid. John looked pale and half dead. My feet were wet and cold, my contact lenses were itching, my brain aching from sleep deprivation. I wanted to burn that cell phone, go home and lock my doors and curl up under a blanket in the closet.

This is the breaking point in a human life, right here. But my whole life had been leading up to this, hadn't it?

From day one it was like society was this violent, complicated dance and everybody had taken lessons but me. Knocked to the floor again and again, climbing to my feet each time, bloody and humiliated. Always met with disapproving faces, waiting for me to leave so I'd stop fucking up the party.

They wanted to push me outside, where the freaks huddled in the cold. Out there with the misfits, the broken, glazed-eye types who can only watch as the normals enjoy their shiny new cars and careers and marriages and vacations with the kids.

The freaks spend their lives shambling around, wondering how they got left out, mumbling about conspiracy theories and Bigfoot sightings. Their encounters with the world are marked by awkward conversations and stifled laughter, hidden smirks and rolled eyes. And worst of all, *pity*.

Sitting there on that night in April, I pictured myself getting shoved out there with them, the sound of doors locking behind me.

Welcome to freakdom, Dave. It'll be time to start a Web site soon, where you'll type out everything in one huge paragraph.

It was like dying.

"WAS THAT ME?" asked John. "That was me, wasn't it?"

I looked down at my coffee and considered flinging it into John's face.

"I'm sorry, Dave. I really am. For messin' up your sleep cycle and for everything that's about to happen, the people that are going to, uh, explode."

I was already up, walking out. I guess John paid at the counter behind me, I don't know. I pushed my way out the glass door, dug out my keys. I opened the driver's door and Molly the dog immediately flung herself out onto the pavement, barking her head off, looking right at me. Then she trotted off across the empty lot, turned and barked some more, then trotted a few steps farther and barked again.

John said, "I think she wants us to follow her."

She scampered off down the sidewalk, glancing back at us to make sure we were coming. I slid into the car.

I pulled out of the space and drove in completely the opposite direction of the dog. John seemed like he wanted to comment on this, but the look on my face probably warned him off. I vaguely heard the sound of the dog running and barking after us as I turned onto the street, but disregarded it. We drove in tense silence.

Finally, tentatively, he asked where we were going.

"We're going to fucking work, John. It's six o'clock and we're opening the shop. There's nobody there to cover for us."

He didn't reply to this. Instead, he leaned his seat back, turned and looked out the passenger window at the passing storefronts and the few early-morning joggers, not saying a word. I eventually asked him how he was doing, got no answer. I could see he was still breathing. That was good. Sleeping, that's all. I guessed that was good, too.

If he gets sick and dies, Robert Marley, they're gonna find you in a ditch somewhere.

I stopped at a red light, feeling foolish as always for stopping at an intersection at an hour when the streets are deserted, just because a colored lightbulb told me to. Society has got me so fucking trained. I rubbed my eyes and groaned and felt utterly alone in the world.

Thump!

Scratching, on the window.

Like claws.

I flinched, turned.

It *was* claws.

Molly's. She was on her hind legs, her paws pressed against the window.

"Woof!"

"Go away!"

"Woof!"

"Shut up!"

"WOOF!"

"Hey! I said shut up! Get your feet off my car!"

"WOOF! WOOF! WOOF!"

"Shut up! Shut up! Shut! Up!"

This went on for longer than I care to admit, and it ended with me getting out and leaning my seat forward so Molly could jump into the back. Yes, the entire spiraling trajectory my life took since that night was because I lost a debate with a dog.

She sniffed around John and then barked at me, the sound deafening in the enclosed space. Still, John didn't stir.

"What do you *want?*"

That seemed like a perfectly reasonable question at that moment. The dog clearly had intentions, somehow, and wasn't going to leave me alone until I acted on them.

"*What?* Do you think I'm your master? Did little Timmy fall down the fucking well? What do you—"

I stopped, my eye drawn to her jingling collar, and the little metal tag there.

I'm Molly.
Please return me to . . .

She stopped barking.

THE PLACE WAS way the hell out of town, out near the big drain cleaner factory. At one point I took a right turn and Molly went into a barking fit. I did a U-turn and she immediately calmed down.

I saw a big, run-down Victorian house standing off by itself at the end of the block, and realized the dog had just directed me to the right address. I didn't know if dogs really did that but at that moment I was sure *this* dog could do it—

"Oh, *shit.*"

I actually said that out loud, in the car. Something had clicked so hard in my mind my whole body twitched.

I knew this place. I flashed back to the party, a huge kid with red hair, his back to me, standing with Robert the fake Jamaican.

That was Big Jim Sullivan.

This is his house.

Big Jim was a year ahead of me in school, six inches taller and twice my weight. He got famous around town after a carjacking attempt, which ended with Jim tearing the gun out of the assailant's hand (ripping the skin off the guy's trigger finger in the process) and then beating the man over the head with his own gun. Afterward Jim visited the guy in the hospital and spent several hours reading Bible verses to him. He once won a fight with Zach Goldstein by chucking him bodily over a guardrail.

I had lived in constant fear of the man, and even now I had the urge to flip the dog out of the car window and speed away.

You see, Jim had a sister.

We called her "Cucumber," but I couldn't remember her real name. She was in Special Ed, a couple of years younger than me. People think she got that nickname because of some sexual thing, but it was a reference to sea cucumbers. They have this defense mechanism where they puke up their guts when faced with a predator, hoping the predator will go for their guts rather than eating them. I should know, I made up the nickname.

You see, Jim's sister used to throw up a lot, and I mean *a lot*. Like, twice a week at school she'd wind up vomiting somewhere or on somebody. I don't know what exactly caused it. She had a lot of things wrong with her but at least she got one of the more clever nicknames out of the deal.

My last year in school, after I had gotten sent off and put into the Behavior Disorder program, Big Jim heard me using that nickname and I lived the rest of my school days afraid he would break me into little pieces in the parking lot. The worst part would have been that as I was bleeding and feeling teeth breaking off in my mouth, I would've spent every second of the pummeling knowing I deserved it.

So Big Jim was at the party. With Robert? What did that mean? And why was his dog there? Did he bring his dog to every party? Had he gone blind, and was Molly his Seeing Eye dog? Was it the dog's birthday?

I felt like an idiot. Here I was toting the animal all over town, putting myself at grave risk in the process, when I could have just left her at the party where her owner was.

I scrambled to think of how I would approach him with all this, the soy sauce and Robert and his unnaturally smart dog.

Wait. Driveway's empty.

So? Jim probably tied on a good drunk and was now sleeping it off at a girlfriend's house.

Bullshit. Big Jim doesn't drink, and wouldn't leave his kid sister at home alone all night.

I got out of the car and motioned for the dog to follow. She didn't. I called to her and patted my thigh, which I've seen other people do with dogs so I figured it must work. Nothing. I did this for several minutes, the dog not even looking at me now, sniffing around John again. I realized no amount of thigh slapping, not even an all-out blues hambone, would move this animal. I leaned into the car and started tugging at her collar. She backed off, growling, looking at me with a disdain I didn't think canines were capable of.

"Come on, dammit! You made me drive here!"

Through all of this, John still didn't stir. I think that was what freaked me out most of all. He was laying there in the uncomfortable bucket seat, twisted and slumped like a crash-test dummy. More passed out than asleep. I reached in and grabbed roughly at Molly's collar.

I'm going to skip past the next ten minutes and just say that I wound up carrying Molly up to the house. The plan was to tie her up around back and slip away unnoticed, but as I passed by the front door, it opened.

Not all the way, just the few inches allowed by the security chain. I was hit by that jittery caught-in-the-act feeling. I turned, huge dog in my arms, to see the pale, freckled, utterly confused face of Jim's sister. No sign she even recognized me, or maybe she just didn't want to acknowledge where she recognized me from.

Hey! Weren't you in my Special Ed class?

I quickly propped my chin over the dog's back and spoke. "Um, hey there. I, uh, have your dog."

The door closed. I stood there for an awkward moment, feeling the odd urge to drop the animal and run. I heard Cucumber's voice from inside, shouting, "Jim! The guy that stole Molly is here!"

I sat the dog down and grabbed hold of her collar before she could bolt. The door snapped open again and I half expected Big Jim to show himself, his Irish copper-topped head appearing a foot and a half above where the girl's had been. But it was the sister again, saying, "He's coming. You better bring me the dog now. Or you can have it if you want it."

"What?"

"The dog. You can have it. That one is worth a hundred and twenty-five dollars but you can have it free because it's used."

"Oh, no. I don't need a . . . I mean, uh, it's yours, right?"

"Jim's. But he doesn't like it, either. He's coming."

"What, is there something wrong with it?"

Her eyes flicked quickly from me, to the dog, and back. Is that *fear*? Something make her nervous about this dog?

You and me both, honey.

"No," she said, looking at her shoes.

"Then why'd you pay a hundred twenty-five dollars for it?"

"Have you ever seen a golden retriever puppy?"

"Your brother isn't here, is he?"

She didn't answer.

"I mean, there's no car here. Doesn't he drive a Jeep or something? Big SUV?"

She looked over, then said, "We have a gun in the house. Do you want the dog or not?"

"I—what? No. Where's Big Jim?"

"Who?"

"Jim, your brother."

"He just went down the street. He'll be back any second now."

"Dammit, I'm not gonna attack you. Didn't he go to a party last night?"

Long pause. She said, "Maybe."

Oh, shit, look at her. She's scared senseless.

"Just outside of town, right? At the lake?"

She snapped, "You know where he is?"

"No. He never came home?"

She didn't answer. She wiped at one of her eyes.

"The dog," I said. "Molly, she was at the party. Did he take her there?"

"No. She ran off before that."

So . . . the dog followed him to the party? It was there looking for Jim? Who knows.

She said, "I think Jim's dead."

This stopped me.

"*What?* Oh, no. No, no. I don't think—"

She broke into tears, then choked out the words, "He won't answer his phone. I think that black guy killed him." She looked right at me and spat out, "Were you there?"

This was an accusation. She wasn't asking if I was at the party. She was asking if I was at the scene of Jim's death. This conversation was spinning out of control.

"No, no. Wait, the black guy? Is his name Robert? Got dreadlocks? How do you know him?"

She wiped her face with her shirt and said, "The police called."

"About Jim?"

She nodded. "They asked if he was here but they wouldn't say anything else. There was this dreadlocks guy, he came to the house a few times. He was on drugs. Jim works at the shelter for church and they do counseling and stuff for people like that. Sometimes people come here asking for Jim, asking for, like, rides or loans. The black guy would come here but Jim wouldn't let him inside. Molly bit him. She ran out and bit his hand while he was talking to Jim."

"When was this?"

"Yesterday. He was right where you are. He was yelling."

"Did you hear what he said?"

"He said a dog bit his hand. I think the guy was some kind of Devil worshipper."

"Uh, that's possible. Do you—"

"I'm closing the door now."

"No! Wait! What about the—"

The door closed.

Defeated, I led Molly around to the back of the house where I found about ten feet of chain, ending in a broken link, where Molly had presumably snapped it the day before. So the dog had broken her chain, then walked seven miles to an empty field in a neighboring town where she somehow knew her master was attending a party? Come on.

I tied the chain around her collar and tried to make a knot with it. I climbed back into the car, saw that John hadn't moved even one millimeter other than for the steady rise and fall of his ribs. Still alive. That was good because we had to be at Wally's in a few minutes and I hadn't been looking forward to opening the store all by myself.

IF I HAD known what was about to happen at work I wouldn't have gone, of course. I would also have taken off my pants. But I didn't have the power of future sight—not at that point, anyway—and so I just sat sulking behind the wheel as we ramped into the parking lot to start the 7:00 A.M. shift at Wally's Videe-Oh!, where I had worked for two years, John about two months.

John was always bitching about "Wally" and how greedy "Wally" was and how he should have given me a raise by now. He didn't realize that there was no person named "Wally" in the Wally's organization. That was the name of the DVD-shaped mascot on the store's sign. I never had the heart to tell him.

I parked and engaged in a discussion with John, transcribed as follows:

"John? We're at Wally's. You need to get up. John? John? John? You need to get up, John. John? I can see you breathing, so I know you ain't dead. You know what that means? It means you gotta get up. John?

62

Come on, we gotta go to work. John? Are you awake? John? John? Wake up, John. John?"

I finally climbed out of the car and walked around to his door. I reached for the handle, and froze.

His eyes were wide open, staring blankly through the glass. He was still breathing and blinking, but not really there.

Great. Now what?

If you're thinking, "Call an ambulance," I admit that's what a smart person would have done. What I did was experiment for a few minutes, poking him and slapping him on the cheek and getting no response. Finally I found I could lure him through the door by taking his cigarettes and holding them out as bait. He walked like a sleepwalker, slow and shuffling, otherwise unresponsive.

Once inside I planted him in front of the computer behind the counter, reached around and brought up a spreadsheet to play on the screen in front of him. If anyone came in, he would appear to be sucked into his work on the PC. I looked at the scene, considered, then grabbed his right arm and propped up his chin with it. There, he looked deep in thought now.

I put away returns and boxed up Tuesday's new releases so Tina wouldn't have to. I pretty much managed to look normal for the few customers who accidentally missed the Blockbuster two blocks down the street. When I got some time to myself after lunch, I flipped through the yellow pages, picked up the phone stuck to the back wall and scooted up a chair.

Two rings, then, "St. Francis."

"Yeah, uh," I said awkwardly. "I need a priest."

"Well, this is Father Shelnut. What can I do for you?"

"Um, hi. Do you have any experience with, like, demon . . . ism? Demonology, I guess. Like possession and hauntings and all that?"

"Wellllll . . . I can't say that I've personally dealt with anything like that. People that come to me and say they've seen things or, say, they feel a kind of unexplained dread in their homes or hear voices, we usually refer them to a counselor or, you understand, a lot of times medication can—"

"No, no, no. I'm not crazy." I glanced over at John, still catatonic. "Other people have—"

"No, no, I didn't mean to imply that. Look, why don't you come talk to me. And even if you need to talk to a professional I got a brother-in-law who's real good. Why don't we do that? Why don't you come in and have a talk with me?"

I thought for a moment, rubbed my temple with my free hand.

"What do you think it's like, Father?"

"What what's like?"

"Being crazy. Mentally ill."

"Well, they never know they're ill, do they? You can't diagnose yourself with the same organ that has the disease, just like you can't see your own eyeball. So, I suppose you just feel normal and the rest of the world seems to go crazy around you."

I thought, then said, "Okay, but let's just suppose I honestly, I mean, in reality ran into something from beyond the—OW!"

It was a pinch on my thigh, like a bee sting. I flung myself upright, toppling my chair, letting the handset bang off the wall. I shoved my hand into my pocket, tried to pull out the syringe I had lifted from John's place.

I *couldn't* pull it out.

The blasted thing was stuck to my leg. I pulled, felt skin and hair come loose. I hissed through clenched teeth, my eyes watered.

I yanked, tearing the syringe free and out of my pants, turning out the white pocket with it. I saw a dime-sized hole in the white fabric, stained red. I saw a drop of the black goo now hanging out of the end of the syringe. Now, I'll try to explain this without cursing, but the black shit that came out from that motherfucker looked like it had grown fucking hair.

No, not hair.

Fucking *spines*. Like a cactus.

Did I mention that the stuff was moving? Twitching? Like it was trying to worm its way out of its container?

I ran into the employee bathroom, holding the syringe at arm's length. I thought about tossing it down the toilet, had visions of the stuff multiplying in the city sewer, and then threw it in the sink instead. I ran out, got John's lighter from his shirt pocket and came back and held the butane flame to the squirming blob. It burned, curling up and around like an earthworm. The end of the syringe browned and melted along with it, stinking like charred electrical wires.

The soy sauce, the black stuff from Planet X or whatever it was, burned in the flame until it became a tiny hard black crust in the sink. I shook it off the end of the misshapen syringe and washed it down the drain, ran five minutes' worth of water after it. The syringe went in the trash.

I stumbled back out of the bathroom, shaking as if chilled. I picked up the phone, said, "Uh, are you still there? Hello?"

"Yes, son. Just calm down, okay? Nothing you're seeing is real."

There was a strange, venomous warmth spreading through my thigh.

"Look," I said, "I appreciate your time but I'm really starting to think there's nothing you can—"

"Son, I'm going to be honest with you. We both know you're fucked." Pause from my end.

"Uh, excuse me?"

"Your mom writes on the wall with her own shit. Big changes are coming to Deadworld, my son. Waves of maggots over oceans of rot. You'll see it, David. You'll see it with your own eyes. That is a prophecy."

I jerked the phone away from my ear, looked at it like it would bite me. I slowly hung it back on the cradle—

"David Wong?"

I spun around. A bald black guy in a suit stood at the cashier counter.

"Yes . . ."

"Detective Lawrence Appleton. Please come with me. Your friend, too."

"No, I, uh, can't leave the shop. John and I are the only ones—"

"We've already contacted the owner. He's sending someone in to cover for you. You'll lock the door on your way out. Please come with me, sir."

CHAPTER 3

Grilling with Morgan Freeman

I WAS ALONE in the "interview" room at the police station; the one-way mirror was to my left. In it I saw myself slumped in the chair, the disorganized black hair, the beard stubble that had crept onto my pale face like mildew on white porcelain.

Man, you need to lose some weight.

I had been in there for thirty minutes. Or two hours, or half a day. If you think time stops in the waiting room at the dentist, you ain't never been alone in an interrogation room at a police station. This is what they do, they throw you in here to stew in the silence, all your guilt and doubts burning a hole in your gut so the truth can spill out onto the tile floor.

I should have gotten John to a hospital. Hell, I should have called an ambulance as soon as I got off the phone with him this morning. Instead I've fucked around for twelve hours and for all I know that black shit from the syringe was eating through his brain that whole time.

That ability to see the right choice, but not until several hours have passed since making the wrong one? That's what makes a person a dumb-ass, folks.

Morgan Freeman stepped in and laid a manila folder before me. Thick paper. Photos. A white cop followed him. Something about their manner pissed me off; like they were swooping in on prey. I wasn't the bad guy here. I wasn't the one selling that black shit. But now I get to listen to these douche bags tell me everything I should have done instead of what I did? There was no fucking time for that.

"I want to thank you for coming down, Mr. Wong," he said. "I bet it's been quite a night for you. Been a long night for me, too, as a matter of fact."

"Okay." *You know what helps? A warm glass of go fuck yourself.* "Where's John?"

"He's fine. He's talking to another officer just a few rooms from here."

I actually couldn't name the actor the black guy reminded me of, so I stuck with Morgan Freeman. Though now that I looked at him he bore almost no resemblance. This man was heavier, with round cheeks, a goatee and a shaved head. I couldn't remember what he said his name was. His white partner had a crew cut with a mustache. Almost a G. Gordon Liddy, a cookie-cutter cop from central casting. I couldn't help but think how much cooler he would look if he would just shave his head like his partner. Morgan should say something to him about that.

"John is talking?" I asked. "Really?"

68

"Don't worry, man. Since you're both gonna tell the unvarnished truth, you don't gotta worry about your stories matching, do you? We're all friendly here. I ain't here to make you piss in a cup, or to lean on you about all that mess that happened your last year in school with that Hitchcock kid."

"Hey, I had nothing to do with—"

"No, no. Don't even bother. That's what I'm sayin', I'm not here to accuse you of nothin' at all. Just tell me what you did last night."

I had a knee-jerk impulse to lie, but realized at the last second that *I* hadn't actually done anything illegal. Not as far as I knew. Sounding guilty anyway, I said, "Went to a party out by the lake. I came home just after midnight. I was asleep by two."

"You sure about that? You sure you didn't go over to the One Ball Inn down on Grand Avenue for a nightcap?"

"What's a nightcap?"

"Your buddies were all there."

Well, officer, I really only have the one friend . . .

"No, I had work this morning. As you know. I went straight home."

I knew I should be talking about the Jamaican. Only my knee-jerk impulse to never volunteer anything to the cops was holding me back. That was stupid. Robert Marley should be sitting here, not me. He was the one handing out the black voodoo oil that seems to have put a crack in the universe. That's got to be a felony, right?

I thought about that shit, *moving,* out of the syringe like a worm. Then I thought of that substance being inside John, and shivered.

"You feelin' okay?"

I heard myself say, "Uh-huh."

As I said it, a strange, jittery energy rose up inside me, radiating from the chest out.

The syringe.

In my pocket.

Biting my leg.

The spot of blood.

Moving. Inside John. Inside me.

All of a sudden everything was too bright, like somebody turned up the saturation on all the colors in the room. Everything came into high focus, a high-def signal. I spotted a moth on the opposite wall, and noticed a small tear in one of its wings. I heard a guy talking on his cell, and realized he was on the sidewalk outside the building.

What the fuck?

I looked the detective in the eye. I was startled to find I could see his next question coming before he even spoke it, word-for-word . . .

Have you heard the name . . .

"Have you heard the name Nathan Curry? Guy your age, parents own a body shop here in town?"

My heart was hammering. I muttered, "No."

How about Shelby Winder?

"How about Shelby Winder? Heavy girl, senior at Eastern High? Ring a bell?"

"No. Sorry."

Clarity lit up my mind like a sunrise. Everything was obvious now, all the walls of the maze turned to glass. I immediately knew two things: this list of people had all been at the party last night . . .

And they were all now dead or heading there.

Now how do I know that? How do I know any of this? Magic?

You know damn well why. That black shit John took made blood contact with you. Now you're getting high, partner.

He asked, "What about Jennifer Lopez?"

"Oh. Yeah. I know her."

"Not the actress, now, but—"

"I know. I saw her last night. Is she okay?"

"Arkeym Gibbs?"

"No. Wait, yeah. Big guy, right? Black? I don't know him, but he was the only black guy in my high school . . ."

I trailed off, studied the detective's face. No, this was not another day at the office for this guy. He's seen things, the kind of things that sit in the brain, like a tumor, poisoning everything around it. I saw all through him, just like that.

He's got two kids, two beautiful daughters. He's suddenly very, very worried about the world they'll grow up in. He's Catholic, wears a gold cross around his neck. But today he's taken it off, put it in his pocket. He keeps sticking his hand down there and rubbing it between his fingers. He thinks the end of the world is coming.

It's not that I could read the cop's mind. I couldn't. I just read his face. We all can tell by the look in somebody's eyes that they don't think our joke is funny or that they don't like what they're eating or whatever. It was just like that. The information was there, presented in the subtle play of facial muscles from microsecond to microsecond.

He read off more names. Justin White, Fred something, a couple others. I didn't recognize any of them and told him so. The last name on the list was Jim Sullivan.

So Cucumber was right to worry.

I didn't tell Morgan I knew the name. In the years since I've wondered how many lives could have been saved if I had.

"You're not outta school even three years. You went to high school with most of these people, Eastern. But you only knew the one girl?"

"I kind of kept to myself."

"And then you got shipped off to the other school—"

"Look, I'm not saying anything else until you tell me whether Jennifer is dead or alive. That ain't confidential information and I deserve to know."

Don't bother. He doesn't know.

"We don't know. You see, that's the problem. That's why I got six hours of overtime already today. At least nine people were at the One Ball at closing time, twelve hours ago. Four of them are missing. Your friend is here."

He paused, probably for effect.

"The rest are dead."

It's funny. Up until that point, despite all the evidence that had been provided to the contrary, it had never hit home how much trouble I was really in. I thought about John, again wondering if I had killed him by not rushing him to the ER.

71

I turned and looked at myself in the one-way mirror. The image was distorted, the other cop out of range at the back of the room. What was left was just me and Morgan, the clean-cut protector of the people, standing tall over the slumped, unshaven kid in a battered video store T-shirt that looked suspiciously like it had been wadded up on a car floorboard for two days. Good guy and bad guy. Trashman and trash.

"What about Justin Feingold and the guys John was with?" I asked. "Kelly and—"

"They're fine. I've already talked to 'em, the whole band. They went home before the party moved on. Which brings us to my next question. Your friend is the only known survivor of the One Ball Inn and—now don't take offense at this—but he ain't lookin' too healthy right about now. Did he say anything this morning at work? Maybe while you guys were putting away the last night's porno returns?"

The white cop across the room stepped forward, put his hands on his hips. Waiting for an answer. Morgan left his gaze on me, calmly waited for me to fill the tense silence. Old interrogation trick.

"John called me last night, talking crazy, clearly out of it. Paranoia, hallucinations, the whole bit. This would have been around five A.M. I came over. He was acting, well, crazy. Seein' things. But otherwise okay. Conscious, you know. Not, like, puking or convulsing or anything. I calmed him down, we went and got some food. That was that. We went to work."

"What did he say? Exactly?"

"Monsters in his apartment, said he couldn't remember how he got where he was, so on."

"Did he say what he was on?"

"No."

"You know we can find out anyway, right? We're not interested in booking a bunch of your raver friends for poppin' pills. To somebody like me, the dead bodies are what matters. And if somebody's sellin' poison, right now, as we talk—"

"No. I'd tell you if I knew. You're a cop, you know I'm tellin' you the truth. So, what, that's how everybody died? Overdose?"

"This Jennifer Lopez, she was your girlfriend?"

"No."

I thought about repeating my question, then stopped. Instead I replayed his question in my mind, focused on it, studied every contour of each word, was almost terrified to find I could glean libraries of information from between each syllable. In an instant I learned volumes by what he didn't say, by the way he breathed, the minute twitch at the corner of his mouth, the slight widening of his left eyelid on the third and fifth word.

This detective last ate seven hours and fifteen minutes ago, two Egg McMuffins and four cups of coffee. You can smell it in the oils seeping through his skin. Check out his posture, he hasn't slept in twenty hours. He forces a smoothness into his voice, wants to come across cultured but shrewd. He tells people his hero is Shaft, but it's really Sean Connery's James Bond. In his daydreams he sees himself hanging off a helicopter in a tuxedo.

And then, in a blink, I knew everything he knew. I saw the fate of each of the dead kids from the One Ball.

Nathan Curry had committed suicide, shot himself in the temple with a little .32 caliber pistol he kept hidden under his bed.

Arkeym Gibbs took a swim, fully clothed, in his family's swimming pool—they found him floating facedown a few hours later.

Shelby Winder and another girl, Carrie Saddleworth, were found together. Each dead of a massive stroke. Shelby was missing her right hand, the wrist a ragged stump wrapped with a blood-soaked shirt.

The rest—Jennifer Lopez, Fred Chu, Big Jim Sullivan are nowhere to be found. They were all at the One Ball with John last night.

Now, only John remained.

You know all that, but you still can't remember this cop's name? You're teetering on the brink of Crazy Man Bluff overlooking Weird Shit Valley.

"And to answer your next question," I continued, "I didn't know Jennifer well enough to know who her friends were or where she may have run off to. I'm sorry."

Detective Freeman stepped forward and flipped open the manila envelope. He fanned out four photographs. One was a mug shot of a young black guy. Dreadlocks. I knew this was my fake Jamaican, knew before my eyes focused on the photo.

The next three pictures were vivid splashes of crimson.

Once, when I was twelve, for reasons that made sense at the time I filled a blender with some ice cubes and three cans of maraschino cherries. I didn't know you had to use a lid on one of those things, so I hit the button and watched it erupt like a volcano. The room in the cop's photographs looked like the resulting mess in our kitchen that day, everything a red spray with lumps.

He pointed to the Jamaican's mug shot. "What about that guy? You know him?"

"He was there. At the party last night. Whatever John was on, this guy gave it to him. John told me."

You already knew that, didn't you, detective?

"That's Bruce Matthews. Runs an amateur unlicensed pharmaceuticals operation on the corner of Thirtieth and Lexington."

I nodded toward the red photos.

"What's that?"

Morgan pointed to the mug shot.

"Before."

He pointed to the red-drenched pictures.

"After."

The first picture was just lumps on the floor, on carpet that was probably brown at one time but was now dyed a wet, purplish black. It looked like somebody had tossed down a bucket of raw steaks and chicken bones. The next picture was a close-up of one wall, deep red splatters over half the surface area, occasional bits of meat stuck here and there. The third picture was a close-up of a severed brown hand in a pool of red, fingers curled loosely, a bandage around the palm.

I turned my eyes away, suddenly sweating heavily. There was that tableau in the mirror again, just me and Morgan, face-to-face. Did he think I had anything to do with this? Was I a suspect? In my panic, I couldn't read him. He let the silence congeal in the air, staring down on me. He broke me, and I broke the silence.

"What could even do that to a person? A bomb? Some kind of—"

"Nothing you know how to do, I'm sure of that. Maybe somethin' not, uh, not within our bounds of familiarity."

That fear again, on Morgan's face. I understood it now.

But there's more. Much more. He's buried it so deep even you can't read it.

The door opened and the detective's words trailed off. A fat Hispanic cop ducked in and whispered in his ear. Morgan's eyebrows shot up and the two of them left the room.

I heard a commotion outside, hurried shouts and feet shuffling on floor tile. After about ten minutes Morgan stormed into the room, eyes wide.

No, no, no, no-no-no. No. Don't say it . . .

"Your friend is dead."

CLICK!

A tape recorder, clicking off at the end of a cassette. Arnie had apparently set the thing on the table before me at some point. I hadn't noticed. He grumbled an apology, fished out a new tape and went about changing it. I glanced over at his discarded notebook, saw he had abandoned his note-taking just after the word "Holocaust."

I pushed away the plate of chicken, rice and snow peas that was the Flaming Shrimp Reunion. I had been picking through it for the last half hour, leaving the chicken. That bird, I knew, had lived a very sad life and I couldn't bring myself to eat it. It also had spent its days covered head to toe in bits of other birds' crap.

"When you got your cell phone bill, did it list the call you got at Denny's?"

"What? I'm sorry."

"The call you got from your friend at Denny's when your friend was sitting there next to you without a phone. Was that call on your cell phone bill?"

"I never thought to check."

The waitress swept by and claimed my plate, dropped off a fortune cookie and my ticket. She ignored Arnie. I held the cookie in my hand, tried to concentrate and "see" what the fortune said inside it. I found I couldn't.

Arnie scratched his head, knitted a question with his eyebrows.

"So the black stuff, the soy sauce, it's a drug, right?"

"Well, I'll get to that."

"And it makes you smarter? When you take it, it lets you read minds and all that?"

"Not really. It heightens your senses. I think. I don't know. When you're on it, it's like overload, like if you hooked your car radio up to one of those interplanetary SETI antennas. You get shit from all over the place, can see things you shouldn't be able to see, but I don't think it would help you do your taxes."

"And you still got some of this stuff?" He glanced quickly down at the silver canister.

"I'm getting to that."

"You're on it right now? That's how you did the thing with the, uh, with the coins and the dream and all that earlier?"

"Yeah. I took some today. It's fading though."

"So the effects don't last that long."

"The *side* effects don't last that long. The effects will last the rest of my life, I think."

Maybe longer.

Arnie scratched his forehead.

"So, the kids that died, this is that rave overdose, right? I remember all that a few years ago, seein' it on CNN. They thought they had gotten hold of some tainted Ecstasy or somethin' like that? So you were the guy that—"

"I can't figure out at what point the party got turned into a 'rave' in the newspapers. There was no techno music or dancing or PVC pants and there was certainly no raving. Freakin' rave. It's one of those words they throw around to scare old people."

"What color is the interview room down at the precinct?"

"Uh, white. It's flaked off in places, shows institutional green underneath."

"And if I contact Detective Appleton, he'll remember talking to you?"

"Good luck finding him."

Arnie made notes.

"So?" I asked. "What do you think?"

"I think you've probably got a book here," he said. "Flesh it out a little."

"A book? Meaning a work of fiction? Meaning it's all bullshit?"

Arnie shrugged. "It's nothin' to me. A story is a story. I'm just a feature reporter, so the fact that you think it happened is my story. But it's like Whitley Strieber, writes that book about aliens. Nobody would ever have heard of it, except he sells it as nonfiction, swears to the end that it all really happened."

His eyes flicked over to the little metal canister again. I realized my fingers had been fidgeting with it.

"Well, I'm not into that whole aliens thing, but I don't think it's right to label the guy a fraud, Arnie."

"Exactly. He's got a nice house, though. His own radio show. Played by Christopher Walken in a movie. Wouldn't you like that? You know, I don't remember leaving the house with any change in my pocket. You could have slipped those coins to me."

"Without you feeling it? And the thing with your dream? Come on, Arnie."

Gotta love the skeptic, mon.

"I saw a sleight-of-hand artist in Vegas who, as part of his show, would call somebody out of the audience and steal the glasses off their face. No kidding. He'd send the poor sap back to his seat and he'd be squinting around, tryin' to figure out why he couldn't see all of a sudden. There's no magic, Mr. Wong. Just knowing tricks the other guy doesn't know about."

I stood up. "Come with me. I wanna show you somethin'. In my truck."

We made our way out to my rattly old Ford Bronco II. I bought it after my old Hyundai got totaled a few years ago in a manner that was undoubtedly unique among all vehicles ever totaled in vehicle history.

I approached the rear and dropped the tailgate, revealing a white sheet covering a large box the size of one of those plastic portable dog carriers. Not coincidentally, it was a portable dog carrier.

"What's the weirdest thing you've ever seen, Arnie?"

He grinned, looking over the box. Like a damn kid at Christmas.

Look, everybody! The crazy man carries around a big crazy box! Let's all humor him at once!

"One time," he began, "I was down in my basement and there's just a couple of bare lightbulbs that hang down, you know? So it's all shadows, and your shadow kind of stretches out across the floor. Anyway, one time, out the corner of my eye, you know, it sort of looked like my shadow back there was movin' without me. I don't mean the bulb was swinging and the shadow was just wavering back and forth, I mean the limbs were, like, flailing around. Real fast, too. It was just for a second and like I said, it was just one of those tricks of light you get out the corner of your eye. But I tell ya, I didn't go back down there until it was broad daylight out. Is what you got in there gonna beat that?"

"I need you to get in that mind-set, Arnie. We're out here, in public with lights on and the whole world's solid and lined up real neat. But down in that basement, in the dark, alone, you believed in things. Dark things. I need you to open yourself up like that. Okay?"

"It was just somethin' I thought I saw. I never said there was anything there, Mr. Wong."

"Just humor me. Ready?"

I threw back the sheet. Long pause.

"Do you see it?"

"No. Or, you know, it's an empty cage."

"Turn your head, so you're looking at me. You should see the box out the corner of your eye, just like the shadow in the basement."

"Okay." Arnie's grin was fading. He was losing patience fast.

"Do you ever go in the bathroom at night, Arnie, and for a second, just a split second, you glimpse something in the mirror other than your reflection? Then you turn the light on and, of course, everything's fine again. But for just a half a second, maybe while you're leaving the room, you see out the corner of your eye that it isn't you in the mirror. Or maybe it is you, only changed? And what's looking back at you is something completely different? Something not very human?"

"Let's go back inside, okay? Your story was more interesting."

"You're going to die, Arnie. Someday, you will face that moment. Regardless of what you believe, at that moment either you will face complete nonexistence, which is something you can't possibly imagine, or you will face something even stranger that you also can't possibly imagine. On an actual day in the future, you will be in the unimaginable, Arnie. Set your mind on that."

Silence, for a few seconds. Arnie nodded a little.

"Okay."

"Now, without turning your head, look at the box."

Arnie did, recoiled, yelped, stumbled and finally fell on his ass.

"Oh, shit!" he gasped. "Shit!! What the shit is that? Sh-shit! Shit!"

I threw the sheet back over the box and closed up the Bronco. Arnie scrambled to his feet and backed up ten steps, halfway to the door of the restaurant.

"How did you do that? And what the fuck was that thing? What the fuck?"

"I don't know what it's called. Pretty freaky, isn't it?"

"You—you made me see something. Something out of my own head. You freaked me out so I would see something."

"No, it's really there. I'm surprised you saw it so easy. You must have an open mind. Most people don't see it that fast unless they're stoned or drunk."

Arnie kept stepping back, muttering.

"I was in the Navy. Diver. I saw some shit, deep-sea shit that didn't look like anything that belonged on this world. But that was nothin', nothin' like that . . . that thing."

79

"I want to tell the rest of the story, Arnie. I need to. I need to get it out. But you need to take it for what it is. The truth. Are you ready to do that?"

Arnie looked at me with uncertainty, then nodded. "Okay. Until I figure it out for real, okay."

"Eh, that'll have to do."

After a moment we walked back toward the restaurant. As we passed through the swinging doors (still painted with the slogan HOLA AMIGOS!!) I picked up my story.

"Anyway, so the cop comes in and tells me John is dead . . ."

I WAS OUT of my chair before I knew it, halfway to the door.

"Wha— How??!"

The cop stopped me cold with a stiff arm to the chest.

"Now calm down," Morgan said, not looking at all calm himself. "He went into a convulsion or somethin' and his pulse stopped but— now listen to me here—we got ambulances, they'll be here in thirty seconds. We got Vinny doin' CPR on him. Vinny's a lifeguard in his off-hours. That boy's in the hands of people who know what they're doin'. That don't include you, so you got no business fartin' around out there, gettin' all hysterical and whatnot."

I knocked his hand away from my chest. The white cop dropped his arms and came toward us, though looking a little less shocked than what I would have expected, having had somebody just drop dead in their police station. Apparently he wouldn't have to fill out the paperwork.

Morgan's lips peeled back slightly to reveal gritted teeth. He started to say something, stopped himself.

Oh, shit. This guy's on the jagged edge . . .

"Here's what you're gonna do, son."

He breathed.

"You're gonna wait here. I'll be back in five minutes and you are gonna start telling me the truth. I am gonna get to the bottom of this

80

and if you obstruct me you will live the rest of your days wishing you had not."

He stepped back, made sure I wasn't going to rush the door, then turned out of the room. What chilled me wasn't the cop's threats. It was the single, dark thought I could read pulsing through his head:

The dead are getting off lucky in this deal.

That didn't seem like a normal cop thought to me.

I stood there, lost, listening to the confusion of shouts and controlled panic outside. I heard sirens out front. Ambulance.

My cell phone chirped. On any other day I would have shut the thing off, but that seemed unwise somehow. I looked toward Officer Liddy, now standing placidly in the middle of the room, and I gestured toward my pocket as if to ask if he minded. He said nothing, I answered my phone.

"Yeah."

"Dave? This is John."

"What? Are you—"

Alive?

"—in an ambulance or something?"

"Yes and no. Are you still at the police station?"

"Yeah. We were both—"

"Have I died yet?"

A long pause from my end.

"Um, yeah, according to the cops." I glanced at the white cop, who showed no interest in my conversation.

"Then there's no time to explain all this. Get out of there."

"But—I'll be a fugitive," I whispered, turning away from the cop. "They know where I—"

"Listen. Get up. Walk to the door. Leave the room. Leave the building. Whatever you do, see that big white cop standing there in the room with you? Don't look at him in the mirror."

"Huh?"

I glanced back over my shoulder at the cop. Something was . . . off.

"Just go. Now."

I tried to get a read on the cop, and realized that's what was off. Even with the soy sauce I was getting zero information from the G. Gordon Liddy–looking detective. I turned my head a few degrees to the right . . .

—*Don't look at the mirror don't look at the mirror*—

. . . to the reflective surface of the two-way mirror directly opposite the cop.

It was just you and Morgan in the mirror, Dave. Even after the white cop stepped forward.

In the mirror it was just me. Standing there, talking on my cell. Alone.

I spun toward the cop.

"I don't get it."

"He's not real, Dave. Not in the, uh, traditional sense."

"He's coming toward me!"

"Go, Dave. You're gonna start seeing things like this from time to time. It's important that you not freak out."

The cop was one step away from me now. His mustache twitched, as if he was starting to grin underneath it.

"So he, uh, can't hurt me?"

"Oh, I'm pretty sure he can."

A hand clenched around my face. The cop's fingers dug into my cheeks, squeezing, rigid as iron bars. I thought my teeth would crack into pieces. He pushed me back using my face and slammed me against the wall.

I clawed at his arm, but it was like trying to tear the limbs off a bronze statue. I smacked him across the nose with my phone. His mustache twitched again as if this amused him greatly.

The mustache kept twitching and twitching and then one end of it began to curl up and peel off, like a man's disguise torn off by a hard wind. Finally the mustache detached completely, leaving a patch of pink, shredded skin. The thing flapped its halves like bat wings—no, it really did—and flew over and landed on my face.

The cop's mustache bit me above the right eyebrow. I slapped at the thing with my left hand, then worked my leg up and, with all my strength, shoved a knee into the detective's guts just below the ribs.

A jolt of pain shot up my thigh, like I had kneed over a pile of cinder blocks. But I felt him give, pushed back by the force. The mustache bat flittered over to my ear and clamped down, feeling like somebody doing five piercings at once. I slapped at it again, suddenly realized the cop had reeled back and fallen to a knee on the floor. I should have been free of him but the hand was still around my face—

Ah, look at that. His arm came off.

The man had a six-inch bloody hole on one shoulder now. The detached arm, on its own, whipped around my neck and coiled up like a python. No hint of bone in there now, the arm making two loops around until the ragged stump hung under my chin like a meat scarf.

I thrashed around, tried to pry the thing off. The armsnake was all muscle, tensed and wiry, slowly squeezing off my windpipe.

Colored spots flashed before my eyes, lack of oxygen shorting out the wiring in my brain. I blinked and saw the floor was closer than before. I was on my knees.

The mustache bat flitted around my head, taking stinging little bites on my cheek and forehead. It went after my eye, pulling at the lid, and I couldn't get my hands up to swat it away. Arms not working right.

The meat scarf squeezed tighter. The whole room got dark. I was on all fours and I suddenly realized the best idea was just to lay down there on the floor and go to sleep.

I detected movement from the corner of my eye. The rest of the cop's body. It was up, walking toward me.

Shit!

I crawled clumsily toward the door. Gordon reached for me with his remaining arm and I felt his fingers try to snatch my shirt. I flung myself toward the door, my face banging off it. I reached up, clawing around for the handle. I sucked air through a squeezed windpipe, my head felt like it would pop like a balloon.

Don't be locked don't be locked don't be locked . . .

The handle turned. I banged open the door with my head and spilled out of the room—

—**AND IT WAS** over.

The thick bundle of armsnake had vanished from my neck, as had the flying mustache. I stood up, saw four guys hustling down the hall with an empty stretcher. I stuck my finger in my mouth, it came out bloody. I looked my cell phone over, saw it had the cracks and busted mouthpiece from its tour as a nose club seconds ago. I cursed at myself, sure that whatever freak-ass cellular conduit I just had with John was now cut off.

People rushed past me and I wanted to push my way through to see what was up with John, remembered John's disembodied instructions. Taking advantage of the chaos, I strolled back through the police station, finally walking right out the front door.

I hit the sidewalk, my heart pounding. What now?

A fat man in a shiny business suit strode by without a glance my way.

Without trying, I realized that he was going to die in just two weeks, a heart attack while trying to knock his cat out of a tree with a broomstick.

A pretty late-model Trans Am gleamed past and I noticed from the posture of the driver that the car was stolen and that the owner was dead. The car's fan belt was going to break in 26,931 miles.

Man, I gotta focus on one thing at a time or my brain's gonna melt and run out of my ears like strawberry jam.

Fine. I took a deep breath. Now what?

My car was two miles away at Wally's and I didn't have cash to waste on a taxi, even if one of the town's three cabs should happen by at this moment. To my surprise, my cell phone rang. I put the broken thing to my ear, realized I owed some props to the engineers at Motorola.

"Hello?"

"Dave? It's me."

John.

"Where are you right now, Dave?"

"I'm on the sidewalk outside the cop shop, walking. Where are you? Heaven?"

"If you figure it out, let me know. Right now just keep walking. Go toward the park. Don't freak out. Are you freaking out?"

"I don't know. I can't believe this phone still works."

"It won't for very much longer. Half a block away, there should be the hot dog guy. Can you see him?"

I walked a dozen steps, smelled it before I saw it. The cart was plastered with right-wing stickers, and had a yellow-and-orange umbrella hanging over it. The hot dog guy was painfully thin, looked about one hundred and sixty years old. As much a landmark as this city has.

"Okay."

"Buy a bratwurst from him."

Questioning this seemed a waste of words.

The man and I exchanged $3.15 and a brat wrapped in a hot dog bun and a sheet of wax paper.

For a moment, I hesitated, then drew two fat, neat lines of mustard along its length. It seemed like the right thing to do.

Cell phone balanced between shoulder and ear, John spoke again, as if under water, his voice growing fainter by the second.

"Now put it up to your head."

I looked down at the rivulets of oozing grease, congealing with the now dripping mustard and was thankful that I didn't use ketchup or that brown hot onion sauce.

Glancing around, I tried to be as inconspicuous as possible as I lay the sausage against my ear. Abruptly, my cell phone went dead.

A drop of grease dribbled into the dead center of my ear, creeping like a worm down onto my neck and below the collar of my shirt. A group of men and women in business suits walked by, swerving to avoid me. Across the street, a homeless-looking guy was staring at me, curious. Yep, this was pretty much rock bottom.

As I was about to reach for a napkin and at least get my money's worth by eating the bratwurst while it was still hot, I heard it.

"Dave? Can you hear me?"

John's voice, coming clear as day through the tube of seasoned meat. I glanced down at the cell phone and got the point. The display was black, the glass busted out of it. A green circuit board was poking out of the warped seam along one side.

"All right, all right. I'm hearing you through some kind of psychic vibration or whatever and not the phone. I get it. You could have just told me that." I lowered the sausage and replaced it with the cell. "Okay, what's next?"

Nothing.

I heard a faint sound coming from the bratwurst, put it back to my head.

"Dave? Are you there?"

"Yeah. I can't get you through the cell now."

"You have to talk through the bratwurst from now on."

"Why—"

I sighed and rubbed my eyes, feeling a headache coming on.

"—Okay. What do we do?"

"The only reason you can hear me is because you got some of the soy sauce into your system, from the syringe. But it's not very much and it won't last long."

"What is it, John? The sauce . . . it was alive. I swear it—"

"Listen. You gotta get over to Robert's place. There aren't any cops there now, but there will be. We have sort of a narrow window here. Take a cab to Wally's and get your car, then go to Shire Village on Lathrop Avenue. It's a trailer park, south of town past that one candy place. You should be able to get there in twenty minutes with any luck."

"I don't have any cash. I had five bucks and I just spent three of it on the bratwurst."

"That bratwurst was three bucks? Holy crap. Okay. Give me a second.

86

All right. Check between the sausage and the bun. You'll find a hundred dollar bill folded up in there."

Encouraged that maybe all this black magic could actually produce something positive, I fingered around under the sausage for a few seconds.

"Nothing here, John."

"Okay. I guess I can't do that. Do you have your ATM card?"

CHAPTER 4
The Soy Sauce

TWO HOURS LATER I pulled my Hyundai into Shire Village. The now-cold bratwurst sat on the dash, little smears of mustard on the windshield where the sloppy wax paper contacted it. I put it to my head.

"John?"

I was greeted with a burst of static, but then John's voice came in, fainter than before.

"Dave?"

"Yeah."

"What, did you drive under a bridge just now?"

"No. We're at the trailer park. Finally. Which one is Robert's?"

Static again. Then: "It's wearing off. Don't talk, just listen. Go inside and—"

Static.

"—and as long as you absolutely remember not to do that, you'll be fine. Good luck."

"What? John, I didn't catch the—"

Dead. The voice was gone, the static was gone. It was just a sausage again. I resigned myself to the hope that whatever I had to do next would be apparent from a look at Robert's place.

His trailer was one of only two that had yellow police tape over the porch and door, and the other one looked like it had been abandoned months ago. Meth lab.

I parked off in the grass across the lot and walked toward Robert's abode. Nobody was there, or at least nobody who came in a car. I knocked for some reason, then went in.

They had cleaned up the blood and guts. I guess that shouldn't have surprised me, since I should have known they wouldn't just let the entrails collect flies for twelve hours. Still, I recognized the room from the photos the cop showed me, the scene of Robert's wet explosion. The carpet was still a few shades off from its original color and the walls were forever stained a faded reddish-brown. And there was a smell, awful and organic. Mildew and rotten milk and shit.

The walls were stripped bare, no family photos or framed landscapes from Wal-Mart or movie posters. Did the cops do that? No television. A sofa, a chair pocked with cigarette burns. Was he living here, or squatting?

I glanced into the open kitchenette at one end of the trailer, then turned and walked down a short hallway to the other end. I pushed through a closed door leading to what had to be a bedroom—

—and stopped. I was suddenly looking out over a snow-dusted field, a range of mountains spiking into a stunning violet sky from the horizon. Not a picture, that's not how it struck me. It was like that end of the trailer had been chainsawed off to reveal the outdoors, only if that had really happened I would've only seen the neighbor's rusty trailer and an abandoned Oldsmobile floating among the weeds. What I saw instead took my breath away.

I stepped backward into the hallway, dizzy, disoriented, afraid I would be sucked in somehow. It took almost a minute to realize what I was looking at.

It was a painting. A floor-to-walls-to-ceiling mural. He had painted the walls, the trim on the windows, the damned glass in the window. He painted over the curtains, painted the carpet, painted the sheets and wrinkled comforter on the unmade bed so that, when viewed from the doorway, the effect was beyond photographic. There was a half-full water glass on the nightstand, and a sprout of ice-coated weeds painted on the wall continued on the nightstand and onto the glass. There was a little crack in the glass and the artist incorporated it into the painting, the fracture becoming a glint of sunlight off an ice-covered leaf.

The effect was too much. It gave me a heaviness in my gut like the first time I saw a skyscraper when I was a kid. Picasso could not have done this, not if he had a lifetime to devote to it. Step on that carpet and disturb the texture, or brush against the comforter and the effect would be ruined.

Whoa. Just . . . whoa.

I don't know how long I stood there, absorbing it, overwhelmed by the details.

There's a deer, complete with little hoofprints in the snow. A happy little cabin, the family in the yard . . .

As I took in those little details, my amazement began to sour, congealing into a cold dread.

The cabin on the mountainside, that's not a little tree out front. It's a makeshift cross, with a man hanging from it. His legs have been cut off. The woman standing next to it . . . look at the infant in her arms. It has a single, curved horn coming out of its skull. And unfortunately for the old man, the baby still looks hungry. The frozen pond in back, those aren't reeds sticking up through the ice all across the surface. Those are hands. And that deer? It has a huge cock, making a little trench in the snow behind it . . .

I closed the door, deciding to never open it again. I walked back down the hall toward the living room, passed a bathroom, then did a double take, leaning back to look inside. Nothing unusual.

The toilet is askew.

"So?" I said, out loud.

Damn my curiosity. I stepped into the bathroom, saw that the back of the toilet was indeed sitting a good foot away from the wall, where it ought to be. The stool was bolted to a square piece of flooring that was no longer neatly covering the square hatch below. I scooted the stool out to the middle of the floor, looked down the hatch. Basement access?

This is a trailer, dumb-ass. Probably just a dope hidey-hole down there. The question is whether he kept pooping in this toilet after he disconnected the drain . . .

Two feet below the hatch was the gravel and dirt surface under the trailer, interrupted by a hole that had been dug into the ground wide enough for a man to drop through.

An old well? Wait a second . . . there's light down there. Did this man get his shovel and just dig himself a trailer basement some weekend?

There was a roll-up ladder leading down the hole, the kind some people keep by their bedroom windows in case of fires.

Yeah, climb right down there, dumb-ass. It's not like a man spontaneously exploded just feet from this spot or anything. Go down and be a meal for the infamous Midwestern Tunneling Explodebear.

But John sent me here for a reason. Maybe a retarded reason, knowing John, but I had come this far. I thought about him, thought about spending the rest of my life without him, and a moment later I was sitting on the linoleum floor, dropping my legs down through the hatch. I tried to look down the hole, could only see that, as I thought, there was an open, lit space down there. I grabbed the floor and dropped my body down the mouth of the hole, finding the ladder with my feet.

The rungs were slippery with mud, and the dirt stank like mold all around me. As I went down, I was hit with another smell so strong it seemed to generate its own warmth. Sharp and rotten and fecal.

The hole went down about twice the length of my body before my feet were hanging in a dim, earthy chamber that seemed big enough to stand in. The stench got stronger, and when I dropped down my feet splashed in a slimy puddle of Robert Marley shit.

I stood straight, kicking crap off my shoes. My head brushed a surprisingly smooth ceiling. The room was almost perfectly round, a diameter about the width of the trailer. The light was coming from one of those camping lanterns, on the floor next to the curved wall on my left. An odd, low, rumbly sound emerged from somewhere, seemingly from every direction at once in the round room.

I looked around quickly.

Shapes, on the floor.

I stepped over and picked up the lantern, scanned the room, fully expecting to find at least three corpses. All I saw was a pile of junk off to one side, including a broken television and what looked like yard compost with something like twigs sticking out here and there. There were a couple of empty jars along the wall near it, faded pickle labels on each. There was something that looked like a long duffel bag lying against the wall on the opposite side.

I stepped slowly toward the duffel bag thing, saw with horror that it was something like a huge, fat caterpillar, leathery and probably five feet long. It was segmented like an earthworm, the end a puckered circle of tiny teeth. I would have run away shrieking like a banshee at that point, but the thing was so over-the-top gross that I was sure it was something he made. A sculpture or whatever. And it wasn't moving, obviously. I would have mentioned that by now.

Just to be sure, I stepped forward very slowly and nudged the worm thing with my foot. Nothing. Maybe a novelty pillow of some kind. I watched it for a moment longer and then carefully backed off toward the junk pile. On the way, I took a glance at the walls, wondering if this dirt chamber was going to collapse without supports. Covering

92

the strangely smooth dirt was a clear, wavy substance like glass or ice. I can't tell you what it felt like because I didn't even consider touching it.

I glanced nervously at the worm pillow one last time, then stepped back and slipped in something slimy again. A little wet pile of what I thought were sausages. On closer inspection, I saw they were fingers.

Four severed digits, along with strips of flesh and bare bone. They all had an odd, misshapen look, as if they were somewhat melted.

My windpipe closed. My heart tried to punch through my sternum.

I took two steps backward, covered my mouth with my hand and tried to calm myself.

Get out get out get the fuck out—

I took long, slow breaths. I tore my eyes off the mess on the floor and walked to the other side of the room.

I arrived at the large pile of random junk, including the gutted television. I was startled to see the TV was on. There was a shot of what looked like a view through somebody's intestines, like when doctors send those little cameras in there.

Then the shot changed to a picture of a twentysomething guy with long blond hair who looked vaguely familiar. He was sitting casually in a living room chair, talking to someone off-camera who was referring to him as "Todd."

The scene flicked again, showing a blurred, uneven first-person shot of a car moving down a residential street.

The rumbling stopped. I stood straight, looked around. The worm thing—wasn't it closer to the wall before? Nah.

I turned back to the TV setup. I couldn't see a power cord leading up and out of the chamber but figured maybe there was a car battery or something hidden in there somewhere. I looked closer at the pile of what I had mistaken for twigs and saw it was a sticky collection of some unknown, uh, something. The back of the television had been removed and a strip of what looked like red seaweed led out of it and into a large, dead fish. The gut of the fish had been slit open and bulging out of it was a pink, wet mass of something the size of a basketball, like its innards had swollen to fifty times its normal size. Close to it was an aquarium tank filled with a thick, yellowish substance that could have been slug slime and at the bottom was a wrinkled grayish mass that could have been a human brain or possibly a meat-loaf.

I had the awful realization that I was looking at a machine of some kind and just when I thought nothing here could surprise me, I looked into the television screen and was proven wrong.

A trailer—this trailer—was on the screen.

Small, as if being seen from a distance.

But getting bigger.

The viewer moving closer.

Somebody's point of view, heading this direction. If the feed was live, just a minute away.

I turned, stepped forward, fell flat on my face. The lantern crashed to the floor, rolling, sending light and shadow dancing over every sur-face. It gave me a quick, strobe-light view of the huge slug thing I had tripped over, which was now resting under my splayed legs. It had moved out to the center of the room with startling speed.

I could feel the thing warmly pulsing and quivering under me, its soft mass giving under my legs. I kicked off of it, pushing backward on my ass, saw the thing squish its way after me. The lantern went out, casting me into a darkness broken only by the soft glow of the mutant television and a shaft of yellow light from the bathroom above.

I could hear the thing sliming around me, felt it near my face. I stumbled to my feet, slipped in the huge pool of shit in the center of the room, back onto my ass, bouncing my head off the hard ground. I got up on my hands just as a heavy weight like a canvas bag filled with meat landed on my chest.

The fucking thing had jumped on me.

Pinned me.

A hundred-pound bag of slime compressing my lungs.

I waited for it to bite my face off.

A few seconds later, the low, rattly sound resumed.

After a long moment I realized that it had gone to sleep. I gently rolled the snoring creature onto the floor, careful not to wake it. I very quietly stood and jumped halfway up the ladder. In ten seconds I had my palms down on the sticky bathroom floor, shoulders brown with what was hopefully mud, pants stained with shit. I decided right then I would leave and go home and watch some TV and drink a—

Thump.

I almost pissed myself. It was a faint sound, from the other end of the trailer. The kitchen end. I stepped into the hall, expecting to see a flame-shooting vampire, a hybrid squid/clown, the Devil himself.

Nothing. Probably just wind. A micro-earthquake. Sudden termite migration.

THUMP.

A heavy sound, violent. Adrenaline set my muscles on fire and, like a dumb-ass, I moved toward the sound. Definitely from the kitchen. In seven steps I crossed the Robert Marley estate.

My shoes hit linoleum. I looked around the counter, floor and appliances. No elves, no gremlins, no nothing. Not yet.

Dead silence. I realized I was holding my breath. I realized I was not holding a weapon. I glanced around for something like a knife—

THUMP.

The refrigerator.

THUMP.

No. The freezer section at the top. The little door up there rattled with the sound, like it was bumped—

THUMP.

—from the inside.

Get out. Get out, David. Go. Go. Go. Go. GO. GO. GO!

With one last thump, the freezer door flew open.

A round, frosty lump the size of a coffee can tumbled out of the freezer, fell to the floor, rolled to a stop two feet away from me. I stared at it, stared into the open, empty freezer. I steeled my courage—

—then turned and ran my ass off.

I stomped toward the exit, made it in three flying strides. A half second before my hand would have ripped the knob off the front door,

I happened to glance out the window and see a sedan parked out there where none had been before. Plain white, but too many antennas.

Cop car.

Somebody getting out.

Fucking Morgan Freeman.

He walked toward the front door, ten feet away from me. I spun around, searching for a back exit. Even if there was one, it would mean stepping over the possessed jar or whatever had rolled out of the freezer, which was now sitting on the tile, rocking back and forth, steaming faintly. I saw now the thing was a bundle of duct tape, something wrapped in layer after layer of the stuff.

No thanks.

A look back outside. My cop friend was coming this way, pausing to turn and look back over his shoulder at something I couldn't see. What would I say when he came in? I can usually cobble together a pretty good lie if I have a couple of hours to plan—

Pock!

A hollow snapping sound, from the freezer jar. The thing hopped an inch off the floor and so did I when I heard that sound.

It did it again, jumped higher.

Shit, like something trying to punch its way out from inside—

Snap. Ka-chunk.

That's how I spell the sound of a doorknob turning. Morgan was just two feet away from me now, on the other side of a door-shaped piece of imitation wood, coming in. I ducked down, looked at the jar now with hope that the leprechaun or demon or whatever jumped out of it would distract the cop from asking the rather obvious question of why the hell I was here after walking out on my interrogation. I braced myself for what was sure to be one of the more awkward moments of my life.

The doorknob snapped back into place, released from the other side. I risked a look through a living room window and saw Morgan looking away, toward the gravel driveway and this time saw what he saw: a white van pulling in, parking next to his cruiser. Big logo on the side. CHANNEL 5 NEWS. A guy stepped out of the driver's seat, hauling out

96

a camera and a folded tripod, and a pretty reporter emerged from the passenger side. Not only was I about to be discovered lurking around a restricted crime scene, but my arrest for said offense was about to be broadcast on live television. It would literally be the worst job of secretly sneaking into a restricted area in recorded history.

POCK! POCK!! POCK!!!

There was a bulge now on the side of the jar or whatever it was, strands of duct tape fibers popping out in the center, giving under the strain. All of a sudden being arrested didn't seem so bad and I should have ducked outside with my hands raised high in surrender. But fear kept my ass Velcroed to the carpet. The jar convulsed, and again I wished I had a weapon, preferably a flamethrower.

Outside, I could barely hear cop and reporter having a terse forced-politeness contest.

"Hi, I'm Kathy Bortz, Channel Five—"

"—All inquiries go through the captain, you've got the number. It's all cleaned up in there anyway, you missed the really good pictures by a few hours—"

She may have missed the story, Morgan, but I bet she'd be pleased to capture a live shot of whatever was about to happen to me.

Here's exclusive Channel 5 video of a local man having his brain eaten by a winged gremlin. Local gremlin experts warn that—

FOONT!

The jar erupted, ejaculated, gave birth in a cloud of stringy tape bits. A shotgun hole blew out from the guts of the can and a little blur of an object zipped out and bounced off the paneled wall above me. The offspring fell to the carpet, bounced and landed next to my shoe.

A little shiny metal canister, the size of a pill bottle. Not moving or growling or glowing. Just sitting.

Waiting.

I stared dully, then forced myself to crane my neck up and around to see the scene outside, the cop turned right toward me, gesturing. I threw my head back down out of the way, sat down hard on the carpet with my back against the wall.

He saw you. Did you see the flicker of surprise on his face? He caught a glimpse of your head looking out from the trailer window. Dumbass.

I looked at the little metal vial, scooted back from it. Are those footsteps I hear outside? I raised my foot to kick the vial away, then reconsidered.

You know what's in there, right?

Nope. No idea.

You know Robert had a stash of the shit that infected John . . .

Faint voices, from outside.

"What part of 'no comment' do you not fucking understand?"

Closer than before?

. . . and if he had a stash, he couldn't just cram it under his bed. That black shit moves. It has a will, an attitude. It bites.

And then I realized, all at once, what I had come here for. John led me here, of course. When I was on the stuff, the little hit in my bloodstream I got when it attacked my thigh, I could communicate with—

(the dead)

—with John. When it wore off, I could not. My one chance to save him lay inside the bottle, wicked as it apparently was.

I picked up the bottle, cold as an ice cube. I found a seam and twisted the top half off, expected black oil to ooze out.

Instead, out tumbled two tiny, cold pebbles. Perfect and black in my palm, like two coal-flavored Tic Tacs. The same stuff, I figured, in convenient capsule form for those who are afraid of needles.

You're afraid of needles.

So?

If it had been a hypodermic, you wouldn't have even considered putting it inside you. How convenient.

I closed my eyes, steeled myself like the first time I did a shot of whiskey.

It knew. And what is it you're doing, exactly? For all you know, this stuff oozed out of a crashed meteor. You've found it in the home of a dead man, after following a trail of dead bodies to get here. So go ahead, put it right in your mouth, dipshit.

98

I hesitated, felt an itching in my palm where the capsules sat. I could hear nothing from outside, which fed a little sprout of hope that maybe everybody had just left.

If you do this, there ain't no turning back. Somehow you know that.

I felt the itch again, a crawling sensation on my palm. I looked down and saw the capsules sitting innocently and then—I saw them move. Wriggling in my hand like a couple of fat, black maggots. I flung them to the carpet, flailing my hand around like it was on fire. I stumbled to my feet. The things twisted, changed, grew tiny little black limbs.

Two flat appendages grew out of one of the capsules, began to twitch, move, flap. A blur now. Wings. The black blob made a terrible, insectile fluttering sound against the carpet. Then, the Tic Tac launched itself at me, a faint, dark streak.

I didn't realize my mouth was hanging open until that moment and if I had known I would have closed it, I assure you. In an instant the thing was skipping off my tongue and landing as a horrible, twitching tickle on the back of my throat. I coughed, hacked, convulsed. The soy sauce insect crawled down my esophagus. I felt its little tingly legs all the way down to my gut.

I opened my eyes, looked desperately for the other one. Hard to spot on the dark carpet—

There.

It buzzed, it flew. So fast it vanished from my sight. I clamped my lips shut, slapped my hand over my mouth for good measure. The thing landed on my left cheek and without thinking I brought up my other hand and swatted it like a mosquito.

Pain. An acidic burn, an iron from the fire, jammed into the soft skin under my eye. I suppressed a scream, brought my hand away from my face and found it bloody.

The stab of agony in my cheek became a bright, broad ache that seemed to radiate down to my toes. A pain so big my mind couldn't wrap itself around it, mixed with a weird, buzzing itch that comes specifically with tearing flesh, the feel of whole nerve endings torn from their roots and tossed aside.

I tasted the copper flow of blood in my mouth, felt something moving over there . . .

OH SON OF A MOTHERFUCK THE FUCKING SOY SAUCE IS DIGGING A FUCKING HOLE INTO MY FUCKING FACE.

I fell flat on the floor, thrashing and rolling like a seizure. I forgot where I was, who I was, everything in my mind vaporized by a hydrogen bomb of panic.

OH THIS HURTS THIS HURTS THIS HURTS I CAN FEEL THE THING CRAWLING ACROSS MY TEETH NOW OH SHIIIIIIITTTT.

My face and shirt were wet and sticky with blood. I felt the second intruder crawl across my tongue and down my throat, felt my stomach wrench with disgust. I heard footsteps just outside the door now, felt relieved, knew I would throw myself at Officer Freeman and beg him to take me to the emergency room, to pump my stomach, to bring in an exorcist, to call in the Air Force to bomb this whole town into radioactive dust and bury it under sixty feet of concrete.

And then, calm.

Almost Zen.

I again felt that sensation from the police station, the radiating energy pulsing from the chest out like that first swallow of hot, spiked coffee while standing outside in the dead of winter. The soy sauce high.

The doorknob began to turn. Morgan was coming. Hell, Morgan was *here*. I wanted to run, to duck, to act. Frustrating. The body is slow, so slow—

And just like that, I was outside my body.

Time stopped.

It was so easy for me, I almost laughed. Why hadn't I caught on before? I had a full 1.78 seconds before the detective would step through the door. The only reason we would normally perceive that span as being a short amount of time is because the wet mechanism of our bodies simply can't accomplish very much in that span. But a supercomputer can do over a trillion mathematical equations in one second. To that machine, one second is a lifetime, an eternity. Speed up how

100

much thinking you can do in two seconds and two seconds becomes two minutes, or two hours or two trillion years.

1.74 seconds until confrontation time now, my body and the body of my nemesis frozen in the moment, on opposite sides of the door, he with his hand on the knob, me on hands and knees in suspended agony.

Okay. I needed a plan. I took a moment to mentally step back, to assess my situation. *Think.*

You are standing on the thin, cool crust of a gigantic ball of molten rock hurtling through frozen space at 496,105 miles an hour. There are 62,284, 523,196,522,717,995,422,922,727,752,433,961,225,994,352,284,523,1 96,571,657,791,521,592,192,954,221,592,175,243,396,122,599,435,29 1,541,293,739,852,734,657,229 subatomic particles in the universe, each set into outward motion at the moment of the Big Bang. Thus, whether or not you move your right arm now, or nod your head, or choose to eat Fruity Pebbles or Corn Flakes next Thursday morning, was all decided at the moment the universe crashed into existence seventeen billion years ago because of the motion and trajectory of those particles at the first millisecond of physical existence. Thus it is physically impossible for you to deviate—

I never finished this thought.

I was no longer in the trailer.

Sun. Sand. A desert.

Was I dead?

I looked around, saw nothing of interest except brown and brown and brown, spanning from horizon to horizon. God's sandbox. What now? I thought of John's ramblings his first hours on the sauce, saying he kept falling out of the time stream, everything overlapping.

I saw movement at my feet. A beetle, trundling along in the sand. I figured this might mean something, so I watched it, followed it as it inched along the desert floor. This went on for approximately two hours, the bug heading steadily in one direction. I had begun to form a theory that this beetle was some kind of Indian-vision spirit guide meant to lead me to my destiny—then it stopped. It stayed in one spot for about half an hour, then turned around and began crawling back the other direction.

In a blink, I was somewhere else.

A chain-link fence.

Brown, dead grass.

People around me, in rags like refugees.

This was getting ridiculous. I stood there for a moment, baffled. I remembered John again and was determined to keep my head, to hang on until the stuff wore off. I looked down and saw I was holding a fork, my hand stained with a gray dust, like ash.

A little girl approached me. She was deformed, filthy, a good chunk of her face missing. One eye. She studied me, then ran up, kneed me in the groin and wrenched the fork from my hand. She ran off with it, and when I looked up—

White walls.

Industrial sounds.

Machines.

I was in a large building, very clean, and a man stood in front of me wearing a blue uniform, watching a small computer screen on what had to be an assembly line. To my left I saw a massive red sign that said NO SMOKING OR OPEN FLAME ON THE PRODUCTION FLOOR, with a cartoon explosion underneath it.

I stepped forward, noticed the guy had one of those Far Side flip calendars next to him. It was badly out of date, the current page a couple of years old.

I had to stop this, somehow. I felt like I was a swimmer, getting tossed downstream by white-water rapids. I knew somehow that if I didn't get ahold of myself, I would drift like this, forever.

Not expecting to get a response, I said, "Uh, hey."

The guy stirred, turned. For just a moment I thought I saw his eyes meet mine, but then his gaze swept around the room, seeing nothing. The man apparently decided he had imagined it and turned back to his monitor.

The room was full of people at various machines. It was obvious no one could see me. I was here, but I was not *here*. I looked down and, sure enough, could not see my feet.

My feet, I knew, were still in a trailer in Undisclosed, on a Saturday

102

afternoon. I focused all my concentration on getting back there, to that spot, to that time, to my body. And in a blink, I was back in the trailer, on the floor. Pain in my face, stench of shit on my pant legs.

I breathed a sigh of relief, tried to remember what I had been doing, when Morgan Freeman stepped through the door and stopped cold at the sight of me.

Damn. I suck at this.

I looked up, climbed awkwardly to my feet with my hand on my bloody face, my pants stinking of Robert Marley's feces.

The detective looked me over.

He had two red plastic gasoline cans with him.

He's gonna burn this place down, I realized with perfect clarity.

And he's gonna burn me with it.

Morgan sat the gas cans at his feet, then lit a cigarette. He smoked in silence for a moment, looking off into space as if he had suddenly forgotten I was there.

"So," I began, figuring I would remind him, "I suppose you're wondering why I'm here."

He shook his head slightly. "Same as everybody. You're trying to figure out what in the name of Elvis is going on. Everybody 'cept me. Me, I don't even wanna know no more. I bet you're wondering what I'm doing with these here gas cans."

"I think I know. And I don't think Robert's landlord would approve at all."

He studied my bleeding face, then reached into his pocket and handed me a handkerchief. I pressed it to my cheek.

"Thank you. I, uh, fell. On a . . . drill."

"You believe in Hell, Mr. Wong?"

Five seconds of confused silence, then, "Uh, yeah. I guess."

"Why?" he asked. "Why do you believe in Hell?"

"Because it's the opposite of what I want to believe."

He nodded slowly, as if this answer seemed to satisfy him. He picked up one gas can, unscrewed the cap, and started splashing the orange liquid around the living room.

I watched him for a moment, then took a tentative step toward the door. In a blur of movement Morgan turned, whipped his hand out of his jacket. A revolver was now aimed right at my face.

"You leavin' already?"

My mind was still buzzing and suddenly I saw a flash from Morgan's memory, something too bizarre to grasp. It was a scene from this morning, here at this very trailer. Blood.

And screaming. All that screaming. What the hell did you see here, Morgan?

Then I had another vision, of walls erupting in flame around me. I put my hands up in surrender and he nodded down toward the other gas can.

He said, "Help me."

"I'll be glad to. But first I want you to tell me what happened to John. You know, the other guy you were interrogating?"

"I figured he was with you."

"Me? Didn't he, you know, die?"

"Sure did. He was in the interview room and Mike Dunlow was askin' him the same questions I was askin' you. And your guy was muttering responses like he's half asleep. He keeps sayin' we gotta let you and him go, that you got to get to Vegas, else it's the end of the world—"

Las Vegas again. What the fuck is in Vegas?

"—So finally Dunlow says to him, 'Look, we got dead or missing kids here and we're gonna find out what we need to know, so you're stayin' in this room until I'm satisfied or you die of old age.' Your boy, when he hears that, he falls over dead. Just like that."

"Yeah, that sounds like John."

"And now he's gone. Got a call from the hospital, it's just an empty bed where he was. They figured he skipped out on payin' the bill."

"That also sounds like John."

I picked up the gas can and removed the cap. Morgan put his gun away. I soaked the couch.

"You know a kid named Justin White, Mr. Wong? High school kid?"

"No. You asked me that back at the police station. He's one of the missing, right?"

No, you know him. Think.

Morgan said, "Drives a cherry-red '65 Mustang?"

Ah. I didn't know the man but I knew the car. This was the baby-faced blond kid I saw Jennifer making out with at the party.

"I know what he looks like, that's it."

"He's the guy who called in the—the whatever happened here. Now, this is how my day started. Just so you understand me, so you understand my state of mind. Okay? Kid calls nine-one-one in a panic, hysterical, talkin' about a dead body. This was about four in the morning. I happened to be two blocks away at the time. So I race over and I'm the first one there and from outside I hear screamin'. And there's people runnin' away, kids peelin' out in their cars. Party that went bad and all that."

He stopped splashing the gasoline and sat the can on the ground. He stared off into space for a moment. He sucked some inspiration from his cigarette butt and spoke again.

"I go up to the door, I tell 'em it's the cops. I go inside and I see—

—I WAS THERE. Just like that.

I was still in the trailer, standing in the exact same spot. Only the pain in my cheek was gone, and horrible rap/reggae hammered my ears from a floor stereo across the room. The light was different and a glance toward a window told me it was night. I looked down and again couldn't see my feet.

Here, but not here.

It was like somebody had hit *rewind* on the trailer, the playback from about twelve hours ago.

The room was full of people. I spotted the faces of Jennifer Lopez and Justin White in the crowd. I scanned the room for John, but there was no sign of him. But of course he would have been gone by now, back at his apartment having a rough night of his own.

105

The music thumped but nobody was moving, or talking. All were standing frozen, their eyes fixed on a spot to my right. Holy shit the song was bad. It was "Informer" by the white reggae rapper Snow. "Infooooormer, younosaydaddymesnowblahblahblay . . ."

I turned to see what was so compelling as to draw a room full of frozen stares.

Robert the pseudo-Jamaican's body was curled up on the floor, twitching. He was saying, "I'm okay, I'm okay, mon! Just give me a minute now! I'm feelin' better!"

His words would have been more reassuring if his head hadn't been separated from his body, laying a good two feet away from the shredded pink stump of his neck.

The disembodied head kept offering reassurances, the head scooting around the floor slightly with each movement of his jaw. One of Robert's arms came free at the shoulder, landing softly on the carpet. I realized with revulsion something was wriggling in the exposed guts, like worms.

Someone screamed.

The party turned into a stampede.

I jumped as some girl ran through me, passing through where my body should be. Everybody was circling around Robert, trying to get to the door while avoiding the infested, oozing mess and—holy *shit* is this song bad. It was like the singer was stabbing my ear with a dagger made of dried turds.

The music stopped abruptly. Somebody had knocked over the stereo.

I saw Justin in the corner, screaming into his cell phone. "I said he's dead! And he's talking! But he's also dead! Just fucking get down here and you can see for yourself!"

I watched the partygoers spill out of the door, but never saw Jennifer pass me. I turned and saw the back of somebody heading the opposite way, down the hall. No door down there, dumbass.

But there is a basement under the bathroom.

There was a sound like a garbage bag of pudding dropped off a tall building onto a sidewalk.

Robert had erupted, chunks slapping off the walls in every direction.

Justin let the phone fall from his hand. His mouth hung open. The room had emptied, now just him and the pink pile of what was left of the Rastafarian drug dealer, together in total silence.

A single white insect appeared. It circled above the wet wreckage of Robert's former body, a white streak, creating the faintest buzz in the silent room.

The insect was joined by another. Then two more.

The sound grew. A high-pitched noise somewhere between the chattering of angry squirrels and the screech of locusts.

Dozens now. Each time I blinked, the swarm doubled in size. The bugs were long, like worms, and flew horizontally. Too many to count now, a swirling cloud above the spilled flesh.

I wanted out of this room, out of this town, off this planet. I had no means to move. It was the nightmare we've had a thousand times, a horror we can't run from because the horror has swallowed us whole.

The sound grew with the swarm, I could feel it, it had a gut-level power like the pulse of John's music at the party last night.

Then, in unison, the white swarm flew toward Justin.

He screamed.

The door burst open—

—I BLINKED, AND saw Morgan in front of me. The stench of gasoline flooded my sinuses. Back again.

"I come through the door and this kid, Justin, he's on his hands and knees and just *wailing*. And I think he's been stabbed in the gut but I look closer and he's got something on him. All over him, his arms and his face."

Morgan left the cigarette in his mouth as he spoke, the paper burning away, leaving a quarter inch of ash dangling off the end. Gasoline dripped off the wallpaper around me.

"It looks like, like thick hairs. All over him," he said. "White, maybe like pipe cleaners, or little twisted bits of fishing line. And they're on

107

his eyelids and ears and neck and arms and this guy is screamin', on his hands and knees, just shrieking like a little kid. And I see these things in the air, too, buzzing around him."

A half inch of ash hanging off his cigarette now. My eyes moved from it to the gasoline-soaked floor at his feet.

"And man, I am frozen there, in the doorway. I mean, I look over and on one side of the room I got a guy sprayed all over the walls like he stepped on a land mine and then there's this, and I should go try to, try to render some assistance but I don't wanna touch him. I don't want whatever's on him on me."

Morgan's words trailed off again. He looked down at his own hands, as if to make absolutely sure they were clean.

The long hunk of ash fell off of his cigarette, onto the wet carpet below.

It went out with a soft hiss.

Morgan said, "Then I did what I shouldn't have done: I ran back out to my car and called for the ambulance. I mean, it's already on the way and I shoulda stayed in and, I don't know, found a can of bug spray or somethin' or dragged the guy off into the shower and washed these things off him but I couldn't. I couldn't make myself because of the way the guy was screamin'. But not just that. Bugs, even biting bugs, I'll handle if I got to. But I could . . ."

He paused, testing what he was about to say in his own head. "I could *hear* them. Inside me. Do you understand?"

I didn't, but found myself unable to speak. He opened a closet, doused the contents with gas.

"So I go to the car and I call it in and I'm real vague about what's goin' on, okay? I got a can of Mace in the car and I grab it and I head back inside and I'm thinkin' I should call a hazmat team, guys who could come in and, I don't know, seal this place off, disinfect it. But I gotta try to help this guy first and I rush back inside, and . . . he's fine. Just like that. He's standing there fixin' his hair and there's no sign of these things nowhere, the bugs or whatever. And this kid, Justin, he starts talkin' like normal, like I just got there."

I went down to the bedroom, threw open the door and, without looking in, tossed in the half-full gas can. I shut the door behind me. Morgan saw me, smiled.

"Yeah, you saw that. That painting. That's messed up, ain't it? Ain't no man who could do that. And I tell ya what, you stay in there long enough, that mural gets inside your head. The dude that was takin' pictures of the crime scene, he went in there for half an hour. He had to be dragged out and he was cryin'. Like a little baby."

I said nothing.

He went on. "So the ambulance gets here, and the kid says he's fine but I put him in it anyway, told the guys the kid maybe had somethin' in his blood that could kill him any second. I mean, I know this kid is . . . infested, I guess. And I wanna know what this stuff is, but I never found out because the kid never arrived at the hospital. That ambulance took off from here with sirens and lights and it's goin' to St. John's, which is just ten minutes away. Ambulance crew shows up there forty-five minutes later, laughin' and jokin' and carryin' fast-food cups, and the kid is nowhere in sight. They ask the two guys what happened and they got no idea what anybody's talkin' about. No memory of any of it. Nobody's heard from the kid since and when they go back out to the garage they find the effing ambulance is gone. They still ain't found it. So, do you understand the kind of day I'm havin'?"

I wiped my cheek with the handkerchief, now deep red and sticky. My hands stank of fuel. I tried to process all this, still studying the carpet, wondering if maybe there wasn't a swarm of alien bugs zipping around under the subfloor.

"So," I said, "can you, uh, hear anything? Right now? Like they're still hanging around in here?"

"Not since I got back."

"But you're gonna burn the place down just to make sure?"

"That's right."

"And you're not gonna let me go."

He was silent for a moment, then said, "Those things that were on the guy? I been describing them like they were bugs or worms or something,

109

you know, something you've seen before. But when they flew, I had one fly right across my face, okay, and they didn't have, like, wings or anything. They had this little row of bristles, spiraling down their length like a barbershop pole. They sort of twisted through the air like that, headlong. A corkscrew motion. And the ones that were on the guy, on his skin? That's what they were doin' I think, turnin' and drillin' themselves into him. You understand?"

"You don't think they were from this world."

"You said it, I didn't. I said I heard them, it's like a, like a chittering I guess. You hear it, you don't hear it really but you just get the sound in the middle of your head, like an itch. It's not so much like a swarm of bees but more like a crowd, a crowd at a concert because you can pick out words and, I say it out loud and it sounds insane, but you can hear them talking to each other, coordinating. And more than that, you can hear *their hate*. Okay? I want you to understand this. I want you to understand what I'm about to do."

"I think I do."

The survival part of my brain was scrambling for a plan to get the cop's gun or at least get away from him, but in my current clarity of mind I realized the certainty of it all. The man was going to shoot me and leave me here, no matter what I did. I was just waiting for it now. An odd feeling.

"So," he said, a kind of slow panic creeping into his eyes, "you understand my mood. You understand why I'm out committin' felonies today. There are dark things happenin' and I got the real lonely feeling like I'm the only one who knows, the only one who can do anything about it."

Morgan moved toward the door, blocking my exit. He sat the gas can down, almost empty now, and gestured to it. "Pick it up, and toss it out the door, in the yard."

I hesitated, the detective put his gun on me again. I did as he asked. He pulled out his lighter once more and, holding it in one hand and his revolver in the other, ignited it. The gasoline fumes burned my nose now and I was getting light-headed.

Standing there, a little yellow flame flickering in his hand, he said, "You know, everybody's got a ghost story. Or a UFO story or a Bigfoot story or an ESP story. Sit around a campfire late at night and you won't find one janitor who ain't seen a glowing old lady roamin' the halls in the middle of the night or maybe a hunter who's seen a pair of leathery wings flappin' out of a tree, somethin' way too big to be a bat. Or just somethin' simple, like a little kid at the store who goes around the corner and disappears into thin air a second later. And nobody thinks it's real because they figure nobody else saw it, but everybody's got their story. Everybody."

He gazed into the lighter flame as he spoke, as if mesmerized. His gun was pointed at the floor and with a soft double-click his thumb pulled back the hammer, as if on its own.

"Now what I think," he said to his lighter, "I think all that stuff is both real and not real at the same time. And I think the people who see it and the people that don't are both right. They're just like two different radios, switched to different stations. Now I ain't no *Star Trek* fan and I don't know about other dimensions and all that. But I am an old Catholic and I do believe in Hell. I believe it ain't just rapists and murderers down there; I believe it's demons and worms and vile things that wouldn't make no sense to you if you saw them. It's the grease trap of the universe. And I think somehow, through some chemistry or magic or some voodoo, that faux Jamaican S.O.B. opened the door into Hell itself. He *became* the door."

I nodded, opened my mouth to say something, then closed it again.

"And me," he said, nodding to himself. "I intend to close it."

He raised his gun and shot me in the heart.

I WOKE UP in Hell. Darkness and pain, time standing still. No wailing, though. I was sure Hell would have wailing.

A creak, a floorboard. And then a *FLUMPH* sound, like a lit gas grill.

I blacked out.

111

I came back. How much time had passed? I smelled smoke, was sure I was in Hell this time. Or was I dreaming?

I forced my eyes open, my nose filled with an acidic itch. I was disappointed to find Hell had a cheap tiled ceiling, some browned with water damage.

My chest hurt. Stung. I was shocked to find I still had an arm and could move it. I felt a wet patch right in the middle of my shirt, winced with the pain. I was cold all over, and vaguely realized I was in shock. I thought of Frank Wambaugh.

Frank worked on the Worthington Munitions production line in Plano, Texas, for eleven years. The company manufactures over one hundred types of cartridges for hunting, sport shooting and law enforcement. A couple of years ago Frank was manning his station as a third-line inspector, the last step in a meticulous quality control process. Defective bullets at Worthington are measured in parts per billion, thanks to that three-tiered inspection system and to the fear of legal liability should one of their cartridges explode in a policeman's face.

Nonetheless, there was a bad bullet among the half-million .38 caliber rounds produced that day at Worthington, thanks to a fly that crawled inside one of the casings as it passed from the machine that added its pinch of propellant. The defective fly bullet was the only one that day to pass by both of the first two inspection stations unnoticed. Frank would have spotted it, but at the exact moment the possible defect error displayed on his screen, Frank was distracted by a man behind him.

Or so he thought. He turned, and saw no one.

When he satisfied himself that he had imagined the spoken "hey" that, upon reflection, he heard more in his head than with his ears, he returned to his work and was none the wiser. The defective round thus passed unnoticed, was packaged, sold through a law enforcement catalogue eight months later and finally distributed to Detective Lawrence "Morgan Freeman" Appleton six months after that.

A year later Freeman loaded said cartridge into his revolver and

112

fired it into my chest. The projectile had only a fraction of the normal propellant and thus less than one tenth of its usual impact force. The bullet had punched through my skin, scratched the thick bone over my heart and bounced off.

I opened my eyes, didn't remember blacking out again. So tired. Waiting for the flames now. I raised my head and saw the couch was a bonfire, black smoke rolling up to the ceiling. Fire licked the paneling and it bubbled and blackened under its touch. The carpet below the couch was saturated with high octane. The moment a spark fell it would—

I was moving, just like that, crawling on hands and knees. Damn, smoke filling in so fast now, like breathing wads of hot cigarette butts. Gotta get to the door, gotta get to the door. Can't see shit. I saw something that looked like a door, reached out, touched smooth metal. Refrigerator.

I had crawled in the exact wrong direction. I turned, crawled. Felt along the wall. Carpet on fire now. Shit, hot as hell in here. I crawled. Crawled and crawled. Ah, here's the door. Thank God. I reached out.

Refrigerator again.

My skin burned, pulled tight on my skull. The place was an oven, a blast furnace. Is that my hair burning? I squinted around. The living room was an orange blur behind me. Could I even make it through there now?

I felt this weird twitching in my chest and realized I was coughing. I lowered my head to the linoleum, hoping to find a few inches of fresh air down there. So tired. I closed my eyes.

PEOPLE DIE.

This is the fact the world desperately hides from us from birth. Long after you find out the truth about sex and Santa Claus, this other myth endures, this one about how you'll always get rescued at the last second and if not, your death will at least mean something and there'll be somebody there to hold your hand and cry over you. All of society is

113

built to prop up that lie, the whole world a big, noisy puppet show meant to distract us from the fact that at the end, you'll die, and you'll probably be alone.

I was lucky. I learned this a long time ago, in a tiny, stifling room behind my high school gym. Most people don't realize it until they're laying facedown on the pavement somewhere, gasping for their last breath. Only then do they realize that life is a flickering candle we all carry around. A gust of wind, a meaningless accident, a microsecond of carelessness, and it's out. Forever.

And no one cares. You kick and scream and cry out into the darkness, and no answer comes. You rage against the unfathomable injustice and two blocks away some guy watches a baseball game and scratches his balls.

Scientists talk about dark matter, the invisible, mysterious substance that occupies the space between stars. Dark matter makes up 99.99 percent of the universe, and they don't know what it is. Well I know. It's apathy. That's the truth of it; pile together everything we know and care about in the universe and it will still be nothing more than a tiny speck in the middle of a vast black ocean of Who Gives A Fuck.

I realized the heat was gone. The sound was gone. Everything was gone. Just darkness.

That wasn't right, darkness would have been something. This wasn't even that. Was I dead?

It was the same detached sensation from before, the feeling of floating across worlds without my body. Only there was nothing to see here, nothing to feel. Only . . .

I was being watched. I knew it. I could sense it. There were eyes on me.

Not eyes. One eye. A single, reptilian, blue eye. I couldn't see it, there was no seeing here. There was just the awareness of it. I was in the presence of something, an intelligence. I recognized it and it recognized me back. But not in the way a man sees and knows another man;

it was the way a man sees a cell under a microscope. To this thing, I was the cell, insignificant under its vast, unfathomable perception.

I tried to sense the nature of it. Was it good? Evil? Indifferent? With my mind I reached out and—

RUN.

I ran. I had no legs, but I ran, I pushed myself away, willed myself to escape from this thing.

RUN.

I sensed heat. I was pushing myself toward an unimaginable heat but I welcomed it. I would throw myself into a lake of fire to escape that *thing* in the—

—DARKNESS. REGULAR DARKNESS now, the familiar back side of my own eyelids. Heat all around me, heat so intense I could barely recognize the sensation.

A low sound. Wailing?

From outside. Getting louder. A car coming. A dog barking.

Get back. Get back!

Who said that?

A thunderous, terrible noise. Glass shattering, metal screaming, wood snapping. The kitchen was exploding around me. I was flung backward and suddenly a blast of fresh air washed over my body.

I was looking at the grille of a car, *my* car, the Hyundai "H" symbol a foot from my face.

The car reversed itself and wrenched free of the wreckage that had been the kitchen's west wall. There was now a rupture near the floor, frayed with tufts of pink insulation and shredded aluminum siding. I rolled myself out of the hole, fell hard onto the cool grass outside. I coughed, coughed.

Coughed.

Passed out.

I woke up what felt like hours later.

Or maybe seconds.

The trailer was a fireball behind me. I was too wiped out to appreciate that I had avoided death twice within a few minutes, first by a fraction of an inch then by a few smoke-filled breaths.

I heard a bark.

David? You alive?

That voice again, from nowhere. I struggled to my feet, saw my car sitting about twenty feet away.

Molly the dog was sitting behind the wheel. I stared at this for a good solid minute. She barked, and again I heard words in the sound.

John's voice.

I didn't think it could get any stupider than the bratwurst thing, but I suspected I was about to find out otherwise. I climbed into the car, pushing Molly over to the passenger's seat.

Molly looked at me, with concern. No, not Molly.

John looked back at me, with Molly's big brown eyes. Molly barked, but I heard:

We're in big fuckin' trouble, Dave.

"No shit, fluffy. How did you work the pedals?"

"Woof!"

Listen. There are three people still alive from last night other than me. Big Jim Sullivan, Jennifer Lopez and Fred Chu. I don't know a whole lot else because my own body ain't workin' so well. I know we're all together and we're on the move and once we get where we're goin', something bad, bad, bad is gonna happen.

"Wait, wait, wait. Why are you a dog again, John?"

"Arrr-oof!"

(Sneeze)

Justin White, or the thing that used to be Justin, he's got me. My body, I mean. He stole a vehicle. When I'm in my body I can't see nothin', but I can hear. It's somethin' big enough to hold all of us, some kind of truck. Dave, you gotta find it.

"Is it an ambulance? The cop told me he stole an ambulance from

116

the hospital. So there are actually four still alive from last night, if you count Justin."

"Woo—"

No, no, no. I said there were three that were alive and I meant it. Justin White ain't alive. He's a walking . . . hive or whatever.

"Those things inside him, what are they?"

"Woof!"

Bitch!

This threw me, and I stared in dull confusion for a moment before I noticed the dog was looking past me. I turned and saw a little brown-and-white beagle tied up next to one of the trailers.

"John?"

"Woof!"

Sorry, Dave. My grandpa used to tell me, toward the end when he was going crazy, that talking through a dog ain't like talking through a sausage. Molly is in here with me and I gotta compete for the barker.

"Where is Justin, or this Justin Thing, taking everybody?"

I already knew the answer as soon as the question left my mouth. I said it along with the dog's bark: "Las Vegas."

"So what's in Las Vegas?"

"Woof! Arrrrr-oof!! Grrrr . . ."

You know that Bugs Bunny cartoon, where they spill the ink on the floor and then climb through it as if it was a hole? I think that's what the soy sauce is like. It's a hole, it opens you right up. Those worms, and the other shit in Robert's basement, the sauce let that stuff come into our world, by turning people into holes. And I think if the sauce infects enough people, in one place, it can make one single big-ass hole.

"Shit. Is it worth asking what's going to come through the hole?"

"Woof."

I don't know. But what comes through will have to feed.

I nodded. "Right. And Vegas has all those free buffets."

Molly closed her eyes in frustration. I had never seen that expression on a dog before.

No. Listen. There's a guy named Albert Marconi. He does these confer-ences on the occult, he's having one there at the Luxor, that's the big casino shaped like a black pyramid. We're going to go there.

"Wait. How do you know this?"

Because it's already happened.

"That doesn't make any—"

"Woof!"

CAT! CAT! CAT! CAT!!!

Molly was up in the seat, jamming her head out the half-open pas-senger window.

"John . . ."

"WOOF! WOOF! WOOF! WOOF! WOOF! WOOFWOOFWOOF-WOOF!!!"

Cat!! Cat! Cat!!! Cat!!! CAT!! CAT!!!! CAAAATTT!!!

A filthy gray cat zipped across the trailer park, across the front of the car and off into the distance. Molly pulled her head inside and tromped over to the driver's-side window, stomping on my crotch and shouting "CAT!!!" the whole way. It took ten minutes to get the dog calmed down, at which point she promptly curled up and went to sleep in the passen-ger seat.

"John?"

The dog farted. I got nothing else out of her the rest of the night.

CHAPTER 5
Riding with Shitload

I DROVE TO a convenience store and bought a road atlas. Back in my car I unfolded it in my lap and drew out the path to Las Vegas with an ink pen. Was I actually doing this?

I knew I would need cash for gas and to replace the several vital parts of the Hyundai's drivetrain that would likely shatter over the course of the long drive. I had nothing in the bank. This seemed to be a rather major problem, but within a few seconds of watching the sunset in the convenience store's parking lot, a plan popped into my head, fully formed and alien. I had learned to accept such things in the last few hours.

This wasn't Dave thinking.

This was soy sauce thinking.

I drove downtown, scanning the alleys until I saw a rail-thin Mexican kid standing by a Dumpster wearing a St. Louis Rams jacket. The kid was wearing the jacket, not the Dumpster. I calmly stepped out of my Hyundai, smiled broadly at him.

I had never met him before.

I had no idea what I was doing.

Without hesitation, I heard myself say, "Yo. Mikey said you got a package for me."

What the fuck.

The kid squinted at me, didn't move. "Who the fuck are you?"

The kid moved slightly, the bottom of his Ram's jacket sliding up his skeletal frame. The gun sticking out of the kid's jeans was black and sleek, looking like something that could shoot lasers. The irony that he was able to afford a nicer gun than the Undisclosed Police Department gave Detective Freeman would have amused me if I wasn't busy picturing the kid pumping six bullets into my forehead with it.

Again, I heard myself speaking. A single word that to me, had no meaning.

"Creech."

My soy sauced brain had officially taken off without me. I was operating on autopilot, phrases and words scrolling up into my mind as if fed to me on a teleprompter.

The kid said nothing.

He reached into his jacket . . .

And pulled out an envelope.

He stepped up and gave me a hug, slipping the envelope to me in one smooth, practiced motion.

As the kid turned away, I slowly let out the breath I had been holding.

I would like to reiterate: what the fuck.

Back in the car, I pulled the envelope out, opened it, saw it was

120

stuffed full of hundred-dollar bills. I had no idea what any of that was, only that speaking those words to that person would get me cash, like a complicated PIN at an ATM machine.

I counted six thousand dollars.

Alrighty.

Without knowing my destination, I drove directly to the Merry Nation Bar and Grill, six blocks away. I went to the parking lot and glanced around, still without any real idea of what I was looking for.

I went right to a cobalt-blue Dodge pickup that I had never seen in my life. I found it unlocked, reached in, felt around under the seat.

I pulled out a satin-finish steel automatic handgun.

Fully loaded.

God bless America.

I stuck the gun in the back of my pants, felt strangely comforted by its gouge into the small of my back as I sat back down in the Hyundai. Evening had set in now, on one of the longest, most retarded days of my life.

I was about to point the car west, then realized I didn't want to drive for over 1,500 miles—

1,669

—in these shit-stained pants and bloodstained shirt.

I drove home to change, proving that even on the soy sauce, part of me was still a dumb-ass.

I THREW THE clothes in the trash and showered, paranoid the whole time, thinking I was hearing opening doors and floor creaks and murderous things bumping around outside the shower curtain. It had been that kind of a day.

I dressed and put on Band-Aids, collected my toothbrush and a comb and contact lens fluid and dumped it into my leather duffel bag.

I flung myself down the hall—

I stopped cold.

121

My bag fell from my hand with a soft thud.

A teenager stood there. Right in the middle of my living room, a space that had been proudly teenager-free for years.

Braces.

Black Limp Bizkit T-shirt.

I said, "Justin?"

Standing there with a shit-eating grin on its face, the thing that had been Justin opened its mouth and emitted a rumbling sound, like something boiling up from his lungs. After a moment he closed it again.

He gathered himself and said brightly, "Why you frontin' here? You know what time it is. Stop callin' me Justin like nothin's changed, yo."

I pictured swarms of white worms twitching through his bloodstream and suddenly had to fight the impulse to run away screaming like a toddler.

I took a step back.

Justin took a step forward.

Buying time, I asked, "What should I call you?"

I shifted my feet, felt the nudge of the gun against my lower back. I had never fired a gun before, and certainly never fired one at a man. The thought brought cool sweat to my forehead and a hot, jittery anticipation. Not entirely unpleasant. I had felt it before.

Justin's mouth opened again, struggling to speak words completely foreign to itself.

"Shitload. Know why? It's because there's a shitload of us in here. Now here's what's gonna happen—"

The left side of Justin's scalp disappeared in a spray of pink brain matter. He was thrown backward, my finger squeezing the trigger as fast as it could twitch, the sound shattering the air. Little sprays of blood flicked out from Justin's chest and thighs and gut, shots landing and backing him across the room.

Jesus, Dave.

I had drawn the gun in a mindless reflex, like slapping at a mosquito bite. I tasted blood where I had bit through my lip. I felt electricity inside, the buzz of the violence, sparks raining down inside my skull as if from a blown fuse.

Too familiar.

Shitload stumbled backward one last time and fell against a wall, but kept his feet.

I pulled the trigger again.

Click.

I squeezed the trigger about twenty more times just to be sure there wasn't another shot hiding in there somewhere. Shitload righted himself, looked down at his wounds, sighed like a man who has dropped his pie in his lap.

Oh, you've got to be shitting me.

I saw now that the white rods were binding up each of his wounds, forming a stitching like the back side of fiberglass. I finally realized I wasn't fighting this kid, I was fighting *those things.* The fear was like lead weights in my chest.

He said, "Man, your little nine is useless against—"

His words were cut off when the empty gun I hurled at him smacked off his cheek, knocking him backward once more. He brought a hand to his face.

"Stop that shit! Don't you know we got the same plan?"

He took a step toward me. I looked across the room. The door. The window. I couldn't make it to either without going through Shitload.

He said, "We both goin' to Vegas, right? You all packed up and all."

My hand at my side, I made a fist.

"Uh, I don't think so."

I realized once more that I was about to enter a fight and, again, had learned no fighting skills since the last one. Only this time there was a good chance the fight would end with me feeling the opponent's teeth ripping out my eyeballs.

"Sure you is."

He lunged. I threw a flailing punch that missed by a foot.

The Justin monster fired out a low punch, the impact exploding in my groin. I doubled over, struggled to keep my feet.

"The only difference is . . ."

He advanced and in a blur threw three more punches that each landed solidly on my balls. A heavy sickness bloomed in my gut and I fell back against a chair. I awkwardly kicked at his chest.

He caught the leg and delivered an expert crotch kick that finished me.

". . . *I'm* doin' the drivin'."

Justin clasped both of his hands into one fist, raised it high above his head as if in victory and then with all his might brought it down on my groin.

I blacked out.

DARKNESS, BARKING AND footsteps. I felt Molly's wet nose on my forehead, then felt her walking over me. All four paws managed to hit my aching crotch on the way over.

I felt the floor moving against me and realized I was being dragged. I was hefted over a shoulder like a sack of dog food and dropped onto a metal floor. A door clanged shut, a latch clicked into place.

In the haze I felt the presence of others around me, could sense terrified thoughts darting around their minds like flies. I could sense the sauce in them, the soy sauce, I could smell it on their thoughts like alcohol on a wino's breath.

Vegas.

I had a hallucination, or a vision. It was the road atlas, spread before me, the red highways tangled like arteries across the country. Undisclosed on the right, Las Vegas a red dot on the left, the line of an ink pen scratched along the highways joining the two.

We were going there because *he* wanted us there. Not this Justin monster, either. Who?

The soy sauce? Again I felt the presence of it in this space. Pulsing. A will of its own. The soy sauce was alive, I knew that.

But beyond it, too, there was someone else. Some*thing* else. And every dark thing I had run into was working on its behalf.

124

In my vision, the map rustled. The red spot marking Las Vegas pulsed, as if something was pushing it from behind. Scratching. Like an animal trying to gnaw its way through.

My eyes snapped open.

I was expecting to find myself inside Justin's stolen ambulance. Instead I saw cardboard boxes stacked around me, each bearing liquor logos. There was a sweet, spoiled smell of ancient spilt beer around me.

Sitting on one stack was Big Jim Sullivan, copper hair capping 275 pounds of bulk.

You should call home, Jim. Cucumber is worried about you.

Next to Jim was a very pale and shaky Jennifer Lopez, scratched and dirty, wearing the same outfit from the party.

Lying across a row of green Heineken cases was a little, wiry man with shoulder-length hair and a goatee, whom I had never seen before and who, by process of elimination, had to be Fred Chu. He had his tattooed arms folded under his head and looked unharmed. Molly went and sat down in the middle of them, bored.

On sight of me, Fred Chu said, "Shit."

Jennifer buried her head in her hands and began weeping softly.

Jim said, "Hey, you found Molly."

The engine started and we jolted into motion. I raised my head and looked around the dim cargo area. Among the crude beer-case furniture the passengers had stacked for themselves was a low, unoccupied seat of boxes in the corner, as if they had known I was coming.

For some reason this annoyed me so much I almost failed to notice that sitting in the corner, cross-legged and wearing hospital pajamas, was John. He stared intently at the wall, not blinking.

Big Jim said, "We're moving again." He reached down and stroked Molly.

I sat up. Big Jim turned his eyes on me, said, "We heard the shots. Are you the one who hurt him? I saw his head."

"I was aiming for his heart but, yeah, I did get him."

Jennifer sobbed the word, "Good." An empty, flat, bitter sound. Jim turned toward the others and said, "Okay, we got one more hostage. We can still make it, guys. Just gotta believe, that's all."

I pretended not to hear this, concentrated on not puking from my ball trauma.

I asked Jen, "Are you okay?"

Jen nodded. "Where's he taking us?"

"Las Vegas."

That drew stares from around the room.

"No, seriously."

Fred Chu said, "The rest of us are fine, by the way. But you gotta understand what's happenin' here. The guy who attacked you, he ain't no fuckin' man, okay? He's been invaded by fuckin' body snatchers or whatever."

"Yeah, I—"

"—I mean if you saw what happened with Shelby. The Jamaican guy spat acid on her hand. The muscle and bone fell apart, just, like, dripped off like fuckin' wax."

I thought of the ache in my groin, realized I had gotten off easy.

Jim said, "Justin is—or those *things* inside Justin—are evil. And I mean that as a noun, not an adjective. They're the kind of physical manifestation that could only have been spawned by the Devil himself."

"I don't . . . completely disagree with that."

"Now, we've been praying," continued Jim. "All of us, in a circle. Fred, Jen and me, even John, as best we could involve him. I had to threaten to beat them first but they joined in eventually. We prayed for someone to come along, to save us from whatever dark thing is up there behind the wheel. And then you showed up, like an answer. Now, you faced that thing. You stood up to it. You've been delivered to us, to be the voice to answer a question I have put to God over and over since this whole thing started: *How do we kill it?*"

"No, Jim, that's not the question. The question is, can it be killed at all."

I pictured the map, and the rabid thing trying to claw through. I realized the scale was all wrong. To this thing, whatever it was, the

126

real Las Vegas, the whole Earth, all of mankind, was as insignificant as the red dot on the map. I pictured a blue, knowing eye, in the darkness.

But that's still the wrong question, isn't it? Maybe Justin can be killed. Maybe not. And maybe it doesn't mean a fucking thing.

I looked toward John.

He should be the one doing the talking. He's been waiting his whole life for something like this, just to prove the universe is as retarded as he's always pictured it in his head. I needed John to be here, alive and unafraid. I needed him to be *John*.

I turned toward him and said, "Wake up."

Nothing. I looked back at Molly, then nudged John with my foot. "Wake up. Wake up, asshole."

More nothing. I felt eyes on me, resisted the urge to punch John right in his stupid catatonic face.

"Look, we fucking *need* you. Now *wake up*."

"Hey." A soft voice, from behind me. I turned and Jennifer Lopez's wet eyes met mine. There was sympathy there, and I felt a tug from inside. Though that could have been one of my testicles detaching from the trauma. "Calm down, okay? You're not helping."

Molly stirred, looked around lazily and then trotted over to John's frozen body. I stepped back as she nuzzled him, then flinched when I saw his hand reach over to pet her.

There was a jolt through John's body, like an electrical shock, so fast that we could barely process the change in posture.

Suddenly he was on his feet, confused, looking at his hands like he was surprised to have them. Looking up, he seemed to see us for the first time and said to no one in particular, "I had a really vivid dream that I was a dog."

IT TOOK JOHN a while to come around. He knew we were in a beer truck piloted by some kind of infested evil, but seemed to have trouble adjusting to actually existing inside his body, in one physical location.

127

"I've got such a headache." He searched his pockets, said, "Anybody have any smokes I could borrow?"

No one did. John took the empty seat, then turned his eyes on me and said, "Let's, uh, start over. How many people do you see in here?"

"What?"

"Just humor me."

Jim said, "I know what he's asking. They can make you see what they want you to see. John wants to make sure we can all trust our eyes. Right?"

Going around the room, I pointed out the four other residents of Undisclosed who had the misfortune of depending on John and me for their lives. Five if you counted Jennifer's boobs separately, as I suddenly had the impulse to. Goddamned testosterone.

John nodded, seeming somewhat relieved. "Good. And yeah, like Jim said, I just wanted to make sure I wasn't, uh, projecting, I guess. You know what I'm saying, Dave? Like that cop in the police station, the one who wasn't really there. I wasn't in the room but I remember it anyway, and he looked like a stereotypical cop, like a generic. Standard issue. An extra in a movie."

Jim nodded again and I wondered how much of this same shit he had been through himself. He said, "Hollywood raised us. Your mind processes the world through a filter formed by comic books and action movies on Cinemax. That's why kids put on trench coats and take guns to school. The Devil knows how to control us."

Jim seemed to be seizing on the opportunity to bring up Satan in a conversation where nobody could counter him with rationalism. Devils and angels seemed pretty plausible in this context and Jim intended to ride that horse hard.

John said, "People who wake up in the middle of the night and see those big-eyed alien abductors or a ghostly old woman . . . it's always something they saw in some movie, isn't it? Your mind puts a familiar face on something it can't understand. Only here, somehow it becomes real. At least to you."

We rode in silence, I think all of us wondering what was behind the flowery wallpaper our perceptions had always pasted on the unknown. All the things the mind won't allow us to see, to protect our sanity, or our soul, or maybe just to keep the shit out of our pants.

Fred spoke first, breaking the silence.

"Well fuck 'em. That's what I say."

Jennifer said, "I took a cinema class at the community college last semester. Most of the films were in French and were about people making out in coffee shops, or in apartments over coffee shops. But I don't even have a TV anymore, so that might help."

I closed my eyes and sighed, wishing Jim would pray for longer attention spans. "Okay," I said, "let's set that aside because at the moment we're not talking about ghost stories or vampires. That thing up there in the cockpit is real, real as any of us—"

Crotch-punchingly real!

"—and it can make us really dead. Now do you guys understand what it wants with us?"

Fred said, "Man, I think he's gonna make a fuckin' suit of human skin, using the best parts from each of us."

"Holy crap," said John. "He'll be *gorgeous*."

I sighed again, rubbed my forehead with both hands. There was a very real chance that the conversation had taken a turn that would allow John to talk about his dick, which was a subject it could take hours, if not the better part of days, to come back from. Nipping it in the bud, I said:

"Nooooo. It's none of that. Look, you know the story of the Trojan horse? A few soldiers get inside the enemy camp riding in this big horse statue, then at night they sneak out of the horse and let the rest of their army in the front gates? Well, that drug the Jamaican was on, it let something through. He became the horse. And those things, the white flying wormy things, they came through. Now they're in Justin and now he's looking to open the gate and let their buddies in."

This brought silence. I scanned the cartons around us, the vague outlines of a plan forming in my head.

Fred said, "Dude, how do you possibly know that?"

"I pieced it together through inductive reasoning and information relayed to me by John when he was talking to me through the dog. Long story."

"Okay," Fred said, accepting it readily. I sensed that I was in the presence of the king of the go-with-the-flow types. "But why us?"

"Because we were chosen," Jim answered. "Called. And that's all that matters."

We were chosen all right, Jim. But not by God, unless God is a black liquid in a silver jar. Hell, maybe he is.

I locked eyes with Jim. I thought of his sister saying the Jamaican had showed up at their house. Jim, at the party, talking to Robert.

He was right there, from the beginning.

And he fucking knows more than he's letting on.

Did he light the fuse on this whole situation somehow? Guys like him, the ones who grip the Bible so tight they leave fingernail grooves, they're the ones who are the most scared of their dark side. Always going too far the other way, fighting for the Lord, often just because it gives them an excuse to fight.

Fred nodded and said, "So what you're saying is, if we all die, that's not even the worst-case scenario."

John replied, "I'd still like to shoot a little higher than that, Freddy."

I looked over his shoulder and scanned the cardboard boxes stacked up against the back wall of the truck. I thought for a moment and then asked John, "How much alcohol does liquor have to have in it before it will burn?"

A COUPLE OF hours later, we had a dozen full bottles lined up near the rear door, each with a bundle of wet cloth cut from Fred's flannel shirt jutting six inches out of the opening. When the Justin monster finally stopped, we'd wait for him to open that door and light his ass up.

But the truck didn't stop. For hours we rode in useless silence, slumped against the metal walls, drifting in and out of fitful sleep. John

130

found a little vented slit in the side of the cargo hold and we took turns watching the world flow by outside.

The wait was Hell. Sunday morning turned to Sunday afternoon. We pissed in empty bottles, though I can't remember exactly how Jennifer pulled that off. The view out of the little vent turned from cornfield to desert as hundreds and hundreds of miles of highway skimmed by under us.

Twenty-eight hours, nineteen minutes. That's how long we were in the truck, all told. We found a case of Evian water at the back of the truck but our only source of calories came from warm beer, a diet for which John needed no adjustment at all.

Finally—*finally*—we slowed, taking multiple turns as if having entered a town.

Each of us sprang up, moving to the back of the truck. We started gathering up bottles.

The truck stopped. We all held our breath. But then it started off again, in a different direction.

We had our plan. Or, considering that the plan had come from me, we had given up and were waiting to die.

Big Jim glanced around at us and said in a low, solemn voice, "Listen, now. Because when that thing opens the door, some of us may die. And at that point, you may have a chance to run, to get away, to save yourself. But we have to stay and finish the job. Do you understand?"

We nodded. Again I was hit with the sense that he comprehended a danger far larger than the rest of us did. He continued, "I don't think you do understand. But . . ."

He swallowed.

". . . You guys know my sister, who's back home at this moment. In that big, old house. Well we've always had a mouse problem. And, you know, we work hard to keep the place up, to keep it clean, since our parents passed away. But you can't keep the mice away. They get everywhere. The cabinets, the walls. I got poison set out all over the place for these things."

Fred pulled out a cigarette lighter, flicked it once to make sure it worked.

Jim stared at the floor and continued, "Then, one day I look under her bed and she's got a little saucer there, with bread on it. The bread's all chewed off at the corners. She put it there on purpose."

The truck turned again. We heard the crackle of gravel under the tires now.

Jim looked up at us again, a kind of pleading in his eyes. "Do you understand? She was feeding them. The whole time I was trying to kill them, she was trying to keep them alive."

I pictured her back there, small and alone in that cavernous house, and I did understand. Jim fucking knew something was coming, on its way to this world, through Las Vegas for whatever fucking reason. He knew what was at stake, while the whole world, vulnerable and un-aware, went about its business behind us. I just wished he would use his sister's damned name so I wouldn't have to keep thinking of her as Cucumber.

"John, Fred. You guys, if one of you makes it out of this instead of me, I want you to promise me something. I want you to look in on her, make sure she's—just make sure she's taken care of, okay? She's smart, you know. I don't mean she's—it's just she ain't never been on her own. I want you to promise me."

The truck turned again. Slowing.

John said, "Of course, man."

I thought of John's last pet, a little terrier dog that jumped out of his third-floor apartment window and died while he played video games on the couch. Yeah, Cucumber will be in good hands, Big Jim.

John flicked his lighter. The truck turned for the last time, then slowed to a stop. I couldn't breathe.

John peered through the vent, trying to see where we were. He said, "If I die, I want you to tell everybody I died in the coolest way possible. Dave, you can have my CDs. My brother will demand the PlayStation, since I borrowed it from him a year ago, so don't fight him for it."

Jennifer hesitated for a long moment before whispering, "Um, there's a loose floorboard under my bed. I keep stuff down there. There's some pot and a little notebook with like, some guys' names in it, and—some other stuff. If I die I want one of you to go in my bedroom and get all that stuff out so my mom doesn't find it."

John reached over and lit the wicks on all three of the Molotov cocktails I held. His hand was steady, mine were not.

Fred whispered, "Okay. If I don't come back, and say they don't got my body, like if Justin eats me or somethin', tell everybody you don't know what happened. Make it mysterious. And then a year later spread rumors that you've seen me wanderin' around town. That way I'll be like fuckin' Bigfoot, everybody claiming to have seen me here and there. Legend of Fred Chu."

John nodded, as if he were committing this to memory. He lit his own firebombs, glanced up at me and asked, "You got any final requests, in case this don't end well?"

"Yeah. Avenge my death."

WE WERE POSITIONED in a circle by the front of the door, each with a high-proof cocktail in each hand. I studied the small orange-and-blue flame dancing on the bundle of wet cloth crammed into the bottle. My heart hammered. Molly whimpered behind me.

The moments oozed out like ketchup from a glass bottle. I could hear Jim breathing next to me, felt a trickle of sweat roll down my temple.

The latch clicked and scraped. Every muscle in my body tensed. I looked down and squeezed the beer bottle in my hand.

Jesus, we are going to die, we are actually going to die here.

The door slowly ground up in its tracks. A band of pale moonlight appeared at the floor, a stiff wind whistling in as the door slid upward. There he was, revealed from the shins up. Jeans and shirt and—

Oh, holy shit.

Justin looked mostly normal, skin pale under the moonlight, blond hair rustling in the stiff breeze, a pimple on his chin. Only now both of his eyes were protruding about six inches from his skull.

The pupils at the end of their new white-and-pink stalks twisted horribly in our direction, staring at us for a very long and terrible moment. We were so caught off guard by this that it killed our momentum, all of us frozen and expecting the person next to them to make the first move.

To Jennifer's credit, she broke the paralysis by weakly tossing a flaming bottle at Justin. The Justin monster watched as it missed and bounced harmlessly to the ground, rolling to a stop. The wick flickered and went out. Shitload curled his twin optical skull-erections down and looked at the sad bottle draining its contents into the dirt. After a moment he turned back up to us and said, "Put that shit down and come with me, fools."

He backed away from us, seeming to realize his eyes were dangling from his skull and in a series of sickening, jerky neck movements sucked them back in.

We stood there for a moment, looked at each other with a kind of deflated shame and defeat, then did what he said.

They were waiting for me, I realized, too late. They were waiting for me to push the attack, to lead them.

Welcome aboard the David Wong Disappointment Train, fuckers.

We weren't in Vegas. A quick glance around showed we were squarely in the middle of rural nowhere. It was a windy night and in small-town Nevada that apparently means dust. Justin, the hybrid walking demon hive and Limp Bizkit fan, led us across a dusty yard onto a paint-peeled dusty porch where a pair of ancient and very dusty shoes sat mummifying in the dusty desert air.

The door was ajar and had only a perfectly round hole where the knob should have been.

Propped next to the door was a dust-covered but new FedEx box, which almost certainly was a delivery mistake since this place looked to be in its tenth year of vacancy.

Justin pushed in through the door, indifferently kicking the box inside as he passed.

As we moved inside I noticed for the first time that Justin had an old, mud-smeared glass jar in his hand and I vaguely remembered seeing it or one just like it in the Jamaican's makeshift basement. He placed it on the floor and walked around to us one by one, arranging our bodies, seated, in a semicircle around it. I saw a speech coming and could only pray that I wouldn't come out sounding like a white kid raised next to a cornfield trying to record interlude skits for a gangsta rap album.

Shitload said, "This world is shit, yo."

Oh, goddamnit.

"How do you people be gettin' around in this, all in these bodies and shit? You act all scared that I'm gonna kill ya, when it's the best thing I could do for you, yo. Deadworld, man, it's alternate layers of rot and shit and rot and shit."

I looked around the dim group, saw moonlight from the window cracks reflecting off of tears on Jennifer's cheeks. Big Jim had his eyes closed, maybe in prayer. Fred Chu looked around as if uninterested, stroking his goatee with one hand and fidgeting with a strip of carpet foam with the other. John was staring vacantly at a spot on the other side of the room, already distracted into a dull stupor. Molly licked her crotch.

Ladies and gentlemen: The Undisclosed Hell-Conqueror Strike Force!

To at least feel like I was doing something, I said, "Deadworld? Is that where you're from?"

"No, dude. That's where *you're* from. It's where we are now. This place, it's a horror show. If the guy next to you decides to knock you out of this world forever, he can do it with just a piece of metal or, hell, even his bare hand. You blobs, you sit there, chillin' in this room and I can smell the rot of dead animals soaking in the acid of your guts. You suck the life from the innocent creatures of this world just so you can clock another day. You're machines that run on the terror and pain and mutilation of other lives. You'll scrape the world clean of every green and living thing until starvation goes one-eight-seven on every one of your sorry asses, your desperation to put off death leadin' to the ultimate death of everybody and everything. Dude, I can't believe you ain't all paralyzed by the pure, naked horror of this place."

After a long, long pause John said, "Uh, thank you."

John's eyes never moved as he spoke, and suddenly I saw a look there, a confidence. I followed his gaze, saw what he was seeing, and then quickly looked away again.

I glanced back at the Justin monster, wondering if he had caught on. But he was busy. He twisted the lid off the old pickle jar, and a small, shriveled thing, like a dried-up earthworm, dropped out and landed quietly on the floor.

Shitload went to the kitchen and I heard him messing around with the sink in there. No water. He came back, studied our faces, and pointed to Fred.

"Piss on it," he commanded.

I was so baffled by this that I wasn't even sure I had heard him right. But Fred, having perfected going with the flow to a degree that philosophers could study for centuries, shrugged and said, "Okay."

He stood, unzipped, urinated on the floor, zipped up and sat back down. The little black dried-worm sliver sat in the middle of the bubbling puddle. Nothing for a long time, maybe a minute.

And then, the worm twitched.

Jennifer screamed, everybody jumped.

The shriveled nothing grew. And grew. And grew.

Just add water!

A hand formed. A human hand, pink and the size of a baby's. Stretching out from behind it, instead of an arm, was something like an insect leg. It was a foot long, springing out to length before our eyes like a radio antenna. Something like a shell took shape. I saw an eye, red and clustered like a fly's. Another eye, this one with a round pupil, like a mammal, grew in next to it. Then another eye, yellow with a black slit down the center. Reptilian.

The thing grew and grew some more. It grew to the size of a rabbit, then a small dog, then stopped when it was about a foot-and-a-half high and maybe three feet wide, probably the same overall mass as Molly.

The finished creature seemed to be assembled from spare parts. It had a tail like a scorpion curling up off its back. It walked on seven— yes, seven—legs, each ending in one of those small, pink infantile hands. It had a head that was sort of an inverted heart shape, a bank of mis- matched eyes in an arc over a hooked, black beak, like a parrot's. On its head, no kidding, it had a tuft of neatly groomed blond hair that I swear on my mother's grave was a wig, held on with a rubber band chinstrap.

What was strange about it, or rather, what was *stranger* about it was that the two sections of its body—the hindquarters and the abdomen—were not connected. There was a good two inches of space between them and when it turned sideways you could see right through the thing. But it moved in unison, as if they were connected by invisible tissue.

The little monster stood twitching there on the floor like a newborn calf, still dripping with urine.

John said, "Huh."

Fred said, "Guys, can you all see that fuckin' thing, or is it just me?"

The beast moved in circles, looking around the room. Justin said to us, "Don't move. If I ask it to, it'll kill you, yo. You don't know what that thing's capable of. Shit, lookin' at the thing, I don't even think *it* knows. But that ain't my goal, I coulda capped you all back home if that was the plan. It ain't."

The thing turned and turned, staring down each of us, its dozen eyes blinking at different intervals. It finally stopped, looking my di- rection. Molly stirred behind me, a low growl rising from her.

"All I need you to do is hold still, yo. In a minute ain't none of you gonna remember why you got all worked up and shit."

The creature crouched, then vanished in a blur. I threw myself back, expected the monster to suddenly be on me, but it wasn't. I heard a horrible, high-pitched yelp behind me and turned to find the monster on Molly's back, its legs wrapped around her body, dug into her fur like steel cables.

137

Jennifer screamed, everyone stirred. Justin shouted at us to stay down, stay down. I watched as the thing whipped back that scorpion tail (Did I say it was like a scorpion? The freaking tail had *hair* on it.) and with a flick, the end was buried in the dog's hide. The length of the tail started pulsing and twitching. It was pumping something into her.

Molly whimpered.

And then it was over. The beast jumped off. Molly looked terrorized but kept her feet. I saw the tip of the monster's scorpion tail and noticed a drip of thick, black fluid trickling out.

Soy sauce.

Wait. What? That's where it comes from?

A burst of movement, behind me. Shuffling feet and shouts.

John was making his move, diving in the direction we had been looking earlier. He skidded on the floor and seized the white FedEx box.

Shitload was on him fast, Bruce Lee–fast. He delivered a kick to John's gut that actually knocked him back a couple of feet. He then wrenched the box from John's arms. Shitload looked baffled, moved to throw the box aside but stopped cold.

He looked at the label, then at John, then at me, then at the label again. I stood and moved slowly toward them.

Shitload stared at John and said, "What's in here?"

John said nothing, looked like he wasn't too sure himself. I moved closer still, not understanding. Shitload stiffened his arm toward John in a "Heil Hitler" motion. This confused us for a second—before a slit appeared in his palm and something like a mouth puckered there. A thin stream of thick, yellow liquid dripped onto the floor, gathering in a small, smoking puddle that quickly ate through the floorboards with a soft hiss.

"Tell me," Justin demanded.

I looked down at the label on the box. The package was addressed to John's real name, to this house in this Nevada town. It was dated yesterday, sent via overnight delivery, with John's own small, neat handwriting.

"Tell me, or I'll melt your face, yo. What is it, like, a bomb?"

John shrugged, said, "Why don't you open it and we'll both find out?"

Shitload sat the box on the floor, said, "Take it outside."

"Okay." John bent over to pick it up.

"Stop! Leave it where it is."

"Okay."

He pointed to the wig monster and said, "Open the box."

The thing apparently understood, because it trundled over and started tearing at the flap with its beak. After several long, clumsy minutes of this, during which I tried to show it the little tear strip all FedEx boxes have, it finally stuck its snout inside and pulled out a sheet of wrinkled notebook paper.

Shitload picked it up, saw scrawled on it in big ink pen letters: "JOHN LOOK BY THE BUSH IN THE FRONT YARD."

The Justin monster turned to John and said, "What's out there? A weapon? You tryin' to gank me?"

John didn't answer. Shitload pointed to the wig beast and said, "If any of you try to move, that thing will rip off all of your limbs, leave you alive and plant five hundred eggs in your belly. You down with that?"

We were. Shitload tossed aside the note and strode out the front door.

We could indeed see a bush out there, shivering in the breeze. Had John, under the influence of the sauce, somehow planted something out there ahead of time? How? And what? A gun? A pipe bomb? A trained badger? Nothing would have surprised me.

The creature formerly known as Justin White walked out to the bush and looked down, kicking around at the base of it. I glanced over at John, who waited with the same anticipation, apparently having completely forgotten the plan once the sauce wore off. The wig monster prowled around between us and I wondered if we should all try sprinting out the back door.

Outside, Justin had found nothing. He turned to walk back—

And was blown off his feet.

A thunderous *boom* echoed in the desert air, followed by a faint mechanical *ka-chunk* of a pump shotgun. A second shot sounded, then a third.

The wig beast in front of us hissed, baring its teeth (yes, it had both teeth and a beak), seeming to know that something was amiss and that we should all be ripped to shreds immediately. We were frozen by the thing, all of us desperate to jump up and watch our salvation, but any slight shift of a limb would cause the wig thing to spin in that direction.

A figure moved toward the open door out in the darkness. The creature spun toward it and when I saw who came through, I found myself rooting for the wig monster.

SAY WHAT YOU want about Shitload and his disjointed pet, but neither of them either tried to shoot me or set me on fire. The same cannot be said for Detective Lawrence "Morgan Freeman" Appleton, who strode into the house loading shells into a pistol-grip riot gun.

His eyes caught the jumbled creature on the floor. He raised the gun.

The thing turned toward him and meowed like a cat. It crouched, leaned his direction and vanished right as John screamed, "MOVE!"

Morgan spun and ducked off to his right.

The wig monster appeared in midair in the spot where Morgan was standing a half second earlier, flailing its limbs in his direction. The thing tumbled to the carpet. Morgan lowered the shotgun.

A blast thundered in the room. Bits of monster flew.

Morgan racked the shotgun, ejecting a blue plastic shell. "There any more of 'em?"

Jim said, "No, but that guy out there ain't dead."

We all got to our feet, everyone relieved at their rescue.

Everyone but me.

I still had a puncture in the middle of my chest like a third nipple, where the good detective here had shot me before trying to roast me alive. I wondered if they noticed Morgan didn't exactly read Justin his rights before blowing a hole in him. I mean, I did the same thing but that's why society doesn't let me carry a badge.

Morgan started to speak, maybe to say, "I blew a hole in his chest the size of a football, jackass, I'm pretty sure he's freaking dead," but then his eyes locked on mine, realizing the other guy he'd shot in the heart this weekend was now standing and breathing in front of him.

There was a moment, when my eyes met Morgan's, when once more I got a flash of his thoughts. Nothing coherent, just fear and exhaustion and cold, deadly purpose.

In that two seconds we shared, I knew the detective's mind was working full time to crush any remaining doubts about what he had to do. He had a mission, and had traveled across the country to carry it out. He was saving the world, and in his mind that meant that anyone dumb enough, unlucky enough, or crazy enough to take the sauce, to risk becoming a conduit for whatever otherworldly invasion was waiting to use them as a doormat, needed to die.

Morgan had a decision to make. He glanced over his shoulder, squinting into the darkness for Justin. But he didn't turn, and he still had the shotgun pointing in our direction.

Six of us, maybe we were hostages and maybe we were hives. Maybe he had thought he'd burst in and we'd all be in *Alien*-style cocoons and he could just torch the place and declare it mission accomplished. But here we were, exhausted and filthy and wounded. To this day I don't know if he was struggling with the moral implications of gunning down half a dozen civilians, or if he was mentally counting to see if he had that many shells left in the gun.

John leaned over and picked up the FedEx box. He peered inside, turned it over. A pack of cigarettes and a lighter slid out into his hand. He plucked one cigarette out, and lit it. He reached into the waistband of his hospital pants and pulled out a little bottle of some kind of brown liquor he had lifted from the truck, took a drink. I was surprised he hadn't mailed himself a burrito, too.

I said to Morgan, "It's a long fucking story but we're on your side. John totally lured Justin out there for you, just now."

Just don't fucking ask me how.

Morgan turned, pushing back through the door, leading with the shotgun. I followed, careful not to step in the wig monster chunks scattered on the floor underfoot.

The cop was a lot more surprised than I was to see Shitload was no longer on the desert floor. He poised the gun in front of him, turning like a turret, then spun on the beer truck as it rumbled to life and rolled onto the road.

Morgan ran, ripped off three shots as the red taillights shrank into the distance. He stomped back toward us, said, "Shit!"

"I know where he's going," I said. "And I'll tell you if you promise to take us with you. And not to shoot me again."

He sucked in a breath, scanning the faces of our group. Finally he said, "Okay."

"Luxor Hotel. Don't ask me how I know."

THIRTY SECONDS LATER we were all crammed into Morgan's rental SUV like it was a clown car, pealing down the blacktop.

From the passenger seat I watched the headlights swallowing up the road and said, "There's something like a massive séance planned. It's a guy named Marconi. Apparently Shitload—er, Justin, has business there."

All ten of Morgan's fingers were clamped around the steering wheel as the speedometer crept upward.

"I know."

"You do? How?"

Everyone in the truck lurched first right, then left as Morgan swerved to pass a car.

"Brock Wholesale reported the liquor truck missing yesterday. I happened to catch word of a gas station attendant in Missouri who said a beer-truck driver told him he needed directions to Las Vegas,

142

then punched him in the balls and told him his daughters would be live meat cocoons for the leech pool. Man thought that was strange, phoned it in. I just followed the same directions he gave Justin, drove balls to the wall. Then I came up on this exit and just had a feelin', you know, like an intuition."

The mention of "intuition" gave me a cold feeling in my gut. I glanced back at John. It got his attention, too.

"I followed my gut and there was the truck, parked by that old house."

Morgan scratched the side of his cheek, two-day stubble sounding like sandpaper. The engine growled, the scenery sprayed past my window.

I asked, "If this thing makes it to the Luxor, what happens?"

"Let's just say I came a long way to make sure that *don't* happen."

From behind us, John said, "If you've been following us since we got kidnapped, you must have been up for more than two days."

"More like fifty hours."

We rode silently for a minute. Less than a minute actually, according to Morgan.

"Make that fifty hours and thirty-seven-point-two-three seconds. It's the adrenaline, I guess. I ain't really been tired. The thrill of the hunt."

We drove in silence for a moment. Red taillights appeared up ahead. I reached out and gripped the dashboard.

Morgan said, "That, and those loud, piercing voices in my head."

Morgan's eyes exploded.

He shrieked as two sprays of blood flecked over the windshield. Jennifer screamed behind me, John and Fred bellowed "OH, FUCK," simultaneously.

Little white rods poured down the cop's face, swirled around inside the truck. He let go of the steering wheel. I reached over and grabbed it. We left the road.

We shook, rattled, bumped. The horizon and sky swapped places in the windshield and the roof of the car bashed me in the shoulder. Glass bits rained down in my eyes and ears and up my nose, the dashboard

143

punched me in the forehead, the roof hammered me a second time, and Molly's furry ass rolled over my face.

Finally, the vehicle banged to a stop.

Silence. Only a soft chittering over the desert breeze. And then came the voices.

CHAPTER 6

Meet Dr. Marconi

THAT SUCKED. I pried my eyes open, feeling scratchy little bits in there that could either be sand or glass. I worked the lids open and found myself staring at dirt. Everything was upside-down; I was hanging by my seat belt. I felt like every single joint in my body had been wrenched painfully out of socket. It was agony from head to toe, so dark now that it took me a moment to realize that the massive, spreading pool down on the ceiling was not motor oil, but blood.

I craned my neck over and saw hunks of meat flying off what had been Officer Freeman/Appleton in juicy ragged pink-and-yellow layers, bone and ribs and a spongy mass that must have been lungs. Out from the meaty shreds came rushing masses of the tiny white demon-rod things, swirling around the interior of the truck like rice in a blender.

That's not what caused me to panic, not that or the faint wet, ripping sounds next to me. No, what got me moving, what sent me clutching at the seat belt clasp, was the sound of the swarm.

Oh, that sound. Not something coming through my ears at all but a kind of shrill electricity in my brain, a million sharp, spiky, poison thoughts ricocheting around my head.

Imagine fifty thousand men trapped on a desert island, deprived of food and water and sex but somehow kept alive for fifty thousand years. Then, after they've been tormented a hundred steps beyond insanity, tortured past self-mutilation and cannibalism, somebody drops off a sculpture of a naked woman made from T-bone steaks. If you could then capture the sound of them simultaneously fucking and eating and tearing her to shreds and broadcast it into the center of your skull at ten thousand watts, it would still sound absolutely nothing like what I heard. It was madness and desperation and deprivation and torment gone supernova, screeches and howls and, sprinkled in here and there, my own name.

It blew every thought out of my head, tore my mind open. I was frantic, patting around for the clasp to the seat belt with hands shaking like a Parkinson's patient. I could vaguely hear actual screams around me, right from the backseat, but they might as well have been a thousand miles away. These little white streaks were buzzing around my face now, past my ears, skipping over my skin.

I got my fingers around the little plastic box that held the seat belt but couldn't find a button, couldn't see it, pressed and pulled and finally just started clawing at the thing like a little kid in a tantrum. I felt this itching over my bare arms, and then little pricks like needles and I knew what it was, I fucking knew, and I started contorting my body to crawl free from the belt like an animal wrenching from a trap.

Movement, all around me in the darkness.

Glass shattering in the backseat.

Somebody getting dragged out.

Screaming.

I ran my hand over my forearm and a thousand of the rods scattered off into the air. I heard a resulting uproar in the voices, shrieks like teenage banshees at a boy band concert, except nothing like that at all. The sound—it was so massive and yet so compressed in my skull that it was a physical pressure against my temples. I thought I could feel wheezing, creaking fissures in the bone.

Then, hands were grabbing me, pulling at the seat belt. A hand came into view and with a flick there was suddenly a narrow blade there, a switchblade cutting at the strap. I fell free, crashed down. Four hands were dragging me out of the wreckage by the shirt and shoulders, my back scraping over a bed of glass bits.

It was Fred Chu and John, pulling me free. Everybody was yelling, freaking out. Molly was dancing around and barking—total panic at the sight of the little cloud of white insects blowing around me like pillow feathers.

The worms had settled on my arm again and were landing on my neck and face. I brushed them off, swatted at them in the air. John seized my arm by the wrist, dug out the brown bottle of alcohol from his pants and doused the arm with it.

This seemed to annoy the flying worm things more than anything, and my skin was on fire with their attempts to dig their way in. I sputtered, "That ain't helping! The alcohol isn't hurting th—"

John flicked his lighter and set my arm on fire.

I said before that my skin was "on fire" with the pain but being confronted so soon after that sentiment with the actual experience, I admit that other thing was nothing like my skin actually being on fire.

But even the white heat on my arm was nothing next to the pain that suddenly erupted inside my skull. Hundreds of the worms were burned alive and the psychic outcry was like shoving my head inside a 747 engine. It was a nuclear bomb of sound, earth-shattering, feeling like an explosion of razor blades in my cranium.

And then, silence. John was rolling my arm in the dust, patting out the flames. The skin was beet red and peeling in places.

I sat up, tried to focus my eyes, tried to get to my feet, fell back down on my ass. I saw John had blood running down his forehead and he was trying to wipe it from his eyes, the empty liquor bottle at his feet. He leaned over and puked. Jennifer was on her knees in the dirt, had a chunk missing from her upper thigh and her hair was matted to the side of her head with blood.

Big Jim was pointing and screaming. Molly was barking.

Fred.

Screaming.

Thrashing around as if on fire.

The swarm had found him.

The flying worms poured out of the wrecked SUV like a kicked hornet's nest. All landed on Fred.

He was coughing, choking, the rods gushing into his wide-open mouth. In five seconds it was over.

Fred collapsed.

We all knew he wasn't dead. Jim and John and Molly stared toward Fred in dull shock, a silence settling over the scene so heavy it was almost a solid thing.

Only Jennifer moved. She sprinted toward the dead SUV, a little squirt of blood jumping from her leg wound with each step. She crawled in, grabbed something, then backed out quickly.

Fred moved. He twitched, flopped onto his back, then clumsily got to his feet. Everybody flinched and took steps backward. I forced myself to my feet over the protest of my leg muscles. Fred—if it was still Fred—looked confused for a moment, then brushed himself off and said, "It's okay, guys. I'm okay. I'm okay."

Jennifer ran up, and I saw what she had retrieved from the SUV. It was Morgan's shotgun. The thing was gleaming in the moonlight with a layer of tacky blood. Without asking, Jim took it from her and checked the chamber to see if a shell was loaded. He laid it over his shoulder like he was suddenly the captain of this crew. He said, "We gotta get a car, guys. Somehow."

Nobody moved. Jennifer looked at me expectantly. What was I supposed to do? I could barely keep my feet. I looked Fred dead in the eyes, searching them.

I said to Fred, "Go flag down a car."

Jim nodded like this was a perfectly good plan and followed Fred as he walked toward the highway. Jennifer gave me an exasperated look, went up to Jim and tore the gun from his hands. He spun, asked her what the heck she was doing. She backed away from him and I half expected her to blow a hole through the infested Fred with the shotgun.

She didn't.

Instead she went right to me and pushed the gun into my hands.

Very slowly and carefully Big Jim said to me, "What are you going to do with that, David?"

John, Jen and I stood side by side, facing Fred and Jim from about ten feet away.

Fred said, "Whoa, guys. Guys, we're all shook up here. Okay?"

Jennifer said, "Jim, were you not paying attention to what just happened? That's *not* Fred. Not anymore."

"We don't know what happened," snapped Jim, glancing over at Fred. "Does anybody here understand this? Really? Screw you if you think you do."

Fred said, "Guys, look, I don't know what you think you saw but I'm still Fred in here. Ask me anything, I'm me. I mean, we were all in that car when the cop exploded. Any of us could be . . . infected or whatever, but we gotta hang together. We're like, the fuckin' good guys here. Right?"

Everyone looked at me. I was the armed one. I looked down, as if deferring to the shotgun. It was cold, heavy and sticky with Morgan's blood.

A breeze blew past us. From my right, Molly let out a low growl.

I closed my eyes, let out a long breath and said, "Go flag down a

149

car." Big Jim and Fred turned once more and took a step toward the highway. I let out a breath, took two steps forward.

I raised the shotgun and blew Fred's head off his shoulders.

Blood flew. I saw it mist in the moonlight, for a split second frozen in the air like a snapshot. There was that feeling again, the sparks in my head, the old violence high, the electricity of it shivering through me.

Fred's body slumped to its knees, then fell flat on its chest.

Blood.

Screaming.

Panic.

The old familiar sights and sounds.

I had been here before.

Big Jim recoiled, splattered with Fred's blood, yelling something I couldn't hear. Everything was dull, slow. I craned my head to see John and he had an expression I had seen there a few times before, something like fear, and pity. I wanted to put the butt of the shotgun through his face. I loathed that look. It said, "You are what you are, Dave, and that's that."

I caught a glimpse of Jen, her hands clasped over her mouth. This seemed like such a fucking good idea ten seconds ago, didn't it?

There was movement out the corner of my eye and it was Big Jim, stomping toward me, rage lighting up his face. That was a familiar look for him, too, seen in a dozen high school fights, his fists about to come loose like fighting dogs tearing out of their cages.

Yeah, Jim, you can quote the Bible to me but you and I got the same sickness.

I aimed the shotgun right at his face.

Jim looked into the barrel, took two more steps, then raised his eyes to meet mine.

He stopped.

His eyes never moving from mine. He said, "The day after the Hitchcock thing, back in school. I saw you, you and your buddies, laughing. Laughing in the hallway. Not twelve hours after Billy died. I know all about you, Dave. You got the Devil in—"

I pumped the shotgun.

"This is not a conversation, Jim."

Every muscle was tensed. We faced off that way, seemingly forever, the trigger pressing into the skin of my finger.

Shoot him. Shoot everybody.

John broke the moment. He sprinted up toward Fred's prone body, grabbing and dragging it. "Get him to the truck!" Jennifer went to help him, but the two of them were making slow, halting progress pulling the deadweight through the sand.

John said, "Dave! These things are starting to come out of him!"

Jim stared me down a moment longer and then turned and walked toward them. John muttered something to him but Big Jim knocked both him and Jen aside. He dragged Fred's body back to the wreckage of the SUV and laid him against the rear door. A familiar fuzzy cloud was emerging from the ragged stump that had been Fred Chu's head.

Jim stomped toward me and, with a quick, impossibly strong motion, easily ripped the shotgun from my hands. He turned and aimed at the gas tank of the SUV.

I flinched from the expected explosion, had the sudden crazy urge for a ball of fire to spew out and reduce all of us to ash.

Nothing. Instead there was a patch of little holes in the metal, a heavy rain of gasoline splattering down the rear and onto the prone body of Fred Chu. John stepped up to his corpse, flicked open his lighter and tossed it down.

Fred Chu went up in a ball of flames. The fire licked up the trunk of the SUV, reached the gas tank and ignited the contents with a heavy, metallic *THONK,* sending us flopping to the ground, little bits of metal plunking softly into the sand around us.

Jim got to his feet and walked toward me again, the shotgun pointed at the ground. The adrenaline was draining from me so fast I thought I'd be sitting in a puddle of it soon. So tired. So tired.

Two feet away, Jim raised the gun.

Man, just do it. Just do it and let me sleep out here in the sand until the sun goes supernova and turns the whole world into a charred memory.

151

He threw the shotgun in my gut, and walked away. The barrel was warm. We all got to our feet and watched thousands of the little particles swarm out of Fred, burning like sparks over a stirred campfire. In my head, the concert of damned voices faded and died.

John said, "Do you think that's all of them? The worms, whatever they are? Do you think we got all of 'em?"

I didn't answer.

"Because I got a feeling that if just a few of them get away, hell, if just *one* of them gets out and gets into a body, they'll multiply. Lay eggs and do what they do."

Nobody answered. What was there to say?

It took us fifteen minutes to flag down a car. I convinced Jennifer to stand out by the road alone, shivering and mussed and looking victimized, one shapely leg coated in crimson. Soon a shiny new SUV pulled over, driven by a young guy and his wife, on their honeymoon or whatever.

As soon as their passenger door was open I sprinted out and put the gun in their face, forced them out while Jim apologized profusely, swearing we would bring it back. The five of us and the dog piled in and we drove into the night.

"I DON'T LIKE it," said Jennifer softly, as if afraid the looming, dark thing on the horizon could hear us.

She was looking at the Luxor Las Vegas Hotel, a pyramid jutting into the night sky, big and black and geometric, like something from the year 3000. We were parked in the lot of a massive neon-lined steakhouse maybe a quarter mile away, all of us beaten and stinking of smoke and looking like war refugees.

We had ducked into a truck stop restroom just outside of the city and washed as much blood off ourselves as we could. Jim spat out two teeth. John was pretty sure he had a concussion and would still be vomiting if he had anything in his stomach. I had double vision in one eye, and in general I felt like I had been run through a wood chipper.

152

We bought four first-aid kits and fixed ourselves up as best we could; Jennifer patched her thigh with a roll of Ace bandages and a tampon. We bought armloads of convenience-store food and sat eating as we drove around looking for the Luxor. This parking lot was as far as we got before somebody asked what the plan was.

"The Justin thing is in there. Right now," Jim said, nodding toward the Luxor. "So what are we waitin' for? This whole thing, it could be going down right this minute for all we know and we're out here doing nothing."

John said, "If he summoned Satan, we'd see it from here, right?"

This was the most any of us had spoken since the accident and the ensuing clusterfuck.

I said, "First problem is we got to get into this thing. Guy like Marconi, probably attracts a lot of nutjobs. Got to think the doors will be guarded and I don't particularly feel like shooting my way in there."

Jim said, "*Think*, David. The séance or whatever it is is happening inside *a casino*. You won't get five feet inside the door with a gun before nine guys in suits tackle you."

"And shove your head in a vise," John added, helpfully.

I said, "Well, I don't like our chances without the gun. Unless Jim wants to try to quote Bible verses at it."

Jennifer put up her hands, said, "Guys, let's not make this a dick-measuring contest, okay?"

There was silence for a moment, then John said, "That's good, because it wouldn't be no contest at all."

Silence again.

"That is, I'm referring to my cock being bigger than either of yours."

I sighed and said, "John, I don't think anyone in this vehicle is in the mood to—"

"John, let me make one thing clear," Jim said, cutting me off in his most stern, evangelical voice. "Every man is blessed with his gifts from the Lord. One of mine happens to be a penis large enough that, if it had a penis of its own, my penis's penis would be larger than your penis."

There was a moment of stunned silence, then I heard Jen start laughing so hard I thought she would choke.

"Fuck all of you," John retorted. "You don't even exist. We're all just a figment of my cock's imagination."

Jim tried to suppress his laugher, and failed. One more victim, sucked in by John. You get in the room with him and you just fall into a warm pool of beer and video games and penis jokes, staring out at the universe with him and saying, "Do you believe this shit?"

I thought, not for the first time, that John could start a pretty fucking successful cult.

I looked down at the shotgun in my lap, a heavy, cold, hateful thing still coated in grit and blood. I noticed something else, a broad lump in my pants pocket. I dug into it and pulled out the folded envelope of cash I had gotten from the alley guy yesterday. I wondered if I wound up not using it if I should go find the guy and give it back to him. From behind me, Molly barked.

John was looking off across the parking lot now where a massive, customized RV sat like a beached whale. Behind it was an eighteen-wheeler, painted white with neon outlines, some kind of logo airbrushed on the side. He asked, "I wonder what's in there."

Big Jim said, "Shipment of fags probably."

The asshole's a comedian all of a sudden.

This seemed to anger Molly, who stared out the windshield and went into a barking frenzy. I reached back and, for the first time in my life, smacked a dog across the nose with an envelope full of cash. Jennifer said, "Thank you."

John said, "There might be some clothes in that RV. We could change, look normal. Get Dave an overcoat to conceal the gun. Then charge into the Luxor, find Justin and open a can of kill-ass."

"We can't break into somebody's RV," I said.

John squinted at the logo on the side of the truck.

"That RV doesn't belong to a person. It belongs to Elton John. You know, the band."

Jen said, "Seriously?"

Molly retreated to the rear and started biting at the luggage the newlyweds had stacked in it. They probably had packed some sausages in there or something.

John said, "Yeah, look at the sign. I bet the truck is their concert stuff."

Jim said, "Elton John is a guy, not a band."

"Please, don't get him started," I said. "There was that one video where he was in different outfits and—"

"For the last time, those were all different guys, Dave. I looked it up. They're brothers."

"Oh, Jesus, forget it. Who cares." I gripped the shotgun and considered shooting myself in the head.

A slow smile spread over John's face. He turned to me and said the five most horrifying words he knows.

"Dave, I have a plan."

IF THE ALIENS who helped the Egyptians build the pyramids returned to Earth and opened a casino, it would look like the Luxor Las Vegas. The thing was a massive, gleaming, black glass pyramid with a line of white lights that pulsed up its four corners.

We had just pulled into the Luxor parking lot and were watching two cop cars and a tow truck messing with Justin's abandoned beer hauler, which had been carelessly run up onto the curb. The cops and tow guy all looked a little confused by the scene.

I said, "Let's go."

We filed out of the SUV and strode toward the front entrance, giving the cops a wide berth. Jennifer looked up at it and whispered to me, "I don't like this place."

"You already said that."

"It looks like—like the end of the world. Somehow. Like those huge, scary future buildings in *Blade Runner,* black with the fire coming out the tops and all that."

Big Jim said, "Yeah, yeah, and those gigantic big screens with huge

Asian women on them. I watched that movie when I was a kid and I started cryin'." Big Jim adjusted his cape.

The entrance was ahead, opened wide like a maw, the guts inside showing gleaming solid gold.

"You know what else scared me?" Jen said, reaching up to scratch where a bundle of black feathers was tickling her neck. "*Independence Day*. That alien invasion movie. The first part, where the aliens come and they look up between the buildings and the sky is gone and, like, all they see is metal. Just as far as you can see, that steel ship looming up there. I remember thinking, that's what the end of the world will look like. It won't be wars or a meteor. It'll be something we never could have thought of . . ."

Awe choked off her voice. We all had entered the lobby and stopped in our tracks. The cavernous inner chamber of the Luxor was gold upon gold, gold floors, gold walls, gold ceiling. The place was a temple, and there was no question who God was.

The lobby was a pulsing crowd of people and we were pushed ahead by the current. Everyone stared at us as they passed, eyes flicking from me to Jen to John's naked ass. I nervously adjusted the guitar strap around my neck.

The shotgun was at my side, concealed under my coat. We probably drew the eyes of a dozen security guys working the floor. But at the sight of us, not a single one of them was thinking, "gun." They were thinking "retards," sure, but not "gun."

John said, "Over there."

He had found an entrance labeled EGYPTIAN BALLROOM, outside of which were two huge stand-up posters featuring a smiling fiftysomething man who must have been Dr. Marconi, since his name was boldly displayed under the picture.

A lady sat at a table with a laptop PC and stacks of programs and brochures fanned out on a table. There were two guys in suits with thin cell phone headsets on, guarding the door.

We strode toward them. My heart skipped a beat. This is as far as we had planned.

As we neared I glanced through the partially opened door to see if anything was happening in there, such as Lucifer crashing up through the floor. He wasn't.

What I could see was that the ballroom was huge, a floor like half a football field. In the center was an enormous ice sculpture that had to have been fifteen feet high. It was an angel with its wings spread, hands upstretched to the ceiling. It must have had water pumping up through it because a rain of liquid rolled off its crystalline wings like a waterfall, splashing into a pool at its feet. The crowd sat in rows of folding chairs around it. Every seat was taken. Each member of the audience had their eyes closed.

The amplified voice of Dr. Marconi drifted into the lobby:

"Okay, everyone. Settle down. I know this is frightening for some of you but what we're dealing with is real, real as the person sitting next to you. But I need all of you, all of your concentration, all of that power, that openness of the mind for this to work. Now we've just heard from Betty, who says her husband disappeared under mysterious circumstances last year. His name is Harold Alexander. Let's all concentrate on Harold Alexander. Now clear your minds. Each of you picture, in your head, an apple . . ."

I had left the six thousand dollars from my envelope with a pony-tailed roadie who gave us fifteen minutes alone with the concert truck while he went off to smoke. The guitar slung over my back was made entirely of a crystal-clear glass or polymer. I was wearing a white leather overcoat trimmed in long, luxuriant green fur and an enormous white sombrero edged in a pattern of fiber-optic lights.

Jennifer had donned a tailed white tuxedo/ringmaster coat over her T-shirt and shorts, the coat long enough to leave only bare legs emerging from the hem. A black feather boa gave her an outfit that sort of looked intentional. Big Jim was wearing an incredibly tight roadie jumpsuit with a flashy Elton John logo on the back. He had a huge Casio keyboard under his arm and pulled a dolly behind him loaded down with two black boxes the size of footlockers.

John wore a black jockstrap, a pair of white chaps and a small

157

purple Robin Hood cap that covered his groin. He was naked from the waist up save for a tight leather vest and a bundle of gold chains. We all wore sunglasses.

As we arrived at the table, Marconi's voice boomed, "Now, now, everyone be calm. Who's next? Does anyone else have someone they'd like to contact?"

The guards and check-in lady stared at us in confused amusement as we approached. The lady at the table, trying to suppress a smile, finally said, "Uh, do you have tickets?"

John said, "No. We're Elton John."

"We're, uh, the band," I said, cutting him off quickly. "We're playing in there after the séance. Show us the back entrance and we'll—"

"Dave!" shouted John. "Look!"

It was Shitload. He was at the far end of the ballroom, shuffling between seats, moving toward the stage. He wore an ill-fitting suit jacket, jeans and a cowboy hat that we knew covered a lumpy head wound.

"Yo, I gots an old homey I'd like you to contact for me, fool," he said as he approached Marconi.

Dr. Marconi's smile faltered at the sight of Shitload, limping with joints bent at odd angles, his body puffy and stretched as if ready to burst. The jacket didn't completely conceal the gaping shotgun wound in his midsection.

Shitload said, "His name is Korrok the Slavemaster from the eighth plane, also known in some realms as Baa'aaa'aaa'aab and in others as the Lord Zanthk All-Bzzki'l Shadd'uuul'l L'luuu'ddahs L'ikzzb-lla Khtnaz."

The guards and the door lady all turned their attention to him, not sure if this was part of the show but sensing something was about to go way, way wrong.

I stepped up to the door and ran my hand along my side, felt the long, rigid shotgun hidden behind my overcoat. I was about to tell Door Lady that we were in the midst of an emergency that only rock and roll could solve and thus had to be let in at once.

"GUN!"

It was the guard to my left. I looked down, realized six inches of shotgun barrel was exposed where my coat had folded back.

Quickly, I whipped it out and pointed it at his face, freezing him in midlunge.

John said, "It's not a gun! It's part of our act!" at the exact same moment I said, "I'm a cop! I'm undercover!"

Then, over the loudspeaker:

"AGGGHHH!! MY BALLS!!!"

I spun and saw Dr. Marconi fall to the floor, grabbing his punched groin.

Shitload loomed over him.

Gasps rippled across the audience.

I sprinted into the ballroom. Guards muscled past me, rushing the stage.

Shitload punched the first guard in the groin so hard it flung his body back five feet. The other retreated.

I raised the shotgun, leveling it at Shitload.

"FREEZE!" I shouted, for some reason. A lady screamed at the sight of the gun. Shitload turned his back to us and leaned forward. His pants split. A fleshy, puckering protrusion formed and pushed its way through the slit, looking like the end of a flesh trumpet.

FOONT!!

With a bassy thump and a smell like burnt sulfur, Shitload farted himself far into the air.

The crowd went wild, chairs clanging down all around us. I tracked Shitload with the barrel of the shotgun as he climbed a hazy contrail of shimmery methane. He landed atop the giant ice angel. Shitload crouched on one wing, raised his arms in a "touchdown" motion and said something at the top of his voice that was probably very profound and ominous but was drowned out by the absolute bedlam in the crowd below.

I fired. Shitload exploded.

Hey! That was easy!

159

An eruption of blood and hamburger stained the wings of the angel red and pink. I felt a momentary euphoria of victory, ready to be carried off on shoulders. I should have known better.

Out of Justin's guts poured, not the white buzzing worms, but a shower of black specks that could have been coffee beans. They bounced and flecked off the wings of the angel and plinked into the water below.

I edged up to the pool with the shotgun. Dark shapes started writhing and splashing below the surface.

Oh shit.

A soft hand landed on my shoulder and I turned to see the sharp, brown eyes of Albert Marconi.

"Son, I think we need to get the people out of here."

Big Jim was behind him, still toting the keyboard. Marconi said, patiently, "Don't you think? We haven't much time."

I turned, ran, fired the shotgun into the air and shouted, "Bomb! There's a bomb in the fountain! Everybody run for your lives! Please don't *not* panic!"

The words were completely lost in the stampede caused by my shotgun blast. I bumped into John in the crowd.

"Where's the bomb?"

"There's no bomb, there's something in the—"

"Guys!"

It was Jen. She was yelling and pointing at the fountain. I turned just as one of the seven-legged wig monsters flung itself out of the pool, in a spray of water.

The beast landed on the carpet on its little baby-like hands, looked around, meowed, then disappeared. In a blink it was clinging to the back of an elderly black woman, scorpion tail buried down into the base of her spine.

Another of the little black beasts emerged. Another. Then three more. They crawled, leapt, clamped themselves onto victims. A fat guy went flailing past me with one of the things on his chest; a bearded man was trying to shake one off his leg.

160

One of the wig monsters ran and jumped at Jim. He swatted it like a baseball with his Elton John keyboard, then bashed the heavy Casio in half over its prone body in a spray of white and black keys.

Jen was on the other side of the fountain, kicking one of the beasts to death. I ran toward her, blew a wig monster in half, worked the pump and realized I had no more shots. I flung the gun at another one of the monsters, missed, hit an elderly man in a wheelchair instead, toppling him over.

I was kicking through the sea of blue chairs, closing on Jen. Two of the wig beasts were bearing down on me. No, three. One of them crouched and launched itself at me—

THONK

The beast was batted away by a folding chair, wielded by John.

He screamed "YEAH!" in a dead-on impersonation of pro wrestler "Macho Man" Randy Savage, grasping the folded chair by two legs. He swung again and flattened another of the beasts, screaming, "Have a *seat,* bitch!"

There were at least a hundred of the wig monsters bouncing around the ballroom now. Victims littered the floor by the dozen.

I flinched at the sound of a sharp gunshot, spun to see a middle-aged lady holding a little chrome pistol. She shot one of the things, killed it, took shots at another, missed. The beasts ganged up on her, three stinging her simultaneously. I heard someone shout, "Becky!" from behind me. A tall guy with a heavy brown beard pushed through the chairs. "BECKY! HONEEEEY!"

He punted two of the creatures off his wife with several furious kicks, then John ran in and chaired the last one off, screaming, "You've been sentenced to get the *chair,* motherfucker!"

The man helped his wife to her feet and said to me, "Those things! They're blocking the exits!"

I spun around, saw black clumps surrounding the doors we came in. "Shit!"

The woman looked dazed. The man asked her if she was okay. She nodded, then calmly reached over with her left arm and tore the right

161

arm out of its socket. It made a slimy sucking sound, like tearing the leg off a Thanksgiving turkey. There was no blood. The wound was instantly sealed by a thin, black layer of the soy sauce.

She calmly walked back toward the fountain, casually carrying her arm like an umbrella. Her husband stood in dumbfounded silence. I heard John land two more blows with the chair.

Another bite victim lay nearby, a young man writhing as if in a seizure. Eventually his legs kicked themselves free from the rest of his body. The limbs thumped along the floor on their own like two giant polyester snakes with shoes for heads. Right behind them was a loose head stuck to a single arm, furiously biting and clawing the carpet.

I felt like we might not be in control of this situation any longer.

I heard a scream that I had come to recognize as Jennifer's. She was on her knees with Fred's switchblade, surrounded by five dead wig monsters all bearing ragged stab wounds. I sprinted that way.

I heard a metallic thump from behind me and heard John yell, "You wants the committee, asshole, then you best meet with the *chair!*" I pulled Jen to her feet.

Around us, the disembodied human limbs were piling up, forming a circle around the fountain, fusing themselves to each other like Satan's LEGO set. A wet, pink disembodied spine slithered past us like a snake.

Dr. Marconi jogging toward us, shouting some instruction I couldn't hear in the pandemonium. All around us the wig monsters were closing in, their dark shapes rolling in toward the fountain like oil down a drain.

One of them jumped onto Jen's back. I flung myself at it, grabbed it in a bear hug and ripped it off her. One of its little fists came around and started punching me in the face.

I carried it to the fountain, stepping over a squishy pile of body parts. I shoved the monster into the water, held it under, screamed "Die!" or something to that effect. After a few seconds it stopped moving and black sauce oozed out of it like an oil slick.

Dr. Marconi got close enough so I could finally hear him. He said, "They're trying to get into the water! Don't let them!"

I looked back down at the spreading black pool, heard a splash as another of the beasts jumped in, followed by another, the creatures returning to the pool from which they had sprung.

Nothing good could come from that.

Marconi said, "Follow me."

We sprinted toward a set of doors behind the stage, John smacking creatures with chairs as we went. Marconi unlocked the doors and we filed in. John stopped and spun in front of the open doorway. He faced at least half a dozen of the wig monsters, circling in on him. He whipped the chair around and actually split one of the things in half with the impact, spilling a spray of blood that was reflective, like mercury. John bellowed, "Anybody else want to donate blood to *chair*-ity?"

He ducked into the door, stopped, thought for a moment, then flung the door open again. He swung the chair and bashed one monster right in the wig, screaming, "There's some dessert! With a *chair*-y on top!"

He came back in again, breathing heavily, slamming the door just as something thumped against it.

I said, "How about we just stay in here until they all leave?"

Dr. Marconi took off his glasses and cleaned them with a handkerchief.

John said, "What's happening to them out there? The bite victims?" He looked at Marconi. "We've got friends who took the soy sauce, the, uh, the venom those things out there spit out. Almost all of them died but not like—"

"Out there you have a room full of true believers," Marconi said, sadly. "There's a shift that goes on, you see, physically and mentally and spiritually. They were ripe for this."

Something hammered against the door and one hinge popped out in a burst of plaster dust. Big Jim and John leaned against the door to brace it.

I said, "Wait, you know what's going on here?"

He gave me a dismissive look. "I'll send you home with a copy of my book."

163

Big Jim said, "He's trying to break through, isn't he?"

Marconi nodded. "He or his lackeys, yes."

"Goddammit!" I screamed. "Did everybody else know this was gonna happen but me?"

"I most certainly did not know this was going to happen," Marconi said, "or I would have canceled and issued full refunds. But when I became aware of the 'sauce' as you call it, I knew that it had only one purpose."

There was a scratching from the opposite side of the door that I suspected was the sound of the beasts trying to bite through it.

"And that purpose is?"

"I offer people a window into the spiritual. Someone wishes to turn it into a door."

A blue eye, in the darkness.

Jim whispered, "The Devil."

Marconi said, "Son, the greatest trick the Devil ever pulled was convincing the world there was only one of him."

I held up a hand in a "halt" motion and said, "How. Do. We. Get. Out. Of. This?"

Marconi placed his glasses back on his nose and said, "We're like one German soldier alone on the beaches of Normandy on D-Day, holding a sharp stick. I assure you, son, if any of us were capable of destroying such evil, the world would have killed us long before now. The world turns, son. And now it turns into the darkness."

I said, "So, what do you suggest?"

"I am a retired priest. Did you know that?"

John asked, "Are you one of those priests who can shoot lasers out of their eyes? Because that would be really helpful right now."

"No," he said. "But I can bless water to make it holy. The ice statue, I mean."

John's face brightened and he said, "That's perfect!" He thrust his index finger into the air. "We bless the ice, then we just have to somehow get all hundred or so of those monsters to go lick the statue!"

I stared hard into the face of the older man, said, "Okay, there is no

164

possible combination of English words that would form a dumber plan than that."

"We'll need to buy time, of course," he said, undeterred. "But if I'm right, if they're doing what I think they're doing, it's most likely the only hope we've got. The travelers out there, the beasts I mean, they do have a weakness."

John said, "We know. Chairs."

"Uh, not exactly. They're natural discordians. It's a product of where they're from, you see. When you live in a world of black noise, melody is like a blade to the ears. Angels and their harps and all that."

I asked, "What does that have to do with—"

A hole exploded from the center of the door. A little pink fist and a segmented leg curled through, reaching around between John and Big Jim. John grabbed it by the wrist and Jennifer severed the arm with the switchblade. There was a feline shriek from the other side. John held the detached arm in his hand for a moment, then shoved it back through the ragged hole.

Marconi said, "I see you have your instruments. Can any of you sing? The old spirituals work best."

John said, "I can sing."

I said, "No, you can't, John."

"Well, I play the guitar."

"So can I," said Big Jim. "We have two guitars."

I said, "This could not be any stupider."

John said, "Dave, you remember the words to 'Camel Holocaust'?"

"Ah, once again, you prove me wrong, John."

Marconi looked down at the two carts stacked with amps and cables and said, "How long is it? I'll need several minutes."

John stepped around and lifted the guitar off my back, said, " 'Camel Holocaust' is as long as you want it to be, my friend. I'm lead, Jim is rhythm, Jen sings backup. Jen, just repeat everything Dave sings, only like one second behind. The sound system will be on the stage. We duck out there and plug in and wail. Okay? Guys, *this is just retarded enough to work.*"

165

We set up, then faced the banging door. John said, "You know, I'm surprised the door stopped them, since they can teleport around like that. You'd think they could just blink right through it."

There was sudden silence from beyond the door, a muttering like the creatures had just realized something. From behind me, Jim screamed.

One of the beasts was on his back. A second appeared on his chest, and in a blurred motion it snatched at his throat.

Jim collapsed on his guitar, the white instrument turning instantly crimson.

Jennifer lunged with the switchblade and stabbed one beast to death. She was good with that thing.

I said, "Jim? Are you—"

He rolled over, his throat laying open in shreds and flaps, as if it had been hit with a shotgun blast. His eyes were wide, his mouth working. Then, he was gone.

I opened my mouth to say something when suddenly my vision was obstructed by blackness. There were little pinches on my chest and belly, like something grabbing hold. My vision focused and I saw a dozen mismatched eyes staring back at me.

I fell backward, hit the ground, the wig monster riding on my chest. Its beak opened and I saw a pink, human tongue lolling around inside.

An electric shriek emerged from the ballroom. A guitar.

The creature closed its beak and turned toward the open door where John played, a look of intense annoyance on its face. It trotted away, two tiny hands over its ears.

Marconi said, "Good! Go!"

I stood and pushed through the open door. John played his ax with his legs spread apart, holding the guitar low to the ground. I sprinted around him, grabbed the mic off of the stage. For a moment, I was speechless.

The base of the fountain was now hidden behind a seven-foot-high circle of stacked body parts, the ice angel rising from the center. The remaining wig monsters gathered around the perimeter, facing inward, as if waiting.

There is no possible way this is actually happening.

Well, might as well go with it. I clenched my throat, filled my lungs until my diaphragm pushed out against the gold-plated belt I was wearing, and screeched:

> "I knew a man
> No, I made that part up
> Hair! Hair! Haaairrr!
> Camel Holocaust! Camel Holocaust!"

The creatures spun our way, donned some very disappointed frowns, backed away.

"Brilliant!" shouted Marconi. "You're really annoying them! Let's move!"

We pushed forward toward the fountain, the sound of the music thundering through the room, scattering the beasts before us like a leaf blower. One of the wig monsters spat at me.

> "My melon soul
> Crushed by your Gallagher of apathy
> Sledgehammer! Hammerrrrr!
> Camel Holocaust! Camel Holocaust!"

We reached the length of our cables, still some distance from the fountain. Marconi went forward with Jennifer in tow. They got within blessing distance of the angel and Marconi said, "Father, you give us grace through sacramental signs, which tell us of the wonders of your unseen power. In baptism we use your gift of water, which you have made a rich symbol of the grace you give us in this sacrament. At the very dawn of creation . . ."

> "There's a wolf behind you
> No, wait, it's just a dog
> Oh, shit! Badger! Baaaadgeeeerrr!
> Camel Holocaust! Camel Holocaust!"

We hit the first solo, John ripped into it. Several of the wig monsters were now chewing on John's guitar wire.

The sound died into faint, pathetic guitar pluckings.

The monsters lurched toward us en masse. John, thinking quickly, ran over and snatched the microphone from my hands. He began making guitar sounds with his mouth.

"WAAAAHHHH wah-wah-wah-wah-wah, weet woo weet weet woo—"

I didn't think that would work. I spun on Dr. Marconi, saw him stepping up over the human-parts wall toward the fountain itself. I followed him, climbed up, stepped on a face, a bundle of six hands, an ass.

The pool was black now. Not black like oil, but black like a cave, so that you couldn't see any reflection or ripples in the surface, not even when Dr. Marconi waded out into it. A black rain fell off the angel's wings above us.

John mounted the pile behind us, screamed, *"WAH, DO-DO-DO-DOOOO-DO, DEE DOO DOO—"*

Marconi, knee-deep in black oil, reached out and touched the icy surface of the statue. He said, "We ask you, Father, with your Son . . ."

John had reached the end of his solo, was now making up a third verse to the song.

> *"My hat smells like*
> *lubricant, I don't wanna touch it*
> *Wait, this isn't mine! And it's not a hat!*
> *Camel Holo—"*

John's mic cable was cut. The sound died.

"—on the waters of this font. We ask this through Christ our Lord. Amen."

Marconi stepped back.

Nothing.

John turned to the waves of approaching monsters and said, "NOW LICK THE STATUE!"

The blackness in the pool suddenly rose, covering the feet of the statue, spilling over the edges of the fountain. I leaned over and pulled at Marconi's jacket, pulling him back, not sure what was happening but certain we didn't want to be standing in the middle of it when it did. He waded over to the edge of the pool. He raised one leg out of the blackness and we saw, with horror, that he had no leg. Everything that had been submerged was gone, his pants ending in a neat line with only empty space beneath—

—and then it was back, whole again. Like a trick of the light. The doctor suddenly sprang out of the pool with renewed motivation. I glanced nervously at my white patent leather shoes disappearing under the rising black tide.

John and Jennifer helped us clamber up the wall of human limbs, then we ran our asses off across the ballroom floor. There was a whistling sound, like wind howling through tree branches. I saw a couple of chairs scooting along the floor toward the fountain, suddenly felt a pull like I was running from an electromagnet with a gut full of iron pellets.

One of the wig monsters skittered toward us, but was suddenly lifted out of the air and sucked back to what I was fairly certain was a portal to Hell. The howling sound was loud now, deafening, the sound of a jetliner. Folding chairs were flying through the air as if propelled by dozens of invisible Bobby Knights. The five of us pushed our way forward, somebody screaming around me but the sound lost in the rushing noise. John grabbed my shirt and pointed me toward the small space behind the stage, room to crouch back there. Jennifer screamed something I couldn't hear, something that sounded like "Todd!"

Sparks blew out from the ceiling lights, and we were cast into darkness.

A few small banks of emergency lights clicked on, faintly glinting off the wings of the ice angel in the center of the room. We stumbled back behind the stage, huddled down like tornado victims. We waited.

Silence. I risked a peek back at the dark well. From the blackness, there was movement. Dark shapes rose up out of the portal. They were like freestanding shadows, vaguely human, long and lean figures, eight or ten feet tall each. Their only features were a pair of tiny, glowing eyes like two lit cigarettes.

One by one they slipped out and into the dark room, a crowd of them, shoulder to shoulder, flowing out of the portal. They shambled out like a spreading pool of spilt oil, perfectly silent, filling the room, a constellation of little red flickering eyes.

They were around us now, closing in just feet away, making their advance in perfect stillness.

And then, the silence was broken. There was a low, screeching sound, like steam escaping. Plumes of smoke or steam rose from the base of the ice angel, a bright, white light down there like it was a rocket about to take off.

The sound grew and grew and grew, became animal, a scream of pain.

In the dim light of the emergency lamps, the holy water angel sank, descending into the black hole.

There was a thunderclap, so loud I thought it would split me in half. I clenched my eyes shut, covered my head with my hands, begged God to forgive me for accidentally bringing an end to all of creation.

There was a jolt, then a bodiless, weightless feeling like drifting out of a dream.

A hand touched my shoulder. I flinched as if gouged with a branding iron. Things were quiet again. How much time had passed? I felt like a man waking after a nap to complete darkness, confused about the time of day.

I opened my eyes and it was Jennifer, with John and Marconi standing behind her. Lights were on. She helped me up and I turned to the center of the floor.

Nothing there but empty, red carpet. No fountain, no bodies, no black hole. The room was completely vacant except for us and a few random toppled chairs still scattered about. I sat down on the floor, suddenly exhausted. John and I looked hard at the spot where the fountain had been. We each extended a hand toward it, and gave it the finger.

The doors burst open. Suits and cop uniforms poured in.

Molly the dog came bounding in with them, a bundle of chewed-up papers in her mouth. She dropped the stuff in front of me, barking her head off. I looked down at two tickets to the Marconi show, which she had presumably gotten out of the young couple's luggage. I nudged the tickets aside, saw a CD labeled: *Amazing Grace: The Brooklyn Choir Sings the Gospel*.

A bearded man wandered over, looking dazed, and I recognized him as the husband of the woman we tried to save before she dismembered herself and everything went to Hell.

I said, "I'm sorry. About your wife. What was her name? Becky."

He looked at me, confused, said, "No, I'm not married. What happened in here?"

I couldn't answer. I lay back on the floor, my body shutting down even with shoes shuffling all around me. I hadn't slept in forty hours, every muscle screamed in pain. I had flown off the cliff of a gargantuan adrenaline rush and was crashing fast.

Somebody said my name, asked if I was okay. I didn't answer, the sound of the commotion dying around me as the heavy monkey of sleep rested its warm, furry ass on my eyelids.

DARKNESS AND WARMTH, and then the nasal *EEEK EEEK EEEK* of an alarm clock. I had a taste in my mouth, smoky, like I had licked an ashtray. I felt something itchy and thick around my mouth. I shot my eyes open. Where the hell was I?

I sat up in bed. Not my bedroom. I looked over at a watch on a nightstand. Not my watch. A nicer one.

I looked around the room, the alarm still screeching its complaints from the nightstand. I found a mirror. There was something dark on my face, and I slapped my hand up to it. Hair. I climbed out of bed and walked toward the mirror. I had a thick, full goatee.

What the hell?

I sat heavily on the edge of the bed. Whose room was this? A voice from behind me said, "Are you going to get that?"

I fumbled around and found a button on the alarm. Jennifer Lopez was in the bed. And I mean the actress.

Oh, wait. No, she rolled over and it was just the local Jennifer Lopez. She got out of bed, wearing a tank top and underwear, and she sleepily walked off to what I guess was a bathroom. She had a faint, white scar at the top of her thigh. She farted softly as she closed the door.

I stood, found a cell phone among the stuff on a nearby chest of drawers, dialed John's number.

Operator recording. "This number has been disconnected . . ."

I was in a slow-burn panic now. I glanced out a window, saw a tree in the front yard with leaves turning fall colors. I went back to the phone, scrolled through the quick-dial numbers. I found an entry for John—a different number than I knew—and dialed it.

I heard water running in the bathroom. I held my breath as the phone rang four, five, six times. Seven.

"Hello?" John, sounding sleepy.

"John? It's me."

"Yeah. What's goin' on?"

"Oh. Nothin'."

After a moment, he said, "You don't remember the last six months, do you?"

"You, too?"

"No, I'm okay. This will be the fourth time it's happened to you, though. You lose everything since that night. Is Vegas the last thing you remember?"

"Yeah."

"I think it's a side effect of the sauce. Come to my—well, you don't know where my apartment is now, do you? Meet me at Dairy Queen."

172

Jennifer came out and, much to my surprise, we kissed for several minutes. *Ashtray.*

I went out, took in the neat little white bungalow-style house and was a little relieved to find my familiar Hyundai in the drive.

I drove and found John sitting on a bench outside the restaurant, a brown DQ sack in his hand. I observed that he, too, had grown a thick goatee.

I said, "This sucks."

"You say that every time."

"Do I have to, like, work today? Where do I work?"

"Wally's. You get Sundays off. This is Sunday, by the way. Come on."

John walked me to a very nice motorcycle. He jumped on, slapped the seat behind him. I looked at it for a moment and then walked to my car, said, "I'll follow you."

As we walked down the hall to John's new apartment he said, "It was a big deal, but not, you know, the real big deal. The story that came out was that five hundred people freaked out at a Marconi show, rushed the doors, one kid got killed in the stampede. That would be, you know, Jim."

We stepped through the doors and I said, "One guy? What about the dozens of people who—"

I stopped, taken aback by John's place. He had a brown leather couch, a matching armchair. He had a big-screen plasma TV sitting in the middle of the room; hooked to it were four video game systems, with game boxes littering the floor. A fairly nice DVD player, a one-hundred-disk CD changer in an entertainment center.

"John, are we crack dealers now?"

John opened a drawer on a writing desk and pulled out a big manila envelope. He extracted a bundle of papers, newspaper clippings, a couple of folded-up tabloids, a glossy magazine called *Strange Days* with a picture of a UFO on the front.

He said, "No. Nothing like that. Out in Vegas, we met a guy. He was a pimp. We made quite a bit of money as male whores. They used to call you Rocket Rimjob. You won the gold at the Greater Nevada Sodomy

Olympics back in July, landed a bunch of endorsement deals. You own that house you and Jennifer live in. Paid cash, I think."

He looked dead serious when he said this. I said, "Are you messing with me?"

"No. You really own that house. I made up the whoring thing, though. I like to add a little bit to it each time. Seriously, what happened is Molly won a bunch of money at the casinos."

"John—"

He pulled out a newspaper, a color "Lifestyles" section from the *Las Vegas Sun,* headline blaring "Dog Wins Quarter Million Playing Slots!" There was a picture of John with Molly in his arms, struggling to get away from him. He had his right hand out, making the shape of a finger gun and pointing at Molly, his mouth wide open in a drunken "that's my dog!" expression. Jen and I were visible in the deep background, trying to hide our faces.

"The thing with the Marconi show, the panic, there was a big investigation and everything," he said. "Cops thought he had slipped acid to everybody, freaked 'em out with a light show or something. Everybody called him a fraud; it was kind of crappy the way they treated him. But he came out okay. The death hasn't come out as anything but an accident and all of a sudden his book is a bestseller, people desperate to get to his shows. You've, uh, tried to contact him a couple of times, but he won't take the calls."

It was coming back to me as he told it. Everything was hazy, drunk memories. He handed me the UFO magazine, pointed to a little header in the bottom left:

Legend of Fred Chu:
Is this dead youth haunting his Midwestern hometown?
One local man says "ABSOLUTELY"

There was a noise above me.
I looked up

My heart skipped a beat.

It was hanging off his ceiling on seven little pink hands. The ridiculous thing's red wig was cockeyed on its head. It looked down at me, then let go and landed a few feet away with a soft thump.

"Uh, John—"

"Oh, *now* you see it." He stood, grabbed the Dairy Queen sack, pulled out a sausage-and-egg biscuit and unwrapped it. He set the sandwich on the floor. The thing picked it up with two hands and bit into it.

"When you came in that night, that first night when I called you, it was standing on the wall. You walked in and of course you saw nothin' at all. And, you know, when I told you not to move or make a sound? The thing *was on your back*. It had jumped on you and you just stood there like nothin'."

The wig monster turned about five eyes up to me as it ate. It paused in its chewing, vanished. The sandwich fell softly to the floor.

I said, "Did I spook it? I mean, does it still, like, attack us or anything?"

"No, not since that night. It bit right through my shoe that night, though. I had been kicking it at the time so I call it even."

The beast reappeared, one arm wrapped around a thirty-two-ounce Coke. It had a wrapped straw in its beak. John pulled out the straw, unwrapped it and poked it into the cup lid for it. The wig monster sucked on the straw and picked up its sandwich again.

"So, can anybody else see it?"

"No. My mom came by last month and it was right in the middle of the floor. She didn't acknowledge it at all. But get this: a week later she left her cat here because she was going on vacation and the cat could see it. It hissed at the thing the whole time. The monster would pick up wads of paper and stuff and throw it at him. The cat died the next day but it was unrelated."

I said, "So the paper said we won a quarter-million dollars. What did I do with my share? I bought that house? Did I save any?"

"I dunno. We really don't see each other that much now. This is actually the first time we've talked since, oh, probably August. You and Jennifer, you uh, don't leave the house a whole lot."

"Oh. I'm . . . sorry, I guess."

"No. Trust me, you're not." He gestured toward the television. "Wanna play hockey?"

CHAPTER 7

Arnie Thinks David Is Full of Shit

I STOPPED TALKING, only to notice Arnie Blondestone was staring at me in wide-eyed, silent horror. Not the kind of horror you feel when you find out the universe is full of real monsters, but the kind you feel when you realize someone else's idiocy has just wasted your entire day. I glanced down at the tape recorder, saw that it had stopped long ago. Arnie rubbed his hands over his face like he was washing without water.

"What?"

He looked at me and made a polite effort to hide his deep, pure disdain, but didn't respond.

"Do you, uh, want something to eat? I'll buy."

"No thanks," he said, twisting his face into a pained fake smile. "Let's just wrap this up and I'll be out of your hair."

"Oh. Okay."

"Now, just to clear a few things up, if you don't mind. First of all, let's confirm that that's the little pill bottle there?"

"Oh. Yeah. It's empty now."

"Because you took the last of the, uh, the soy sauce before you came today."

"That's right."

"So you don't have any left to show me. Let me see the stuff crawl around on the table and all that."

"Oh. No. I guess I should have saved some."

"No problem. I mean, that would have been physical evidence to back up your whole story, but we won't worry about that sort of thing."

Asshole. I should cut that smirk off your face with my butter knife.

"And I guess you forgot to tell me that you took the pill bottle with you when you left the trailer? Because you have it now, but in your story you left it behind. You know, when your dog drove by in your car and picked you up. Hey, that would have been something else to show me, the car-driving dog."

"I went back to Robert's place afterward, found the pill bottle among the debris. Completely unburnt."

"Of course."

"I can show you where the trailer was, by the way. I mean, there's another trailer there now but if you look at the ground you can sort of see where something might have burned there once. We can drive out there."

"Uh-huh. And what about the dozens of deaths from the dismembered fans at the Marconi thing? I'm surprised that wasn't bigger news, a crowd of people disappearing like that."

"There's actually a very good reason for—"

"And you told me Jim hauled in a dolly of sound equipment to the Luxor, but later on there were *two* carts of equipment there."

"Of everything that I told you, *that's* the part you have trouble believing?"

"And in your story you kept losing track of how many people were with you. At some point you said something like, 'The five of us and the dog piled into the car' when it was only four of you at that point, by my count. You, your friend John, Big Jim and the girl, Lopez. But you probably got mixed up."

"It's hard to exp—"

"You were probably forgetting you had killed Fred already. Meaning Fred Chu, the guy whose head you blew off with a shotgun."

I didn't answer.

"So there really is a guy named Fred Chu and he's really dead? I could look him up?"

"He's missing. Officially."

"Okay. So is there more story, or should I pack up? Do you have any documents you'd like to copy me on, like your tax returns from the year your dog won all the money at the casino? Which form does the IRS have you fill out for that?"

I took a deep breath, said, "Look, not every little single thing in the story is true, but the meat of it is. I swear it. I admit I get silly when—when the truth is hard to explain. It's my way. But those people in the Luxor, they *did* disappear, Arnie. And I mean they totally disappeared. That guy with the beard who lost his wife? He came back later and said he had no wife and, you know what? *He didn't.* He didn't have a wife named 'Becky' and there was no 'Becky' at the show. They went down the guest list; everybody is accounted for."

"So she was never there. Okay."

"Would you please stop doing that? Patronizing me? You saw the wig monster out there in my truck, in the cage. That's what it was, you saw it."

"I saw something. I saw what you wanted me to see. Some people are manipulators, I know that much. Oh, hey, you said those monsters, they ooze the soy sauce, right? So you can go out there and get some?"

"You seriously want to go try?"

"No, I don't. Let me ask you, did they do any psychological testing on you when you had your incident in school? The one that got you sent away? And the report they wrote, did it have the word 'sociopath' on it?"

I groaned.

"Don't make this about me. The people in Vegas, the ones who vanished? They never existed, Arnie. No, listen. This is hard to understand, but the moment they were sucked into that hole, or whatever it was, they didn't just stop existing in the here and now. *They were erased from the past, too.* That's why there's no report of them being gone. At that moment, they were never born. If I had fallen in there, you'd be able to go back and see that my mom never had a male child and she never named him 'David' and we wouldn't be sitting here right now."

"Assuming this is true, which, incidentally, I'm not drunk enough to do, how can you possibly prove that?"

I took a breath.

Here goes . . .

"I have dreams, Arnie. And in my dreams the whole thing from the Luxor plays out, only we're with another guy. And I know his name. Todd Brinkmeyer. A year older than me. Long blond hair. In the dream he's with us, he's toting the second dolly of sound stuff, he's with us in the SUV. He's carrying the second guitar—"

"Okay, okay, back up—"

"I heard her say his name, Arnie. I heard Jennifer shout 'Todd' plain as day. I think that was him getting sucked into the hole, the vortex thing. And as of that moment, he was gone, he got sucked in and he was zapped out of the past, present and future, out of our memories. They have that power somehow. But one night, me and John got really drunk and we sat around telling Todd Brinkmeyer stories, real stories,

180

stories that happened but didn't happen. I think of his face and sometimes I can see it, and it's like a dream you can't quite remember the next morning. And I go back and go over the chain of events and there's places, holes where I know Todd should be. He was there and he helped us, Arnie. He fought with us. And I'm not even allowed to remember him, to mourn his death. At least Jim got a funeral. But Todd, I can't find his picture in the yearbook. Can you even imagine what that's like?"

Arnie sighed and for a quick moment looked genuinely sympathetic that someone could dream up something this elaborately sad. He said, "We both got places to go tomorrow. Is there any more?"

You act bored, Arnie, you act like you're miles above it all. But you're still sitting here, aren't you? You're still listening. I know you got reasons but I don't know what they are yet. God knows I would have split by now if I were in your shoes.

I said, "You gotta understand . . . Vegas was just the beginning."

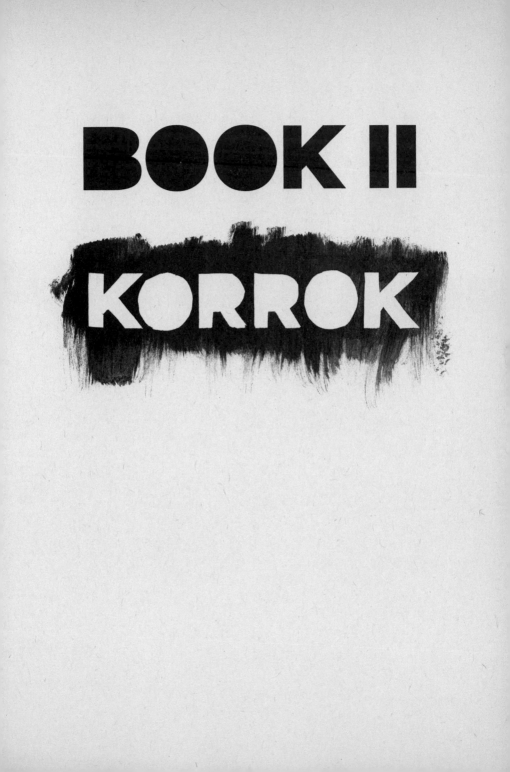

BOOK II

KORROK

A yellow legal pad was found during an inventory of the items inside the Chevy Tahoe belonging to James "Big Jim" Sullivan after his disappearance. The following was handwritten on the first page. It appears to be part of an unfinished novel titled *Jameson and the Invasion from X'all'th'thu' "thuuu.* No other pages from this work have been discovered.

---

she held the blade before him and in the torchlight Jameson could see it was incredibly sharp and haunted with the ~~ghosts~~ *blood of countless slain Terrans. Jameson stared into the wicked beauty of the woman before him, the* one blue eye that was not hidden behind an eyepatch shined like a shiny blue jewel.

"Xorox," said Jameson. "I should have known it was you. I could smell your evil before you came in the door!"

"You should not talk so, when it is I that hold this incredibly sharp blade!" ~~And it is you who are~~ She slid the slender razor-sharp blade lightly up Jameson's bare thigh. Jameson strained against the chains that bound him to the wall and gritted his teeth in rage.

"The mighty Captain Jameson," said Xorox, "bound in my dungeon while my mighty army amasses for the invasion of Earth!"

With a flick of her delicate wrist, she cut Jameson's loincloth, which fell to the floor. Her eyes grew at the ~~sight~~ magnificence of Jameson's exposed naked body, his exposed manhood a thunderclap of flesh.

"Mighty army?" said Jameson with a sneer. "I have slain larger armies on my way to battle!"

"Insolent dog!" She held the blade at Jameson's ~~scrot~~ groin. "If I did not require your seed to infiltrate Earth, I would cut off your manhood and mount it like a trophy over my throne!"

"My seed?"

"Ha ha ha! You still do not get it, dog! With the seed of your manhood in my womb, we shall breed a race of Terran and Reptillian hybrids that cannot be detected by even your most sensitive R-Meters! They will walk among the earthlings as my agents, and not even they will know that their true loyalty is to me! Until the day when they strike! Now you will make love to me, or die!"

~~"No!"~~ "Never!"

Jameson gathered his strength and pulled free of his chains. He seized Xorox's wrist in the iron grip of his right hand and tore it free of her body as blood spurted like a fountain. He then stabbed Xorox in the belly with her own hand.

[insert Jameson one-liner here]

186

CHAPTER 8

The Carpet Stain

MY MEMORY OF the next few months after Vegas is spotty. I know John went to jail for a couple of weeks that winter. It was because of a fight over a girl or something, no big deal. Jennifer moved out of my place and then moved back in because of a fight we had over something or other. My roof started leaking and I learned about the joys of home ownership when a bill for four thousand dollars showed up in my mailbox after I got it repaired. On my birthday I went and visited my adoptive parents and it was a little awkward, as always. But they're good people. My birthday gift from John was an envelope full of baked beans.

Jen and I didn't talk about Vegas. We didn't talk about Big Jim and all the things we saw and did over those two strange days. That's why she never got along with John, I think, because John loved to talk about it, loved to read about ghosts and dimensions and demonic conspiracies. He was soaking this stuff up from the 'Net and telling us all about it over empty beer bottles and greasy pizza boxes. He'd talk and she'd fidget, change the subject. I usually took her side.

But I still made a habit of watching, looking for alien white insects zipping around outdoors, studying the shadows for the dark figures we saw float out from that portal to who-knows-where. I kept a lookout for, well, anything. And I saw things from time to time. Or maybe I didn't. A dark shape slipping around a corner, a pair of lit eyes like burning coals, floating through the night. Always out the corner of my eye or in the reflection of a window. Or in the paralyzed state between deep sleep and wakefulness in those dim morning hours. Nothing you could trust, nothing you could admit to seeing.

John got me alone one night, I guess it would have been that next spring after Vegas, and asked me straight up if I ever saw anything strange. Because he did, he said. All the time, he said. He got a job working as a janitor in the Undisclosed Courthouse and he said he saw an old man walking around the basement, a ghost, semitransparent but very real and "There, man. Just *there,* there as a brick wall. I mean, he was just, so incredibly *there.*" John rattled off more stories, told me he watched a baseball game on TV and the announcers made some comment about how the stands were half empty, how the team was having trouble selling tickets. "But man, the stands were full, Dave. I'm tellin' ya, to my eyes every seat was filled and I think it was the undead, I think I was seeing thousands of walking souls that nobody else could see, watching the game. Isn't that bizarre?"

I told him the truth, sort of. I said I didn't see spirits or demons or walking shadows or anything that couldn't be written off as a trick of the eyes. I told him I thought the soy sauce made us see all that and it had been months since we'd ingested it and no matter what the stuff was or where it was from, surely it had worked itself out of our systems by now. An awkward silence followed, John letting the implication of that statement hang in the air. Without coming out and saying it, I had just told him I thought he was either full of shit or losing his mind.

A week later I was in John's apartment, flipping through a magazine while he sat on the couch playing some game or another. I glanced at the TV and it looked like one of those first-person shooting games where you wander around hallways looking over the barrel of your gun, tearing bad guys in half with splashes of digital blood. I was never that into them.

"You still got that pill bottle?" John said, trying to sound offhand while he hammered a control pad with his thumbs. "You said you went back and found it at Robert's old trailer, right?"

"Yeah."

"And was there still sauce in there?"

"No. It had two—capsules, or whatever they were—in it originally and I had taken them both."

"Oh."

On the screen, John shot and killed some kind of demon creature and a little box fell out of him. The screen displayed, YOU'VE GOT A BOX OF SHOTGUN SHELLS.

It wasn't until later that I realized, with amazement and disgust, what John was saying: *he would have taken the fucking soy sauce again if I had any left.*

I started avoiding John after that.

JOHN DOESN'T MAKE avoiding him easy, though. He kept showing up at my house with a video game console curled under one arm, kept calling me to come play basketball, kept asking me if I was avoiding him. He was "let go" from his janitor job and he asked me if I could get him back on at Wally's. I did and then I saw him every day whether I

189

liked it or not. But when he tried to bring up anything vaguely spooky, I did what Jen did: I changed the subject.

And then, one day at Taco Bell there was this old woman sitting two tables away from John, Jen and me. The old woman isn't eating. Just sitting there, both hands holding her purse in her lap.

A group of four college kids come in, frat guys, and they sat right at the old lady's table like she wasn't there, one guy sitting right on her. *Through* her. He's sucking on this Burrito Supreme with this old woman's elbows sticking out of his torso the whole time. Finally she just sits up out of him and daintily walks out through—literally through—one of the glass doors.

All three of our heads were fixed right on her, even Jen's. There was no pretending we didn't see it, we were all staring. It was the pink elephant in the room, the thunderous fart in the elevator. Denial would have been ridiculous. We finished our food and walked out and piled in my car, then Jen put her face in her hands and cried. John had this satisfied look that I wanted to punch off his face. He knew better than to say anything.

I decided right there that I could outlast it, ignore stuff like that for the rest of my life if I had to.

I was wrong, of course.

In the summer John read on a Web site about a lady in a neighboring state who claimed she had bloodstains that kept coming back and back in this one spot in her carpet. She had it steam-cleaned back to bleach white, but a week later, there was the stain again. Then they replaced the carpet. The stain came back. They had video and everything.

John told me about it and I blew him off. Then he got me drunk and told me about it again and suddenly I was fascinated. We called the lady, told her we were experts in new carpet-cleaning techniques and asked if we could come up to take a look. So based on one moment of drunken curiosity, we wound up burning up a whole Saturday making the seven-hour drive to go check out the magical carpet stain.

We heard screams from inside the house as soon as we pulled into the driveway. We banged on the door and were greeted by a six-year-old girl holding one of those sippy cups. We walked in and saw the parents watching some award show on TV while in the center of the room lay a screaming man, a flow of crimson running from his groin and staining the carpet underneath. The mother, a pleasant, heavy woman in her forties, pointed to the shrieking man and said, "That's the stain."

We told her we had to get some supplies from my car, then drove away. We did a search at their local library—that is, John did a search while I curled up in a chair and went to sleep—and found a story from a few years before where a man had died after getting his penis caught in a spring-loaded mole trap he was working on. He bled to death. We went back to the house the next day, asked the family to leave the room and tried talking to the bleeding guy.

We told him it wasn't his house any longer, that his wife had sold it, that he was staining the carpet from beyond the grave. He didn't react to us, just kept screeching and thrashing around and clutching his groin. But after about an hour of us badgering him, he vanished. Off to wherever they go. No more stain.

The carpet family was so impressed they apparently told everybody they knew about it. They knew it wasn't some magical detergent, either.

After that we got about a dozen calls and e-mails asking us to come check out some situation or other. We thought only one was worth checking out because it mentioned "shadow people," but it turned out to be bullshit, a college kid with a budding case of schizophrenia. In fact, of the contacts we got over the next three months, exactly one of them turned out to be a real haunting-type thing and that was Frank Campo, the guy with the spidery car. We fixed him just by telling him that he wasn't crazy, that the horrors he was seeing were real. He seemed oddly comforted by that. He was a lawyer.

But the rest were nothing, scared and lonely old ladies and attention seekers who thought it was better to be crazy than unnoticed.

But John and I saw things. Oh yes. By then, just walking around and going about our lives, we saw things. There seemed to be a knack to it, a tuning of the eyes. Like focusing on the dirt on your windshield instead of the road outside.

191

I woke up one morning to find four pairs of huge eyes peering over my bedspread, inches from my face. Short little dwarf people, standing along the side of the bed with eyeballs three times bigger than a person's should be. I blinked. They were gone. I didn't tell Jennifer. I didn't tell her about any of it. I told myself it was just one more thing to adjust to. That's what life is. Adjustment.

Then, in the fall, everything went to hell.

CHAPTER 9

The Bratwurst Prophecy

IT WAS RONALD McDonald's eyes that haunted me.

I had gotten hungry for bratwurst and had been walking toward the entrance of one of the four McDonald's franchises in Undisclosed (if you think it's weird getting a bratwurst from a McDonald's, then you're not from the Midwest). I glanced at the cartoon clown logo in the window and let out a scream.

Just a little scream, and a manly one. But I still frightened one little girl on the sidewalk so badly that she screamed, too.

I couldn't help it. It was one of those clear plastic static

193

signs, pressed to the inside of the glass with the cartoon image filling most of that pane. The cloud of red hair, the size sixty red shoes, the yellow suit, and the, well . . .

I reached out and brushed my fingers over the glass.

The image is so perfectly drawn, I thought. *So vivid.*

Other late-night customers brushed past me and cast quick, stealthy glances my way, looking at the crazy man with the beard stubble and the ruffled dark hair. But they didn't see what I saw, I was sure of that.

No, they saw the happy clown with his arms spread wide, one leg cocked at a forty-five-degree angle with one red floppy clown shoe tipped up into the air, big smile spread across his red-and-white face, welcoming paying customers into his burger factory. I remembered it from the last hundred times I had been here.

What *I* saw at the moment was a clown standing there with his gut split raggedly open, as if cut with a dull utility razor. He was—how can I put this delicately? In this perfectly rendered and shaded cartoon he was using his own white-gloved hands to feed a rope of his own intestines into his mouth.

Detailed. Yes. It was very, very detailed.

But it was those eyes that got me. His expressive cartoon eyes pulsed with a terror about to boil over into madness. Tears streaked his face, sweat beaded his forehead. Those eyes pleaded with me, looked right into me and screamed to be put out of his misery. Those eyes told a story, not just of a man eating himself, but of a man *being forced* to eat himself.

And only I saw it.

I closed my eyes, looked again. Still there. Not shimmering like a mirage in the desert or some blur out the corner of your eye. It just clung to the window in its brazen thereness, real right down to the little plastic corners peeling up from the glass.

I turned away, tried to clear my head, to concentrate. Then I spun back at the image. There. For just a split second, I saw the normal logo, the way everybody else saw it. Happy corporate clown. Then it blurred back to the corrupted version again. This time there was text.

The usual MCDONALD'S–I'M LOVIN' IT! slogan was replaced by a jumble of crazed red letters saying,

MCWONGALD'S–SHIT LUNCH TURDWOMAN

Some would have doubted their sanity at this point, but by now the part of my mind that issued doubts about my sanity had melted from overuse. I went back to my car and just drove around town for several hours, my appetite gone.

It had my fucking name in it. McWongald's. What the fuck.

They haunt minds.

Someone was talking to me, from that other side. I pictured floating black figures and eyes like cigarette embers. I pictured a single blue eye in the darkness. I felt sick.

My orbit around the town finally degraded and I crash-landed at John's apartment. I told him the McWongald's story, hoping he'd say something like, "That's some weird shit" and start untangling two controllers from one of his many game consoles. Instead, he said, "Get up."

I stood and realized I had been sitting on a stack of three cardboard boxes. He opened the flaps on one to reveal that it was full of hardback books.

"Wait, what's all that?"

"Dr. Marconi's book."

"You have a hundred and fifty copies of it?"

"Oh, right. You don't remember. In Vegas, we were walking out the back and Marconi makes some comment about how we should read his book. You were all 'fuck you old man' and I said sure. Then I grabbed a dolly and wheeled out a whole stack. Just staring at him coldly the whole time I was wheeling them backward out the door. Daring that fucker to stop me."

"Why?"

"They were free, Dave. Anyway, he says something in here . . ." John flipped pages. "It's around the beginning somewhere. I don't see it right now—maybe it was in a different book—but anyway he says that when you read the Bible, the Devil looks back at you through the pages."

195

"What, like his Bible was possessed? Holy shit, he must have been the worst priest ever."

"No. He says when you're dealing with any kind of supernatural beings, Gods and Devils and angels, you tend to think about them like hurricanes or earthquakes, some kind of mindless force of nature. But if they're real, then they have minds. They know *your name*. So even reading about the Devil tips him off, he knows instantly he's being read about and that you're somebody he may have to deal with. And I'm thinking what you did in Vegas went way, way beyond that."

"What 'I' did? What about *us*? We were both there."

"Yeah but I cut my hair since then. They probably think that was a different guy."

I closed my eyes and collapsed onto John's futon. I said, "The thing. The wig monster. Does it still come around?"

"No, haven't seen it in months. Except about three weeks ago I was eating a corn dog, the thing appeared, snatched it out of my hand, and disappeared again. Never saw it after that."

"No more of this. Okay? It's over. No more chasing after this stuff. They've set up camp inside my head, John. It's gone too far."

John's mouth said, "Okay" but his eyes said, *What makes you think you can just walk away?*

"Let's order a pizza."

THE PIZZA TASTED like rotten eggs. Just to me, not to John. The rest of that week, every meal smelled like formaldehyde or paint thinner. I decided it was them, messing with me. Punching random buttons in my brain. When they got bored with that, they switched senses. I would hear my name as I drifted off to sleep, as if spoken six inches from my ear. Over and over again.

Molly started to get agitated, growling at things in the darkness, prowling around our bed at all hours of the night as if keeping watch. Early one morning she woke me up, pressing her wet nose against my

196

elbow. I went to let her outside, and she went sprinting down the street. She didn't look back.

Not long after that, they—whoever "they" were—tried something new. The radio. I would hear entire songs changed, twisted. I got dancey and lighthearted beats under lyrics about prison rape or incest and, once, a version of "Stairway to Heaven" with my name edited in throughout. This new version that blared over the speakers of a busy shopping mall (though only I heard it, of course) was a list of all my chronic sins and vices, a musical rundown of all the reasons I, David Wong, was destined for Hell. It got to me, I admit. Even if their version of "Stairway" barely rhymed. What rhymes with masturbation?

I slowly came to the realization that these shadowy beings had the crude sense of humor of fourteen-year-olds.

That's when things started to disintegrate between me and Jen. Our entire relationship had been a process of slow disintegration, I think. She knew something was up, mainly because there were so many more '80s power ballads around the house than usual. She pestered me until I came clean and told her what was going on.

She nodded and said she understood, then left to go to her friend Amber's house, ostensibly to help out with Amber's new baby. She seemed to have taken all of her clothes with her, though, and didn't come back that night. I sat there, depressed, thinking about coming home to the silent house night after night. Without even Molly for company.

On an evening a few weeks later, I was driving home from work with one thought cycling through my brain: I would go to the grocery store, buy a pie, and just eat the whole thing. In one sitting. A whole pie.

My radio was playing a supernaturally reworked version of an '80s song by some Duran Duran soundalike band. It was the one with the word "Africa" in the chorus, and this version had been twisted into some kind of a racist diatribe against blacks. I tried to block it out, turning my attention to the call. Toto, that was the band's name.

My cell phone rang.

Shocked, as always, that I had actually left it on, I fished around inside my jacket for the chirping thing. Caller ID showed John's number. I punched the button and said:

"No."

"Dave, glad I caught you. I just got a call from my uncle. He's asked us to come in on a case. Like consultants."

"Your uncle? The exotic dancer? Exactly what kind of 'consulting' would we be doing?"

"No, no, Uncle Drake. The cop. They got weirdness and they want us to come look at it. The crime scene is at Eight-eighteen West Twenty-third Street. By the mall."

This stopped me. The *cops* called us? What, they got a ghost they want us to check out? Like we're fucking Scooby-Doo?

"No. We talked about this. I'm going home to eat a pie."

"I think they found Molly."

"What?"

Molly? What, did she steal another car?

"Come get me. See you in a few."

"I'm not going, John. I—"

I was talking to a dead phone.

I cursed and rubbed my forehead. The radio sang its bigotry in perfect '80s pop harmony.

Let's send 'em aaalllllll ba-ack to Aaaaafrica . . .

I reached down to the knob, to find the radio was already off.

Here we fucking go.

I PICKED UP John at his building, since it turned out his supernatural powers couldn't stop the bank from repossessing his motorcycle.

We turned onto 23rd Street, a lineup of perfect new houses with trendy coffee-cream-colored siding and a shiny SUV in each driveway. Finding the house was easy—it was the one with the swirling red-and-blue cop lights out front, the collected cop cars making it look like the ship from *Close Encounters* had landed there.

198

One guy tells us to turn back, and we go, I thought as we pulled up a block away from the commotion. *Any one of those guys says "boo" and we turn around and never come back here.*

We passed a blue Jeep in the driveway, license plate STRMQQ 1. John studied it, frowning a little. Four cops stood out on the front lawn, looking unsure, like they all needed each other's armed company right now. Eight eyes landed on us.

"Don't worry," John said to them. "We're here."

Each cop was individually pissed off by that, I could see, and it was only the arrival of John's uncle Drake that spared us the confrontation with these guys who clearly had no idea who we were. Drake was a big guy, with a uniform that stretched and bulged around the middle. He sported an uneven mustache that I think he grew to cover a scar on his upper lip.

"Hey, Johnny. I really appreciate you comin' by like this."

He gave John a hard, manly handshake.

"So what's goin' on?"

"Do you, uh, know whose house this is?"

"Strom Cuzewon?" John offered.

A moment of confused silence from Drake.

"Um, no. It's Ken Phillipe, the Channel Five weather guy."

"Oh," said John, seeming unsatisfied. I glanced back at the plates, STRMQQ 1.

"The Qs are supposed to look like a pair of eyes," I informed John. "The license plate means 'Storm Watcher.'"

John looked at the plates, then back at me, then at the plates again. I noticed for the first time that the big bay window into the living room of the house had been bashed in, the curtains behind it rustling in the breeze. Finally John said, "So somebody killed the weather guy?"

Drake grunted. "Sorta. Damnedest thing you ever saw."

"I highly doubt that."

"We ain't been inside the house yet. There's this, dog." To me he said, "John here said he thought it sounded like yours."

I couldn't see around the bay window curtains, so I walked up to

199

the front door and peered into the decorative little window, into the living room. A girl sat on an overstuffed leather couch, maybe a few years younger than me, silken auburn hair pulled into a ponytail. Little wisps of bangs drifted down over her smooth forehead, just above her gorgeous almond eyes. She wore cutoff sweatshorts and had the most perfect pair of tanned thighs I have ever seen. I felt my hand instinctively go up to straighten my hair and I was suddenly horribly aware of every physical flaw on my body. Every ounce of fat, the little scar on my cheek.

If I looked like that, I would wear shorts in October, too. I'd quit my job and spend all day at home, gently caressing myself. Did I shave today?

On the floor next to the couch was a bloody dead person.

"That's the weather guy?" I asked.

"Yeah," confirmed Drake.

"Do you see the girl sitting on the couch?"

"Look, buddy, I told ya we've tried to get to her in there, but the dog . . ."

"I wasn't being sarcastic. I just wanted to know if you could see her."

"That's Krissy Lovelace, their neighbor. She's been sitting like that since we got here, frozen. We even tried to signal to her but she won't respond. Like she's just blanked out."

"So she killed him?"

"No, his throat was torn out. By the dog. It's still in there. That's the problem. Every time we try to get in, it—"

"Damn," I interrupted. "It's too bad this city doesn't have a special department to, you know, control animals. Oh, wait. We do. It's called Animal Control. Do you want their number?"

"Wait a second," said John. "You're saying Molly did that?" He turned to me. "Dave, we sat there and poked at Molly with a stick for exactly twenty-three minutes that one time before she even growled. She couldn't do that to a man."

"No," Drake said. "You still don't understand. My guys won't even go in and I don't blame 'em. It's somethin' . . . unnatural."

I peered in again. "Well, I don't see a dog. And I'm not seeing why we can't just—"

Molly came into view. It was her all right, the rusty coat of an Irish retriever or whatever she was, now shampooed and combed to perfection. Her new owner apparently groomed her more than I had. This combination of girl and dog could make a good living as models in the dog-supply industry.

The only other thing that was different about Molly was the blood staining her muzzle and the fact that she was floating three feet off the floor.

Molly's legs were stiff below her as she moved, buzzing slowly across the room as if on a track and hung by invisible threads. When Molly came near the door she turned her head my way and in a clear but guttural voice said, "I serve none but Korrok."

Molly continued to float around the room like a shaggy little blimp.

Here. We. Go. Again.

I TURNED FROM the door. John had this look on his face like this was all routine. *Ah, yes, a floating-dog scenario. We have the parts in the truck.*

Drake said, "A neighbor saw it, said Krissy was just walking the dog along the street out there and all of a sudden the thing takes off. The damned thing breaks its leash and races across the lawn like it was fired from a cannon. It then jumps through the plate-glass window. She said the dog jumped into the air and tore out Phillipe's throat in half a second. I guess Ms. Lovelace ran inside after it, started bawling and then she just shut down. Too much for her. I kinda feel like doing that myself. Not the bawling part, mind you."

I said, "Wait. Did you hear what the dog said just now?"

"Said? She barked . . ."

"Ah. Okay. And when you look at the dog right now, she's . . ."

"Floatin' a few feet off the floor."

You'd think the fact that other people could witness the weirdness

201

would have comforted me. It didn't. It meant the rules had changed already.

"John and I need to have a word about this. We'll, uh, be right back."

On the way back to my car, I said, "We're driving away as fast as we can. Right to the bakery counter at the grocery store."

"Dave, those guys could see her. All the cops. They saw her floatin' around and doing supernatural shit. That's new."

"*That's* new? Why is she floating at all, John?"

"Gotta be the sauce, right? She got more of it than any of us. I was always amazed she survived. Maybe, you know, they got to her finally."

"After all this time? None of this makes sense."

"Did you hear what she said?"

"She said, 'I serve none but Korrok.'"

Speaking that meaningless word made the hairs stand up on the back of my neck, though I couldn't pin down why. My mind almost made a connection, then abruptly steered clear of it nearly hard enough to make the train of thought go flying out of my ear.

"You sure?" said John. "I thought she said, 'I serve none but to rock.' I was about to agree with her."

"Whatever, John."

"So who's Korrok?"

"Don't know."

And keeping it that way is making my brain's denial gland work overtime.

"You still got the mints in your car?"

"I don't know. I think so."

John dug around in the glove compartment and pulled out a little roll of candies somebody had mailed to me a while back. Crazy people mail me things. Most of it I throw on a shelf in my toolshed and forget.

We went back to the front door of the house, and I shook one of the candies out into my palm. I very slowly turned the knob and pushed the door in, just enough to lean my head and my right arm through.

Molly the Hoverdog was about ten feet away, behind the couch and her incredibly hot new owner. I held out the candy, which immediately caught Molly's attention.

I tossed the candy on the floor and quickly ducked back out. Molly floated over to it, tilted in midair until her snout was just over the white morsel. She lapped it up.

For a moment, nothing. John was about to supply the "it's not working" when, with a wet, tearing *KERRRAAAAACTCH* sound, Molly exploded like a meat piñata at a birthday party for very strong, invisible children.

A couple of cops behind us cheered. Drake walked up. "What the hell was that?"

John answered for me. "It was a TestaMint. Little candies with Bible verses printed on them. You can get them at your local Christian bookstore. We were sort of hoping it would just drive the evil out of her, but . . ." John shrugged, businesslike. *These things happen sometimes.*

Drake said, "Fine. Now let's get one thing clear. I don't want to hear any more about this after tonight. This gets written up as a dog attack. Somebody'll be here later to clean up the scene and there'll be a funeral and all of these here men will go home to their wives and try to act like the world ain't gone crazy."

I said, "Yeah that's probably for the best—"

Drake's head snapped toward me.

"Shut up. I ain't done."

Back to John he said, "Between you and me, I need to know some things. That was your dog, right?"

"Well, Dave's dog. But she's belonged to several people . . ."

"Hey. *Look in there.* He's dead. You understand me? Now, you and I both know, things . . . happen around here. In this town. Always have. My daddy wore this uniform before me, he told me stories. But I ain't never seen anything like *that.*"

John put up his hands defensively and said, "Neither have we."

"But the last time things got weird, you were there. With the party and all those kids that died, the detective that left and never came back. Don't be playin' games with me. If you know somethin', tell me. Tell me so I can prepare for it."

John said, "We don't know the situation. Not yet."

On the word "yet" I had the urge to punch John in the kidneys.

"But let us take a shot at the girl." We all glanced toward Krissy, still frozen on the sofa. "Before the psychiatrist gets here or whoever you bring in to reboot people like her."

Drake stared John down, then decided to roll the dice. "You got two minutes."

"Great." John ducked through the front door. Drake reached out and grabbed his elbow.

"Hey."

"Yeah."

"This the end of the world?"

He said it in the earnest, stiff-jawed manner of a middle-aged man asking the doc if it's cancer. It scared the fuck out of me.

John said, "We'll give you a call if we find out."

John went to the couch, but I couldn't resist stopping by the red, six-foot circle of dog mush.

I found Molly's collar near her head. The bloodstained tag:

I'm Molly.
Please return me to . . .

"Good-bye, Molly," I muttered. "Of all the dogs I've known in my life, I've never seen a better driver."

Just before I turned away, I noticed something else. Out of the pile of dog salsa stuck one of the paws, straight up into the air. On the foot, on the pad where the palm would be on a human hand, was a marking, like a tattoo.

It was a little black symbol, something like the mathematical symbol for pi. I pointed this out to John, who suggested I take the severed paw home for further study. I decided it wasn't that important. Maybe something the breeder put on there, I didn't know. I hadn't noticed it before but how often do you look at a dog's feet?

Krissy Lovelace wouldn't make eye contact with us and she wouldn't respond to our voices, but we did get her to her feet and led her outside. We took her to the backyard, saying generic, soothing words to her the whole way.

Once we were out of sight of the cops, John put his hands on Krissy's shoulders and turned her to face him. He held up his smoldering cigarette.

"Miss? You see this? You start talkin' or I'm gonna burn you with it."

No response.

"Ma'am," I offered. "I'd do what he says. I'm a good guy, a reasonable guy, but my friend here? He's a wild man. And once he gets goin' I can't stop him. Now wouldn't you rather talk to me?"

Nothing.

John jammed the lit cigarette into the back of her hand with a *pssssst* sound.

She yelped and yanked her hand back, shaking it madly. "What the heck *are you doing?*" she screeched.

"Ma'am, we got a serious situation here," John said, in a voice devoid of sympathy. "We got a dead guy and maybe a lot worse on the horizon if you can't help us. Now I'm real sorry you saw what you saw but we ain't got time for you to curl up into some psychological shell. Help us and you can just repress the memory later."

She looked around for a moment, bewildered. Then:

"Molly!" she gasped. "Molly attacked Ken!"

"Yes, we know," I said. "But we don't get why—"

"And you say he died?"

"It's—yes, he died. It's a strange thing and we need you to tell us—"

"I'm gonna puke." She leaned over. "Can I go to jail for this? Because it was my dog? Can they charge me with murder?"

"No. I—look, I don't know. But we need to—"

"Miss," John interrupted. "We have reason to believe your dog was possessed by some kind of Hell demon. Has Molly ever spoken to you before?"

Pause.

"Who are you guys?"

"Just answer the question. Please," John said. "Has there ever been any levitation?"

"What? No."

"Are you sure?"

"Ma'am," I said, "if your dog was dabbling in the occult while you had her it's best you tell us now. We're experts."

"What? No, no. I've only had her for a few weeks, she showed up at my house and I went to return her to the address on her tag but the owner was this weird girl and she told me to keep her. I was just walking her and we ran into Danny Wexler."

She said that name like we should know it, like it was a mutual friend or something. She saw the look of nonrecognition on our faces and said, "The Channel Five sports guy. I . . . know him. He goes to my church. He pulled up alongside the road, like he was gonna stop at Ken Phillipe's house because, you know, they work together. He gets out and he pets Molly and then he drives off. Just like that."

I glanced at John, then turned to her.

"Ma'am—"

"Please stop calling me that. You sound like a cop when you do it. Call me Krissy."

"Krissy," I said, "tell me exactly what Wexler said to you. Word for word."

"I don't think he said much of anything. Just, 'pretty dog you got there.' Then he drove away. A second later Molly went nuts."

"After he touched her?"

"Yeah," she said. "Just to pet her, though."

I flashed back to the beer truck, John touching Molly and waking up with a jolt, his soul jumping from her to him like a spark of static electricity.

"And he didn't say anything else?" I asked. "Didn't use the word 'Korrok' or anything like that?"

"Um, no, I'm pretty sure he didn't."

"Okay." I turned to walk away.

"Wait!" said Krissy. "There's something else. When Danny drove up, he was wearing a mask. Or it looked like it, all black. But he must have taken it off because when he pulled up it was off. But I know I saw it. That's weird, isn't it?"

"Could you see any of his face? When he had the mask on?"

"No, but . . . it was dark. Why would he do that? Is Molly okay? Do you think they'll take her to the pound?"

"Uh, if you go around and talk to the police, they'll explain everything."

As I walked away, John thanked Krissy for her cooperation and let her know that we would contact her if any more leads developed. He hurried to catch up with me and said, "Fuck! Dave! The shadow people. She saw a fucking shadow people . . . person."

"The what people?"

"You know goddamned well. Those things, the men made of shadow we saw in Vegas. They're here. Or at least one of them is. I've seen them, Dave. I've seen them around."

"No, they're not and no, you haven't."

When our butts landed in my car a minute later, John lit up another cigarette and asked, "Okay, what now?"

THE THING ABOUT video game basketball is that the computer decides whether or not the ball goes in when you shoot. So say you're playing against the computer team, you're down by one and let's say you take a last-second shot to win the game. It's the same program you're playing against that decides whether or not the digital ball goes through the digital hoop on that final shot. So it can arbitrarily make you lose or arbitrarily let you win. The whole thing is bullshit.

But we were playing anyway, on my sofa. John was Kobe Bryant's Lakers and I was the Chicago Bulls, led by Pierre Manslapper (you can name your own players if you want). It was an hour after the thing with Molly and the dead weather guy.

"So," John said, glancing at his watch. "You think the cops talked to Wexler?"

"Who?"

"Danny Wexler, the sports guy? Because of the thing with the weather guy getting killed?"

"The weather guy was killed by Molly. That's how it'll go down, dog attack. Case closed. And Molly is dead so . . ."

"You're being stupid, you know that? You think we should call Marconi?"

I shrugged. "You do what you want. Hey, did you know that the number-one all-time rated show in Korea was the premiere of that '80s show *Joanie Loves Chachi?* It turns out that in Korean, 'chachi' means 'penis.' "

John paused the game.

"It's after ten. I wanna flip over, see if the news has got anything about it."

He did, before I could object, and I was immediately reminded of why I hated local newscasts. We sat through a lengthy tribute to the departed Ken Phillipe, showing old video clips of the idiot standing knee-deep in rushing floodwater while wind pummeled his microphone, another shot of a shaky camera trying to track a tornado on the horizon while Ken shouted his report.

They transitioned from that to a scandal at a local nursing home where dishwashers rinsed bedpans and dinner plates in the same load, then to a house fire that wouldn't have made the newscast at all had their crew not arrived in time to get video of the pretty flames. Then they got to sports and I admit, that part was . . . different.

The first thing that was strange was when they cut to the two-shot of Danny Wexler and the anchor, Danny's face was black. I saw immediately why Krissy thought he was wearing a mask earlier. At first glance it would look like he had on a black ski mask, one without the eyeholes.

But when they cut to the closer one-shot of his head, you could see the effect went way beyond that; Danny Wexler appeared to be a statue carved from solid shadow. Only John and I saw this, of course, because the other anchors didn't react in horror. Or at least, not until Danny Wexler opened his mouth:

"I'm Danny Wexler and this is Channel Five sports! The [Undisclosed] football team has been raped in the ass by fate once again, booted from the first round of the playoffs as they failed to carry their inflatable turd past a chalk line in the grass as often as their opponents did. Here's Hornets quarterback Mikey Wolford, flopping that right arm around like a retard while he tries to pass to a teammate that apparently only he can see. Aaaaand, it's intercepted. Nice pass, 'tard! Now here's Spartans fullback Derrick Simpson, pumping those nigger thighs down the field like pistons on a machine designed for cotton picking. Ooh, nice tackle attempt there, Freddy Mason! I bet you could tackle that fullback if he was made of *dick*, couldn't you, Freddy? But, he's not, so final score, forty-one to seventeen. May every Spartan die with a turd on his lips. All hail Korrok."

Danny didn't get to read any more highlights, as the newscast abruptly switched back to a visibly shaken anchorwoman, who announced they would be right back. Commercial.

John clicked off the TV and I let out a long, resigned sigh. Without a word, we put on our jackets and walked out the door. We stopped by my toolshed.

THE MORBIDLY OBESE security guard at the Channel 5 building told us Wexler had left early. We almost gave up at that point, but got a huge break in the case when John thought to look up Wexler's home address in the phone book.

After getting lost, briefly, we pulled into the lot of Wexler's building and found a Buick with the license plate 5 SPRTS, which, after some debate, we decided must stand for Channel 5 sports and that it must be his.

"You still got the mints?" John asked as we strode up to the four-story apartment building. "You knock on the door and when Wexler answers, you cram some mints down his throat."

"If he's acting normal, we don't do anything. Just find out what he knows. About Molly and, you know, everything else that's happening. If it's something we can fix with a mint then fine. If not, then we leave Dr. Marconi a voice mail and drive until we find a town that doesn't keep showing up in books with titles like *True Tales of the Bizarre*. Marconi can come down and do a whole show on it for all I care. Write another book."

I had my old-school ghetto blaster; John was carrying a satchel containing several items he collected from my toolshed. We didn't have any holy water. Where do you even get it? Off the Internet?

We positioned ourselves on either side of the door to Wexler's third-floor apartment. I set down the stereo, facing its speakers toward the closed door. John unzipped the satchel and pulled out a weapon he had made, a Bible wrapped around the end of a baseball bat with electrician's tape. He brought it up to the ready. I pushed "play."

The smooth-yet-screechy sound of Cinderella's "Don't Know What You've Got 'til it's Gone" filled the hall.

We let it play for the duration of the song, one guy down the hall poking his head out of a door in confusion and then closing it quickly at the sight of John and his bat. Wexler's door remained closed.

We shut off the stereo, listened. Nothing from the other side of the door. I tried the knob. Unlocked. I gestured to John and he ducked inside, Bible bat at the ready. My gesture had meant, "Wait, we should reconsider this."

I followed John in, reluctantly. I left the door open behind me.

Wide open.

Lights on, but nobody home. The television was on and I jumped when I saw it was me and John on the screen. Then I noticed a tripod and camcorder facing us from across the room, aimed at the sofa in front of us. It was apparently positioned to tape whoever was sitting there, the TV set to show the live feed. The sofa was empty now.

We split up and quickly searched all five rooms of the small apartment, but the place had an empty feeling to it and my heart had slowed down by the time I peered in the last doorway. Nobody here.

The place was neat but cramped. Furniture too close to the TV, a kitchen table that would have to be pulled away from the wall if you wanted to seat more than two people. Movie posters in the bedroom. Bachelor pad.

"DAVE! IN HERE!"

I ran. I found John lying prone on the floor of the bedroom.

"JOHN! WHAT—"

At the sight of me he sat up and thrust both hands out. In one hand he held a large, folded envelope, ragged where it had been torn open. In the other hand he held a small, silver canister.

Just like mine.

He said, "Under the bed."

I let out a long breath and said, "Oh holy mother of fuck."

"Yeah."

I sat on the bed. I shook my head slowly and said, "Man, we can't go through this again."

"Look."

He gave me the envelope. I flattened it out, saw the address was written in an aggressive jagged scrawl that had to be a man's.

"ATTN: KATHY BORTZ, REPORTER
CHANNEL 5 NEWSROOM"

. . . and then the P.O. Box number of the TV station.

John said he remembered her from the newscast earlier, said she was the lead reporter who did the nursing home story. So if you were a citizen and had something big to share with the world, such as a vial of a black, oily goo from Planet X, you'd mail it to a Kathy Bortz. Or, at least, that's what James "Big Jim" Sullivan would do.

I can say that because his name was scrawled in the return address corner, followed by an address I had seen many times and had long

211

memorized, always following the words, *"I'm Molly. Please return me to . . ."*

I rubbed my hand over my mouth, tried to think through it. I said, "Jim had the soy sauce."

John shrugged. "I guess so."

"Why didn't he tell us?"

"For the same reason you haven't told anybody else. That night, I was surprised Jim hung around as long as he did, even after the needle came out. But, maybe he was there because he *did* know what it was. Trying to control the situation. And he did try to tell somebody, you know. He mailed it to the damned TV station."

"Before he died."

A shrug. "Probably."

"Son of a bitch. I knew he knew more than he was letting on. We should have sweated him down and got some answers. So he got it from the Jamaican?"

"I guess."

"Where'd the Jamaican get it from?"

"The wig monsters, right?"

"What, you think Robert Marley had a ranch full of them somewhere? No, I think saying soy sauce comes from those monsters is like saying Pringles come from Pringles tubes. The sauce has a mind of its own, those things are just carriers. And these little silver vials that keep turning up, you don't buy these at the hardware store. No, somebody was supplying Robert."

I found myself about to suggest calling Drake the Cop, but I stopped that in midthought. I pictured all sorts of questions about the Las Vegas trip, and the missing detective, and so on. Then I thought again about calling Marconi, but that felt hopeless. John had looked up a number for his office but it wasn't like that was a red phone that rang at his bedside. We'd get some voice mail tree asking if we wanted to order a copy of his DVD.

I wandered into the living room and sat on the couch, seeing myself do it on the TV screen at the same time. I waved to myself. I looked depressed, rumpled and tired enough to sleep on a sidewalk. People would stop and put change in a cup for me.

John went and did something in the kitchen, banging around plates and opening drawers. A minute later he sat down beside me, carrying a sandwich and a soda.

I noticed a VCR atop the TV was recording the camera's feed. I hit "stop" on the VCR and then "rewind."

John reached over to an answering machine on the end table. He skipped through eleven worthless messages before we heard the unmistakable voice of Action Weather Watcher Ken Phillipe:

Beep.

"Danny? It's Ken. Call me, buddy. What you saw, I don't want you to misunderstand. Krissy and I, we been neighbors a long time, I knew her mom from way back—look, I want you to know that she and I were talking but we were talkin' about you, Danny. You got her scared, the way you've been acting. Anyway. Give me a call, Danny, and I'll be over with a six-pack and we'll shoot the shit. I hope you're well, buddy."

Beep.

I started the VCR from the beginning of the tape. Empty sofa. Then Danny Wexler leaned into the frame, glancing over at the feed on the TV. He sat down, looking worn and beaten and drained, in a sweat-stained T-shirt and jeans. The door we had just entered through was visible over his shoulder. He said:

"Hi, honey. Are you there? Answer me if you're there."

I looked at John. "Was he talking to somebody behind the camera?" John didn't answer, just squinted quizzically as Wexler continued.

"Come on. It's okay."

A pause, Wexler staring into the camera in silence for a few seconds.

"Just say hello."

[Another pause.]

"I know. It's been a rough couple of weeks. Baby, I've done somethin' really stupid. I've gotten wrapped up in something. Something you can't imagine."

"That's bizarre," said John. "It's like listening to one half of a phone conversation."

"If I told you the details, you would wish I hadn't," he said. "But you know by now that I'm not myself. I come and go, and right now I'm fine, but I have to fight for every second of control. It's draining. Baby, it takes so much energy to keep myself on top, on the surface, at the wheel. As soon as I relax, he'll take over. *It* will take over. And I'll just be a spectator. Helpless."

He broke down into sobs.
Wexler babbled on, those long pauses here and there.
I said, "So, he was on the sauce, right?"
"At some point, yeah. Maybe he thought it would improve his sportscast. And now that I think about it, it sort of did."
"Or maybe he didn't take it. Maybe it took him. The same way it happened to me. The reporter lady gets the envelope, she glances at it and assumes it's from a crazy person, she tosses it in the trash . . ."
John picked it up. ". . . Then Wexler's dumb ass wanders along, gets curious and says, 'What's this?' and fishes it out. Horror ensues."
"Fast-forward toward the end of tape. See if he mentions where he's going before he leaves."

John never got the chance. On the screen, Wexler flinched and looked up. The sound of Cinderella's "Don't Know What You've Got 'til it's Gone" filled the room.

Wexler jumped off the couch and walked out of the frame. A couple of minutes later we watched ourselves burst through the door.

John and I leapt up from the couch as if our asses were spring-loaded.

"We just missed him!" John screamed. "We just missed him! Shit!"

On the TV, John and I walked passed the camera, then headed off to search the apartment.

On-screen, a shape appeared above us.

Some kind of creature, clinging to the ceiling.

Wexler.

On the screen, he scrambled upside down to the doorway, clutching the top of the door frame and pushing himself into the hall. Weightless. Moving fast as a salamander, an inhuman blur.

John hoisted the ghetto blaster, punched "play." "Sweet Child O' Mine" blasted. He held the stereo over his head like John Cusack in *Say Anything* and charged into the hall.

We pounded down the stairs, power ballad in our wake, stupidly hoping Wexler had hung around the building.

In the parking lot, a minute later, John spun with the ghetto blaster, warding off the night. No sign of Wexler.

The parking spot was empty. The song ended and we stood there like idiots, chests heaving, chilled air frosting the sweat on my face.

John said, "Maybe he went back to the TV station?"

I shrugged. "Or to Ken's house. Or Krissy's house. Or to the hospital. Or that twenty-four-hour tattoo place. Or the airport where he has a flight waiting to take him to Thailand. You know where I think we should check first? The nearest all-night bakery."

We trudged around the building and back through the row of hedges that separated the visitors' lot from the reserved spaces. Black as pitch out here. I glanced up and noticed the lights were off in the lot—

—of course they are—

215

—and there was no moon. Dark as hell. It was chilly, that wet-autumn-night kind of cold, but I knew part of the cold I was feeling was coming from inside. Fear was creeping up on me, working from the guts out.

Just go back, man. Go back home, to the warmth and the light. You did your best. Now it's over. You won't find him. And dark like this, true dark, belongs to bats and rapists. You did what you could.

I walked on, feeling already like this was wrong, totally wrong, my car keys clutched in my hand like a rosary, our shoes crunching dead leaves with each step.

Crunch . . . crunch . . . crunch . . .

I blinked, trying to adjust to the dark, failing. Eyes watering from the chilled air, a little soreness in my knees from bouncing down the steps, a tickling around the hairs of my ankles. Every nerve alive and standing at attention.

I blinked and could see a little now, my Hyundai just twenty feet away, one of two cars in the lot. The low, cloud-filtered gloom made the blue compact appear a few shades too dark.

I suddenly had this flash of visual memory, the glimpse of parking lot as my headlights swept across it when we pulled in. Flat asphalt under circles of lamplight. That memory knotted in my gut for some reason, something I couldn't put my finger on. We walked.

Crunch . . . cranch . . . crinch . . .

Something's wrong.

Seeing it again, the lights flashing across the lot as we turned in, a newly paved lot with fresh, dark pavement against sharp, yellow lines . . .

Crunch . . . cree-unch . . .

. . . and completely devoid of fallen leaves.

Cruuuuunch . . .

That tickling at my ankles again. I stopped, looked down.

From behind me, John screamed.

The ground was rippling.

Pulsing, as if pelted by a heavy rain.

Twitching.

Cockroaches.

My legs were covered with them. I squealed and crazily slapped at my pant legs, trying to knock the things off me, dropping the duffel bag and my car keys in the process. If this was one of our patented hallucinations, it was a five-senses hallucination extravaganza. Once, while half asleep, I had a cockroach crawl across the back of my neck. It's quite the unique feeling and hard to mistake.

This was real, quite real, so very tinglingly and itchingly real, and my heart was pounding, my skin crawling and I mean *literally* crawling. In that instant I was sure the insects were not only on my skin but under it, burrowing through muscle tissue, spindly legs flicking over nerve bundles.

Every thought was blown from my mind.

You would think that under those conditions nothing would surprise me. You'd be wrong. I was quite surprised, for instance, when I looked down and saw that my fallen car keys were running away from me, floating as if carried downstream.

They're taking my keys! The roaches are stealing my car keys!

I trotted toward the car, itching in a hundred places. I saw then that it wasn't the autumn night that made the paint appear darker. It was the couple-hundred-thousand roaches swarming over the body.

I took off my jacket and used it to sweep the bastards away from the door and window. I yanked open the latch, squishing a roach between my fingers and the handle as I did. I swung the door open—

There were a lot more roaches on the inside than out. They had puddled in the floorboards and they poured out onto the pavement like the jackpot from the Devil's slot machine, the bugs raining down with a sound like frying bacon.

There was a lump on the driver's seat, invisible under a rippling blanket of roaches. But then the lump grew and pulsed and I realized the lump *was* roaches. They scrambled over one another, twitching legs entangling and knotting, piling higher and higher.

You see people in horror movies standing there stupidly while some special effect takes shape before them, the dumb-asses gawking at it instead of turning and running like the wind. And I wanted to run, to do the smart thing. But this was *my* car, dammit. My only car. I'd be damned if I was gonna walk to work every day.

The roach pile in the seat grew and grew until it was a grotesque, lumpy column two feet high. Bugs were pouring around my shoes like floodwater, flowing up the tires and across the fenders and into the driver's seat. Their stampede made a soft sound like someone crunching cereal from across the room and I could *smell* the things, an odor like an old fryer full of dirty cooking oil.

In the seat, two smaller columns jutted from the base of the bug pile like tree roots, hanging off the front of the seat, building down toward the floorboard. The lump now had legs.

They were, I saw, forming themselves into a human figure.

Hey, why not?

Arms formed a few seconds later. Finally, a head. A full replica of a man sculpted entirely from cockroaches now sat comfortably in the driver's seat.

The compacted ball of roaches that was its skull rotated toward me, as if it had turned to look me in the eye.

It spoke.

"A cockroach has no soul. Yet it runs and eats and shits and fucks and breeds. It has no soul, yet it lives a full life. Just like you."

Time froze. I was locked in this moment, with this thing. I spoke, but I don't think my mouth ever moved.

I said, or thought, "Who are you?"

"Who are *you*? Who are you to one like Korrok, who fills his belly with great men, swallowing them as a whale swallows swarms of krill? The desires and ambitions of men who towered over you are, in Korrok, digested over eternities, fermenting into an anguish that exceeds the sum of all of living mankind's suffering through the ages. Populations of worlds roil in his guts, the mad screams and desperate longings of seven trillion souls escape every time Korrok farts. *And he does fart.* So let me repeat my question: who are *you*, you shit-spewing crotchfruit?"

"I'm nobody," I found myself saying. "I'm nobody. Why not just leave me be? I have nothing you can take."

"Korrok enjoys bitter food, and he has decided to let you rest on his tongue. Then, he will swallow. You wish to be left alone? You will get that wish. You will die alone, with shit in your pants. That is a prophecy."

I blinked, and realized that the time standing still wasn't an illusion—no time had actually passed. The whole conversation was relayed directly to me via a conduit the soy sauce granted me all those months ago.

The roach man raised its hand. My car keys. It started the Hyundai. Its other arm clasped the open door with fingers of knotted insects, and pulled it shut.

The roach man shifted into reverse, backed out of the space and drove to the parking lot exit. It signaled a right turn, then drove off into the night. I looked down and saw the lot was now clean of insect life.

John threw away his cigarette and said, "Shit. I knew that was gonna happen."

Shakily I said, "What now?"

"You okay?"

"It . . . spoke to me. I think."

"What'd it say?"

"Just . . . I don't know."

"Man, how are you gonna report this to your insurance company?"

We heard an engine from behind us, a white Ford Focus rolling into the parking lot. Out the side window popped the pretty head of Krissy, the girl from the couch at the crime scene. I stepped closer and saw that, yes, her body was attached.

"Hey, I'm glad I caught you guys. Did you see that newscast?"

John trotted up, carrying his satchel. "Yes. Wexler's gone. We need your car."

"What? Why?"

John circled around to the passenger-side door and said, "Car chase."

She smiled. "Cool. Hop in."

"Wait," I said, digging out my roll of TestaMints. "Here. Eat one of these."

"And who are you, again?" she asked.

"I'm the only man here who has his head on straight. This ain't a situation for the dogcatcher anymore. There's something else, something dark. We're talking every bad thing you've ever thought didn't exist, demons and witchcraft and gremlins and Sasquatch and I don't care if you believe or—"

"All right, all right. Stop talking. I know what I saw tonight." She reached into her sweatshirt and pulled out a gold cross dangling on a thin chain. "See? Could I wear this if I were some kind of a devil or vampire or something? Now are you getting in or not?"

I studied her as best I could, judged her on the spot. I got in the car. The tires chirped as she pulled out of the parking lot, turning the same direction roach man had gone.

Traffic was dead at this hour and we hummed along with the speedometer hovering just over the seventy-five mark.

So freaking dark. No moon and no stars and we're all on our own down here—

"There!" said John. Taillights way up ahead. Small and close together. It was my boy, all right. It was at this moment I realized we, again, had no plan for what to do once we caught up to it. The same thing apparently occurred to Krissy, who asked, "What do we do now?"

"Get up alongside," said John. "And then ram it off the road."

"I'm not doin' that! Who's gonna pay for the—"

She cut off her words with a scream. We were close now, close enough for her to see the driver. "What *is* that thing?"

"You don't wanna know," John said. "But don't be afraid. Get up close again, I got a plan."

She looked confused, but faced forward and pressed the Focus up to eighty. We ran up alongside the blue compact. "Keep us even," John said as he rolled down the window. Roach man had his window down, too, one roachy elbow resting outside the window like a trucker. The occasional roach dripped off his arm like candle wax, flicking off into the wind.

John started to climb out of the window, wind whipping his hair around his face and I had the crazy idea that he was going to try to fling himself over to the other car like Bruce Willis. Instead he leaned his torso back against the car and braced his knees against the inside of the door. He unzipped his pants.

Roach man turned his roach head toward us just in time to take a windblown spray of urine to the face. The creature flailed and convulsed; the Hyundai wobbled in its lane. The little tires lost traction and the car went soaring off the side of the road. It plowed through weeds and tipped nose-down over an embankment, landing in a culvert with a white explosion of water.

Krissy pulled over and we all spilled out.

"What was that? Huh?" I screamed at John. "What the hell was that?"

"Hey, we stopped him."

"The goal was to get the car back. My car. Intact. And not splattered with urine."

"Look! Oh, man—"

A dark shape.

Floating up from the Hyundai.

A black plume of smoke.

With two glowing eyes.

I felt it. It was as if the shadow man had reached out to me, cold fingers running through my skull and down my spine.

Then, it was gone, slipping soundlessly off into the night. I heard a breathy sound from Krissy. She had slapped a hand over her mouth, eyes wide.

John said, "They're here, Dave. They're here. They're here, they're here, they're here. Shit."

I hissed, "What are they?"

"Don't know. It's probably in Marconi's book but I can never finish it, it gets so slow after the first two chapters."

To Krissy I said, "Don't worry, it looks like it left. You saw it?"

She shook her head. "I *felt* it. It just ran through me, this sort of heavy feeling like—like there was nothing here. Like everything was nothing, everything everywhere. There's like molecules and stuff but behind it, nothing. Just cold and dark . . ."

She fell into silence.

I said to John, "When it spoke to me, it mentioned Korrok. Just like Molly."

"Was that thing Korrok?"

"No. I'm sure of that."

Krissy wasn't following this conversation at all, and instead focused her attention down toward the crashed Hyundai, two-thirds submerged in the standing water, its rear stuck into the air like the *Titanic*.

"Ew! What's that?"

A layer of cockroaches two inches thick floated out from around the car like an oil slick, clumps here and there still holding the shape of limbs. A half dozen old fast-food bags floated up from the interior and hung nearby like buoys.

"Roaches," I said. "You can see them?"

"Yeah. Where'd they come from?"

"My car was really dirty." I turned to John. "What the shadow guy here did with the bugs? I think he did the same to Molly. Just reached out and took over."

John said, "And Wexler, too, I guess. So. They can do that."

"This is indescribably bad. What now?"

Krissy asked, "Are they, like, demons?"

"Well, they're evil," said John. "You just saw one of them steal a car."

"Molly!"

Krissy, pointing down the road.

Sure enough, the dog that was standing about twenty yards away, it was either Molly or an exact replica.

To me John said, "Ghost?"

"Krissy can see her."

"Zombie then. Well, she's earthbound, that's a positive sign."

Molly barked, trotted off down the road, then turned and barked again.

John said to Krissy, "She wants us to follow her." He said it to her, not to me. Leaving me out of the decision. Asshole.

I glanced at my watch. "Anybody want to go to Denny's? Maybe this thing will sort itself out."

They both went to the car. I started listing all of the things that were retarded about this plan, and by the time I reached the end we were all rolling down the street with the copper dog in our headlights.

After a few minutes, the dog, looking perfectly healthy despite having exploded in half earlier that evening, turned and bounded off the road. She streaked across an expanse of weeds, gravel and busted concrete.

We were at the Mall of the Dead.

That's what we called the half finished and subsequently abandoned Undisclosed Shopping Centre. The city sank forty million dollars' worth of tax breaks and infrastructure into getting the thing built before three of the five investors disappeared (I always imagined that all three simultaneously shot each other, like in the movie *Reservoir Dogs*). Now, three years and thirty lawsuits later, raccoons nested in the one hundred and fifty empty store slots and rainwater puddled in the halls.

It lay there in the darkness, broken and rotting like a decomposing animal carcass that was slowly picked apart by scavengers.

Molly zipped off toward the building and was swallowed by the darkness.

Krissy said, "Do we follow her in there?"

The radio kicked on, mandolin plucking the intro to an early '90s song by REM called "Losing My Religion." John and I reacted, Krissy didn't. It only took a few seconds for me to realize this was not the song as Michael Stipe had written it.

223

"Oooohhh, knife
plus nigger
Equals you, and Jews are dead meat . . ."

"I know people around here," John said, "who would like the song better that way."

"You can hear it?"

"Yeah."

Krissy said, "Hear what?"

"Never mind. Look over by those Dumpsters," John said. "Wexler's car."

5 SPRTS.

"Well,"I said. "Nothing to do now but wander the fuck into that abandoned building, totally unarmed."

John opened the satchel and drew out a long, metal flashlight, clicked on the beam to confirm that it still worked. Then he pulled out a wadded-up hand towel and handed it to me.

I unwrapped it and found myself holding the stainless-steel automatic pistol I had stolen from the pickup during the Las Vegas thing. I had planned to ditch it, to throw it into the river or something. Not only was the weapon stolen, but for all I knew it had been used to hold up four liquor stores and shoot two policemen before I got hold of it.

"Why do you still have this? I thought you were gonna make it disappear."

John shrugged. "Never got around to it. I keep it hidden. And I scratched off the serial numbers there. Should be safe."

I ejected the magazine.

"What? Why is it loaded?"

"Oh, Head bought bullets for it. He borrowed it a month ago, I think he had to threaten a dude with it. Brought it right back though."

Krissy said, "You're not going to shoot Danny, are you? If he's possessed or whatever, you know that's not his fault."

"You belong to a church, right?" I asked. "You know anything about performing exorcisms? That sort of thing?"

She shook her head.

"You know your Bible?" John asked. "You could show us the part that's got the spells and incantations and stuff and read them right from there."

She just stared at him. She heard the chorus as the bastardized song continued. Chorus now.

> *"That's me in the porno*
> *That's me in the spotlight*
> *Losing my religion*
> *Tryin' to beat a tight-assed Jew . . ."*

Krissy dug into her purse and pulled out a little black plastic thing that I thought was a flashlight but when she pressed the button a blue spark jumped across the end.

"It's a Taser. A, uh, stun gun. I don't think I've got anything else in here." She sifted around in the purse. "Nail file . . ."

"No, let's go."

Our hearts hammering, the three of us approached the sprawling building, none of us making a sound other than the crunching of gravel under our shoes.

I made my way to Wexler's car, edged toward the window with the gun.

Nobody inside.

Ahead was the tall, rusted metal framework that I supposed was going to be a fancy awning for the main entrance. Beneath it was a row of huge windows and a bank of doors, all boarded over with plywood.

Among the graffiti, something had been painted in bold letters two feet high. On closer inspection we saw the letters were twitching, moving ever so slightly.

Slugs.

A couple hundred of them had slimed their way up the boards to spell out a phrase that I was certain was right from "Korrok," whoever he was:

YOUR DOOMED

His spelling, not mine.

One panel of plywood had been pulled partially off its frame, presumably by Mr. Wexler.

John said, "Dave, you got the gun. You should go in first."

"You got the stereo! Besides, if I go in and get killed right off the bat, you're all fucked. But if you get attacked I can rescue you with the gun."

"Maybe Krissy should go, like as a decoy."

She moved toward the opening but I shouldered her aside.

The stink hit me one foot inside the place. Rot and mildew and dead rodents.

The empty storefronts were boarded up, giving us a single, impossibly long corridor. The floor was littered with paper cups and candy wrappers and cigarette butts and other teenager droppings. I saw a used condom under my shoe.

Our only light was from a huge skylight running down the length of the building. Parts of it had been boarded over, other sections were spiderwebbed with breaks and clouded with mounds of accumulated dead leaves. When we walked under the boarded-over sections of the glass we found ourselves in pools of absolute blackness.

John lit the flashlight. He fired up the stereo.

"Home Sweet Home" by Mötley Crüe.

We plunged ahead, a creeping pool of light and music in the dead space.

A sound.

Shoes scraping on floor tile.

I raised the gun.

"Wexler?!"

No answer.

We reached a bend in the mall, the hall taking a ninety-degree turn to the right. Blood was pumping in my ears. Palm sweat greased the handle of the gun.

Ahead of us, shoes scraping tile.

A shadowy shape.

Not shoes.

Hooves.

Moving fast.

It was as tall as a man. It passed into a shaft of moonlight.

John screamed a profanity.

I squeezed the trigger.

Gunshots hammered the air.

Krissy shrieked.

Yellow flashes from the gun barrel. Glimpses of brown fur and antlers in the darkness. A deer?

Maybe it had been one, once. This creature had grown several new sets of eyes. Each of its antlers ended in a snapping set of lobsterish claws. It looked like it had a novelty chandelier from a seafood restaurant on its head. Looking back, I have to say it was the stupidest-looking thing I had ever seen.

It stumbled as it got close and my wild shots started to land, blossoms of red opening up on the beast's chest and neck.

It tried to turn away, showing me its rib cage and taking several broadside shots for its trouble. The mutated deer collapsed, thrashing on the dirty floor tiles and leaving red smears like a child's finger painting.

It twitched one last time, and was still.

My hands were shaking. The gun looked broken, the top half of it pushed an inch from the rest of the mechanism. After fiddling with it for a few minutes I realized this is what the gun naturally did when it was empty. I pushed in the button to release the empty magazine. Great job conserving ammo so far.

We approached the fallen was-a-deer, kicking brass casings as we went. I pushed at its furry hide with my foot. As solid as a dead deer. I turned to Krissy, asked, "You see it?"

She nodded, eyes still wide.

"Oh, look!" yelped John. "Look at its ass!"

The deer's ass was melting, puddling on the floor like candle wax. In less than a minute the entire hindquarters were a brown pool on the floor, the ribs quickly caving in like a punctured balloon at a Thanksgiving Day parade. As the front legs and head flattened, the liquid residue from the hindquarters dissolved before our eyes, leaving dry floor behind.

There was one part that didn't melt, a section in the middle of the animal that protruded from the pink and brown slime. Square. A box about six inches to a side.

I scooted it away with my foot. Heavy. When the goo dissolved from it, I saw that it was a green-and-yellow box marked . . .

"Shotgun shells," John said. "Too bad we don't have a . . ."

His voice trailed off as his gaze shifted to a lone wooden crate over by the wall, presumably full of floor tile or coils of electrical wiring and other mall fixin's.

John delivered a series of hard kicks to the side of the crate, cracking and splintering the boards. He plunged his hands into the opening and pulled out a dark length of plastic and metal that I had already guessed was a shotgun.

Growls emerged from the darkness, followed by the scratches of claws. Many claws.

I clenched the empty gun in my hand, pointing it stupidly into the darkness. John frantically loaded the shotgun.

"WHOA, LOOK AT the time!" said Arnie, standing to leave. "Mr. Wong, it's been a hell of a lot of fun talkin' to you. But I should start my drive back; I got six hours ahead of me. The piece may not run next month, but soon. They may want to run it on Halloween, you know."

"Arnie, please. You came all this way. Don't walk away thinking what you're thinking."

He dug his car keys from his pocket. "I'm not here to judge, I said that already. The shotgun, hey, the roofers could have left that behind. And maybe that deer got fed up with the local hunters and ate one of them, including the shotgun shells the poor guy had in his pocket."

He pulled out a cigar from an inside pocket and jammed it into his mouth.

"No, it's nothing like that. The thing in Wexler, it had the power to call up on these things I guess, to try to kill us. But I think Wexler was still inside there, too, and he was working from the other end, helping us out. He was on the sauce, you know, and he used it."

"After you told me the part about Las Vegas, you know how I said it was the stupidest story I had ever heard?"

"You didn't say that."

"Well, I was thinkin' it. But I've decided I owe that Las Vegas story an apology because this last thing made that one look like *The Grapes of Wrath*. I'll see ya around."

Arnie walked toward the exit. I followed, stopping quickly to pay the lady at the counter.

"Wait," I stammered as he pushed through the door. "I got, you know, all that paperwork on the Hyundai and the accident and all that. The insurance company, they took pictures of the scene and, well, you can't really see anything but they describe the scene in the report, the dead roaches and all that. I went back that next morning and I got a hand, a clump of the bugs in the shape of, of the fingers. I got it at home . . ."

Nothing from Arnie. He didn't even nod.

"In my toolshed, in a jar. I can show it to you. I mean, what kind of a person would fake that, would sit at home and glue a bunch of roaches together? 'Honey, what are you doing?' 'Oh, I'm making a roach hand. You know, to aid my credibility with the press.'"

Arnie said, "The kid you say you killed during the Las Vegas thing? Fred Chu? Say I go looking into that, his disappearance."

I hesitated. "Do it. Those records are out there. I've been honest with you, I keep saying that."

"So you admit killing him?"

"Off the record, yeah."

"And the other kid that died, Big Jim—"

"He's really dead, too. You can look it up."

"I already did. But Big Jim, he would have gone to the cops about Fred, wouldn't he? That you shot Fred? He didn't seem too happy about it."

"I—I don't know. We'll never know."

"Worked out pretty good for you that Big Jim died then, didn't it?"

"Fuck you."

"Don't you see? You got all this ridiculous shit swirling around in your story, Wong, but then you got the parts that are real, the parts that can be verified. And they're all felonies. A dead kid. A missing kid. A missing *cop*. So why don't I do both of us a favor and pretend we never talked? Because I'm not sure I wanna hear the rest of it."

He unlocked the door to a white Cavalier and ducked inside.

"Wait!"

I jogged up to the car and circled around to the passenger side. I gently smacked the window with my palm. Arnie hesitated, then reached over and unlocked it. I leaned in.

"Can I sit down?"

He paused once more, not wanting to prolong this but not quite sure how to get rid of me. Maybe he was afraid I was dangerous, liable to fly into crazy-man violence if turned away. He used both hands to scoop up a bundle of notebooks and folders from the passenger seat. I ducked in and arranged my feet around a pile of recording equipment and cassettes on the floorboard.

"Here," I said. "Look." I pulled a single folded sheet of paper from my pocket. "It's been in my pants all day so it's kind of wrinkled and, uh, moist, but read it. I copied that from Dr. Marconi's book."

leaving it looking like a jar of pickled eggs that had been eaten and then vomited by a gorilla.

The strange ritual was done in service to a deity who to my ears sounded like "Koddock" (the tribe had no written language). I was told that each member bore the mark of this god and I was allowed to witness the branding ceremony each member undertakes at the age of manhood.

The young man was forced to lay facedown on a mat, naked. The priest then brought out a clay jar containing the writhing maggots of bot flies. The larvae were placed on the back of the young man, arranged in the shape of Koddock's symbol. The maggots then chewed through the top layer of skin, digging holes a half-inch deep. I was told the larvae would, according to ceremony, be allowed to remain in their warm, wet tunnels in the young man's back for seven days. If the young man succumbed to the itch and scratched the spot, he would fail the test of manhood and would have to wait a year before attempting it again.

On the seventh day the larvae are extracted by the priest and the wound treated. What remains will be the trails of scar tissue, following the paths eaten by the worms. These scars would form the "brand" of Koddock. The priest showed me the finished symbol and the pipe literally fell from my mouth.

Once more, it was like the symbol for pi, only rotated ninety degrees to the left. The same symbol I had seen a Manchester toddler draw in his trance state months before.

 As soon as I got back to Lima, I phoned Dr. Haleine, the Egyptologist. Shouting to each other over a poor connection, he described for me again the hieroglyph he had discovered in his dig, nearly 7,500 miles from where I stood.

I was so stunned by what he told me that I could not keep my feet. Sitting on the floor of my hotel, I pondered the enormity of the revelation and sought out my flask.

Haleine explained that there was an Egyptian god named Kuk, who was already known to Egyptologists (in the Ogdoad cosmogony, Kuk

231

was a frog-like god who represented darkness and chaos). Haleine, however, believed he had stumbled upon a cult that worshipped his rash and destructive son, Kor'rok. This god was represented symbolically by a man punctured by two spears, one in the mouth and one in the groin, the twin centers of desire for mankind.

In the cult's mythology, Kor'rok was a reckless and cruel slavemaster, who used men's bodily desires to lure them to their destruction for his own amusement.

Dr. Haleine's hieroglyph and the symbol of "Koddock" I had copied in my notepad, when laid over one another, were nearly identical in shape. Here we had now three peoples, living on opposite corners of the planet, separated by oceans of water and time, independently identifying the same deity.

It was the single best piece of evidence for the supernatural ever discovered by science.

Another day of travel took me back to the village. I arrived in such a state of excitement that the priest had me restrained by several strong men and forced me to drink a potion to "cool the embers in my head." After some time I got alone with the priest and asked him about Koddock and the symbol.

The symbol, he told me, was a representation of the god Koddock himself. Koddock was a young god, he told me, hotheaded and prone to fits of rage if not pleased. The vertical line was his body. The top horizontal line was a stream of vomit, the second horizontal line was a stream of urine. For, you see, the tribe believed Koddock liked to drink to excess, and when he was intoxicated he interfered with the affairs of man and caused great destruction. This was the tribe's explanation for all suffering and misfortune in the world.

Arnie skimmed over it, then let out a long sigh.

"See? That's Korrok. That symbol, that's what was on Molly's foot, it's what's on . . . look, you're a journalist, these are independent sources here confirming the same thing. It doesn't matter if it's crazy, this is evidence, right?"

"What am I supposed to say, Wong? What do you want from me?"

"I need somebody to know about this. I have to get this out. Before . . ." I shook my head. I ran out of words.

"Before what? A monster catches you in an alley and eats you?"

Tell him about Amy.

"No. It's nothing like that. Well, I mean, that's a possibility, but it's bigger than that."

Arnie let out a sigh.

"Just listen," I said, begging a little. "Just listen a little bit longer and then everything will be clear. You'll understand how much is at stake here. Seriously."

Arnie sighed and looked off across the parking lot. "I ain't got much time, Wong. It's getting late."

"I know. Just . . . I need you to drive somewhere. We go there and I can show you. Everything will be clear, you'll know what's true and what isn't."

"Where?"

"The mall. *The* mall."

He gave me a long, hard look. He was probably sizing up his ability to take me down if I went nuts on him and tried to bite through his neck. He apparently judged his physical prowess to be superior because he twisted the key and revved the engine to life.

"Turn right out of the parking lot here."

THE SKITTERING FOOTSTEPS grew louder in the mall's cavernous hallway. John pumped the shotgun and raised it.

"Sister Christian," by Night Ranger, slowed, garbled, ground to silence. The last of the juice in the ghetto blaster's batteries.

233

Scratching claws.

Approaching fast.

Two gray blurs.

They were coyotes, muscular, with matted fur and red eyes. They both skidded to a stop at the sight of us, took in deep breaths, and breathed plumes of fire.

The three of us dove behind the crate. John leaned over with the shotgun, fired and tore a fist-sized chunk out of the first coyote head. He fired at the second one, missed.

Pumped.

Fired.

Missed again.

The beast lunged at me, knocking me over like a linebacker. It stood on my chest, its breath smelling like burnt electrical wires. It sucked in a huge breath that I knew would take the flesh off my skull.

A hand shot out.

Punching into the coyote's side.

Krissy hit the Taser.

Blue sparks flew.

The coyote's abdomen, swollen with flammable breath, exploded like the *Hindenburg*. Furry chunks hit me in the face, a beautiful orange fireball rolling up toward the glass ceiling.

I scrambled to my feet, my face hot and tight, brushing slimy red chunks of animal off me and cursing. I wasn't sure if it was coyote blood or my own piss on my pants.

Something heavy bounced off my shoe. John shone the flashlight, revealing a box of bullets.

Laying next to it was a key with the number "1" etched into it.

"A key," said John, clicking shells into his shotgun. "Good. Now, if I know what's going on here, and I think I do, we'll have to wander around looking for that door. Behind it we'll meet a series of monsters or, more likely, a whole bunch of the same one. We'll kill them, get another key, and then it'll open a really big door. Now right before that we'll probably get nicer guns. It may require us to backtrack some and it might get really tedious and annoying."

"Oh, fuck you," I said. "I'm staying here." I sat on the ground, pulled open the box of bullets and tried to put one in the pistol. It fit. Hey, why the hell not. I started pushing rounds into the pistol magazine one at a time. "You go find the door."

A metallic thunder filled the hall.

We all flew into action, bullets spilling off my lap and rolling in every direction.

Ahead of us something huge dropped from the ceiling, blocking our view. The clanking roar finally ended in a crash that made all three of us jump.

We advanced, guns drawn. It was one of those enormous drop-down gates that malls use to button up at closing time.

"Well," Krissy said, "I guess this is the big door. There's a keyhole at the bottom, near the latch."

"All right," said John, nodding. "All right. Big door. Sooner than I expected, but whatever. Now, that means there's a boss behind there. A huge bad guy."

He focused on Krissy. "I want you to be prepared for this. This evil that has Wexler, it's impossible for us to imagine what form it's taken with him. Expect tentacles. And a whole bunch of eyes. Or just one eye. I don't know what exactly to expect but I know it'll be a way bigger asshole than we faced out here—"

"Krissy!"

From behind us. We spun on the voice and I involuntarily squeezed the trigger. The gun clicked. I hadn't chambered a round.

It was Wexler, trudging up in the shadows behind us. He looked pale but perfectly human. I posed casually with the gun, so as not to be too blatant about the fact that I had almost killed him with it just now.

Krissy moved toward him.

"Don't," he said. "Stay away from me. He'll be back. Any second now, he'll be back."

He bent over and broke down in a coughing fit. Blood splattered the floor.

"Dude," said John, "let's get you to a hospital, we'll protect you and—"

"No. Listen. I'm falling apart. I'm falling apart inside. When he comes back, I won't hold up. Now, how much do you know about this place?"

"If you're talking about this town in general," John said, "don't even get us started. We're the experts."

"No. No. I'm talking about the doors. This building—"

Coughing fit.

"—the doors, under it, or somewhere. I don't know where. Hidden. This building and others, I think."

"We can go over all that later," I said. "Where's the shadow man? The, you know, the thing, the one who's possessing you? Where is he now? Is he behind that gate?"

"He'll come back here. Let him. Let him enter me. Then kill me—"

Krissy screamed, "No! Danny!"

"—Kill me and burn my body. Then burn this place down on top of me. Find the other doors if there are more, and burn them down, too. In fact, just burn the whole town. Just to be safe."

"Doors? I don't get—"

Danny coughed, spat, then coughed and coughed some more, hacking until he finally passed out.

Krissy ran to him, but couldn't get him to respond. He was still breathing, though, so we dragged him over to the wall, leaning him against it.

John and I trained our guns on him, and waited.

Krissy looked back and forth at us and said, "What are you guys *doing?*"

John and I glanced at each other.

"Well . . . you know," I said meekly. "We're waiting for the thing to come back into him so we can, uh . . ."

"We are *not* doing that."

To me the guy looked to be on his last legs anyway, so this really did seem like a more reasonable plan than getting eaten by whatever monstrosity waited behind that gate. Shouldn't we honor his final wishes?

We were unable to convince Krissy of this. She took the key and started working at the lock of the huge gate.

I sighed and went to her, the pistol clasped in both hands. John nudged her aside and knelt with his hand on the gate handle.

Krissy pulled the Taser from her pocket.

John looked up at us and said, "We stay together. Look for a weak spot, like an eye or something. If there are crates around the room, cover me and I'll open them, see if there's a rocket launcher or something in one of them. If either of you find a big, green, polka-dotted mushroom, set it aside. We may need it later."

The blood, pounding through my ears again, my skull sounding like the inside of a seashell. I blinked hard to try to clear the spots pulsing in front of my eyes.

I knew this was the thing to do, but every fiber screamed to retreat and try again some other day, when we had more on our side, when I wasn't so tired, or so nervous, or so fat. I struggled for something to cling to, the way soldiers in foxholes picture their families, or a flag.

My car, I thought crazily. *This fucker crashed the Wongmobile. And for that, he must taste death.*

It would have to do. I reminded myself to breathe. John pulled up the gate, rolling it up on its tracks with a sound like tank treads.

We entered a huge octagon of a room, more storefront blanks where food counters were to go. There was some broken glass and dead leaves on the ground, where one of the panes in the overhead skylight had broken out.

Nothing else.

John gestured to our left and said, "Check it out."

It wasn't a monster. But still I stopped in my tracks, let out a long breath and said, "Shiiiiiiiiit."

There was a painting on one wall to our left. On the wall, on the ceiling, on the floor, on the two-by-fours stacked next to the wall. I recognized the style.

The painting was abstract, yet strangely realistic. It was a three-dimensional picture of a ring intersecting another ring in a way that seemed to shift as you looked at it. Like the landscape I saw in Robert Marley's bedroom, it seemed to draw you in, to take on complexity as you stared.

It's a picture of time.

I tore my eyes off it and said to John, "I think your Jamaican friend was here."

"I think he was actually living here."

He nodded toward a nearby nest made up of an ancient sleeping bag and about half a dozen plastic milk crates. The surrounding floor looked like the aftermath of a bloody battle between empty Captain Morgan bottles and faded candy bar wrappers.

I thought about Wexler, ranting about hidden doors. Now here was where our guy, our Patient Zero, had set up camp all those months ago. I felt like there were dots that I was intentionally not connecting. I wanted to go somewhere warm and bright to think about all this. Or, even better, not.

I wandered out to the center of the floor, crunching glass and leaves underfoot. John lit up a cigarette and said, "Man, if you could flood this place in the winter and let it freeze up, you'd have a kick-ass place to play hock—"

A shriek, from behind me. Krissy, screeching my name.

A shotgun blast split the air.

I spun, scanning the room through the sights of the automatic.

John screamed my name, bellowing instructions I couldn't make out. Then I saw it, the black shape zipping through the air, like a Hefty bag blown around in a hurricane. I spotted it, lost it, caught it again, then—

It vanished. I spun around. No sign of it. John and Krissy were staring at me, horrified.

"It's okay! I'm okay! Where did it go?"

I *was* okay, now that I thought about it. Felt great, in fact. The adrenaline must have been working because all the fear evaporated in an instant.

A veil lifted from over my thoughts.

John and Krissy. Two of six billion humans on the planet. One American, I heard, consumes enough calories to keep forty African children alive.

John routinely burned half a gallon of gasoline to get a pack of cigarettes. The girl bought special shampoo for her dog while Somali children starved. She warded off her guilt with a gold symbol around her neck, the intersecting strips of gold the last thing millions saw before their limbs were ripped from their bodies in medieval torture machines. Two locusts, standing before me, blazing through resources by the ton.

I had been such a fucking fool.

"Uh . . . Dave?"

John dragged me here for one reason: his attention span demanded new and loud experiences, links to add to his chain of distractions until the day he would finally drink himself to death.

And the girl, I could save her life a dozen times over in this room and she would still climb into bed with the guy with the great eyes and the promising TV career. She could never contaminate her precious genetic material with mine.

When was I going to stop letting the world bleed me dry?

"Dave, can you hear me?"

Without a word, I took a step toward the pair. I kicked something metal. It was a rusty utility knife, an inch of blade protruding from the end. I stuffed it in my pocket, thinking I would need it later.

The gun aimed nonthreateningly at the floor at my side, I strode toward the girl and was pleased to see a look of crippling fear ooze into her eyes, an expression that broke those sculpted porcelain features like a hammer.

Have you ever been truly scared of anything, princess?

I had a second to look over Krissy from the neck down, those perfect thigh muscles, soft curves under softer skin. The hint of perfect little breasts hiding under the sweatshirt. I suddenly had an idea for this girl that would win my dick the Nobel Prize.

Footsteps.

John, running toward me.

I spun.

Raised the gun.

Shot him in the head.

He tumbled forward, spray of blood droplets arcing through the air as he fell face-first onto the floor.

I moved toward him, to put a second and third and fourth round into his brain.

Movement behind me—

POP! POPBZZZZZZPOP POP POP!

Pain.

A crackling sound, like popcorn.

Every muscle in my body first clenched, then went slack. The tiled floor rose up and smacked me in the face.

I lay there, plywood pressed against my cheek, a bug's-eye view of the world. I was paralyzed, my brains scrambled.

Looks like Krissy needs new shoes. Hey, look! A smashed cigarette butt!

I felt the gun twist out of my fingers. With a huge effort I turned my head enough to look up and see Krissy holding the gun on me while she inspected John. He shifted and moved, sitting up.

He took off his flannel shirt and pressed it against a wet wound on his scalp, his hair matted with blood.

She helped him to his feet. They towered over me, Krissy with the Taser in her hand.

I strained to move a limb. Random muscles started to flex under my command again, but I couldn't organize them.

John, bloody rag pressed to his skull, looked me right in the eye.

"David, if you're still you at all, you know why I'm doing this. Are you in there?"

I met his gaze. I tried to talk, tested a few words to get my lips moving.

"John . . . John, I understand, and I'm sorry. I don't know what came over me just now. Really. But I'm thinkin' clear now. It's me. Don't let her shoot me, okay?"

He studied my face. I grasped the situation, with growing horror.

"John," I said, eyes pleading. "Please."

All I needed was for him to turn his back. I had the utility knife. Just hide it in my hand and, with a quick and decisive move, I could slit his throat. Use him as a shield, get the pistol away from the girl. After that, then she'd do whatever I wanted under the barrel of a gun.

Everything would be fine.

John took Krissy aside. They whispered to each other while she kept the gun on me, the barrel tipping up and down in her delicate hand.

I tried to move my legs. I could feel them but couldn't make them obey me. I ground my teeth so hard I felt like they would shatter.

Gotta stay cool. I couldn't hear, but the girl was doing all the talking now, the bitch trying to convince John to do something. He finally agreed, and came back to face me.

"Dave, here's what I think. I think the thing that was in Wexler was in you. Maybe it still is, maybe it isn't. Now, we're gonna do something here. Krissy's gonna give me the gun and I'm gonna put it on you, it's nothin' personal. And on top of that, she's gonna press the zappy thing against your skin while she does this. So do not move. You know I won't kill ya, Dave, but you jump or grab for her or anything, she'll zap you and I'll shoot you in the thigh. Then I'll come over there and kick you in the crotch repeatedly."

I showed no emotion, just nodded.

Get the arms moving, get them moving now. You get the Taser away from the girl and immobilize John with it. Move move move . . .

Feeling rushed into my right arm, I could flex the muscles all the way up. I was sure I could get it to respond.

I focused everything on readying the limb for a quick, violent move. A chop to the throat, make her drop the Taser.

Krissy handed the pistol to John. She came around me, pressed the Taser against my shoulder with her left hand.

With her right, she reached around her neck and took off her gold necklace, the one with the dangling cross.

What the—?

She dropped the necklace over my head at the exact moment I swung my fist—

My stomach clenched, my hand frozen in midair.

It's poison. They've coated it with some kind of toxin that can seep through my skin like a nicotine patch, into my bloodstream, eating through my lungs and liver like acid . . .

I thrashed away from her and got my hands up, but my coordination was even more screwed now than from the Taser. I fought like a toddler. My body convulsed, organs thrashing around inside like they were making a jailbreak from my gut.

I fell, hard.

Hands on my arm.

Soft hands. The girl.

Everything stopped.

The seizure, or whatever the hell it was, ended abruptly. I was tired, confused. I blinked, trying to take in my surroundings.

I sat up and saw the girl stumbling as if she had been cracked over the head with a pipe, dazed, out on her feet. She bent down at the waist, breathing hard. She vomited on the floor.

I felt like doing the same. I had this greasy feeling like I was rid of something unclean, like I had just passed a tapeworm. And there was this lingering, sick shame, the feel of a man who sobers up just enough to realize he's been making out with his best friend's mother.

John stared at Krissy, terrified. He turned on me, questioning, suspicious.

"What are you looking at me for?" I shouted. "Go help her, you ass!"

John nodded, apparently convinced that I was fine. Krissy was not fine. Krissy was screaming. She went to her knees, then thrashed onto her back. I scrambled to my feet, moved toward her. John grabbed my jacket, holding me back.

"No!" I screamed. "It's in her! The thing is in her! Let me touch her, let it pass back into me and then shoot me in the temple."

"Not today."

"It's killing her!"

"No. It's not. She's killing *it*."

"What?"

Krissy looked up at us with eyes that had turned bloodshot pink, sweat-soaked hair hanging down in strands. There was a deep, black hatred in that stare so profound that it was like a punch in the gut.

I had never seen anything approaching that look on a human face before. The intelligence behind it was so hateful it was alien, unfeeling, unreasoning, infinitely terrible.

I serve none but Korrok.

A blue eye, in the darkness.

He controlled you just like the cockroaches.

I wanted to curl up into a fetal position and start sucking my thumb, let my tears and dripping saliva pool under me.

Sorry. I tried living, tried being sentient. Can't do it. Can't live in the same universe with that.

She screamed again, loud. Opera-singer loud. Impossibly loud. She clutched at her hair and pressed her eyes closed. A sound erupted in the air around us, a long roar like an ocean wave crashing against a dock. Flecks of glass smacked me in the cheek.

A hundred panes of glass skylight exploded at once, a circular wave of airborne shards overhead, spreading like a ripple in a pond. Glass poured down around us, a high-pitched ringing as shards pelted the floor, raining down on our heads and shoulders.

Silence. She lay still.

Whoa. She's dead.

No . . . chest moving. Breathing.

"MOVE! MOVE!"

John, pulling at my sleeve, lifting Krissy to her feet.

A metal beam crashed down behind her.

The room was coming apart. We ran, half dragging her out of the food court. Ceiling trusses and light fixtures and cables and boards and glass came down in an avalanche.

We tumbled through the gate and into the hall, falling on our asses. The entire food court ceiling collapsed behind us, debris piling in front of the door, a wave of compressed air and dust rushing past us like a sandstorm.

Krissy tried to sit up, looking utterly exhausted. She wiped grit from her eyes.

I took the necklace from around my neck and handed it to her. She took it without hesitation, put it on.

"She broke it," John said. "Like a fever. It passed from you into her, but it couldn't live in her."

He turned his attention to the girl.

"How do you feel?"

"Like I could sleep for a thousand years."

MY BULLET HAD creased John's scalp and he said he was okay but, damn, did it bleed a lot. The wad of shirt he held against it was soaked.

We wandered around the mall looking for Molly and any additional monsters. Nothing on both counts.

Krissy stayed with Wexler, calling for an ambulance on her cell. She insisted he was alive, though we could see no sign of it. Then, as the first sirens faded in from the distance, Wexler climbed into consciousness long enough to smile at Krissy, brush a strand of hair out of her face with his fingers. He said something to her that we couldn't hear and wasn't any of our business anyway.

Paramedics arrived, with many, many questions. John told them the truth. And I mean he literally told them I was possessed and that killing the demon destroyed the food court. He refused treatment.

After the ambulance left we made our way out to Krissy's car. She asked John, "Are you going to get your head looked at?"

"Nah, it's just a cut. I was gonna shave my head anyway. Are you gonna go see Danny in the hospital?"

"Yeah. But . . . there's something I'm supposed to do first. He asked me if I had watched the tape. Do you know what that's about?"

I said "no" and John said "yes" simultaneously.

"The video he was shooting," John said. "In his apartment."

A HALF HOUR later, Krissy sat down on the couch in Wexler's apartment while John rewound the tape and let it play. Wexler, looking tired and beaten, appeared on the screen as before.

"Hi, honey. Are you there? Answer me if you're there."

Krissy looked at us, confused. We had no answers. She turned her eyes back to the screen, waiting.

"Come on. It's okay. Just say hello."

"Um, hello," said Krissy, looking embarrassed. A tear ran down her cheek. "Danny. You look awful . . ."

"I know. It's been a rough couple of weeks,"

Danny said, replying to the camera a full three hours before Krissy made that comment.

"Baby, I've done somethin' really stupid. I've gotten wrapped up in something. Something you can't imagine."

"What?" Krissy said, sobbing. "What did you get into?"

"If I told you the details, you would wish I hadn't. But you know by now that I'm not myself. I come and go, and right now I'm fine, but I have to fight for every second of control. It's draining. Baby, it takes so much energy to

245

keep myself on top, on the surface, at the wheel. As soon as I relax, he'll take over. *It* will take over. And I'll just be a spectator. Helpless."

He broke down into sobs. So did Krissy, sounding utterly drained.

"Are you okay?"

he asked, through hitching breaths.

"Were you hurt in all of this?"

"I'm fine. I'll be fine. This is so strange."

"I don't even know how I'm doing it, any of this. Right now. I see things, I hear things across time and space and . . . it's better if you can put it out of your head, Kris. It's better to live the rest of your life believing things like this aren't possible. But there's other things I need to tell you. Things I've been wanting to say for a long time. And if I'm still alive, I probably won't have the courage to say them in person. But first . . ."

Wexler's eyes shifted slightly. A chill ran down my spine.
He was looking at me.
I shifted to my left a couple of feet, and his eyes followed me.
He said,

"You're David Wong?"

No! Say no!
"Yeah . . . I guess."
Video conferencing across time. Man I need pie, and fast.

"I don't know all the details, things are . . . confused in my mind right now. But you're under the eye. You understand what I'm saying, don't you?"

I found I couldn't answer. My mouth had gone so dry it had glued shut.

"David, you alone fully understand what is at stake here."

A thousand questions popped into my mind but all I could do was peel my lips apart and say, "But . . . I don't . . ." before trailing off.

"Kris and I need to have a private conversation now, okay? Glad you made it out alive."

I BEGGED OFF from John's offer to stay the night at his place and drink many beers with him. I was hungry, and had something else to take care of first.

I took a cab to McDonald's and had it dump me in the parking lot.

I took a deep breath, steeled myself and approached the sign. I prayed I'd find it back to normal.

Nope. There was Ronald, cutting himself, gutting himself, eating himself. I felt something rigid in my jacket pocket and pulled out a rusty utility razor I didn't remember putting in there. I dropped it like it was a rattlesnake, then picked it up with two fingers and threw it in a trash can.

I stared down the poster again.

I was hungry.

The inside of the restaurant was closed but they did have a twenty-four-hour drive-through. I walked up to it and, shivering in the chill of the autumn air, ordered two bratwurst.

I sat on the curb across the parking lot and, looking right at the sign the whole time, ate them both.

ARNIE ROLLED TO a stop in the weed-and-dirt field that would have been the mall parking lot had they ever gotten around to paving it.

"So," Arnie said. "Christian mints, crosses, Bibles. This whole long story is just an elaborate setup to get me to subscribe to *Guideposts*, isn't it? You're gonna leave me with pamphlets with pictures of Jesus, then go start telling this whole story to the next sinner? Got to be less roundabout ways, Wong."

"No. That stuff, the crosses and all that, either it works because we *think* it works, or because the bad guys think it works. Or maybe there's some power everybody can tap into if they just know how."

"It's Scientology, isn't it?"

I said, "We never saw Krissy or Wexler again. Not even on TV. They moved out of town as soon as he got out of the hospital. Together. So, yeah, he was porking her."

He squinted at the sprawling skeleton of the mall and said, "This is the place?"

"You think a town could have *two* places like this?"

I ran my hands through my hair and stared at the darkened sockets on the decomposing mall where windows should have been. I heard the faint sound of a plastic tarp snapping in the breeze somewhere. "You scared, Arnie?"

"Should I be? Is this place haunted?"

"Nothin' so simple as that. I wish it were. You say it's haunted and you picture the ghost of some old lady wandering around aimlessly. The things that come and go around here, I don't know that they were ever human. Or maybe they just don't remember it. Try to imagine a Hitler or a Vlad the Impaler or even the nasty old man at the dump who steals people's cats and buries them alive. Now imagine those guys but strip them of all their limitations. No bodies, so they never die or run down or get tired. Give them all the time in the world.

Imagine that malice, that stupid black mass of hate drifting through eternity, just burning on and on and on like an oil well fire."

Arnie waited for me to go on. I didn't.

I was realizing all of a sudden how hard it was going to be to tell this next part. I thought it would feel good to unload the whole tale on somebody. But this next bit, this felt more like a confession.

I got out of the car and walked toward a concrete ramp, a would-be loading dock for a stillborn mall department store. I heard Arnie's door click and thunk behind me and knew he was following.

I said, "There was a girl here in town. She disappeared last year. It wasn't a big story, but you can look it up."

"Let me guess. You were the last person to talk to her."

I didn't answer. I climbed up the loading ramp and reached a doorway, greeted by the familiar smell of mildew and urine.

I tore aside a strip of yellow warning tape and stepped into the cool darkness within.

"Now, this is going to sound crazy . . ."

CHAPTER 10
The Missing Girl

IN THE SUMMER of the year after the Wexler thing, I realized someone was watching me through my television.

I could sense it, the way you sense someone staring at your back. A presence behind the screen, a pair of watching eyes.

I ignored it as long as I could, telling myself no one would want to secretly watch a single twenty-three-year-old on his couch eating Taco Bell bean burritos day after day (eighty cents apiece, two and a Coke for three bucks). But I knew better, of course. There were, apparently, parties who had a very good reason to keep eyes on me at this point, aside from my perfectly-sculpted Statue-of-*David* buttocks.

One night, with the television on some History Channel special about history's Top Ten Deadliest Warships or some shit, I turned away from the TV and toward the mirror on the far wall. I went to pull a brush through my knotted hair and froze.

I had glimpsed the TV, playing in the reflection over my shoulder.

A face.

It was an oddly shaped face, with features that were human but *off*. A Michael Jackson face, a face like a mask. Wide, too-large eyes, a nose not quite centered. Looking right at my back from the TV, plain as day.

I spun on the television, the hairbrush flying from my hand, a terrorized breath sucking through my teeth.

Back to normal now, the *Bismarck* getting sunk in a plume of smoke.

Again, I suppose most people would have feared a mental illness at that point. By now, though, mental illness would just mean some tests and a prescription. Big deal. No, my fear was of somebody actually watching me through my fucking television.

I told John about it and he came right over, as a best friend would. We cursed at the television for half an hour, then he dropped his pants and pressed his balls against the screen. Like he said, there was no need to change our routine. He suggested I get some rest, that I was stressed because of Jennifer, who had moved in and then moved back out again twice in the last six months. Then we drank and played PlayStation hockey until the sun came up.

That became my routine for weeks after, sleeping too little and drinking too much and playing too much hockey. Things started to spin out of control. Soon we were playing without the goalies, skating six on six and scoring games 74 to 68. Finally, when we started both playing on the same side (Red Wings) against an inept team controlled by the computer AI and winning the games 126 to zero, I knew I had hit rock bottom.

251

I also knew I was still being watched. I knew this was a bad sign, that things were moving again, that I had to get my head on straight.

I threw out the bottles and shaved my face and even considered cleaning the house. I started ironing my shirts again. Somebody mailed me a little bottle of what they claimed was holy water and I kept it on my nightstand. I hung a garage-sale crucifix from my front door.

Then, just after Christmas, things got weird again.

THE END BEGAN when I came home from work on a frigid Friday night. I was plowing my truck through the worst winter storm the area had seen in years, the world looking like the aftermath of God's sno-cone machine explosion.

I pushed in through the front door, snow melting off my leather coat. A prickly feverish sweat was breaking out all over me as my skin adjusted to the fifty-degree temperature difference between my living room and the night air outside. The wind shifted, the whole house creaked, there was a tinkling of ice chips flicking off the windows.

I had just left a nightmarish sixteen-hour, soul-numbing double shift at Wally's Video Rental Orifice. The night manager had claimed she couldn't get out in the storm and asked if I could please work for her, saying that she owed me big-time, that I was such a sweetheart and that if I ever needed anything, anything at all, just let her know. I don't think she meant that. But I put my head down and plowed through a one-thousand-minute, dead-quiet, customer-free battle against exhaustion and my urge to beat my coworkers to death. Now I just wanted to dry off and curl up in—

I saw something out of the corner of my eye that stopped me in midthought. I leaned back to see through the open door of my bedroom.

The drawer on my nightstand was open.

The drawer where I keep my gun.

My butt cheeks clenched so tightly that not even light could have escaped. I listened for burglar sounds. Dead quiet. I took a soft step forward, wondering if I could fake kung fu if I had to. I once saw Arnold Schwarzenegger kill a man in a movie by grabbing his head and twisting it until the neck broke. Was that difficult? Could a man do it without a lot of practice?

I keep the gun in a hollowed-out copy of the Koran that John got me for Christmas. And there the big book was, tossed on the bed, open and gunless. Nothing else disturbed. *They actually checked my Koran to see if there was a gun inside.* I knew I was dealing with a sick son of a bitch.

I stepped carefully and quietly through the bedroom doorway, glancing this way and that. Nobody here. I checked under the bed, the sheets still smelling faintly of girl even now, months after I'd spent my last naked night on them with Jen. Or maybe it was my imagination.

Either way, you should probably change those sheets . . .

Nothing under the bed. I checked the other rooms in the dark little house, stepping slowly across the carpet. Somebody had called, I noticed, the little red "new message" light on my answering machine blinking in the darkness like a time bomb.

Nobody here. I wandered toward the answering machine, my gut full of snakes. Snow melted in my hair, a droplet of ice water running into my ear. I reached up to brush it back—

And sucked in a shocked breath.

I had found the pistol.

It was in my motherfucking hand.

I dropped the gun like it was made of bees. It bounced onto the sofa and I stared stupidly at it, then stared even more stupidly at my empty palm, fingers pink from the cold. What the—

Now that you ask, it's a whole ten-foot walk from your heated truck to your front door. Why does every inch of exposed skin feel windburned? Why do you seem to have a pint of snow in your hair?

There's that feeling again, that fluttery feeling of mental weightlessness, like the times when you wake up in the dark, on the hood of a car, a bottle in your hand, no idea what day it is, some girl shouting at you in Arabic.

I tried to collect myself. Tired. Tired like a zombie. An overworked zombie, one who got hired as a salaried assistant manager at a zombie video store, only to find out "salaried" just means he doesn't get paid for overtime. My skull pounded, my knees were ground glass. I sat heavily on the sofa and stared vacantly at the little beads of water standing on the sleek, chrome surface of the Smith. I glanced at my watch. Right after midnight.

Okay. You got off at eleven. You came straight home. It's a twelve-minute drive, figure maybe twenty for the weather. You came right in. So where did the other half hour go, Dave? Did you maybe take a detour and shoot your boss?

No, if I'd shot Wally's manager Jeff Wolflake, I wouldn't have deprived myself by repressing the memory, would I?

I picked up the gun and ejected the magazine. Still heavy with bullets. I sighed with relief. If I had indeed stopped by Jeff's house to murder him, I would have emptied the gun. I reinserted the magazine.

This was no way to start the weekend. I punched the "play" button on the machine, listened to the message. It was John. It finished, I hit "play" again, listened closer, then hit "play" again. By the fourth time I was pretty sure that John had said, "bag full of fat."

I decided to try once more:

Beep.

> "Dave? It's me. Amy's missing and we got what looks like a bag full of fat here. It's weird. And I mean 'bad' weird, not 'clown' weird. It's almost midnight and—I guess you're not home yet. Or maybe you're in bed. You're not in bed, are you? I know you haven't been sleepin'. Are you there? Wake up, David. Wake up. Okay, so you're not there. Call me when you get this, I don't care how late. Oh, and when you come over, watch out for a jellyfish. See you."

Beep.

Bag full of fat. I picked up the phone and dialed John on his cell. One ring, and then—

"I TOLD YOU TO LEAVE ME THE FUCK ALONE, VINNY!"

"John?"

"Oh, Dave. Sorry. I had been having a heated argument here on my phone and then I hung up in disgust. Then when the phone rang I just assumed, without checking, that it was the person I was having an argument with, so I just blindly shouted insults into the phone. How embarrassing."

"I'm getting sick of that one, John."

"Are you on your way over?"

"I, uh, got somethin' going on here."

"What's your thing?"

"I've got a—"

I paused, made a decision.

"—batch of brownies in the oven. I don't want them to burn, or else they get gummy."

"Yeah, they'll stick, too. Did you grease the pan?"

"Uh, yeah."

"Good. Anyway, Amy is missing and the scene is weird as shit. The situation has a real Lovecraft feel to it. Though, you know, if you come over it'll be more of an Anne Rice situation. If you know what I mean."

"Who's—"

"Because you're gay."

"Who's missing, John?"

"*Amy*, Dave. A-M-Y. I think my signal's breaking up—"

"I don't know any—"

"Amy Sullivan? Big Jim's sister?"

That stopped me.

Memories of an entire day spent locked in the back of a truck, sick with fear and boredom. A promise made to a dead man. I hadn't thought of that day in months.

"Oh. You mean Cucumber."

"Do you not feel the need to learn people's real names, Dave?"

"We called her that in school. She was in that Special Ed class, always throwing up for some reason."

A silent pause on John's end.

"You know, like a sea cucumber? They're these eels that—"

"Anyway, Dave, we're at her house now. The cops, too. How soon can you be here?"

How about June?

Even that wasn't going to be enough time to piece this together. I pictured Big Jim on his back, a crimson stain across his neck and the floor like a scarf. The dead man had circled back into my life somehow. I glanced at the gun, trying to make it all fit and failing.

"What'd you say on my machine? Bag full of—"

"I can't hear you, you're breaking up. Just get here as soon as you can, we gotta go deal with this flying jellyfish thing."

A pause on my end now.

"What?"

"See you in a few—UNDER THE CABINET! NO, THE CABINET! THE—HERE, LET ME—"

Click. Dooooooooooooooooooo . . .

I disconnected and did what I usually do after hanging up with John: sat in dumbfounded silence and contemplated all of the poor choices in my life.

I shrugged out of my coat, pulled off my Wally's shirt, smelled it, then hung it back in the bedroom closet.

As I pulled on a new shirt I grabbed a bottle of caffeine pills from my desk drawer. I washed down four of them with a warm, half-empty bottle of red Mountain Dew I found on the kitchen counter.

I pulled on the coat and, after a moment's hesitation, dropped the Smith & Wesson in the pocket, the weight pulling the whole left side of the coat down on my shoulder. I felt like Bruce Willis.

Is it just me, or is the barrel slightly warm?

I pushed through my front door and plunged into the cold, but made it no farther than the doormat.

Footprints.

The thin blanket of white across my front lawn should have been clean, save for a single trail of prints from the driver's side of my Bronco to the spot I was standing. Instead, there was a haphazard circle of tracks in loops around my front yard, then trailing off around the back of the house. The trail of prints emerged from the other side and eventually led to the front porch, where I was now.

I stepped off the porch and into the crunchy snow/ice shell that coated the ground. I leaned down, squinting against the storm. Boot prints, zigzag treads. I had a very dark, very lonely realization.

The prints were mine. All of them.

I glanced around in the darkness, seeing nothing but sparkling flecks of ice passing through shafts of street light. I made the silent decision to never tell anyone about this, and got in my truck.

Missing time. That's what they call it. John's got a missing girl, you've got a missing half hour. Shit.

I twisted the ignition to life, thought for a moment, then pulled the Smith from my pocket. I pressed the button on the handle and again popped out the magazine. I made a little pouch in my lap with my shirt and, with my thumb, flicked out the bullets one by one. I counted as I went, hoping—no, praying—that none were missing.

One, two, three, four . . .

The bullets were, uh, unusual. The heads were silver with a bright-green plastic tip. A guy had mailed me these, anonymously. They were lined up in rows in a heavy white cardboard box, a tag on the inside typed with bullet jargon I didn't understand. Something about "proximity fuses" and long serial numbers. John and I test-fired them, shot a pumpkin and watched it explode into flaming bits of blackened shell.

. . . seven, eight, nine . . .

That's what people do these days, they mail me things. Crystals. Shrunken heads. Doctored pictures of angels in clouds and of bleeding statues. Bundles of blue-lined notebook paper full of scrawled, rambly stories about Satan sending hidden messages through mass e-mail subject lines. I've gotten chunks of stone stolen from haunted castles in Scotland, hunks of supposedly cursed black volcanic rock from Hawaii, dried Bigfoot turds. John and I have this reputation now and everybody wants to help.

. . . thirteen, fourteen . . .

I let out a long breath.

One missing. One.

THE TWO-STORY *PSYCHO-STYLE* house "Big Jim" Sullivan had lived in with his mentally handicapped sister would have cost most of a million dollars had it not been run-down and located in a weedy, desolate section of town a block from a chemical-drain-cleaner factory. I guessed the sister, Amy, lived here by herself now that Big Jim was deceased under circumstances I am rarely able to adequately explain in mixed company.

I swung my headlights into the yard of the Sullivan *Psycho* house, between John's 1978 Caddie (bearing the cryptic license plate, CRKHTLR) and an Undisclosed cop car that was parked along the road.

It really was a shitty, shitty neighborhood. The next house over looked empty. The neighbor down the hill on the other side was an expanse of white parking lot dense with a wormy pattern of tire treads. It led to the ass of a huge building lined with a row of roll-up garage doors. The rear trucking entrance of the Drain Rooter plant. There was a single semi backed into one of the stalls, bearing the logo of a cartoon plumber with a big red "X" through him. I wondered if the bathroom drains at the plant ever got clogged to the point that they had to call in a plumber and, if so, if anyone was able to make eye contact with the guy while he was there.

Through my windshield I saw two figures in the front yard. One was John, arms jammed in his pockets, the stiff breeze sucking away cigarette smoke in a horizontal stream. The other was a bear of a man who I recognized as John's uncle Drake, still the only cop in town with whom we were on a first-name basis. Drake spoke, John nodded, the ember of his cigarette bobbing slightly in the darkness. John was growing a beard. He had been working construction off and on after having been fired from Wally's a year before. He had gotten caught bootlegging DVDs and giving them away to customers, right there at the store. Not selling them, mind you. Giving them away. I climbed out and was immediately assaulted by the freezing wind.

The looming house didn't just look empty, it looked abandoned. It had gone downhill since I had last seen it on the night I tried to return Molly. Peeling paint, filthy windows, no tire tracks in the driveway.

Big Jim had looked after Amy in the years since their parents died, but I don't know who was looking after her now. Apparently nobody, since she was lost and all. Man, was it cold.

Drake looked shabbier than I did, the man inflated in full cop uniform and parka, complete with one of those navy blue fur earflap hats. The blue blimp of weariness.

"Wong," he said, with a lack of enthusiasm usually reserved for door-to-door Mormons.

I don't enjoy our little encounters either, Drake. But here we are, just the same.

"How long's she been missing?"

"Don't know. Neighbors saw her dog walking around the neighborhood this afternoon. They tried to return her and couldn't get anybody at the door. I came by and saw the—"

A skipped beat, a quick glance at John.

"Uh, I thought you guys might know something."

Tell him about your missing half hour!

I pushed that thought from my head and pretended it had never been there. Besides, I knew exactly where I had been during my missing time. Walking around and around my yard in circles. Right? Perfect sense.

John flicked away his cigarette and crunched toward the front door. "Drake is gonna see if Amy is at a friend's house. She knows the Hoaglands, so he figures maybe she got scared off by the, uh—"

The two of them shared a second "let's not discuss this now" glance.

Opening the door to his cruiser, Drake said, "You find anything, you call my cell, right? Then I handle it." Making it clear that we weren't cops, that a missing person was still a cop thing no matter what weird-assedness lurked inside the house.

John tipped a finger at him and said, "Yep. Thanks for calling us, Drake. You're the kind of man a man wants when a man wants a man."

Just inside the door was a little entrance hall with a black-and-white tiled floor, like a chessboard. There was a plate-sized chunk of tile missing near the wall and the bare wood had been painted in to match the pattern with what looked like Magic Marker and Wite-Out.

I glanced into the kitchen.

I froze.

Molly.

No question it was her. A red Labrador whatever, fast asleep on the linoleum. I had the same thought from when we glimpsed her outside the abandoned mall that night.

No way. Just another dog of the same breed. Surely.

"Oh, that's her," said John. "Go look at the collar. Got the address on there and everything."

"But . . . how?"

"Don't know. She answers to Molly, though. Or at least as well as she ever did."

I wanted to go look closer but, I admit, I was afraid to. Something coming back from the dead was almost always bad news. Movies taught me that. For every one Jesus you get a million zombies.

"So the dog we saw explode, that wasn't Molly?"

"Don't know."

"Or maybe that was Molly and this is, what, an imposter?"

He shrugged. "You should have seen me, when I saw her here. I freaked out."

"You think she's responsible for what happened to Amy? Maybe she, I don't know. Ate her."

"Withhold judgment until you see the jellyfish."

I didn't ask. I reluctantly turned my back on the resurrected dog and we pushed through a living room with a green couch that looked to be from 1905. Up a stairway, into a darkened hall. There was an unlit light fixture on the ceiling and one of those old brass switch plates on the wall, the kind with the black buttons. I punched the top button, nothing happened.

John stepped carefully down the hall, squinting into the darkness. He turned and said, "No, that doesn't do anything. Hand me the flashlight."

"You didn't tell me to bring a—"

He held a hand out to shush me and ducked into a side door. We both stepped into a large room that, in the dim glow from the window, looked like a library of shelves mostly filled with odd shadowy shapes that were not books. I saw what looked like a bundle of cobweb hanging from the ceiling and reached out to brush it aside—

POP!

A shower of blue sparks flashlit the room. A bone-rattling electric sting flared up my elbow.

The fixture on the ceiling blinked once, twice and then bathed the room in light. About a foot in front of me was what looked like a bundle of wet string, suspended in the air by nothing at all. It didn't look so much like a jellyfish as a man-o'-war, the slimy things that float lazily on the ocean surface and let their stringy tentacles hang down in the water. The creature drifted slowly up to the ceiling, toward the light. It wrapped its tentacles around the fixture and, to our utter astonishment, began frantically humping it like a puppy on a bunny slipper.

The lights dimmed, finally flickering out to darkness again. The room was silent except for the soft rattling of glass vibrating against metal with each of the creature's spastic thrusts.

"You ever seen one of those before?" John whispered, somewhere in the darkness. Above us, a little blue spark jumped from one noodly tentacle to another with a soft *FZZZZT* sound.

"I like to think I would have mentioned it if I had."

"Uncle Drake shot it, didn't seem to bother it much."

"He could see it?"

"Yeah. It's real."

So that put it in the category of the mutants at the mall, and not the wig monsters and shadow people. I'd have to make a spreadsheet somewhere to keep track.

And don't forget, just because Drake can see it, doesn't mean another stranger from around town would. Lots of chances for a cop to get infected in this town. Ask Morgan Freeman.

Now there was another train of thought badly in need of derailing.

I said, "You got your lighter?"

John flicked his Zippo and cast a pool of weak yellowy light around us. I glanced around, saw that only a couple of the shelves contained books, worn paperbacks with white fold lines. Tolkien, C. S. Lewis, somebody named Terry Pratchett. *Babylon 5* novelizations. The first, third and fourth *Harry Potter* novels. Jim must have figured three was the most he could allow without risking turning Amy to witchcraft.

The rest of the shelves were crammed with stuffed animals and junk. I saw a row of plates on little wire stands painted with the faces of *Star Trek* characters.

The creature on the ceiling didn't react.

"Well," I said, letting out a tired breath, "I was hoping it would attack your hand. I guess it's the electricity it likes and not the light."

John slapped the lighter off and said, "I thought about opening a window and just shooing it outside."

"Uh, that doesn't seem like such a good idea." I thought for a moment, wondering vaguely if I had remembered to turn on the porch light back home. "Can it, like, pass through walls?"

"It hasn't yet."

"Follow me."

We stepped out into the hall and I closed the door behind us.

"Okay," I said. "As long as nobody ever opens that door . . ."

"Right. We'll put a sign on it or something," John said, the first problem solved. "The *weird* thing is down here. Check this shit."

We went across the hall and he gestured into an ancient bathroom, complete with enormous cast-iron tub and a yellowing vanity with a cracked mirror. A steady stream of drips plunked from the faucet. A pair of scissors were wedged under one of the knobs, presumably to keep the valve from running freely. He punched the switch and the light flickered on, this one apparently unmolested.

On the floor was what looked like a clear plastic bag, filled with a marbled pink-and-yellow substance, about the size of one of those giant bags of dog food. There was writing on the side in an odd, angular font.

John said, "That lock was bolted from inside. We had to jimmy it to get in here. Water was running in the sink, toothbrush laying on the counter with dried toothpaste on it. That window is painted shut, so there was no way out of the room. So she was in here and then she wasn't. And she never left the room. Right?"

The lock was one of those little slide bolts like you'd see on old public toilet stalls. The "jimmy" of the lock had been accomplished by smacking the door, probably with their shoulders, until the little metal loop on the door frame popped out of its screw holes. I leaned over and inspected the window. It looked to have been sealed long before I was born. Not that it made a difference; even if Amy had locked the door and crawled out of the window for some reason, dropping fifteen feet or so to the ice below, how would she have gotten the window shut behind her?

"Can you think of a way that somebody could get that door locked from the other side? Like if they snatched her and then slid the bolt closed behind them?"

What you're asking, said the irritating voice in my head, *is whether or not you could have done it, Dave.*

Bullshit. Forget that. I was sure my bout of missing time, during which a bullet had left my gun, had nothing to do with this person who suddenly went missing on the same day. Two completely separate events. In fact, the event I was repressing was probably Amy coming to my house to borrow a bullet, and me calmly handing it to her.

"Sure," said John, "you could probably get the bolt slid in there with the door closed. Give a guy twenty minutes, a bent wire coat hanger. Let him try it about forty times. What would be the point, though? Just to mess with us?"

.I nudged the bag on the floor with my foot. Dense liquid, a bag of sludge. He said, "The writing on the bag, that's a weight, right?"

"I guess." I leaned down. "Forty-four-point-four-two kilograms." I scratched my head. "I give up."

"You, uh, think that's her? In the bag?"

"Ew. No, let's assume not for now. That's just gross."

"You think the jellyfish ate her?"

"Bones and all?"

"We're talking about a tentacled flying lamp fucker, Dave. What are you prepared to call unlikely?"

I stepped out of the bathroom and wandered down the hall, passing a room stacked with cardboard boxes and some broken chairs. There was another door that had been nailed shut, that seemed to lead out into midair.

John said, "You know what that is? They used to build these old houses with doors that just led to a big drop, to fool burglars. They'd label that door TREASURY or something like that. The guy busts through the door and finds himself falling straight down. They'd put spikes or something down there. They used to call it an 'Irish Elevator.'"

"Or, John, they tore a balcony off here years ago and just never bothered to take out the door."

We passed a bare guest room that smelled of dust and old varnish, then at the end of the hall came to a door standing open with a band poster stuck to the inside, a group called VNV Nation.

I leaned into a chaotic bedroom, crammed with furniture and carpeted with wrinkled clothes. Posters on every wall, bands I'd never heard of and one of a shiny Angelina Jolie as the Tomb Raider. There was a very nice laptop computer, a Mac, propped up on a pillow on an unmade bed.

"The computer," I asked, "it was like that when you got here?"

"Yeah. We didn't touch a thing."

On a nightstand off the bed there were four empty plastic bottles with orange juice labels and half a dozen brown prescription bottles. There was a box of Froot Loops on the floor, open.

I saw all this from the doorway but didn't step inside. I felt dirty just for peeking my head in, invading this person's space. John pushed past me, though, and I realized we probably didn't have a choice if we were serious about this. Cops do this every day, rifling closets and digging through your dildo drawer. I noticed the bed laptop was on, ironically in sleep mode, a single power light glowing along one side. I tapped the space bar, the screen fading up from black to reveal a white screen with blue text scrolling down.

"Check it out." John nodded his head toward a dresser, one drawer half open, a couple of bras trying to escape. Atop the dresser sat a little black object, round and not much bigger than a roll of film. A lens in the center.

"A camera," I noted.

"It's one of those wireless camera deals," he said. "For the computer."

"What, like a webcam?"

"Yeah, or something."

"Was this Jim's old room?" I asked, for some reason having trouble picturing Amy "Cucumber" Sullivan knowing how to shop for and use computer gadgetry. Before I encountered her while trying to return Molly a few years before, my only memory of Amy was from the Life Skills class at the Pine View Alternative School for Mentally Fucked Students where I had spent my senior year. She always had her head down on her desk, asleep, to me just a mop of red hair spilling over bony forearms.

I think I only heard her say a dozen words my whole time there and most of them were "please move or I'm going to puke on you."

John muttered, "dunno," in the way that people do when you ask a useless question that deserves nothing more. I glanced around and saw a second camera, a square one, sitting atop a shelf on a department store sortawood computer desk across the room. It wasn't aimed at the chair in front of it like you'd think a webcam would be, but sideways, toward the hall.

"This camera is aimed over at the door," I deduced. I looked up and saw a ceiling fan with a set of four little canister lights aimed around the room. Taped to one canister was another of the wireless cameras. "And another one," I said. "Aimed right at the window. All the entryways covered, like a security system."

A little tingle of nervousness rose in my gut for reasons I couldn't wrap my sluggish brain around.

"Okay . . ." John said, moving toward the laptop. "You know, I just thought about something. Why would she lock her bathroom at all if she lived here alone? You'd just poop with the door open, right?"

I nodded and said, "So maybe she was already scared. If this were an episode of *Law and Order* we'd have a nice shot of her getting abducted right on camera. And yes, before you give me that look of yours, I do realize whatever happened, happened in the bathroom and not in here. She didn't have a webcam in her bathroom, did she?"

"I want you to think about what you just asked."

John picked up the laptop and sat down with it in the computer chair.

"Well," I said, "she could have caught somebody in the hall."

That feeling again. It was like a faint alarm in the back of my skull, like the creeping sense that you've left something important at the house just as you're leaving for vacation.

He's going to look for the webcam stills on there.

So? I shoved my hands in my pockets and wandered around the room, wondering how our getting first-look at the evidence would fuck up a prosecution should this turn out to be a run-of-the-mill kidnapping and murder, flying jellyfish notwithstanding. Welcome to Undisclosed.

I fingered a loose key in my pocket that had apparently fallen off the key ring. I ran my other hand through my hair, which was drying in a mushrooming Carrot Top spray. I said, "Is there any place open in town that sells that red Mountain Dew? I had some today, it's like somebody melted a box of cherry Jolly Ranchers and stirred in some crack cocaine. Is that one convenience store on Lexington a twenty-four-hour deal?"

John wasn't listening. He was studying the flat monitor on the laptop.

FOR THE WEBCAM STILLS. TO SEE WHO TOOK AMY.

My mouth was going dry, my heart thumping just a little too fast. The caffeine, probably. I leaned over John's shoulder and saw the phrase MY CAT PEED ON MY BED at the top of the screen. It was a series of broken lines, each beginning with a name in brackets. I knew the format.

That's a chat log. She was on there when she got up to brush her teeth. Then somebody took her, maybe somebody or maybe some thing. But the key is she knew they were coming, somehow. She knew because she set up cameras so she would have evid—

OH, SHIT.

I stood bolt upright.

WHAT ARE YOU GOING TO SAY IF THAT'S YOU ON THE CAMERA, ASSHOLE?

That thought—like a hammer to the balls. John actually glanced over at me and I suddenly felt naked. I tried to remember what my body language looked like when I was at my most casual and innocent, then the whole effect was ruined when I pulled my other hand from my pocket and saw what I was holding.

It was the key to the toolshed in my backyard.

I normally keep it on a nail near my back door. I do not normally keep it in my pocket.

Oh, what did you put in your toolshed, Dave?

I held up a declaratory, "I've got an idea" finger and said, "Wait."

John turned to me, his sudden attention like a heat lamp on my face. I realized I had absolutely no idea what I was going to say next.

"We shouldn't, uh, we shouldn't do that yet."

"Okay. Why?"

"Because, uh, I think it would be better if—look, we have one witness to this thing, right?"

"We do?"

"Yeah, the thing. The jellyfish thing. I mean, we're up here dicking around with computers and that thing could take off in the meantime, go back to wherever it goes. The computer isn't going anywhere."

John glanced into the hallway and said, "You think it talks?"

I looked him straight in the eye and said, "I think *you* can make it talk. Whether it wants to or not."

He scratched his chin thoughtfully, then said, "I'll need a toaster."

"I saw one in the kitchen. Here, hand me the laptop, you go beat some information out of that slimy bastard."

John strode out of the room with newfound purpose. I took his seat. The desktop wallpaper on the laptop was a photo of Orlando Bloom, in full *Lord of the Rings* costume. I waited until I heard John's footsteps clomping down the stairs before I started clicking through folders, as fast as my fingers would go. Sweating a little now, my heart thumping against bone, my knee bouncing.

I eventually stumbled across a folder full of little icons that came up as grainy camera stills. I clicked on one, saw a dim image of a lump sleeping soundly under the covers of the bed. Another, same thing. A third, a shot of an empty bed. A fourth, the lump again. There were hundreds.

I heard John stomp back up the stairs and I glanced toward the hall, not returning to my task until I heard him open the library door.

I was stuck. Deleting the pictures was out of the question. I was not covering up a crime here and at that point I fully intended to tell John if it somehow turned out I was the culprit we were after. But I wanted him to find out *my* way. I needed time to figure it out, to process it, to have some control over the revelation. I needed options.

I cut the whole folder of pics and moved them to the most obscure location on the hard drive I could find, inside a subfolder of a subfolder of a subfolder of a subfolder of printer drivers. I closed up the computer and leapt out of the chair, suddenly a bundle of nervous energy.

You've got to get home. You've got to see what's in that toolshed.

Yes. That was right. I plunged a hand into my pocket and clutched my car keys so tightly they etched marks in my palm. I strode out and down the hall, feeling a cloud of guilt around me like a stench. I passed the library just as John came flying out, slamming the door behind him.

He said, "That dangly bastard knows something. I can read it in his body language."

I said, "I have to go."

"Why?"

"I just have to run home. I'll be back."

"Yeah, you probably gotta check on the brownies. Can you get me some rubber gloves while you're at it?"

"Okay."

He opened the library door again and said, "Where'd you go, *asshole?*" then once more closed himself inside the room.

I fled.

DRIVING AGAIN. DEFROST heat blowing on the windshield, ice crystals melting on contact with the glass, swept aside by the wiper blade a second later. Wheels floating under me, no traction in the ice. The roads all to myself.

If there's a body in your toolshed, say, of a skinny, retarded redheaded girl, just come clean. To John first. Tell him exactly what happened. No need to plan beyond that. Gotta see what's there first. Gotta see . . .

I turned on the radio, looking for something to blast the thoughts out of my head, hoping the moist nighttime air would blow in a rare non-country station. I ground through static and static and static, then recoiled at the shrill, choking sound of a man apparently squealing through a crushed larynx. After a moment I realized it was simply Fred Durst and the group Limp Bizkit—Shitload's favorite band. They're the ones who invented the musical technique of feeding a list of generic rap phrases to a goat, then reading its turds into a microphone over heavy metal guitar.

This was the song "Rollin'," judging by the fact that the chorus was Fred saying that word several dozen times. Perfect. Rollin', rollin', rollin' . . .

Just tell the truth, that's all I had to do. Just tell the truth. If I did it, I did it. I blanked and found a dead girl. No cover-up, no hiding the body or any of that. Just face the consequences.

Sure. Your "dad" will fly up and he'll tell you not to talk to anybody and he'll make noise about your record of mental illness and use lots of big words. You'll get off, because he's damned good at getting people off, and instead of jail you'll get a stay in an institution smelling of ammonia and spoiled food, surrounded by people mumbling to themselves and smearing feces on the walls. It will work. It worked for the Hitchcock thing. No, don't think about that. Keep rollin', rollin', rollin' . . .

From the darkness behind me, a very cold and very bony hand reached up and closed around my mouth.

The hand squeezed, pulling my head back.

I expected a blade on my throat.

Instead, something long and cold and wet and twitching slid across my neck and down my shirt.

I cranked the wheel and clawed at the hand. The truck skidded in the snow, jumped a curb and smacked a newspaper machine with a crash of ruined metal and glass. With a jolt, the front tires blasted through a snowdrift and landed back on the street, wheels spinning, grabbing, then spinning again.

The thing on my neck snaked across my collarbone and slid down my shirt, something with the texture of a slug or a leech but long, its tail snaking up from my chest around my collarbone. A cool, twitching, itching weight on my skin.

I screamed. I admit it. I blew through an intersection blinking yellow lights, I stomped around with my feet until I found the brake and went into a powerslide, the rear of the truck trading places with the front.

"No, no. Keep driving," said a soft voice in my ear. "She will not bite if you keep driving."

Fuck that. Fuck that idea like the fucking captain of the Thai Fuck

Team fucking at the fucking Tour de Fuck. I stomped the brake and cranked the wheel. We skidded to a stop and—

I screamed again. A terrible, pinching pain pierced my breastbone. It was unreal, like my bones were sprouting razor blades. I screamed again and grabbed at the monster on my chest. A hand reached around and snatched my wrist with a quick, clean move.

"Be calm," said the voice. "Drive. Just drive. She will leave you alone. If you drive."

I didn't even hear this, not really. I got my other hand into my pocket and clawed free the pistol. A pain ripped through my chest again, unimaginable, like being torn in half. It crippled me. All of my limbs stopped in protest.

The hand reached up from the backseat and very slowly took the Smith. Once more he said, "Drive. Just drive."

The pain relented. Huge gasps of breath tore in and out of my lungs. I squeezed my eyes shut, opened them again, and eased my foot onto the accelerator. I tried to look down at the thing that had me, its tail sticking out of the neck of my shirt. It had inch-long stalks all along its back, each ending in what looked like a small black eye. Several of the stalks tickled my chin as it wormed its way around, the end of the creature resting over my shoulder, squirming gently back and forth on the leather of my jacket. I heard the figure behind me shift on the upholstery, as if it was sitting back in the seat. I drove into the night, desperately trying to remember where I was going. I felt a drop of some kind of liquid crawl down my belly.

I tried to say something cool, wound up stammering something like, "WANNA YOU WANNA WEENIE ME?" The end kind of trailed off in a shrill, choking warble.

"Just be calm. You're doing fine. Now tell me what you were doing before I made myself known."

"Who—who the fuck are you?"

"My name is Robert North."

"Congratulations. Now who are you and what's this fucking thing you—"

271

"Please answer my question. Where were you going in such a hurry?"

"Home. Why? What's it to you? What's happening tonight?"

I reached up and adjusted the rearview mirror to see in the backseat. It was just a man, thin, in his thirties. Brown hair, buggy eyes and a beak-like nose. Looked sort of English, but no matching accent. He spoke robotically, with difficulty. It's the way some deaf people talk, not able to hear their own inflection. He was wearing a white, furry woman's hat, what looked like a blue Wal-Mart vest with a little plastic toy sheriff's badge tacked to the breast.

He nodded toward the rear of the vehicle, where the stereo speakers were. "That man, in your, whatever you call it, your communicator. Does he need help?"

"What?"

"He sounds wounded. Does he need your assistance?"

"You're not from around here, are you?"

"Why do you not respond to my questions directly?"

"That's just Fred Durst. On the radio. He's not talking to us."

"Are you certain? It sounds as if he is crying out while someone is strangling him."

"I know. That sound is entertainment to many of us. It's called a 'song.'"

"I know songs. But—I thought they rhymed."

I looked back again and saw the man was holding my gun by the barrel, studying it with detached curiosity. He had never held a gun before.

I said, "I'm turning off the radio so we can hear each other. Look." I very gingerly reached out and clicked off the power button. "Okay. I'm driving home. I live there. Can you tell me who you are, and where you're from? Or even better, who sent you?"

"I'm from right here, so far as you know it. Who sent me means very little right now. Why you are travelling home with such urgency, in these conditions, is of great importance."

"Did I kill the girl?"

"I do not understand the question. My interest is only in you and in your desperation not to answer my question. I assure you that your own safety depends on your honesty."

The thing on my chest began pulsing gently, making gulping twitches.

Okay, this bullshit has got to end. I'm neither brave nor reckless, but this was simply pissing me off too much.

"I'm going to reach out again," I said, "to make an adjustment to the heat in here. Okay?"

I very slowly and nonthreateningly punched in the cigarette lighter.

"Now," I said, "I am going home to check something. In my tool-shed. The, uh, the little building behind my home where I store things. Okay?"

He stayed silent for several seconds. A quick glance in the rearview showed a very grave expression on a bony face bathed in shadow and flickers of passing streetlights. The look of a man who's going to have to put his dog to sleep.

"Fascinating."

"What?"

I glanced down at the lighter. The slug on my chest slowly curled its tail around, coming to rest along my neck and earlobe. It gave a little shiver.

North stared off into the passing night and said, "They harvest insects here, do they not? For their honey? Do the bees know they make the honey for you? Or do they work tirelessly because they think it is their own choice? Have you never noticed that, after hearing a new word for the first time in your life, you'll hear it again within twenty-four hours? Do you ever wonder why sometimes you'll see a single shoe lying along the road?"

A single tear rolled down his cheek. It occurred to me that the man was batshit insane.

The lighter clicked. My heart leapt with anticipation and I realized, with disgust, that the slug thing could feel the change. It twitched and fluttered as if it were feeding off the excitement.

Or the increased blood flow.

I shifted my hands, the left on the wheel, the fingers on my right resting on the knob of the lighter.

North didn't seem to notice me plotting my escape, but said, "I am at a loss. I have been watching you for some time, but there are great gaps in my knowledge. You know, I observed a man who masturbated until he bled. Did he want to do that? And you, when you were alone you—"

I yanked the lighter free, the coils orange with heat. I slammed on the brakes and cranked the wheel with my left hand. With my right I jammed the lighter onto the lump in my shirt where I guessed the creature's head would be with a sharp *hiiiissssss.*

The slug thing shrieked and thrashed wildly inside my shirt. The truck spun and tilted up on two tires for a sickening moment.

The truck fell back down on four wheels with a thud. The lighter tumbled to the floor, a streak of orange in the darkness. A small yellow flame danced around a hole in my shirt where I had singed it with the lighter.

I grabbed around for the slug thing and for several terrible seconds I felt its teeth brushing against my skin, jaws working, struggling to grab on. I wrestled it free and suddenly I had it tight in my hands, slimy and writhing, slipping under my fingers. It had a little circle of tiny teeth, each curled and needle-sharp, like fishhooks. There was a thin, strawlike appendage emerging from the center, about as long as my finger and whipping around, flecking little droplets of blood.

I took one hand off it and opened the driver's-side door. I flung the flopping thing out into the snowy middle of the street.

I spun around in my seat and saw Mr. North pawing around the floorboard, the gun nowhere to be seen. I threw a wild punch at his face. North flung himself back in an effort to dodge it and gave me a shot at the gun, laying half under the seat below me.

I threw my torso back there, my feet kicking around at the windshield. In a scramble of elbows and hands I grabbed the pistol and twisted my body around. I jammed the barrel under his chin.

We sat like that for a long moment, both of us breathing puffs of

274

steam as the icy wind poured in the open door. I thought I could hear a soft thumping sound, our slug friend trying to deal with life in a world of ice.

"Okay," I breathed. "Okay, okay. This thing I've got pointed at you, you know what it does?"

He nodded, said, "I believe I have an idea, yes."

"And have you ever heard the old human saying, 'I want to shoot you so bad, my dick's hard'?"

"I have not. But I believe the context makes its meaning clear."

"Shut up. Don't move."

I crawled back into the front seat, keeping the sights on him until I dropped my legs out of the driver's-side door and stood up into the wind. I looked around the street for the squirming monster. It had crawled all the way to the sidewalk.

I crunched over toward the creature, lifted a boot and stomped on it. I grunted random curses under my breath as I pounded the thing, again and again, hammering with my boot heel. The slug exploded in a spray of brown and red. The red blood, I assumed with disgust, was mine. I kept stomping, little flecks of ice spraying with each impact, until the monster was a wet, twisted stain.

I kicked the shredded remains into a sewer grate nearby, then stomped back toward the truck. Sweat freezing on my face, my nose running freely. My teeth were clenched, my hand squeezed on the gun so tight I could feel the pulse in my palm. From a few feet away I could see that the back door of the truck was open now and when I got there I was not surprised to see that North was gone. I slammed his door. I got in. I drove home.

I SAW JUST one other vehicle while I was out, a snowplow. I passed a cop in a convenience store parking lot, messing with the chains on his tires. He shot me a look as I passed, like I was insane for even leaving the driveway in this mess. I had to pull over once and go over my windshield with my ice scraper, the wipers unable to keep up with the storm.

I pulled alongside the road by my house and left the engine running. I crossed the yard, the network of footprints now just soft craters under new snow and ice. I clasped the toolshed key in my left hand.

You have an alibi. You were at work, all day. Alllllll day. Right?

Sure. Yeah, that's right.

But who knows when she actually went missing. It could have taken days for anyone to notice. Even if it was last night . . .

I was in bed last night. Eleven P.M.

Were you? Can you account for every minute you think you were asleep? There's one period when you distinctly remember being a pirate, raiding a cruise ship full of naked women. Could you have been up and prowling and imprisoning a girl in your toolshed?

No. No way.

Maybe you had her tied up out there all day and you came home and decided you finally had to get rid of your plaything? Or put it out of its misery? So you came in and got your gun and—

I suddenly pictured the answering machine, on the little table by my front door. John had called, the red light blinking, slowly.

Slowly.

The new-message light blinks fast, like a strobe. The machine tonight was signaling a saved message. One already played.

No. I'd remember.

Would I? I thought of last summer, a month after Lopez and I broke up; she showed up at a bar where John's band was playing. I had drunk, oh, probably seven hundred beers. I wound up back at her place, a rented house she shared with some other girl. The night was a lost blur. I remember sweat in my eyes, my own breath blowing back to me off her neck, damp sheets. And a fly. This fly that kept buzzing and landing on my back and my neck, tickling me, waking me up again and again through the night. The rest is lost. Days later it gets back to me, through one of Jennifer's friends, that I had gone on a drunken, tear-filled rant about how Hell was waiting for me and there was nothing I could do to avoid it. I said it was bullshit, that Jen had made it up to make me look stupid. But had she? How would I know? Some memories bury themselves so, so deep . . .

And just like that, flashes of memory came pulsing in, like forgotten fragments of a dream.

You do remember. You remember rushing into the house and digging out the big book from the nightstand. You yanked the gun free and plunged out into the cold—

With the key clasped in my hand, I crossed the yard, continued around the house. The trail of prints that led back there were gone now, the space between the houses a wind tunnel that seemed to burn my ears right off my head. The Andersons lived next door; they were in Florida. The next house over was vacant, a Realtor's FOR SALE sign buried under snow in the front yard. A single gunshot, carried by the wind? Who would call the cops? You wake up and you're not even sure you heard it.

In the backyard now, dimly lit by a dusk-to-dawn light off my back door. Just enough light to see the pool of pink slush right in the middle of the snow. A metal wire tightened around my gut.

Did you actually feel sorry for yourself a few minutes ago, having to live your life in an institution or jail? That's an actual girl's actual blood, Dave. She was warm in her home and ready to curl up in bed and next she was wrestled away or knocked cold. What do you remember? You remember the flare of light and the gun jumping in your hand, then digging around the snow for the brass casing and not finding it, night-blinded from the muzzle flash, ears ringing with the sound. And just like that night with Jennifer, you knew it was the last thing you wanted to do but still you did it and did it and did it. You never stop, Dave.

I reached the door and tried to wedge the key into the frozen padlock, my fingers shaking. I dropped the key once, twice, then wrapped the frozen lock in my palm to warm it. Finally I got the key in and twisted it and popped the lock free.

A burst of fire in the darkness, the sharp crack of a gunshot, night blindness, panic, frozen breaths, blue canvas—

I pulled open the door, scraping it along the frozen ground. The piano wire around my gut tightened again and I thought I would have been sick, had I eaten anything.

I have this tarp, a blue one, one I always used to keep my firewood dry before I ran out of firewood. Right now it was in a loose roll along the gravel floor of my toolshed, above another frosted stain of cranberry-colored slush. There was something wrapped in the canvas, something the size of a body, something I knew *was* a body, rolled up like—

A murder burrito!

—a gutted deer in the bed of a pickup. I could have confused this for a slain young deer, in fact, had there not been three pale fingers extending just over the edge of the canvas.

I turned away, stepped outside, put my hands on my knees.

Breathe.

Slow, deep breaths. I stood upright, let the steam rise past my eyes, my soul making a run for it. Knees felt like Jell-O. I lay back against the door frame of the shed, then felt it sliding against my back. My ass was cold suddenly. Snow soaking in. I was surprised to see I was sitting, legs splayed out in front of me, no strength to stand.

You guys know my sister, who's back home at this moment. In that big, old house.

If one of you makes it out of this instead of me, I want you to look in on her, make sure she's taken care of.

She ain't never been on her own.

I want you to promise me.

In the end, the people riding in the back of that beer truck couldn't protect her. They couldn't protect her from me.

There was no question in my mind I had done it. I didn't want to do it, to be sure, but I had done it just the same. And the thought, the gargantuan thought that swallowed me the way the impossible idea of eternity will swallow me upon arrival in Hell, was that nothing would ever, ever, ever be right again.

Christ. The weight of it.

No shit, asshole. That's why you have to act. She's dead, you're not.

Think. Do you know what they do to guys like you in jail? The river isn't frozen over yet, just take the body and dump it, cut off the head and the hands and dump it. This isn't your fault—

No. I wouldn't do that. I had a vision of friends and family—and she had to have family, somewhere—living the rest of their lives not knowing what happened to Amy Sullivan. No, they deserved to know. They deserved to know I did it and to see me strapped to a table with a needle in my arm.

I made myself breathe. One step at a time, that was the only way to handle things after they spun out of control. Step one: breathe. Step two: stand up. Go inside the shed, take a look, make sure it's her—

Oh, hey, that's right. You might have a whole collection of corpses stacked around here—

—then go to Amy's place and tell John. Just tell him, no bullshit. Then call Drake and show him the body. Tell him the truth, tell him I blanked out and there she was. Let's face it, if I'm this dangerous it's better that I be locked up. For everyone's safety.

I climbed to my feet, put my hand on the door—

Okay, fine, just go in and unwrap her and face this thing, just face what you did—

—and closed it. I snapped the padlock shut, then trudged inside the house.

CHAPTER 11

By the way . . .

LOOKING BACK, IF I had gone in and seen what was in the toolshed, I would have put a bullet in my own skull one minute later.

CHAPTER 12

Amy

I FOLLOWED MY own tire tracks as I made my way back through town. I kept the dome light on and threw nervous glances behind me every four seconds or so. At Amy's house I found John hunched under the hood of his Cadillac. I walked past him, the horrible news coiled inside me like one of those chest-bursters from *Alien*. I said, "Your battery dead?"

"I hope not." I noticed a set of jumper cables coiled in the snow around his feet. Hooked around one elbow was a knotted string of what looked like Christmas tree lights.

"Christmas is coming *late* for that motherfucker. As soon as I find it. You got my gloves?"

"Uh, no."

"Okay . . . can I have a brownie?"

He caught a glimpse of my face as I passed. He stood upright, alarmed. "Dave? What's up? Did you change your shirt?"

"Put that stuff back. I, uh, think I got it figured out."

"What? You do?"

I stepped into the warm house, thinking this was going to be another of life's little awkward conversations. I absently rubbed the cold from my fingers. I heard John approach the door and suddenly ideas hit me, quick and desperate. Panicked wild fastballs of thought.

I could tell them it was an accident.

Yeah. You can make it work. You can march people up to testify about the time you severed an artery in your arm trying to carve a pumpkin. You can pull the emergency room records from the time Jennifer had to rush you to get half a cup of candle wax scraped off of your scrotum. There was the hot glue-gun incident. People would believe it, would see that you're not a murderer but are merely an incredible dumb-ass. You see, officer, I was driving past the house and I observed through the window what appeared to be some kind of shaved baboon, apparently escaped from a nearby circus. The animal was clearly thin and malnourished, which I believed made it an even greater threat to the inhabitants of the home. Naturally I produced a weapon and subdued the creature with a single gunshot. Now, interestingly, it was at this moment that my penis accidentally fell out and I found myself—

CRUNK. CREEE-UNK.

Above me.

Creaking floorboards.

I stopped, held my breath, listened. The wind? Above me, a door clicked shut.

I stepped quickly and softly toward the stairs, eyes on the darkened doorway at the top. I glanced back at John, the startled look on his face

282

told me he hadn't invited any company over. I pulled the Smith from my coat and pointed it up the stairs.

Come on down, fuckers. Come on down. Come see David on the worst day of his life, destined for forever in jail or worse, still with fourteen bullets left to spend. Whatever you are, you picked the goddamned staircase on the wrong goddamned day.

Come on down.

I heard another door open, then close. Are the most dangerous creatures the ones that use doors or the ones that don't?

I eased myself up the stairs one at a time, softly. My feet hit the creaky wood floor of the hallway. Every door in the hall was closed but one, the bedroom. The library seemed like the logical one to check first. I quietly cranked the brass knob until the door clicked free. Nothing but darkness. I tried the light and it came right on.

No jellyfish.

I backed out, took a step and tried the door on my right. The bathroom. No need for the light. I could see right away that the room was empty and—*look at that*—the fat bag was gone.

Toward the bedroom now, the gun in front of me in both hands, arms rigid, like the turret on a tank. The old sensations again, blood pumping past my ears, sparks flying in my brain, that cool sweat again. My clothes must have stank of it.

Something moved in the shadows.

A thin figure, almost as tall as a man.

A gray torso, like a rhino.

It saw me and froze.

A trickle of sweat crawled down my forehead, landing as a burning speck in my left eye.

Holy shit! It's a shaved baboon!

Through the sights of the pistol I saw a young, very thin and pale girl draped in a gray University of Notre Dame sweatshirt that she wore like a dress.

I said, "Oh! Amy! Hey!"

An avalanche of relief buried every thought in my mind.

Amy took several steps backward. She was holding a toothbrush and was nervously rubbing the bristles with her thumb as she retreated toward her door. Her other arm ended in an empty sleeve.

"Hi," she said, in a too-loud squeak. "Can I, uh, help you?"

"No, no. It's fine. We were just worried about—"

I made a huge mistake. I reached out, casually, I thought (it's hard to come off casual with a gun in your other hand, I guess) to take her arm. I had to see if it was her, if she was solid.

I wrapped my fingers around a very solid and very real forearm, but then she pulled away and when I went to catch the spot where her hand would be, I grabbed only air.

She ducked back through her bedroom door and slammed it shut. I looked stupidly down at my empty fingers and realized two things:

Amy Sullivan was alive, and she no longer had a left hand.

"Wait! Hey!" I said, screaming and pounding on the door while wielding a handgun, in exactly the way an armed rapist would. "It's me!"

"Okay!" She said as I heard something scoot across the floor and jolt the doorknob. She had braced the door with some piece of furniture, probably the chest of drawers.

"No! It's fine! I'm not armed! I mean, I'm armed, but not in a bad way. We've been looking all over for you."

"I'm here!" She said in the artificial-sweetener tones you'd use to soothe a rabid dog. "You can leave!"

I stuffed the gun in my jacket pocket and leaned toward the door. "Hey, where have you been?"

Nothing from inside. I could hear her talking faintly in there, like she was mumbling to herself. Poor kid.

I wandered back to the stairs, one question answered with several dozen new ones replacing it. First off, who did I kill?

John came up the steps, saying, "Who was talking up here?"

"I found her. She was in her bedroom."

He glanced that way and said, "Damn. You're good. So, she was here the whole time? Like, folded up in a desk drawer?"

"I don't know, John. And I don't care. She wants us to leave."

"You sure?"

"John, we have to talk."

I turned him around and we stepped down into the living room, just in time to see red-and-blue lights pulsing across the bay window. We reached the front door just as Officer Drake pushed his way in.

"What's the deal?" Drake said, brushing snow off his shoulders. "We got a nine-one-one call from Amy saying there was an armed man in the house."

DRAKE WENT UPSTAIRS to calm Amy down while John and I waited down at the diner-style chrome-and-green table in her kitchen. John pulled out a small package of what looked like tobacco and asked, "You think she'd mind if I smoked in here?"

"John, I killed somebody."

As the words hung in the air I had a split second to wonder how many people had ever uttered them and still gone on to live happy lives.

I said, "There's a body in my toolshed."

"Is it Jeff Wolflake? Does that mean the manager job is open?"

"No. A guy showed up, a guy but maybe not a guy, on the way home. He put a thing on me like a slug or something and asked me a bunch of questions."

"And you killed him."

"No, no. He got away. I killed some other person, completely unrelated to that guy apparently. I was just putting that out there."

"Okay, so who is it?"

"Dunno. I didn't check. I remember doing it, though, sort of. I shot them with the Smith. There's a bullet missing and everything. I remember doing it but I don't remember *wanting* to do it."

John eyed me carefully. He looked away and pulled his hair back, then tied it with a rubber band. He pulled out a small box and shook out a rolling paper, then opened the tobacco.

He said, "You think it was like the thing with Danny Wexler? The demon thing we ran into at the mall?"

At the mall, he says. Like we saw it folding pants at American Eagle. *I serve none but Korrok.*

"You know," he said, "the way they could take hold of people, move them around like puppets? Then you shot me?"

"You gonna bring that up again?"

"You think it was Jennifer you killed?"

I hadn't thought of that.

"No, I . . . I mean that was amicable, right?"

He didn't answer.

I pulled out my cell phone and pulled Jennifer Lopez's number off my speed-dial menu. One ring. Then three. Then six. Eight. Finally . . .

"Mmmm . . . hello?"

I knew the voice. Sleepy and drunk, sure, but hers. I broke the connection.

"She's there," I said.

"Well, that's everybody you know."

"But if it was . . . that *thing* controlling me, it wouldn't be somebody I wanted dead. It would be somebody *it* wanted dead."

Holy shit, this is madness.

John said, "So it could happen again?"

I opened my mouth to respond, then closed it. I actually hadn't thought of that, either. John started laboriously sprinkling tobacco onto a cigarette paper.

I said, "She may not want you to smoke that in here, John."

"Eh, I gotta make them ahead of time anyway. I get the urge to smoke, I don't wanna sit and mess with it. You get the tobacco too clumped in the middle and it doesn't stay lit. Rolling is a pain in the ass."

"You know, I think you can buy them now where they're already made." He started rolling the thing, unrolled it, tried again.

I lowered my voice and leaned in. "Hey, John, when I saw Amy, I think her *hand* was missing."

"Well, yeah. It's been like that for a long time. She was in an accident."

"Oh. And she lives here alone?"

"Yeah. Why?"

"There's nobody who, you know, comes by to take care of her?"

John studied me for a moment, then said, "Well, Dave, I think one of the neighbors comes by to put out food and water in a bowl for her. Let her out, you know."

"What?"

"Nothing."

We snapped into silence as Drake appeared in the doorway, Amy barely visible behind him. She squeezed around him, the girl now fully dressed in street clothes and even shoes. She wasn't going anywhere, not at this time of night and not in this weather. Must be her hosting outfit. She had chin-length copper hair that looked like she had cut herself. Something weird with her eyes. The wrong shade of green.

On top of all that, she still didn't have a hand. As she came into the room I averted my eyes from the handless arm that didn't swing quite right when she walked, then realized it was becoming obvious that I was averting my eyes, so I looked at the scarred stump where her wrist ended, then it became so obvious I was looking at it that she actually folded her arms, her wrist disappearing behind her shirtsleeve. She glanced past me and said, "Hi, John!"

"What's up. This is Dave, the one you saw in your hallway. He's not a psychotic killer or anything," he lied.

"Oh, I know. We went to school together."

Yes, Amy, let's reminisce about the Pine View Behavior Disorder Program. "Remember that time they had to restrain schizo Bobby Valdez and one of the aides broke his arm! Hahahahahahaha!!!"

I said, "Hey, I'm sorry about the, you know. Almost shooting you. We just have some questions and we'll leave you alone."

She looked at me with the too-long stare of someone with no social skills or diminished mental capacity. Like John said, I knew she had

287

been in an accident as a kid. Brain damage? Was that her thing? I thought about the pills on the nightstand.

She held her gaze as she said, "It's okay!" She waved a dismissive hand in the air and smiled. "So are you guys with the police or what?"

Damn, you're cheery. Does one of those pill bottles contain Vicodin, dear?

"Oh, no. John knows Officer Drake here and he just called us to help out. We're, uh, sort of experts on—"

"Oh, I know," she said brightly. "I've read about you guys. There's this Web site I go to, like a News of the Weird sort of thing. I think you guys are mentioned in every other article. The thing with Jim, when Jim, well, you know. I did a lot of reading. Do you want something to drink? I have, um, cranapple juice and . . ." she spun and opened the fridge, ". . . and . . . water. And pickles."

"No, thanks."

She closed the refrigerator and took a chair at the table opposite John and me. Drake said, "She doesn't remember a thing. She lost about twenty hours, as far as I can tell."

I said to her, "What's the last thing you remember?"

"Brushing my teeth. I had the brush in my hand, I had gone downstairs to let Molly out so she could pee and roll around in the snow. She likes that. I came up and was putting toothpaste on the brush and then, the light was off. All of a sudden, just like that. The toothbrush was back on the shelf and the water was off and I don't remember anything in between. Then I heard somebody in the hall and it turned out it was you."

"And you were on your computer, right? Before you went in?"

Hesitation. Hiding something?

"Yeah, I think so."

"Nothing strange happened?"

"When?"

"That night, the nights leading up to it."

"No," she said, studying my face as some bad liars do, always seeing if you're buying it. No practice, this girl.

"Are you sure?"

On cue, John stood up and moved toward the door, saying, "I'll be right back." I turned to Drake and said, "Well, no crime committed here, right?"

He fixed me with a dismissive glance that told me he was the cop and that he'd leave when he damned well felt like it and not a moment sooner.

Amy said, "I'm okay, really. Just tired."

Drake and I stared that way long enough for him to establish that he would indeed leave but that his dick was still well bigger than mine. He grabbed his hat off the counter and pulled it over his ears. "Yeah, I gotta get back." To Amy, "But you tell *me* if something like this happens again. You got that?"

Emphasis on "me."

"Yeah. Thanks."

With the slam of a door and a puff of frigid air, he was gone. I experienced the unique awkward silence that comes from being alone in the room with someone for whom you once made up a humorous nickname behind their back. Sea cucumbers, you see, vomit up their guts to distract predators, and around the third time she threw up on somebody's desk we . . . well, I think I mentioned that earlier. Anyway.

She studied the scratched surface of the kitchen table and drummed her fingers. My eyes bounced around the room, from the calendar on the fridge (monkeys posed in Victorian costumes) to the stump where her hand should be to the sleeping dog on the floor apparently indifferent to both its own resurrection and the return of its master, to the package of plastic picnic cups on the counter and finally back to Amy's missing hand. What the hell was taking John so long?

Amy leaned forward and said, "So, like, what's the creepiest thing you've ever seen?"

I thought, then said, "I was at Cracker Barrel the other night. And two tables over from me, there's this group of four old women. They're all wearing big, red hats. Red hats and purple coats. I keep glancing back at them and they're all there just drinking coffee, not eating. So I get up to leave, right—"

"You were eating by yourself?"

"Yeah. So I get up to leave, right, and I pay, and on the way out the door I see another table and there's another group of women there in red hats. Purple jackets."

Amy thought about this for a moment, then said, "Weird."

She looked down at the table, then said in a low, conspiratorial whisper, "Have you ever heard of spontaneous combustion?"

"Yeah."

"I have a friend, Dana, who was in the grocery store one day, and her arm, like, bursts into flame. Just like that. Just her arm. And she's screaming and waving her arm around and around, flames shooting everywhere. Finally the cops showed up and arrested her."

"Arrested her? Why did—"

"Possession of an unlicensed firearm."

A great, heavy silence settled over the room. She looked down at the table again, a smile playing at her lips, looking extraordinarily pleased with herself.

I said, "You know, in the Middle East a woman can be flogged for telling a story like that."

John burst in at that moment, carrying a plastic squeeze bottle that used to hold dishwashing liquid but now held a clear, thick substance that might have been mistaken for hair gel, though if you did you would likely never have the chance to mistake anything for hair gel again.

I stood up, John next to me. Interrogation mode.

"Okay," I began, "we know you knew something was going on. You knew something was coming and you had your room wired up to catch it on camera."

Long, long pause from Amy.

Finally she said, "It's happened before."

"Missing time?"

She nodded. "At least half a dozen times, that I know of. I'm sure it's more. Little things, starting probably two weeks ago but who knows, you know? I'd turn on bathwater, blink, and it's all over the floor, the tub overflowing in two seconds. Once I woke up in a different room, another time I was suddenly in bed, my shirt turned around, backward. I had been up watching TV and then a second later there I was, lying down."

John said, "And you never see anything?"

"No."

I said, "What do you think it is? UFO?"

"No, no. No. Sleepwalking, you know. Blackouts. I thought something with the medication maybe."

I'm sick of your lies, scumbag!

I said, "John?"

He pulled a saucer from a strainer in the sink. He squirted some of the fluid from the bottle onto it, then found a spoon on the counter.

He said to her, "Imagine something. A physical object."

"Like what?"

"Anything."

She actually smiled, amused, ready to play along. She pushed her hair from her forehead and I noticed that, tragically, her bangs were the exact length to fall right into her eyeballs. She squinted into an almost comical expression of concentration. The gel in the saucer began to bubble and rise, twisting and spilling upward like the wax in a lava lamp. At the top it slowly spread outward, like a mushroom. After a moment it held the shape of a tree, six inches tall, like one of those little crystal sculptures some old people keep on their shelves.

Amy was impressed. "How . . ."

"We have no idea," I said. "Somebody mailed it to me. Guy said he worked for an oil company and they found the stuff stuck to the end of a drill bit that had been about a thousand feet down. They thought it was lubrication or something, like they had a leak. Until the stuff killed one of them."

The tree was already beginning to melt and puddle back into a gel pool. John held the spoon just above it and said, "Yeah, it's pretty impressive that it can do anything at all, considering it's just a big *faggot.*"

The gel turned bloodred. The shape shifted, grew a hole in the center. Spikes emerged from the edges. Teeth.

"Ooh, you don't likes that, do ya?" John taunted. "I've seen gel that could make shapes twice the size of you. If you're so special why don't you go out and get a job, you pus—"

With a blur and a *clink,* half of the spoon was gone. The gel creature had it in its jaws, bending it and crunching the metal shard like a dog on a bone. A chair clattered to the floor and suddenly Amy was standing, arms wrapped around her abdomen.

"Just wait," John said. "It always calms down after a second." The color of the thing faded from crimson to pink and back to clear again. It eventually settled into a puddle, the chunk of bent spoon wading in the pool.

I said, "We got a whole collection of weird shit like this at home. The stories you heard about us? They're mostly true. This is what we do. We have a talent for it. We have seen shit that would fuel your nightmares. So you need to understand, Amy, that there is nothing you can say that will make us think you're crazy. But we need to know everything if we're going to help you. Do you want our help? Because weird things are happening tonight. Big, weird, stupid things."

She brushed her hair from her eyes, nodded, then said, "Okay."

"Talk to us."

She said, "The basement."

THE DOOR TO the basement was hidden behind a shelf. Not a cool pull-the-book-off-the-bookcase-to-make-it-swing-open Batman secret passage, but a regular old bookshelf that somebody had set in front of the slim door in the storage room to discourage strangers from going in. Strangers, or a thin girl without the upper-body strength to move a bookcase. It took John and me both to scoot it aside, even without a lot of books on the shelves.

Amy shoved open the door, then reached around in the darkness until she found a pull-string for a dangling lightbulb, the once-white string now a greasy brown.

Cobwebs.

Bare brick walls.

A smell like a pile of wet dogs.

I realized about halfway down the creaky stairs that we were letting the girl take point on our adventure into the dark basement and how utterly unheroic this was.

I reached out and, with a small move of my body, did something that would change my life forever. I gently moved Amy aside and stepped down ahead of her, putting myself between her and the shadows.

Cold down here. I saw little rectangles of white floating in the darkness to my left, ground-level windows buried under snowdrifts.

Around a corner I saw something long and jagged poking out of the darkness, like a tree branch. In the dim light my imagination went wild, seeing razor-sharp claws on the end.

I stepped around the corner, blinking to get some night vision back. In my adrenaline-charged state, I saw a monster, the "arm" ending in a squat body, covered with pointed plates like an alligator's back, tall legs like a grasshopper, jointed backward and sticking up in the air, giving the creature a "W" shape. The head had twin bundles of eyes, clustered like an insect, which wrapped around to the back of a narrow skull. The mouth was long and equipped with mandibles that ended in points as sharp as hypodermic needles.

I stared at the thing, blinking, thinking it would reveal itself to be, I don't know, a hot-water heater or something. Then I realized the monster-shaped shadow was, surprisingly, a monster.

Amy rounded the corner. I screamed "GET BACK!!!" and threw out a hand to stop her, catching her right in the face. I had the gun in my hand, yanking it free and firing in one motion, the sound deafening in the basement. I was sure the shot was wild, as likely to hit my foot as the beast.

The creature's shoulder exploded in a shower of yellow sparks. The extended arm flew off, tumbled to the ground, the jagged end aflame.

I kicked the creature in the chest, knocking it to the floor. I picked up the severed arm and clubbed the beast with it over and over again, screaming at the top of my lungs over the *thunk thunk thunk* of the beast's own limb smacking its crotch.

After a moment it became apparent that the monster was not fighting back. It lay there, its limbs splayed stiffly into midair, as if petrified. I gave it seven or eight more thumps with its arm and then dropped the limb on the concrete floor with a thud. I sucked in huge breaths of dank, moldy air, trembling.

John approached, looking down at the broken beast. He said, "It wasn't very agile, was it?"

"Guys . . ." Amy pushed past us. She squatted and picked up the monster, setting it on its feet again.

"It's not real, you guys. It's a model. A prop. Jim made it."

She balanced the thing on its feet, then stumbled past some strewn cardboard boxes and found another switch. This one turned on a fluorescent shop light overhead.

The creature was actually a lot more horrifying under the glaring lights. The other arm was curled at its side, with talons that looked like they could cut down trees. I could see my reflection in each of the hundred little bundled eyes, a kaleidoscope of my own very tired and pale face.

I said, "Oh. I'm, uh, sorry about that."

She turned to me, eyes bright, looking like that was just about the most entertaining thing she had seen all year. I looked the monster over. It was, at the very least, an astonishing work of creature art.

John said, "Look at that. At the arm, the tendons and all that."

I examined the broken arm on the floor, the wound ending in a frayed spray of torn bone and connective tissue. Big Jim had sculpted the inside of this thing, the musculature, tendons, bone, presumably organs as well. Impossible.

"He was into that stuff," Amy said. "He had all of those sci-fi magazines, and he used to have subscriptions to magazines about makeup and effects and all that stuff. Always mixing big buckets of latex. He wanted to do that stuff when he grew up. This one took him two months. He would come down here after work and just stay. I wouldn't hear him until early the next morning. Just hours and hours . . ."

She trailed off, the memories of her dead brother taking her mind elsewhere. It seemed like a bad time to mention that I thought it would take a six-man crew from Industrial Light & Magic to make a prop like this, on a budget of a quarter-million dollars. This was soy sauce craftsmanship.

Jim, you crazy fucker. I'm starting to think we could have been friends.

"Come on," she said. "Over here."

She went through a short doorway that John had to duck through, a corner of the basement that may have been a coal room decades ago. She knelt down and plugged in a yellow extension cord, bathing the room in a harsh glare of light. Two halogen work lamps stood on thin metal stands, illuminating a small work space including two folding metal tables and dozens of jars and tubes, dye and latex and plaster and every other thing. White five-gallon buckets were piled high in one corner.

Amy said, "He had boxes and boxes and boxes of sketches and notes. He used to write these science fiction stories, really bad ones. He wouldn't let me read them but I'd sneak looks and the hero would always wind up tied up and naked and at the mercy of these beautiful female alien princesses who would 'torture' him. Jim, you know, he kind of went a long time without a girlfriend."

She was kneeling over a stack of cardboard banker's boxes. She pulled the lid off one and brought up a series of sketch pads.

"He was doing something bigger, a novel or a screenplay. I'd tell him that they wouldn't let him do his own props and write the movie both. He said James Cameron did his own designs and models for the robot in *Terminator,* though. You know that scene in *The Matrix* where they've got a shot of Keanu reaching out to open a door and you can sort of see the reflection of the camera crew in the doorknob? Jim saw that the first time he watched it. Just a total expert. He had all these plans, always talking about selling the house and moving and . . ."

She shrugged, cutting off the words, I think, to keep tears from spilling out with them. She handed me a bundle of four or five art pads. I flipped through them, saw sketches of joints and muscles and hands and claws and eyes. I flipped further and saw something that caught my eye.

It was a group of men, walking with three beings that were not men. They were pure black, their limbs represented on the paper by heavy swaths of charcoal. Drawn like they were men made of shadow.

The men in the picture were in a small room, at a doorway. One of the dark creatures was reaching out as if to open the door.

I flipped more pages. I saw another sketch of a doorway; this one was familiar. I had just seen it an hour ago. It was the abandoned balcony door upstairs.

I glanced back at the broken sculpture and said, "All this, that thing back there, Jim said it was for a story he was working on?"

"He never talked about it. But I saw his notes. You know, after. He kept a journal with all that stuff and I had to sort through everything."

She wiped at her cheek with her sleeve and I felt like an ass for asking. We didn't ask another question, but she said, "It was parallel-universe stuff. Typical sci-fi, alternate reality and all that. I think his story was about the people on an Earth, a parallel Earth, you know, that was real close to this one and they were trying to build some kind of bridge between the two. Then they would . . . you know—invade."

"And that creature back there?" I asked. "How did that figure in?"

She shrugged. John said, solemnly, "I'm gonna guess that was the thing that tied him up so the naked alien women could interrogate him."

Amy laughed and I suddenly remembered why I keep John around. I glanced back again at the one-armed creature and said, "Let's get the hell out of here."

I COULDN'T HAVE known at the time, right? That maybe all of our answers were there, in Jim's stuff? That maybe he had pieced the whole thing together?

At that moment, on that night, I just wanted out of there. The rotten smell of guilt hung over every thought. Especially on the subject of Jim.

So, yeah, we clomped up the stairs and flipped out the lights. All of Jim's materials were thrown under a blanket of darkness, never to be seen by human eyes again.

I never went back down there, from that day until the day we burned the house to the ground.

BACK UPSTAIRS JOHN asked Amy if she had ever seen a jellyfish-looking thing around the house or a huge bag full of what looked like butcher trimmings. To my complete lack of surprise, she said she had not.

She also said that she had never caught anything on the webcams, that they were set to click on at the sign of movement.

"It's always just me rolling over," she said. "I move around a lot in bed because of my back and all that."

"The other times you went missing," John thought to ask, "how long ago was it?"

"It happened for sure Sunday night, then Tuesday night. Then last night, you know."

"Every forty-eight hours," John observed. "As far as we know."

"But it's not usually as long. The most time I had lost up until now was about six hours, from midnight until early morning. This is the first time I lost a whole day."

"Is it always around midnight?" I asked.

"Yeah, I guess."

Amy declined our offer to help her stay and sift through her webcam photos from last night. I was desperate to see what would show up but this was her bedroom and I suppose she had a reasonable fear of two creepy males clicking through shots of her dressing and doing the things girls do alone in their bedrooms. Lighting farts or whatever.

She promised to look through them and let us know. I told her that I was pretty sure I had moved the photos to a folder buried in printer drivers. On accident. John volunteered to stay the night and stake the place out, but Amy recoiled at that idea and said the night was mostly over anyway.

And so, feeling like men trying to work a jigsaw puzzle blindfolded and using only our butt cheeks to grip the pieces, we left.

I CAME HOME to see 3:26 A.M. on my wall clock. I turned on every light in the place, checking every room for any damned thing at all. I finally collapsed into a chair, thinking there was no way in hell I was getting to sleep that night. Too much adrenaline, too many nasty dreams waiting for me behind my eyelids.

I fell asleep.

THE ROOM CAME back into focus. How much time had passed? I tried to move my arms, found that I could not. Somebody here. Footsteps behind me. Tried to move again. Limbs not responding.

I've had this dream before. Just got to–

OH SHIT.

A thin face appeared, leaning down in front of me. Huge nose. My friend Robert North, from my Bronco.

He asked, "Can you hear me?"

I couldn't answer. I was paralyzed, a brain inside a statue.

"Blink your eyes. Blink if you can hear me."

I blinked, not to answer him, but to see if I could blink. I could. Is there a way to kill a man using only your eyelids?

He said, "Good."

He walked out of view, then came back and extended his palm to me. On his palm, something was moving. He held it up to my face.

A spider.

Huge, a body the size of a chicken egg.

Black legs with yellow stripes.

It looked to have been bred for war.

North offered it on the palm of his hand and said, "I want you to eat this."

I was able to move my lips enough to say, "Fuck you."

"I'm going to say some words. I need you to listen very carefully. Tractor. Moonlight. Violin. Clay. Thumbs."

This went on for several minutes, North rattling off dozens of words. Maybe over a hundred. He held the arachnid up, legs twitching.

"Red. Sandstone. Trombone. Stain. Linger."

And just like that, I was dying. I could feel a poison living in my body, shutting me down, rotting my guts, burning my veins. And there was only one cure—the thing in North's palm. Suddenly the spider was my salvation, the narrow, bright window out of this dark room. I gathered every ounce of strength and leaned forward with my head—my hands still numb and useless—and then I sucked the spider into my mouth with greedy lips. I chewed through rigid, wiry legs and felt a hot, salty fluid burst into my mouth when I bit through the body. I quickly choked down the bitter bundle of legs and gristle and—

I SNAPPED AWAKE and leapt out of my chair. Alone. Still dark.

The clock on the wall said 6:13 A.M. I ran a hand over my mouth, a lingering bitterness on my tongue. I whipped my head around, confirmed that I was alone.

That was a dream, right? Eating a spider? What the hell did that symbolize?

Look at the bright side. At least it's not a workday.

My phone rang.

299

I WOULD LIKE to pause for a moment, to talk about my penis.

My penis is like a toddler. A toddler—who is a perfectly normal size for his age—on a long road trip to what he thinks is Disney World. My penis is excited because he hasn't been to Disney World in a long, long time, but remembers a time when he used to go every day. So now the penis toddler is constantly fidgeting, whining, "Are we there yet? Are we there yet? How about now? Now? How about . . . now?"

And Disney World is nowhere in sight.

Thus, one of the many awful things I can admit about myself is that the two years I spent with Jennifer live in my mind mostly as a series of frantic, breathy memories. Clawing hands tugging off clothes, heartbeat thumping in my ears, fingernails digging down my back, salty tastes lingering in my mouth. It's biology. It's hormones. As time passes I can recall fewer and fewer of our conversations and I couldn't give you the details of our five most-fun dates (though I have a fairly graphic vision of how each of them ended).

If upon hearing this you pump your fist and wink knowingly, you can kiss my ass. She was a good friend to me. She put up with my bullshit and at times not even *I* can put up with my bullshit. But all that is gone and what is left is a big, black hole where the sex used to be.

The thing with Jen ended with a pregnancy scare. She had seen my world and didn't want to bring a baby into it. This led to some violent arguments during which I pointed out, loudly and in sprays of spittle, that if she got an abortion the fucking unborn fucking fetus would likely fucking haunt us—I mean literally haunt our home—until the day we died and possibly beyond. It turned out that was the wrong thing to say.

It also turned out the pregnancy was a false alarm but I was spooked after that, found myself backing off more and more, making excuses because, gosh, I gotta get up real early in the morning and it's gonna be a busy day with inventory and all that and I'm just not in the mood right now, Jen . . .

We slowly went hands-off after that, Jen thinking this had something to do with me not loving her anymore, though the loving part of me and the penis part of me rarely speak to each other. She cried a lot. She slept a lot. We argued a lot. She left.

So I had been off the sex wagon for six months as I stood there at the counter of Wally's Videe-Oh!, having dragged myself in for yet another unexpected shift on yet another frozen morning. It was going to be a bad day. The hormones come and go like the tide and some days it's no big deal and some days it's like being fifteen again. The other night a coworker had insisted I take home a movie called *Ghost World*, which turned out not to be about ghosts at all, but was instead some kind of coming-of-age story about a girl who, I noticed, had a fabulous collection of very short dresses. All I remember from the plot is two hours of Thora Birch's bare thighs.

But I digress. It had been my coworker Tina on the phone this morning, asking if I could cover her morning because, gosh, even though the roads have been scraped clean she hears there's supposed to be more snow today and she doesn't want to get trapped at work, and I'm just the nicest guy ever, she really, really owes me. Tina, by the way, is short and blond and bouncy and full of cheerleader energy. So I got dressed and drove in, cruising on those few hours of fitful chair-sleep. Tina is also engaged, by the way, with a kid. On days like this, Mr. Penis isn't big on logic.

How about . . . *now?*

I folded up this morning's newspaper and dropped it in the trash can at my feet. I had scanned it for news of a missing person, a manhunt, anything of the sort. Nothing. The front page was a shot of kids playing in the snow. The person in my toolshed was apparently not noticed missing yet, or they were such a total asshole that the town had gotten together overnight and decided that it was better left unsolved.

Three hours passed without a single paying customer. I looked down at one point and noticed the newspaper had fallen onto the floor. The day before we had put balloons up around the store for a promotion and during cleanup one of my coworkers had stuffed a balloon into the little trash can. Inflated. It literally filled the whole container, so that no more trash could be put in. This fascinated me for some reason. I heard the door open.

Officer Drake sidled in the door the way cops do, still in uniform. He sidled all the way across the floor and desidled near the counter. I found my hands clenching a nearby DVD case.

Tell me, Mr. Wong, you wouldn't happen to know about a guy from across town who went missing last night? Your name was written on the wall in blood and a pair of your gloves was left behind and we have video of you killing him.

Instead he said, "That's downright beautiful, isn't it?"

I had no clue what he was talking about. He turned and looked out the glass doors and nodded. Out there was the aftermath of the ice storm, a world coated in crystal. The little landscaping trees in the parking lot gleamed with branches of blown glass. It was still sort of dark when I came in and I hadn't noticed.

"Uh-huh. What's up, Drake?"

"Haven't been sleeping," he said. "Neither have you, from the look of it."

"Yeah."

He shrugged. "Eh, probably just need a new mattress, right? Maybe one of those machines that make soothing noises. Like the sound of a waterfall or a jungle, something like that."

"Jungle sounds?" I said, my face taking on great weight. "I don't think the jungle sounds would help me sleep. Reminds me a little too much of *Vietnam*."

Drake didn't laugh.

"Me, it's my little girl that's been keeping me up," he said. "She's four. Wakes up every couple of hours, crying about a doll. We come in and ask her about the doll and calm her down. So two nights ago, I'm walking past her room, she's not in there at the time and I see this doll. I never saw it before, a big china-doll lookin' thing, the kind with the glass eyes, big, puffy dress, you know. And it's sitting on the edge of the bed. I figure my wife bought it at a garage sale, because I ain't seen it before then. Then I walk back by and look in there, not two seconds later, and there ain't no doll there. Just an empty bed. I ask my wife about it, and she says she's never seen such a doll. Never."

"Yeah," I said, as if that shed some light on it. What did he want me to say?

"You figure out what that thing was, floatin' around in the Sullivan house?"

"I don't know any more than you, Drake. Just weird, that's all. This town, you know."

"You know there was a cop, a detective that went missing a while back? Name was Appleton? Black guy? Started ranting about the end of the world, then vanished like a puff of smoke?"

"I think I heard about that."

Drake said, "You know who was the very last person he interrogated before he went missing?"

"Me?"

"That's right. That's right. And they never found him."

Being a cop in Undisclosed is not a path to long-term mental or physical health, Drake. Check the suicide rate. And I'll tell you something else, too. The look I saw in the eyes of that guy before he went off the edge is the same look I see in yours now.

Out loud I said, "Why are you here, Drake?"

"I need a movie," he said brightly. "Gonna stay in tonight."

"Okay."

"Why don't you recommend something for me? Something fun."

I reached over and plucked the first movie off a pile of returns to my left. *Mulholland Drive,* some David Lynch movie I had never heard of. There was no anti-theft tag on the case of this one. Almost like we wanted it to get stolen.

"Here," I said. "This is a good one."

"It's something my kid will sit through?"

"Sure."

I rang him up and he sidled from the counter. Drake put his hand on the door as I picked up another DVD and let out the breath I had been holding. Then, just as he was stepping out into the cold, I heard myself say, "There wasn't anybody else reported missing today, was there?"

He stopped, and turned. He let his gaze stay on me for a moment before saying, "No. Why?"

He's gonna remember you asking when somebody does come up missing, you stupid fuck.

"No reason," I said. I recovered with, "Whatever happened to Amy, I didn't want it to happen to somebody else."

"Yeah."

He waited for a moment, like he had something else to say, but turned and walked out instead. My cell phone rang. Everybody had taken to downloading songs to replace the ringers on their cell phones but me; I just set mine to ring again. One less thing to worry about. I pulled it from my pants pocket and saw John's name on the display. I answered, "Hello?"

"I TOLD YOU TO LEAVE ME THE FUCK ALONE, VINNY!"

"You called *me*, John."

"That's right. Sorry. Have you seen the trees? Isn't it pretty?"

"That guy came back, John. The guy who showed up in my car last night. He came back and I thought it was a dream but I'm starting to think it wasn't."

"Did you kill him?"

"No, John. And thank you for asking me that over a cell phone."

"Speaking of which, did you find out about the you-know-what in your toolshed? As in, a name?"

"No, the dead body in my you-know-what is still a mystery. I have to get back to work. What do you need?"

"You gotta leave the store."

"I can't, I'm the only one here."

"Close the store, then. Close the store and get outta there."

"What? Why?"

"You'll see. Meet me at the safe house. Noon. You're not gonna believe this shit."

"THE SAFE HOUSE" was our code name for Denny's.

I arrived and saw John at a far corner booth, a bundle of papers in his hand, a pair of boobs next to him attached to a girl. This wasn't Crystal, the tall girl with the electric blue eyes and short hair and the peasant skirts, nor was it Angie, the sexy librarian girl with the dark-rimmed glasses and ponytails and capri pants. It wasn't Nina, with the criminally short skirts and green streaks in her hair, or Nicky the Bitch.

This one was Marcy. Oh, Marcy. Contrary to the wisdom of the gay men who run the fashion industry (who, coincidentally, prefer their female models to look like thin males), the hottest girl I ever saw in real life weighed probably one hundred and fifty pounds. And her name was Marcy Hansen. And she was John's girl. Rusty reddish-brown hair, about the same color as Molly's, wide cobalt-blue eyes that looked at you like you were the most important person in the world.

I sat, we greeted each other. Out of the corner of my eye, off to the left of Marcy's boobs, John waved around the papers and said, "You gotta read this."

At that moment I realized I was boob-staring and I took the papers from John. Marcy wore tan cargo pants and a skintight T-shirt that said, I SWAM THE NAKED MILE! Marcy was one of those girls who seemed to have an endless supply of stories that involved some kind of hilarious sexual misadventure and/or accidental nudity. I took the papers from John's hand. I studied Marcy's boobs carefully. I caught myself, again, and held up the papers to obscure the supple swell of her bosoms. The papers were a printout, a log of the chat Amy was on the night she got abducted last time.

"I saw Amy this morning," John said. "I stopped by to, you know, make sure she was still there. She was pretty freaked out, reading that."

I read, but didn't understand until the last third or so and, at that point, everything changed.

This, I thought, is the end. One way or another, this is gonna be the end.

CHAPTER 13
The Chat Transcript

* JOHNNY_5 HAS LOGGED OUT *

{faierydust} asshole
{MustacheGirl} Still there girl?
{faierydust} hes banned
{EVLNYMPH} dialup sux
{amy_sullivan} still here
{EVLNYMPH} anybody else lagging?
{faierydust} this is the creepiest thing ive ever done
{MustacheGirl} You should look out the window. See if there's lights.

{EVLNYMPH} stop with the ufo thing

{MustacheGirl} Have you thought about getting hypnotized? They can recall memories of those nights . . .

{amy_sullivan} no

{amy_sullivan} i don't even know where ppl go to have that done

{amy_sulllvan} sounds like a good way to get molested

{MustacheGirl} Almost midnight.

{EVLNYMPH} iam so freaked out right now i read a book about a navy ship that disappeared

{EVLNYMPH} they found it latr but the crew was all gone and some guys turned up hundreds of miles awy w/no memory

{EVLNYMPH} they think it was sum kind of time pocket or somethin

{faierydust} oh shit

{amy_sullivan} that was a movie. the philadelphia experiment

{MustacheGirl} Yes.

{faierydust} it had tom hanks. the expriment gave him aids

{MustacheGirl} The movie was based on a true story though.

{amy_sullivan} molly is staring

{amy_sullivan} she jumps up on my bed and stares at me til i take her out

{MustacheGirl} I assume the true story wasn't as interesting.

{EVLNYMPH} im putting on music the quiet is freakin me out

{faierydust} what if its like a wormhole or something

{EVLNYMPH} bob dylan. you gotta serv somebody

{EVLNYMPH} serve

{amy_sullivan} im taking molly outside BRB

{MustacheGirl} AMY!!! Are you nuts?!?!

{amy_sullivan} BRB

{EVLNYMPH} serve

{faierydust} wormhole. i just got the weirdest picture in my head when i thought of that. ugh. worms.

{MustacheGirl} Stupid dog. I'm literally on the edge of my seat and she walks away. This is hurting my butt.

{MustacheGirl} Ew. The cat peed on my bed.

{EVLNYMPH} serve

{MustacheGirl} She NEVER does that.

{faierydust} my science teacher says if all of the worms in the world came up to the surface the world would be buried 20 feet deep in them

{faierydust} he said there are 100000000000000000000-000000 sea worms in the ocean 10 w/ 26 zeros

{faierydust} they would flow around the streets like aflood

{EVLNYMPH} serve

{faierydust} there is a world like that i have seen it

{faierydust} people die choking on them

{faierydust} they are consumed from the inside out

{MustacheGirl} All of us find that exact same fate.

{EVLNYMPH} serve

* S_GUTTENBERG HAS LOGGED IN *

{S_GUTTENBERG} HEY GIRLZ!!!!!! I'M TYPING WITH MY COCK. CYBER?

{MustacheGirl} Our race was created as food for worms that do not die. Our eyes are as sweet as candy to them.

{faierydust} eye

{EVLNYMPH} serve

{faierydust} I

{MustacheGirl} None find life outside of the throat. His jaws are like a lover's embrace.

* S_GUTTENBERG HAS LOGGED OUT *

{MustacheGirl} None

{faierydust} I

{EVLNYMPH} serve

{MustacheGirl} None

{faierydust} BUT

{EVLNYMPH} K

{MustacheGirl} O

{faierydust} R

{EVLNYMPH} R

{MustacheGirl} O

{faierydust} K

{MustacheGirl} It is done.

{faierydust} i just blanked out what time is it KORROK THE SLAVEMASTER KORROK THE KNOWING KORROK THE WISE KORROK THE LIVING KORROK THE FAMISHED KORROK THE CONQUERER KORROK THE GIVER KORROK THE ALMIGHTY I SERVE NONE BUT KORROK

{EVLNYMPH} faierydust are you o

{MustacheGirl} She's food.

{MustacheGirl} //////////

{MustacheGirl} //////////////////////////////////

{MustacheGirl} //////////////////////////////////

{MustacheGirl} //////////

{MustacheGirl} //////////

{MustacheGirl} //////////

{MustacheGirl} //////////

{MustacheGirl} //////////////////////////////////

{MustacheGirl} //////////////////////////////////

{MustacheGirl} //////////

* MUSTACHEGIRL HAS LOGGED OUT *

I FOLDED THE pages and ran my hand over my mouth, unshaven jaw like sandpaper. Korrok the Slavemaster.

A blue eye in the darkness. Populations of worlds roil in his guts.

As much as I hate being right, I hate it even more when *John* is right.

Marcy said, "Isn't that just the weirdest?"

I glanced at Marcy, then at John. Keep in mind, these two had been going out all of ten days.

John said, "Somebody's got to stay with Amy tonight."

"Oh, and don't even get me started on her, John." I tossed the prints aside. "I mean, did you notice that she's not even retarded?"

Silence from John's end, then, "Was she supposed to come back retarded?"

"They had her at that school. Pine View. The alternative school, where they put the retarded kids."

"That would be the same facility where *you* went to school for a year?"

"Yes. Pine View."

A pause on his end, then, "Anyway, I was going to stake out her place tonight—"

"Good plan."

"—but, Steve called and he needs me and the whole crew on a job site. A chunk of roof caved in, from the ice they say—"

"John, you just made me close down Wally's so—"

"No, listen. Guess where the job is."

"Your mom's ass?"

"The Drain Rooter plant. Right next to Amy's house. We gotta be on site at five thirty in the morning."

"I don't get it."

"Neither do I, but they gave Steve all these requirements about who could go where, what part of the plant we could be in. Sounded weird, all of it. Plus, I really, really need the money. They're paying triple time. So can you stay with Amy tonight? See if anything horrifying happens?"

"John, did you read the chat log? Do you remember the—"

A glance at Marcy.

"—thing. In my toolshed? She's not safe with me, John."

Marcy's eyes widened. "You mean there's something in there *other than the dead body?*"

I closed my eyes and silently counted to ten.

"Dave, we've made it this far. What else are we gonna do, chain you up in your room? I got something else to show you. You see it, you're gonna want in on this. You ready?"

John unfolded a white piece of paper with a color photo in the center. A printout from a color printer.

"Camera still. From two days ago."

A grainy shot of Amy's bedroom. Good light, early evening. Amy standing right there in the center, arms held up, bent at the elbows, one foot lifted off the floor. Motion blur.

I said, "What is she *doing?*"

"Uh, I think she's dancing. But that's not the weird part."

I knew what the weird part was. There was a black shape behind her, standing there, in the form of a man. Like a body painted in tar, head to toe. The now-familiar image of a man who had been neatly cut from reality . . .

I closed my eyes.

Shiiiiit.

I said to Marcy's boobs, "What did Amy think?"

"To her," John said, answering for them, "it's just a picture of her in the empty room."

"How is that possible, John? It's ink on paper. Either it's there or it's not."

"Wouldn't you be surprised if I somehow knew the answer to that? Marcy doesn't see it, either. Just you and me. Anyway, I was thinking maybe you could put on a red wig and pajamas and pretend to be Amy. Sleep in her bed, see if they'll abduct you instead. Will you stay with her?"

Notice the subtle transition from "can you do it" from a few seconds ago to "will you do it." If I had jumped in and answered "no" to the first one, I'd have been saying I can't, it's impossible. If I refuse now, though, I'm saying I *won't* do it. I can, but I choose not to because I'm an apathetic asshole. Smooth.

Hmmm . . . what would Marcy's boobs do in this situation?

"Fine."

"And watch out for Molly. See if she does anything unusual. There's something I don't trust about the way she exploded and then came back from the dead like that."

"I gotta get back to work. Good to see you, Marcy."

I stood, she stood. She leaned forward and, to my utter shock, threw her arms around me and squeezed.

She sat down and smiled and said, "You looked like you needed a hug."

How about . . . NOW?!?

"Um, thanks." I stood awkwardly for a moment, then walked away. From behind me I heard her say to John, "Where was I? Oh, yeah. I ran outside and just then realized I wasn't wearing pants . . ."

I WENT BACK to the store and worked the rest of my shift because I'm a huge dork. Jeff came in at six, took one look at the storm that was salting the air and declared the shop closed for the day.

I stopped by the house to change and saw I had a package in the mail, a thick brown envelope, from an address unknown to me. Handwritten, blocky letters. Little kid writing.

I tore it open and found a pair of cardboard glasses with plastic lenses, a *Scooby-Doo* logo on the earpiece. A prize from a Burger King kids' meal. It said "GhostVision" in spooky letters on the side. I put them on, saw a faded cartoon ghost smiling at me. There was a Post-it note inside the envelope that said, "HELP IM A GOST LOOKER 2 MOO MOO MOOOOOO FUCKASS."

Nice.

I flung it in the passenger seat of the truck, then almost fell on the ice four times on my way to my front door. I knew I needed to shovel the walk before the mailman broke his neck.

Sure. The shovel's right back there in the toolshed . . .

ABOUT AN HOUR later I emerged from the hardware store with a brand-new snow shovel. It was getting late so I went straight to the Sullivan place.

Amy opened the door with the too-happy-to-see-me look I associate with crazy people and dogs. She wore thin wire-framed glasses—she didn't have them last night but I guess she didn't wear them to bed—and seemed to have put a lot of work into her hair. Jeans and bare feet with tiny red toenails. It made me cold just looking at them. I observed that she still didn't have a left hand.

"Hi!" she sang. "Come in!"

Molly was standing in the entryway, looking at me with utter disinterest. Amy turned around and gestured to me, said, "Look, Molly! David's here! You remember David!"

The one who made you explode!

The dog turned and walked away, making a sound that I swear was a snort of derision. Amy led me through the living room. The television was on, displaying nothing but the face of a white-haired old man staring quietly at the camera. PBS, probably. There was a picture on the wall, a black velvet Jesus painted in comic-book tones. There was only a lone table lamp in the room, which left about half of the space in shadow.

Of all the creepy places to spend a night . . .

She said, "You look tired! Your eyes are pink."

"Eh, I haven't been sleeping. Got a headache."

Feels like elves tugging on fishhooks in my brain . . .

"Be right back!"

Amy vanished into the kitchen, almost bouncing.

Vicodin.

I sat on the couch and glanced at the TV again, same old guy. Odd-shaped face. He leaned over, whispered to someone just out of frame, then looked back toward the camera again. Weird, because he seemed to be looking at me.

Amy bounced back in, a green Excedrin bottle in her hand and a red Mountain Dew bottle in the crook of her elbow. She nodded her

313

head toward the TV and said, "Cable's out. I hope you brought something to read."

I looked at the old guy, looking right back at me.

Oh, SHIT.

The screen blinked, went to black, then came up on MTV. Some reality show with teenage girls screeching at each other.

Amy set the bottle in front of me and said, "Hey, it's back! I got that cherry Mountain Dew. John said you liked it so blame him if it's not . . ."

It's not cherry, dear. It's RED.

"No, it's fine, thanks."

I studied the television. Nobody home but the screeching girls.

Amy said, "It comes and goes. John says that he saw a bunch of birds on the lines and they were flapping their wings but couldn't take off because their feet had frozen there."

Without breaking my gaze with the TV, I said, "To John, something being funny is more important than being true." I glanced at a grandfather clock that was ticking but was off by approximately seven hours.

The television blinked back off, switching to snow.

Amy said, "See?"

I said, "When the TV goes out, it's just snow?"

"Sure."

"Never anything else? Like—other programming?"

"No. Why?"

I shrugged. She couldn't see the old man.

By responding to her attempts at small talk with nothing but ambiguous grunts, I was able to drive Amy back upstairs to her room. I glanced at the grandfather clock . . .

12:10 A.M.

. . . realized again that it was utterly useless, then looked at my watch instead:

7:24 P.M.

This was gonna be a long damned night. I thought absently that maybe if Amy got taken at midnight again I'd be able to duck outta here and go sleep in my own bed. Nobody would notice.

There was a coffee table in front of the sofa and I noticed some magazines resting on a shelf on the end of it. I sifted through them. *Cosmo.* I picked up the top one and flipped through the pages. Topless woman. Another woman, naked, except for some whipped cream on her naughty bits. Two more pages, a naked man's ass. I had seen less nudity on Cinemax. I glanced up at the velvet painting and suddenly felt sacrilegious ogling naked models. I stuffed the magazine back in the coffee table and nodded an apology to Badly Drawn Jesus. I looked at my watch again.

7:25 P.M.

I leaned over on the couch and put my feet up. Like lying on a pile of felt-covered bricks. I wondered if I could set all of the clocks ahead to midnight, maybe fool them into coming early.

John and I had looked into the case of a Wisconsin guy who spontaneously combusted while driving his green Oldsmobile last year. We had one witness who claimed the flames formed a huge, satanic hand at the moment of explosion. We went up there, talked to a few people, came up with nothing. Eventually we get a call from a goth kid up there who was heavily into Satan worship. The kid said he had made a pact with Satan to kill both of his parents, then backed out of it when his mom unexpectedly bought him a video game console. The kid, as it turned out, also drove an olive-green Oldsmobile.

The avenging demon—or whatever it was—got the wrong car, barbecued the wrong guy. So they can make mistakes. They can confuse identities. The kid felt terrible about it and from then on spent every night on his knees, praying to God for another chance. For my own safety I pray that Brad Pitt doesn't do anything to piss off the dark realms.

Eyes getting heavy. A shadow moved on the far wall, probably from passing headlights in the street. My eyes closed.

Open again. Darker. Had time passed? Shadow on the wall again, elongated figure of a man.

No, just the tree outside the window . . .

Another shadow, next to it. Another, a forest of shapes. Moving, slowly. Was I dreaming this? Suddenly there was darkness right in front of me, pitch-black. Two orbs of fire appeared right in the center of it, two burning coals floating right there, inches away.

I flung myself upright, my muscles on fire with adrenaline. The room was normal again. There was still a lone shadow on the far wall, which was in fact just a tree backlit from the front yard. I walked over to it, reached out, and touched it. The shadow didn't react. That was good.

My watch:

11:43 P.M.

I pounded up the stairs and burst into Amy's room, terrifying her. She was on the bed with the laptop, legs crossed under her, a handful of what looked like Cheetos frozen halfway to her mouth.

I caught my breath and said, "How can you eat those and type on your computer? Don't you get that orange shit everywhere?"

"Uh, I . . ."

"Come downstairs. If this thing's gonna happen, it's gonna happen. But I want to be on the ground floor and near an exit."

"Why?"

In case we have to run screaming out of this place.

"And put some shoes on. Just in case."

11:52 P.M.

The television was back to regularly scheduled programming, the basic cable package of somebody who doesn't watch a lot of TV. No movie channels. I turned it off and turned to Amy, who was sitting stiffly on the stiff sofa, biting a thumbnail.

She said, "What are we waiting for?"

"Anything. And I do mean anything."

"Can I ask you something?"

"Sure." I stalked around the walls of the room, stopping to peer out of the big bay window. Not snowing, at least.

As long as you don't bring up your brother . . .

"You said yesterday that, like, most of what people say about you guys is true. So—there are some things that I've read that, you know . . ."

316

"What do they say, Amy?"

"That you guys have, like, a cult or something. And that Jim died because of something you guys were into."

"If that were true, would I admit it?" I glanced at my watch, something that was becoming a compulsion with me.

11:55 P.M.

"I don't know. You were there, though, right? In Las Vegas?"

"Yeah."

"And John says he didn't die in an accident, the way the papers said."

"What did John say?"

"He said a little monster that looked like a spider with a beak and a blond wig ate him."

Awkward pause. "You believed him?"

"I thought I would ask you."

"What are you willing to believe, Amy? Do you believe in ghosts and angels and demons and devils and gods, all that?"

"Sure."

"Okay. So, if they exist, then to them we'd be like bacteria or viruses, right? Like way lower on the ladder. Now the trick is that a higher being can study and understand the things under it, but not vice versa. We put the virus under the microscope. A virus can't do the same to us. So if there are things that exist above us humans, beings so radically different and big and complex that they can't fit inside your brain, we'd be no more equipped to see them than the germs are equipped to see us. Right?"

11:58 P.M.

"Okay."

"I mean, not without special tools."

"Okay."

"John and I have those tools. But just because we can see these things, these odd and weird and horrible things, it don't mean we can actually understand them or do anything about them."

"Ooooo-kay."

317

"Now let me ask you something. Big Jim, he was into some things, he had unusual hobbies. He built model monsters. But he knew some people, too, didn't he? Weird people? You know who I'm talking about, right? The black guy with the Jamaican accent?"

She said, "Yeah, I think we talked about that, didn't we? He was homeless. They found that guy and I heard he, like, exploded. I always wondered about that. Do you think Jim was into something, too?"

There was no short answer to that, so I said nothing. Amy looked at the floor.

11:59 P.M.

Amy said, "So what are we expecting?"

"Anything. Beyond anything."

She looked very pale. She wrapped her arms tightly around herself, rocking slightly.

"What time is it?"

"Almost time."

"I'm scared to death, David."

"That's good because there's lots to be afraid of."

I glanced at Badly Drawn Jesus, then pulled the gun from my pocket. On Judgment Day, I'd be able to proudly state that when I thought the hordes of Hell were coming for a local girl, I stood ready to shoot at them with a small-caliber pistol.

I said, "Keep talking."

"Um, okay. Let's see. Keep talking. Talking talking talking, doo doo doo doo doo. Uh, my name is Amy Sullivan and I'm twenty-one years old and, um, I'm really scared right now and I feel like I'm going to pee my pants and my back hurts but I don't want to take a pill because I think I'll just throw it back up and this couch is really uncomfortable and I don't like ham and—this is hard. My mouth is going dry. What time is it now?"

I held my breath, my heart hammering. Anything. Ridiculous, the idea that anything can happen. Impossible. But we should have known from the start. The Big Bang. One moment there was nothing and then, *BAM!* Everything. What was impossible after that?

318

12:02 A.M.

I glanced back at Amy. Still there.

"Well," I said. "They're late."

"Maybe they won't come with you here."

"Maybe."

"Or maybe their clock isn't the same as yours."

Another good point.

She asked, "Are you scared?"

"Pretty much all the time, yeah."

"Why? Because of what happened in Las Vegas?"

"Because I sort of looked into Hell, but I still don't know if there's a Heaven or not."

That stopped her.

12:04 A.M.

She finally said, "You saw it?"

"Sort of. I felt it. Heard it, I guess. Screams, bleeding over into my head. And I knew, I knew right then what it would be like." I took a breath and knew I was about to spill a giant load of stark-raving lunacy.

"It was just like the locker room," I said. "That day at the high school. Not Pine View where we went to school together, but before that, before they shipped me off there. Billy Hitchcock and four friends. Their hands on me like animal jaws, twisting me, pushing me to the ground. So easy. So fucking easy, the way they overpowered me, and that look, that look of stupid joy on their faces because they knew, they knew that they could do whatever they wanted and they knew that I knew. And that fear, that total hopelessness when I realized I wasn't going to kick my way out of it and the coach wasn't gonna come in and break it up and nobody was going to come to my rescue. Whatever they wanted to do was going to happen and happen and happen until they got bored with it and they got *so high* off that power . . ."

I felt the Smith's plastic grip digging into my palm, knew I was involuntarily squeezing it.

"Before that, Billy's neighbor had this little yappy dog, expensive

319

thing. One day the old lady comes home and finds the little yapping thing in her backyard, only it's not yapping because Billy has taken a hot glue gun and glued its jaws shut. He decided to do the eyes, too, and—look, the point is I think that people live on, forever, outside of time somehow. And I think people like Billy, they never change. And I think they all wind up in the same place, and you and I can wind up right among them and they have forever, literally forever, to do what they want with us. In whatever way people live, maybe you don't have a body they can cut or bruise or burn but the worst pain isn't in the nerve endings, is it? Total fear and submission and torment and deprivation and hopelessness, that tidal wave of hopelessness. They never get tired, they never sleep, and you never, ever, ever die. They stay on top of you and they hold you down and down and down, forever."

I let out a breath.

12:06 A.M.

She said, "Billy Hitchcock. He was the kid who di—"

Her words broke off and she let out an enormous snore, like she'd suddenly fallen into a deep sleep in midsentence.

I turned, and where Amy had been sitting there was now a human-shaped thing with jointed arms and gray rags for clothes, legs sticking stiffly out in front. Like a department store mannequin crafted by a blind man. The red hair looked to be made of copper wire. A hinged jaw clamped shut and the snoring sound was clipped immediately. Two seconds later the jaw yawned wide open again and the enormous snoring sound poured forth—a sound that was more mechanical than human. Artificial.

I got to hand it to them, I thought. *I really wasn't expecting that.*

I heard a *clump* and realized the gun had fallen out of my limp hand. I also realized my jaw was hanging open. I tried to pull myself together, forced my legs to step forward. I reached out toward the thing—

The gun was back in my hand. Amy was back on the couch, sitting bolt upright, looking blankly into space. I immediately looked at my watch—

3:20 A.M.

SHIT.

Amy slowly turned her head, coming to. She saw me, saw the look on my face. Realization washed over her and her hand flew to her mouth, her eyes suddenly wide.

"Did it—did it happen? It happened, didn't it?"

I said, "Go upstairs and pack as much stuff as you can carry. We're getting outta here."

SHE BOUNDED DOWN the stairs seven minutes later, a satchel over her shoulder and the laptop under her arm.

We found Molly in the kitchen, standing on a chair and eating from a box of cookies that had been left open on the table. After some coaxing and threats we got her to follow us out to my truck. We loaded up, the engine growled to life. The windshield was a solid sheet of white.

Amy found the cardboard GhostVision glasses on the dashboard and examined them with a quizzical look. I found my ice scraper from under my seat and jumped out to scrape the ice from the windows. Outside I turned toward the house–

I stopped in my tracks.

I mumbled, "Oh, shit, shit, shit."

There was a figure on the roof, silhouetted against the pearly moonlit clouds. Nothing but silhouette, a walking shadow. Two tiny, glowing eyes.

"What are you looking at?"

Amy, trying to follow my gaze.

"You can't see it."

She squinted. "No."

"Get back in the truck!"

In a series of frantic bursts I managed to scrape a lookhole in the powdered-sugar crust of ice on the windshield, then jogged around to the back to do the same.

I heard Amy say, "Hey! What's he doing up there?"

321

I leaned around the truck and saw Amy was wearing the *Scooby-Doo* ghost glasses and was staring right at the spot where Shadow Man was standing. She pulled off the glasses and looked at them in amazement, then looked through them again and said, "What *is* that thing? Look! What is it?"

"What—are you using the damned *Scooby* glasses?"

"I can see it! It's a black shape and . . . it's moving! Look!"

I did look, long enough to see the shape spout giant black wings. No . . . that wasn't right. It *became* wings, two flapping wing shapes that didn't quite meet in the middle. It flitted into the sky, a black slip against the clouds, higher and higher until it vanished.

I heard barking. Molly had gotten out of the truck, was at my knees.

Amy kept staring up, her mouth hanging open, steam jumping out in little puffs. She said, "David, what was it?"

"How should I know? They're shadow people. They're walking death. They take you and you're gone and nobody knows you were ever there."

"You've seen them before?"

"More and more. Let's go, let's go."

We climbed in, called to Molly. She didn't move, stood stiffly, trembling, growling at the sky. I called to her again, got out, picked her up and threw her inside.

I jumped in, floored it.

We fired down the road, fishtailing on the glaze of skating-rink-caliber black ice left over from the road graters. The house shrank in the rearview mirror. Beyond it, the low, flat Drain Rooter factory.

Amy twisted in her seat and peered back through the rear window, then did the same with those stupid ghost glasses. Molly was up and dancing behind us, bouncing around, probably thinking she'd be safer out on foot. Amy squealed, "Look! Look!"

I gave it a glance in the mirror, saw high headlights behind us, probably a Rooter truck leaving with a load. I did something they don't teach you in driving class, which was to lean my head out into the blistering wind and look up, steering blind with one hand.

Black shapes were swirling overhead, winged things and long, whipping forms like serpents. Swirling, stopping, turning, like bits of debris in a tornado.

They were congregating around the factory.

Most of them were. Some of them were breaking off and following us, dark shapes flitting across the sky and into the shadowy trees and houses around us, vanishing from view. I pulled in my head and focused on the road.

Amy sat forward and strapped her seat belt on, screamed, "What do we do?"

"We're doing it."

Another glance into the mirror, headlights closer now. Trucker hauling ass, hauling drain cleaner.

A shadow flicked across the hood.

I stomped the brakes, the Bronco spun out, skidded, plowed ass-first into a bumper-high snowdrift alongside the road. Silence for a second, then the apocalyptic sound of eighteen wheels skidding on ice.

The semi jackknifed, the front end stopping and the heavier rear still pushing forward, toward us. A giant cartoon plumber, a red "X" through him, loomed in the windshield.

The trailer skidded to a stop about six feet from the bumper, then rocked threateningly back and forth, deciding whether or not it wanted to tip, clumps of snow spilling off the roof with each sway.

Silence, save for the tick of the engine and the rushing of the wind. Finally, Amy said, "Are you all right?"

"Uh, yeah."

I was scanning the sky for shadows. I glanced at the red cab of the semi, could see somebody moving inside. An elbow.

A hand clamped on my arm. Amy whispered, "There. Over there."

She was pointing, with her handless wrist, God bless her, at a black shape growing on the side of the semi, several shapes, molding together, forming something like a spider. Sitting there on the white wall of the trailer like a piece of black spray-painted gang graffiti.

The little hand clamped tighter on my forearm, hard, like a

blood-pressure cuff. A low growl from Molly, who had backed up all the way to the rear wall of the Bronco, pressed against the rear door like she was trying to escape by osmosis.

"David, go. Go." Amy was whispering it hard, harsh hisses of "GO GO GO GO GO . . ."

I slammed on the gas. The tires spun. Spun and spun and spun. Four-wheel drive. Two wheels buried in packed snow, two wheels spinning on ice.

The shadow spider moved, blurred, flicked across the length of the tractor trailer and appeared right next to the cab. Just a few feet from the driver inside. I threw the Bronco into reverse, then forward, rocking out of the ruts dug by the spinning tires, praying for traction.

"David!"

I looked up. The spider shape was gone.

I heard screams, curses. Rage. The driver had stumbled out of the cab, a big guy, tall and fat, a goatee.

The man was ranting, spit flying from his mouth, staring us down, fists clenched. Face pink with the effort of it. He turned his eyes on us. A rabid dog. "Cunt blood fucking cunt motherfuckers—"

Maybe he thinks we're plumbers . . .

He stomped toward us and I could see them now, shapes moving around him, shadows wrapping around him like black ribbons twisting in the wind. And his eyes. His eyes were pure black now, the pupils and the whites gone in coal-black holes.

A few feet away from us now, trudging toward us like a robot. I slammed on the gas again, spun again, felt the rear end shift and then settle in, the tires making a pathetic, wet whine against the slush. A thin arm shot across my chest and it was Amy, reaching over and slapping the lock shut on my door a millisecond before the truck driver started clawing at the handle.

Crazed curses muffled by the door, his breath steaming up the glass. Tires whirring against ice. "FUCK YOU MOTHERFUCKING MOTHERFUCKERS EAT YOUR FUCKING—" A meaty hand smacked the glass.

The curses were replaced by a long, howling scream. The man stumbled back as if shot, a hand flying to his forehead. He stumbled, went to a knee, screeched like a saw blade on metal plate.

He exploded.

Limbs flew, flecks of red splattered over the windshield, Amy screamed. A head tumbled through the air, landed on the road and bounced out of sight. The tire sounds stopped. I realized I had let off the gas, was gawking at the looping remains of the man's intestines, steaming in the frozen air.

The shadows, restless again. Crawling over the truck and the snowy ground around us, the things as stark as black felt in the snow-reflected moonlight. A tall one grew in front of us, almost the shape of a man but without a visible head and with too many arms. Molly went wild, barking and barking and barking, then melting into high, breathy whimpers.

I stomped the gas pedal one more time, got the tires spinning, heard bits of ice and dirt smack the fenders. The shape moved toward us, melting into the hood, walking through the engine block, moving across the hood like wading into a pond. It reached up with an arm, an arm as long as a man, then plunged it into the hood. The engine died instantly. The headlights went dark.

Shadow everywhere now. Movement, hints of it through the moonlight. Amy breathing next to me, quick, nervous gasps. For a long time, nothing happened.

She mumbled something, too low to hear. I glanced at her; she leaned in and said, "I don't think they can see us."

I didn't get it at first but it almost made sense. Whatever they were, they didn't have corneas and pupils and optic nerves. We couldn't see them, normally. They were sensing us, feeling us out, searching without seeing.

I looked up, saw one shape flit away and disappear into the sky. Another, floating past the semi trailer, crawling over the plumber logo, then dissolving into the darkness.

I nodded, slowly, whispered, "They don't belong here, in this world. They're flying blind, with no eyes to—"

325

A soft thump on the window. Amy screamed.

Outside my window, inches from my face, was the severed head of the truck driver. A six-inch hunk of spinal column dangled from his neck, hanging in midair. His eyes were wide open, no sign of lids, two orbs twitching this way and that, taking us in. Amy was still screaming. Some lungs, that girl.

"Amy!"

The head pressed up against the window, squishing its nose, cramming its eyeball against the glass to get a look in. Its mouth hung open, lips pressed against the glass, teeth scraping.

"Amy! Plug your ears!"

She looked at me, saw me pull out the gun, pressed her forearms over the side of her head. I started rolling down my window.

I created a gap of about six inches when the head tried to ram into the opening, jaws working, teeth snapping. I jammed the gun in its mouth and squeezed the trigger.

Thunder. The head disintegrated, became a red mist and a rain of bone chips. I glanced at the gun, impressed, wondered about the loads the stranger had sent me. I leaned to the window and screamed, "You should have quit while you were a—"

"David!"

I turned. Darkness was falling around us now, pooling, the clouds over us vanishing behind living shadow. Suddenly it was dark, cave dark, coffin dark. I opened my mouth to tell Amy to run, to run and leave me behind because it was me they wanted and not her, but nothing came out.

I twisted the key, the engine turned over, stalled. I tried again, it fired to life, I stomped the gas. I floored it and we went nowhere, nowhere, nowhere and then lurched forward, across an unseen street, smacking into the drift on the other side of the road. I threw it in reverse, floored it again, spinning out and then crawling forward—

We were off. Out of the blackness and into the night, eating up the street, my hands strangling the wheel. The speedometer crept up, tires floating under us, like driving a hovercraft. I felt a hand on my arm

326

again, Amy, breathing, whipping her head around, trying to see everything at once through the ridiculous cardboard glasses.

The night outside got darker and darker, shapes swirling around, blackness closing in, swimming in it, like being downwind from a forest fire.

And suddenly, Amy was gone. An empty seat.

And then I felt stupid.

Of course the seat was empty—I came out here alone and we had never found Amy; the house had been empty and we all knew she was actually wrapped up in a tarp in my—

The darkness swallowed me. The passing scenery outside was gone, no houses or grass or snowdrifts, like driving in deep space.

Shadow poured into the Bronco like floodwater. A blade of ice pierced my chest, cold flowing in like poison. My heart stopped. It was like strong, cold fingers reaching behind my ribs and squeezing.

And then I was gone, out of the truck, out of anywhere. A storm of images exploded in my head, crazed mental snapshots like fever dreams:

—looking down, a black crayon in my hand, drawing pictures of three stick figures. One drawn with long hair, one shorter with a spray of red at the top—

—under my car, my old car, my Hyundai. On my back, another guy next to me, long blond hair. I'm holding up a muffler and he's threading in bolts, and I tell Todd we're missing a bolt, that it rolled away, and he's saying that the jack is tilting and GET OUT GET OUT BECAUSE THE CAR IS FALLING—

—running, breathing hard, through a ballroom in a Las Vegas casino. Chaos, then seeing Jim and knowing what I had to do, raising and firing and watching him go down, clutching his neck—

—blue canvas, knees in the snow, rolling a body, rolling it up because somebody could show up any second and it's sooooo hard to move the deadweight—

Back. In the truck again, fingers clamped on the wheel. Plowing through deep snow, a mailbox flying toward me.

"David!"

I was driving in somebody's front yard. I cranked the wheel, ground through a drift and landed in the street again. I saw Amy was back, in the passenger seat, pale as china. I reached over and grabbed her by the arm, pulled her over, like I could somehow stop her from getting sucked out of reality again if I hung on really, really tight. She screamed, "The light! Go to the light!"

No idea what she was going on about. Then I saw it, a pool of light in the pitch blackness just ahead. A flat of parking lot, a hint of an unlit red sign.

It was getting darker, blackness eating up the landscape around me, a power outage during a lunar eclipse. I cranked toward the embankment and jumped the curb, climbed over a little hill then landed with a lurch. I slammed the brakes, spinning on a white plane as flat as a hockey rink.

THUNK!

We smacked a pole, light bathing the interior. I saw out of the rearview mirror the sign for a new doughnut shop, the place still under construction but the parking lot lights on. And then I saw nothing at all, because blackness settled over everything outside the little island of lit snow we had settled in. In a second we were cut off from the universe, nothing in any direction, like we had submerged in a lake of oil five hundred feet under the ocean floor. Just black and black and black.

Silence. The sound of two people breathing. I felt a wet nose at my ear, saw Molly poking her head up, wagging her tail, bouncing back and forth on her paws, growling low under her breath.

Amy said, "They can't get us! They can't get us in the light! I knew it!"

"How did you—"

"David," she said, rolling her eyes, "they're *shadow people*."

She rolled down her window, poked her head out into the night and screamed, "Screw you!"

"Amy, I'd prefer that you not do that."

She pulled back in and said, "My heart's going a thousand miles an hour."

I looked out into the nothing, found the gun in my lap and squeezed it. A good luck charm at this point, and barely that.

Amy said, "Ooh! Look at that. What is—"

Little bits of light, moving around in the darkness in pairs. Twin embers, small as lit cigarettes, floating slowly around us. There were a few and then a few more, until dozens of the fiery eyes were peering in at us. And then, through the windshield, I saw color. A thin line of electric blue across the darkness, like a horizon. Then the blue line grew fat in the middle, expanding, widening like a slit cut in black cloth. It expanded until blue was all that was visible through the windshield.

It was an eye. *The* eye. Vibrant blue with a dark, vertical reptilian slit of a pupil. The hand on my forearm again. I thought Amy was going to break the bone with her grip. The eye twitched, taking us in. Then it blinked, and was gone.

The shroud of blackness was gone, too. Just the night now, shrouded stars and moonlit snow and a sad, dormant doughnut shop.

Amy said, "Are—are they gone?"

"They're never gone."

"What *was* that?"

Well you see, Amy, it's like this. We are under the eye of Korrok. We are his food, and our screams are his Tabasco sauce.

Instead I said, "I'm not leaving the light."

"No."

Amy craned her head around, looking in all directions again, then took off the cardboard glasses. I looked down at the Smith and realized something, probably several minutes too late. I grabbed the barrel and offered it to Amy, butt-first.

I whispered, "Take this."

"What? No."

"Amy, that thing, with the truck driver? You saw how they took him over, used his body? Well that same thing can happen to me."

And don't ask me how I know that, honey.

"No, David—"

"Amy, listen to me. If I start acting weird, if I make a move at you, you need to shoot me."

"I wouldn't even know how to—"

"It's not complicated. The safety is off. Just squeeze. And don't get cute and try to go for my arm or some shit like that. You'll miss. Just aim for the middle of me, jam it into my ribs. Shoot and get out, run for it. Don't, you know, keep shooting me. Please, take it."

To my surprise, she did. She turned the pistol over, the gun looking huge in her little hand. She said, "Well, what if it happens to me? What if they take me instead?"

"I can overpower you if I have to, get the gun away. But I don't think it'll happen. Not with you."

"Why?"

I leaned back, suddenly feeling lighter without the gun. I swear the things generate their own gravity.

"It's just a theory I have."

Amy pulled her feet up on the seat and scrunched against me, shivering. The gun was in her right hand, laying across her hip and pointing vaguely at my crotch. There would be some real symbolism there, I thought, if this turned out to be a dream.

I said, "Besides, I don't need the gun." I held up my hands and said, "They passed a law that said I couldn't put my hands in my pockets. Do you know why? Because they would become concealed weapons. I can kill a man with these hands. Or just one of my feet."

She snorted a dry, nervous laugh and said, "Yeah, okay. I'll watch out for you then."

I again gripped the steering wheel with both hands, tendons tensing across my forearms like cables. I sat like that, in silence, for an eternity of minutes. A whole bunch of words trapped behind clenched teeth.

Finally, I closed my eyes and said, "Okay. Look. You need to understand something. About this situation, who you're trapped in here with."

330

"Oookaaaay . . ."

She twisted around to face me. Those eyes were so damned green. Like a cat. "Don't, just—just listen. Do you know why I was in the special school, why I was in the BD class in Pine View?"

She said, "Sort of. The thing with Billy, right? The fight you got into with him? And then later when he—"

"Yes, that's right. Listen. Men are animals. Get us together, take out the authority figures, and it's *Lord of the Flies*. Billy and his gang, a couple of guys on the wrestling team, they used to make these videos. The kid, you know the Patterson kid, kind of fat? Anyway, they got him after school and tied him to a goalpost and shaved his head and all that, and it was hours before somebody found him, and by then, you know, the skin on his face was all blistered from the contact with the feces . . ."

Maybe you can cut back on the details a bit, hmmm?

". . . and they have this party and they show the tape, show the tape of them torturing this fat kid and him just *screaming*. And they sat there with their beers and watched that tape over and over and over and that's the way it is in high school. Shit that would get an adult put in a straightjacket is just brushed off. 'Boys will be boys.'"

I hesitated, scanned the night for something, anything. I saw a lone bird on a power line, flapping its wings, but it didn't seem to be going anywhere.

"Anyway, the Hitchcock guys, I had gym with them and they picked me outta the crowd. It became this daily thing. Little shit at first but they kept pushing it further and further and it took more and more to keep them entertained. And the coach there, he hated me, so he would make sure and not be there. I mean, I literally saw him turn his back and leave the room when they came after me one time, made sure I saw him do it. And one day they got on me and took me to this equipment room in back, this little storage area with shoulder pads and wrestling mats stacked all around and it's hot as an oven and there's this moldy smell of old sweat fermenting in foam padding.

And things got crazy. Like, prison yard crazy. And eventually it ends and they leave me there and they're walking out through the locker room and . . ."

Hmmmm . . . would she notice if I suddenly changed the subject?

"Well, I had taken to bringing a knife to school, not a switchblade or anything cool but a little two-inch blade on my key chain. It was all I had. And I get this blade free and I get behind Billy and I slice him, right up his back, a shallow little cut up his spine. It wasn't deep but it got his attention and he fell over, thinking he was dead, blood all over the bench and the floor. And I got on him, sat on his chest and I started jabbing at his face, cutting, the blade bouncing off bone in his forehead and blood and . . ."

I thought long and hard about how to dress up this next part, but couldn't think of a way. I wondered when the doughnut shop was scheduled to open.

Filling in the silence, Amy asked, "What did they do to you?"

"Let's put it this way. I'll never, ever tell you."

She had no answer, which either meant she was totally unfamiliar with the concept or very well familiar. I pressed on.

"So, I wound up—"

—cutting out his eyes—

"—hurting him pretty bad, he lost his eyesight. I mean, like, legally blind. I wound up getting charged with aggravated assault and several other things that are all synonyms for aggravated assault. The school was talking a permanent expulsion. My dad—my adoptive dad—he's a lawyer, you know, he had a series of meetings with the school and the prosecutor and it was a mess. They wound up testing me for mental illness, which I knew even at the time was a way to get me off because the case could be made that the school should have protected Billy from *me*, should have diagnosed me, whatever. I met with a counselor who had me talk about my mom and look at inkblots and role-play with puppets and draw a picture of how I viewed my place in the world. . . ."

"... and I knew it was a scam, a lawyer trick, but I kept picturing Coach Wilson turning his back, again and again and I figured, hey, screw them. The prosecutor, this bearded Jewish tough guy, didn't want to push the charges. He said it was a five-on-one fight and shit happens, didn't want to see me disappear into the jaws of the juvie justice system. The school backed off on the expulsion under threat of lawsuit and, bada-boom, I wind up spending my final year at Pine View."

A speck of crystal landed on the windshield. A lone snowflake. Another landed a few inches away.

"So," I said, "four months later Billy is adjusting to life without eyes, saying good-bye to sports and driving and independence and knowing what his food looks like before he eats it and never knowing if a fly has landed in his soup. He takes all of his pain pills at once. Demerol, I think. They find him dead the next day."

Silence. Desperate to hear her say something, anything, I asked, "So how much of that story did you already know?"

"Most of it. There was a weird rumor that went around that you had snuck into his room and poisoned him or something stupid like that, with rat poison or something, which was stupid because the police would have noticed that."

"Right, right."

I started that rumor, by the way.

"You must have felt horrible when you found out. About Billy, I mean. That'd be awful."

"Yeah."

Nope.

What followed was the longest and most tense conversation pause of my life, like being stuck on a Ferris wheel with somebody you just puked on. Exactly like that, by the way. The truth was, I didn't feel sorry for Billy. He teased a dog and got his fingers bitten off. Fuck him. Fuck everybody. And fuck you, Amy, for somehow getting me to tell you this. Sure, yeah, I felt bad about it, Your Honor. And that day years ago when I heard about the kids shooting up the school in Colorado I shook my head and said it was a tragedy, an awful tragedy, but inside I was thinking the look on the jocks' faces when they saw the guns must have been fucking priceless. So, yeah, as far as you know, I felt just as bad about Billy as a good person would. And I'll never, ever tell you otherwise. Never.

She said, "Still, who knows what he would have done to somebody else if you hadn't—"

"I don't feel bad about it, Amy. I lied about that part. When I heard, I felt nothing at all. I thought I would, I didn't. The guilt just wasn't there because I'm not that type of person. And that's what I've been saying, that's why you're in danger here. I don't think those things, those bits of walking nothing can use you, but I think they'd know me as one of their own. So keep the gun on me. And keep your finger

334

along the side of the trigger and be ready to squeeze it as hard and as fast as you can."

Silence again. Did I say that last silence was the longest and most awkward of my life? The record didn't stand for long.

I would give everything I own to somehow take this conversation back.

I said, "We have no idea what they were doing to you, Amy, when those things took you all of those times. But they're not going to do it again. This being scared bullshit, it's exhausting for me. And you know, I reach a point where I say, you can kill me or tear off my arms or soak me in gasoline and set me on fire, but you won't keep me like this, imprisoned by fear. Now, after everything I've seen, I'm not really scared of monsters and demons and whatever they are. I'm only scared of one thing and that's the fear. Living with that fear, with intimidation. A boot on my neck. I won't live like that. I won't. I wouldn't then and I won't now."

After a long time she said, "What do we do?"

"We sit here. Just keep the gun on me, okay? We'll sit here and wait for the sun. Then I'll talk to John. John will know what to do."

I can't believe you just said that.

CHAPTER 14

John Investigates

4:20 A.M.

John had decided to go to the Drain Rooter job site early to get a look around on his own. So while Amy and I sat camped out in my Bronco at the unborn doughnut shop, John was rolling his Caddie up the snowy road past Amy's house. He didn't get far, of course, arriving at a bundle of vehicles trying to unstick a jackknifed Drain Rooter semi tractor trailer.

Now, I wasn't there, so this story is hearsay. If you know John, you'll take the details for what they're worth. Please also remember that, where John claims to have "gotten up at three thirty" to perform this investigation, it was far more likely he was still up and somewhat drunk from the night before.

John says he pulled up to the scene, which was roped off with yellow-and-black tape that announced it as a Hazardous Material Area. Several guys in yellow jumpsuits were milling around and cleaning the scene with some urgency, so of course he immediately decided to cross the DO NOT CROSS tape. Two steps in, John found himself standing on a faded pink stain on the snow, as wide as a car. He deduced that this was blood, though the truck driver's body was gone. He stood over this large bloodstain and said, out loud and in the presence of several bystanders, "This is blood! David must have been here."

At this point two elderly security guards in parkas, the guys who normally work the front desk at the plant, asked John to step behind the tape. John claims that here he told the guards that he could not speak English and when this failed to persuade them, he faked a violent seizure. I am unclear as to the purpose of this part of his plan. John flung himself down and began rolling around in the snow, thrashing his limbs about and screaming, "EL SEIZURE!!! NO ES BUENO!!!" in a Mexican accent. Half a dozen pairs of boots came mushing through the snow toward him.

From the ground, John saw something that stopped him cold. The semi trailer was, according to him, "bleeding from the ass." John saw gallons of a red liquid running freely from the rear cargo doors of the truck, pooling on the road below, the stuff almost black in the moonlight. Several gloved hands seized him and dragged him through the snow, men in jumpsuits and protective masks. John squinted through the bustling team of men around the truck and saw several guys haul out a couple of blue plastic barrels, stained on the sides with the red substance that now seemed a little more like transmission fluid than blood. Dark and thick and oily.

Right behind them, several casket-shaped boxes were hauled out, the men carrying them like pallbearers. John stressed that these containers were not caskets but were merely casket-shaped, coated with several stickers that seemed to indicate some kind of biohazard. Not the sort of thing you would use to ship bottles of a household chemical to the local True Value.

Here's where things get hazy. John claims that the men hauling him away from the scene were escorted by other men carrying submachine guns, though when pressed, he admitted that they may have been flashlights. Either way, John says the men threw him down and intended to execute him, at which point he kicked one of the men in the face and backflipped to his feet. He then wrestled away the man's gun and "dick-whipped" him with it. I am unclear as to whether or not this means he struck the man in the groin or merely slapped him in the same manner in which he would slap a person with his dick. I never ask John to clarify such things. Anyway, he said he swung again and slammed another man's skull with the gun, so hard it "made the batteries fly out."

Next—according to John, of course—in one continuous motion, he "triple-kicked" a third man in the face, while shooting a fourth "right in his damned cock." John, of course, knew that he couldn't leave that man just lying there, screaming in pain. So he grasped him by the sides of his face and mercifully snapped his neck with a sharp twisting motion of his bare hands. At this point John says the rest of the hazard workers noticed what was going on and a chase ensued; he escaped by stealing a nearby horse. This is the first inconsistency in John's account, because when the story picks up he is calmly driving his Caddie back down the road, past Amy's house and away from the Rooter plant. I suspect that, in reality, either the men at the cleanup site didn't see John at all or they merely gave him a dirty look until he turned around and drove away. Again, I wasn't there and I do not wish to cast an unfavorable light on John's personal credibility.

Undaunted, John turned off on a country road not far from the house. He wasn't the first to have this idea tonight, he figured, because there were tire tracks in the snow leading up, and John figured the last person who came this way was doing what he was doing: getting around the accident.

A few minutes in he became sure he was right because the road seemed to circle back around to the rear of the old industrial park, which contained the Rooter plant along with an abandoned beans-and-wienies cannery, a Best Buy distribution center and a closed Hanes jockstrap jockstrappery. Just across the highway from that was the abandoned Undisclosed Shopping Centre with its rows of decaying stores where the only inventory was mildew, bats and squirrel families building nests out of used rubbers.

The gravel road and fresh tire tracks that John followed took him through a narrow strip of woods alongside the Rooter property. It was while passing through the leafy darkened canopy that he saw a flickering of lights off to his left, flashing between the tree trunks.

He slowed and stopped, seeing bouncing white beams that had to be men with flashlights, maybe a half dozen or so.

Shots rang out.

The lights vanished and John sat there for a few minutes before he picked them up again, farther down in the trees. He pulled forward a little down the road, peering into the woods, saw the flashlight beams stop and then blink out one by one. Whatever the men were looking for, be it a raccoon to boil or one of the guys' contact lenses, they had apparently found it. He peered into the trees looking for more activity, decided that the group could have been mere redneck poachers or fraternity scavenger hunters, and stepped on the gas. The big Caddie crested a hill and when John saw what was below, he slammed on the brakes. A truck was down there, a heavy truck that looked military but didn't have a military paint job. Flat black from head to toe. This was apparently the source of the tire tracks he had been following.

A group of men carrying what had to be rifles stood around the vehicle, and John immediately reached out and punched the switch to kill his headlights. Then it occurred to him that the lights suddenly going off might have been more noticeable. So he punched them back on, thought he saw two of the men turn toward him, and then quickly turned the lights back off again. Now he felt the strobing of his headlights was almost impossible not to notice; in fact, all of the men seemed to be looking up the hill at him. The group might have either pursued him or raised their rifles to perforate his windshield had a gorilla riding a giant crab not leapt out of the woods and eaten two of them.

You heard me.

John said the thing was as tall as the truck and walked on six legs that looked horned and armored like something seen at a seafood buffet. But there was a part that had the feel of a mammal, too, fur and arms. Please remember that from John's distance the beast would have been the size of a dime, so I won't criticize his crab-riding monkey description even though we all know it's retarded.

The thing crawled away—sideways—with the legs of one man still kicking from its mandibles. Cracks of rifle shots rang out and little flares of muzzle flash lit up the snow at the foot of the hill. The men raced into the woods. John waited, then threw the Caddie into reverse and backed far enough down the other side of the hill as to be out of view of the army truck, though he claims that from that vantage point *he* could still see the *truck,* so that's probably physically impossible.

Shots rang out from the woods. An animal screech rang out from the woods. Shots rang out from the woods again. More howls and then more shots, dozens, rattling over each other. Full auto fire. Screams.

There was silence for a moment and then John says he saw a single figure sprint out of the woods and head to the truck. The man jumped into the back, pulled out two small cases the size of lunch boxes and ran into the woods again. After a moment, more shots hammered the night air. The bestial screams again. More shots. More screams. More shots. There was a low, animal moan from the woods. The gunfire fell silent. John threw the Caddie in gear and was prepared to drive past the truck before the men returned, but he was too late because here was the lone man, running back. He was carrying the small cases, which seemed lighter now. He ducked into the truck again, emerged with two *new* cases, and returned to the woods. Gunshots resumed, followed by the screams of the monkey-crab.

This went on for about half an hour and then finally the noises stopped. Four men wandered out of the woods and mounted up in the truck. The truck pulled away. John followed. He passed a turn that led back to the Drain Rooter plant, probably to the employee lot, but saw that it was sealed off with a chain-link gate. If this had been an action movie, John thought, he would have rammed through it. Unlike a movie prop car, however, John was depending on the Cadillac to get him to work the next morning, and a punctured radiator would cost a week's pay.

But more importantly, the truck he was following didn't turn off at the gated road and he was now very eager to see where it went. John hung far back, content to follow the trail of the tire tracks. They kept going through the main access road for the industrial park and across the two-lane highway that intersected the road. The truck had continued onto the white canvas that was the parking lot of the dead Undisclosed Mall. It had circled around to the back of the eastern wing, one fork in the mall's U-shaped floor plan.

John waited what he thought was a sufficient amount of time for the men in the truck to dismount and go wherever they were going, then cautiously drove around the building so he could see the truck parked near the ramp and boarded-up entrance of what would have been a department store had the mall ever bothered to open. John staked out the spot, saw nothing. He finally grew impatient and, being totally unarmed and without a flashlight or any kind of survival instincts, tromped over to a doorless doorway and walked in like he owned the place.

The cavernous space was as cold as a meat locker. Some moonlight spilled in from a framed hole in the roof, the skylight that had the glass shattered out of it last year. Snow had sifted down through the hole, leaving a coating at the center of the floor like spilled flour. Right across the edge of it were footprints. Five or six leading to an elongated skid that John assumed was created by a guy slipping in the snow and falling on his ass. John didn't make the same mistake, circling around the dusting of snow and following the direction of the tracks. They led to a metal MAINTENANCE door and John paused to wonder if maintenance on this place was the easiest job in the world or the hardest. He found the door locked and claims he picked it. I've never known John to know how to pick a lock but I don't claim to know all of his secrets. Maybe the guys just left it unlocked.

Anyway, John says he picked it and inside found a small, dirty, windowless room that seemed to be home to a lot of spiderwebs and dark scurrying shapes, but no exits. He flicked on his lighter and confirmed it. No doors, no hatches, no tunnels. Just like Amy's bathroom, the trail led there and stopped. John turned to leave, and out of the corner of his eye he saw a doorway. He felt like an idiot because, how do you miss it, right in the middle of the wall like that? Tall, arched at the top, ornate. Totally out of place in a room like this. Then he turned to face it and saw that it was only a blank wall again.

He turned to the side, once more saw a blurry glimpse of the big door out of the corner of his eye. There, but not there, like an optical illusion. John went over to the wall and pawed around on the surface by the warm glow of the butane flame, looking for a lever or a seam or hidden hinges or something. After several minutes, he found it only to be a solid wall. He glanced at his watch—

5:06 A.M.

—and realized he had to be at the job site in less than half an hour. He left, guessing—rightly—that he would be back.

5:18 A.M.

I alternately turned the Bronco's engine on and off so we could run the heater without poisoning ourselves with carbon monoxide, as I heard could happen if a parked car was left on too long. Especially this one, which smelled like rotten eggs from time to time anyway. I had always credited it to some sort of emissions problem, and I was sure it would remain even if I gave the truck a thorough cleaning, though I had never fully investigated that scenario.

Amy's hair smelled like strawberries. She was leaning on me, her feet on the armrest of her door, the gun pointed somewhere in the direction of the glove compartment. There was a coating of white on all of the glass now, as if a sheet had been thrown over the Bronco. For the second time that night I had the very odd, weightless feeling that we were the last two people on Earth.

I said, "Can I ask you something?"

"Nope."

"Why were you in Pine View? There's barely anything wrong with you. And I have a right to know, you know, as a taxpayer."

"The car accident. I missed school for a few months, had all kinds of problems when I came back. They had me on antidepressants and everything else. Wellbutrin. I bit a teacher and wound up with the crazy kids."

"You *bit a teacher?*"

She sighed and said, "Okay. One day me and Mom and Dad were driving, going shopping for school clothes. I was fourteen, about to start high school. I fell asleep in the backseat and woke up and felt like somebody was shaking me. Then I was upside down, my cheek pressed to pavement. Glass everywhere, blood everywhere. Dad had been thrown from the car, he died right there, two feet in front of me. His face was just—it was like a rubber mask. Just, nothing there. Mom was laying there, legs pinned under the hood, screaming. I was mostly okay but my back was twisted around and my legs were numb, my hand was caught under a door and I just laid there and told Mom to calm down, that help would be here soon. We laid there *forever*. And I could hear cars passing. I could hear them and it's like, 'why don't they stop?' Somebody, you'd think . . ."

She trailed off, turned to look out the side window, at nothing.

"They pulled me out and my hand was like, hamburger. Tendons and stuff curling out of it and, just gross. It was just barely on, hanging by like, a little strip holding it to my wrist. They're putting me on a stretcher and my hand is just dangling, swinging back and forth. Mom died at the hospital. Jim wasn't there, of course, he had stayed home so he was okay and he was freaking out, like it was his fault. They did surgery on my hand, put it back on. Then they did surgery on my back where I cracked a vertebrae. They put a little metal rod right—" she

343

reached around and pointed to a spot between her shoulder blades. "—there. It made me a half inch taller. Isn't that weird? I had a lot of pain, they'd put me in traction every now and then to kind of stretch me out and take pressure off it. And so the hand, it was a big problem. It worked for a few years, into high school, but then I lost feeling in these two fingers . . ."

Amy did something very creepy, which was to hold up her stump and point to a spot in space where the last two fingers would be.

"And they did surgery again. And again. The pain was unbelievable. That and my back, and I was on these pills, pain pills every four hours and they made me sick constantly. So they'd lower my dosage but those would wear off and I'd spend the last two hours counting the minutes to pill time again. So I was having to live with either the pain or the puking and I kind of had to pick."

Antidepressants. The thought of this girl actually being depressed made me want to grab the whole planet and throw it into the sun. Well, more than usual anyway.

"And I bit a teacher. So eventually my fingers went numb again, al-most all of them, and I couldn't grip anything. I was dropping things. They had me staying with Uncle Bill and Aunt Betty and they were in the process of splitting up and they didn't want me there. One time I dropped this glass thing, this little figurine, and Bill freaked out. I mean it's not his fault they didn't want me but what could I do? He yelled, and anyway the doctors said we had one last shot, one last chance to get the hand to work because the nerve tissue was dying off."

She looked down and picked something off her sock. "So they did the surgery and I woke up in the recovery room and I was half out of it and I was dreaming that my hand was gone and I woke up and there it was. Gone. Just an empty space, white sheets where my hand should be. It looked so weird. I cried and cried and cried. Just, bawling. For hours. They knew, David, they knew they'd have to take the hand off. And they didn't say anything. And I was just lying there and I knew, all at once, that I'd never be able to blend into a room again. You know?"

344

I grunted.

"And, no matter what I did or what I said, it'd always be, 'Amy, you know, the girl without a hand?' Everywhere I went. And the worst part is when you, like, meet somebody new and they don't notice the hand right away, they don't see it and you sit there talking to them and you're just waiting, anticipating that moment when they're going to notice. That look in their eyes at the moment they see it. Like they're *embarrassed* for me."

She went quiet.

I said, "This world kind of sucks."

"I left. I went and stayed with Jim after that. I can still feel the hand, you know. It's true what they say about that, ghost feeling in the limb and all that."

"What, it itches or something?"

"No, it's, like, clenched. I can feel my hand clenching and I can't release it. Isn't that weird?" She held up her good hand, squeezed in a tight fist. "Like this. I can actually feel the fingernails digging into my palm, on the hand that isn't there. All in my head, I guess, something with the nerves. And it's like that all the time. If I *really* concentrate, I can make it let up a little but it goes right back that way a minute later. That little twinge of pain is always there, a couple of inches into space where my hand should be. I wake up with it."

I thought about telling her my own tragic story of the scrotal candle-wax incident, but figured it wouldn't impress her. She crossed her arms and rubbed the cold from them and I put my arm around her to help. The gun was on the floorboard.

I said, "You know I was confused when I first saw you, right? At the house? I didn't know where your hand went—"

"Well, I still had it in school—"

"—but John knew."

"Well, yeah," she said. "He used to come by."

"Let me tell you everything you need to know about John. The reason I was surprised by your hand was because John never once described you as, 'the girl with the missing hand.'"

5:36 A.M.

I don't know what John did in the intervening time between when he left the mall and when he showed up at the Drain Rooter roofing site, but from past experiences with John I will extrapolate that he told a series of humorous stories about his penis, drank some sort of off-brand alcohol and then had sex with yet another girl who I secretly had a crush on but never got the courage to talk to. At some point he also changed into his roofing clothes, layers of flannel and coveralls stained with tar.

The semi accident scene had been neatly cleared away by the time he passed it again, only a flat of tangled tire tracks as evidence. Steve the Roofing Guy was already at the rear of the building, talking to a security guard about roof access. This was one of the guards John saw at the trailer crash site. He didn't know if the guy would recognize him or not, so he took a newspaper from the trash and held it in front of his face as he approached. Again, this is just what John told me, so, you know. Grain of salt. By six o'clock, thirteen men in Steve's crew were swarming above and below the ragged roof hole, working as snow and ice runoff poured mini-waterfalls into the Drain Rooter break room. The drenched carpet and waterlogged candy bar machine were ruined.

John got on the roof and immediately saw that the hole was no ice collapse. Everything was flung upward, debris and boards and tile scattered on the roof like something blew out from inside. Tyler Schultz, a big blond Nazi Youth–looking kid who had jammed with John's band off and on, made the same observation and said wasn't that some weird shit. John told Tyler that frequently during sudden cold spells the warm air inside a heated building will expand, causing a building to partially explode for much the same reason balloons will burst if you fill them with warm air rather than cool. Tyler asked John if he was making that shit up and John said that he could look it up, knowing he wouldn't.

John then took the stairs down to the wet break room, tape strewn across the hallways to keep employees from wandering in. The first thing he noticed was that the break room snack machine looked like it had been hit by a car, glass smashed in and shreds of candy wrappers all over the ground. While the guys were stomping around above him, getting a tarp set up and shoveling snow away from the ceiling wound, John wandered around and noticed a section of hallway that had been blocked off with the same black-and-yellow DANGER tape he saw earlier.

For the second time that day John ducked casually across some DO NOT DUCK CASUALLY ACROSS THIS TAPE tape and saw another hole, one in the wall, again like something blew through it. Something the size of a car or a giant crab with a monkey strapped to the back of it. And at the edges of the hole, there were scars in the drywall like scratches. Claw marks. John leaned in and peered through the jagged tear in the wall.

He saw a room that was clearly not on the floor plan. It was small, maybe the size of an average living room, and had absolutely no features. Four bare walls. Then John turned away from it and, as he did, saw a perfectly round hole in the floor as wide as the room, going down. Way down. John said it was the kind of chasm thing they have in all of the space stations in the *Star Wars* movies, for some reason. The ones crisscrossed with catwalks with no handrails.

When he looked directly at it, it was not there. A tiled floor. Just like at the mall. So the crab beast escaped from here, but the crew of guys sent to take it down returned to the abandoned mall. Everything came back to the mall, didn't it? John thought about Robert Marley, the soy sauce Patient Zero who had squatted in the food court, and about Danny Wexler ranting about invisible doors. John decided this whole thing required a shitload of further investigation.

I SPLASHED WATER over my face and studied my own bloodshot eyes in the mirror. Glad to be back home, back in my bathroom. I pulled off my shirt and felt something catch back there. Something itchy. I turned to the side and looked into the mirror at my back. My breath caught in my throat.

There was something elongated, maybe a half inch long, protruding from my shoulder blade. Thin, like a needle. Pink.

Thump.

A knock at the door.

I leaned in close to the mirror, examining the growth and reaching back with my fingers, afraid to touch it. A shiver of revulsion twitched through my body.

Thump-thump.

A muffled voice, at the door.

"David? Hey."

John's voice. What was he doing here?

Thump thump thump.

"Hold on," I said, pulling up a hand mirror from the drawer in the vanity. "I'll be out in a minute. I'm, uh, shaving my balls."

I held up the mirror, angled it to see the thing on my back, and almost screamed. The little protrusion on my back was a stalk that ended in an eye. A tiny black slug's eye that twitched as the stalk began curling this way and that, as if getting a look around—

I JOLTED AWAKE.

THUMP.

I was cold. A searing pain in my neck. I smelled the sweet but artificial chemical smell of strawberry shampoo flavoring. Come to think of it, strawberries don't have a smell. They just smell wet like grass.

Focus.

I felt something like a steel cable around my chest. I couldn't move, a weight holding me flat. I pulled my eyelids apart, saw a set of eyes peering down at me through frosted glass. I blinked, looked down and saw copper red. A head full of red hair on my chest. An arm was around me, squeezing, a fist full of my shirt, twisting it.

I was lying with my head against the door of the Bronco, window roller pressing into my back, feet splayed across the bench seats, boot resting against the door across from me. Amy, however, looked rather comfortable since she had me to use as a self-warming mattress. She was curled up on top of me, breathing erratically, her eyelids twitching. Nightmares.

Get used to it, kid.

I craned my head and saw the blurred shape of John's face through a hole he had wiped clean of snow. He waved at me, standing there in full work gear. My watch:

8:07 A.M.

My truck had died at some point because the engine and the heat were off. Amy and I untangled ourselves and I pushed out of the door, standing up in the refrigerated air, joints feeling lined with thick steel wire. I glanced back into the truck and saw Molly fast asleep in the back, paws twitching as she dreamed of clawing somebody to death, probably me.

John said, "It's your first date and you make the girl camp out at the doughnut shop with you? You know they don't open for three months, right?"

There were five guys standing around aside from John, though Tyler was the only one I knew. They had come in two tall delivery trucks with ANDERSON ROOF AND GUTTER painted on the side. I glanced at the strangers and said to John, "We, uh, had to leave the house. Shouldn't you all be working?"

John said, "We had to get a load of shit from Home Depot. We've been fucking around for two hours. Passed by here and saw your truck. What happened at the house?"

Amy came around then, arms wrapped around that huge parka of hers and immediately pressed herself up against me.

"Hi, John. Ugh, I'm freezing."

She reached back and pulled my arm around her, saying, "Warm me up."

"Uh, I've got to have a word with John." I grabbed her by the shoulders and sort of sat her aside, then motioned to John to follow me across the parking lot. We walked around the edge of the lot, me squinting as my eyes adjusted to the light. John said, "You look like shit."

"I'm burning out, John. Seriously. I don't know if I'm up for this. I feel stretched out, like too little butter scraped over too much waffle. And then it all falls down into one of the waffle holes and there's none left for the rest of the waffle and you sort of have to tilt it to make it run out."

"They got some serious weird shit going on at the Drain Rooter plant, Dave. Mall, too."

This was when John told me the somewhat dubious story of his experience at the semi crash site and everything that followed. I saw his story and raised him our experience with the shadow people.

I looked back at my truck, where Amy was sitting sideways in the open door and fishing through her purse. She pulled out a brown pill bottle.

"Well there you go, Dave. It looks like the Drain Rooter plant is making more than drain cleaner. In fact, you could say they're manufacturing *evil*."

"No, we couldn't say that."

"I wanna see where that hole goes. I think that monster came out of it."

"We can't get into the place, John. There's three shifts at the plant, working around the clock."

We completed our circuit of the lot and arrived back where Tyler and one other guy leaned against the truck smoking cigarettes and sipping coffee from steaming insulated mugs.

John said, "There may be another way."

John told me about the mall, and the ghost door that was there but wasn't there. "Wanna know what I think? I think all those secret doors lead to the same place. Hell, there may be doors like that all over town. Like Wexler said."

I nodded resignedly, sighed and said, "Well, we're not waiting for them to just come get Amy again."

"Absofuckinglutely. We'll meet at noon."

"What happens at noon?"

"We're done with the roof job. They just want us to brace it for now and cover it. Keep the snow out."

"You're still going to fix their roof?"

"They paid Steve in advance. Plus, I really need the money."

I noticed ghosts of exhaust rising from my Bronco; Amy had turned it on to get warm.

I said, "I don't know what to do with her. That house of hers is eighteen different kinds of screwed." I glanced at Tyler, saw he was listening intently, and lowered my voice. "She's got people watching her through the TV, like me."

Amy saw us and emerged from the truck at that moment, a twenty-four-ounce bottle of red Mountain Dew in her hand.

She came up and said, "Can I have this?"

"You keep that red shit in your truck now?" John asked me. "I think that's one of the twelve warning signs, isn't it?"

"I eat all of my meals there at work. If you eat in your car, nobody tries to talk to you."

John looked at me with something like pity. I said, "It's yours, Amy."

She twisted at the cap, shoulders hunched against the cold. Somebody handed John a cup of coffee. John said, "Break time."

"Shit yeah," said Tyler, in his dickish way. He was wearing wraparound shades. He watched Amy as she tried to open the Mountain Dew bottle one-handed, trying to keep it still with her elbow. She concentrated on the task, grunting, the wet bottle sort of spinning in place.

I asked John, "Where's the safest place to keep her while we do this?"

Amy said, "While you do what? Can I come?"

Tyler reacted to this for some reason, looking at John with a "when are people gonna learn" look, and then he spat on the ground. Tobacco spitting is a kind of nonverbal communication in many parts of the Midwest. He must have spilled his coffee a lot as a kid because he had one of those big spill-proof mugs, the kind that flare way out at the bottom. It looked like he was speaking into a megaphone every time he took a drink.

I said, "We'll talk about it later."

Amy dropped the bottle, made a frustrated sound like somebody stepping on a cat. I reached out as if to help her and she slapped at my hand, then went back to twisting at the cap.

I continued, "She can't go back to that house. I don't know if she has any money but we can work something out. She can sleep on my couch if it comes to that."

John eyed me as if to say, "really?" but didn't say anything.

Tyler got a sly look in his eyes and said, "I got an interestin' story. My brother, he and his wife gave birth to a Down's kid. He drools all over the place, he shits himself. They made my ma babysit a few times, and then some more times, and then it was every night. Every damned night. You know what happened then?"

"Your brain fell out?" I noticed Amy had stopped messing with the bottle and was sort of just looking at it, frozen. I said, "Look, I gotta—"

"Listen, man. Listen. They left the kid there. At Ma's house. They come by to visit every now and then. My ma, she's basically got stuck feedin' and cleanin' this thing now, every day, it's her job. Full-time job. She can't go to her bingo games or date or any of that shit because she's got this thing to take care of, because she wanted to be a nice person. It's like bein' in prison."

Amy glared at him, like she really had something killer to say to him, then she got this look on her face, sour, like biting an apple and seeing half a worm. She spun and took two steps toward my truck, then put her hand over her mouth and leaned over.

Tip: if you ever feel a puke coming on, do not, *do not* put your hand over your mouth to try to catch it. It's reflex but it doesn't work at all. Vomit kind of sprays everywhere. So Amy stood there in the snow, leaning over at the waist, her eyes clamped shut, her hand dripping, a puddle at her feet. It was an awkward moment. There were some comments from the crowd behind me. Somebody muttered something and somebody else chuckled.

I walked to her and said, "Over here." I guided Amy toward the truck and sat her in the open door.

"Don't move."

I ran back to the rear door of the Bronco, opened it, reached in and grabbed a red-and-white flip-top cooler. This is my emergency kit. It contained a roll of duct tape, a spare pair of pants, an envelope with two hundred dollars, two bags of dried fruit, two packages of beef jerky, three bottles of water, a roll of those thick shop towels you see mechanics use, a small metal pipe—just right for cracking a skull with—and a fake beard. Look, you never know.

I pulled out a bottle of water and soaked a shop towel. I went to hand it to Amy, realized stupidly that she had no hand to take the towel with since she only had, you know, the puke hand and the non-existent hand.

"Here," I said. I took her arm by the wrist and wiped vomit from her fingers. Amy wrinkled her nose in disgust at this, but to be honest I had never attended a party of John's where someone didn't either vomit on me or near me. I was kind of inured to it.

As I worked I said, "When I was in seventh grade, I took Emily Parks to the Fall Festival. First time I had ever been anywhere with a girl. We wandered around and ate elephant ears and saltwater taffy and lemon shakeups, all of that festival stuff. We get on the Ferris wheel, and riiiiight as the ride is about to end I lean over and puke in her lap. The ride slows to a stop, you know, so they can unload all of the riders. And we wind up at the very top. Waiting. She's sitting up there, with a lap full of vomit, crying. And we're up there for-ev-er."

Amy's hand seemed pretty clean. I tossed the soiled rag in the snow and gave her a new one and the bottle of water. I stepped back and said, "I didn't ask another girl out until I was a junior in high school. Seventeen years old before I even held a girl's hand. All because somewhere, in the back of my mind, I knew I would wind up puking on her."

Amy didn't react. She drank some water and wiped splatters of vomit off her pants and her shoes, her fingers having to be frozen now doing wet work in this weather. I caught a glimpse of her face and saw that look, a familiar look, a sort of embarrassment that is almost numbing. Like she wanted to dig a hole, bury herself in it and let grass grow over the top.

A warmth spread behind my eyes. Everything turned red in my brain, my skull suddenly filled with Tabasco sauce. There was a tingling in my gut, muscles tensing. I picked up the used towels and walked back toward a trash can in the parking lot, near where Tyler and the guys were standing. I tossed in the towels and Tyler leaned over, whispering, "You're a nice guy, Dave. So all I'm sayin' is watch, that's all I'm sayin'. Watch out bein' a nice guy because you can get fucked."

A blink. A searing pain in my hand. Blood.

There were arms on me, grabbing my jacket, pulling me, and there was blood on my knuckles and blood in my mouth. My jaws were clenched, I had bitten my tongue and tasted warm copper. Tyler was on his hands and knees, blood dripping from his nose and mouth, grunting that they had better hold me back because I was a fucking psycho and that I had broken his fucking nose. Then John was there, in my face, saying okay, okay, back off, just go, get outta here. I looked down at my throbbing hands and saw the knuckles were split, like I had been punching concrete. John pushed me back from the group, looked over my shoulder and said, "Get him outta here."

A fat blond kid was standing over Tyler, looked like a bloated version of him and I realized this was Tyler's brother or cousin or something. And the fat kid was saying see, see what happens when you run your fucking mouth, Tyler, that one day talking shit was gonna get him killed because he was gonna say the wrong thing and some nigger was gonna shoot him in the back. John turned and joined the group, and I was standing there in the parking lot by myself, lost, disoriented. Tyler outweighed me by seventy-five pounds and, where I spent my days shelving DVDs, he spent his days carrying roofs up ladders. But the strangest thing, the sickening thing, was the urge that flashed through my mind as I was standing over him—

—*the urge to BITE*—

—and I knew this was it again, that I had lost time, that I had lost

354

myself. Then I felt a pull on my jacket and the unique sensation of a handless arm reaching around my midsection.

"Come on. Come on, David."

Amy circled around, her hand on my sleeve.

"Amy, I—"

"Come on. It's okay. Come on."

She started turning me back toward the truck and I felt everyone staring. She got behind me and started pushing me toward the Bronco.

"Come on, David. Take deep breaths. You're fine."

"Amy, don't—"

"Nope. Come on. Keep going. Vrrrooooommmm . . ."

That last part was Amy making an engine sound as she steered me toward the truck, like she was driving me. She reached around me and opened the door, then pushed me into the seat like you see cops doing with handcuffed suspects. She slammed the door, circled around and sat in beside me. We sat that way for a moment; I glanced out my window and saw the whole group watching. I reached up with a shaking hand to twist the key and realized the engine was already running. I tried to slow my breathing. I couldn't keep my hands still.

Amy asked, "Are you okay?"

"Just, give me a second."

"You kicked that guy's ass."

"Amy . . ."

"Come on, let's go. Before he gets up and beats the crap out of you."

WE GOT BACK to my house to find it ransacked. It was difficult to tell because I'm not the world's greatest housekeeper myself, but by the time I was in the kitchen I knew they had been here: I don't normally keep the oven open. I whipped out the gun and prowled around the house, finding it empty. Amy asked what they were looking for. I dodged the question by pointing out what a pity it was they tossed the place because it was immaculate before they got here and that it was too bad she didn't get to see it when it was clean. I went to the kitchen and ran water over my bleeding knuckles.

"Look," Amy said, from behind me. "They threw laundry all over your floor in there."

"Yeah. And they wore the clothes first, the bastards."

"And what were they looking for again?"

A pause. I was on the verge of revealing what was probably our biggest and most dangerous secret to someone whom I had known for all of a day. I let out a breath and looked right into her eyes. The irises were too green, that was the thing. Like grass after a week of spring rain. And there was a piercing, electric intelligence in those eyes that I was too stupid to notice before. Seeing right through me. And I suddenly had the very dismaying realization that I probably could not lie to this girl, for one very simple reason. She was smarter than me.

I said, "They were looking for the soy sauce. I know they didn't find it, though."

"The what?"

I didn't answer. I did a walk around the house, saw if anything was broken. It looked like they had taken the batteries out of my clock for some reason, and the glass fixture on my ceiling fan was cracked.

Amy followed me around, pestering me with questions, suddenly desperately curious. The truth was, I wasn't sure how to explain it. After about the fifth time she turned the conversation to it, I held up a silencing hand, made a shushing sound, and put a single finger to her lips.

"All will become apparent in good time, sweet Amy."

For a second, I seriously thought she was going to punch me. I went outside and did a walk-around of the house, glancing nervously at the toolshed and praying that the door wouldn't be standing open.

What are you talking about, dipshit? If they came and took the body off your hands that'd be a blessing.

I noticed the flag was up on my mailbox. This was Sunday. I went over and opened it, found a palm-sized package inside. There was no name, no address, no postage. I stared at it with some trepidation, then

356

peeled it open, thinking it might be the world's tiniest mail bomb. Inside was a necklace, a little gold cross on a delicate chain. I had seen it before, though seeing it close I noticed that the cross was formed of two tiny nails, bound together by thread-like wire. There was a piece of paper inside, too, a folded piece of stationery bearing a cartoon puppy with a pencil in his mouth. The writing was in sparkly pink:

Hi! I had a dream
& an angel told me to
give this to you!
It's always brought me
luck!!
God Bless!
(Smiley face)
—Krissy Lovelace

All of the I's were dotted with big, friendly loops. Everybody wants to help.

When I went in, Amy was in the bathroom running water. She emerged, stuffing Altoids mints into her mouth from a tin. I went to the fridge and said, "You want something to drink? I have, uh, some fruity Leinenkugel's beer and, uh, some kind of terrible plum-flavored liquor John's friend from the Czech Republic sent him. It tastes like the juice from a single plum was squeezed into a fifty-five-gallon drum of paint thinner."

The cans of Leinenkugel's had masking tape on them with JOHN'S printed in ink. Amy looked around me and said, "John is protective about his beer, isn't he?"

"I put that label on there. When company comes I want them to know the Leinie's is his, not mine. Do you want it?"

"Uh, no. I don't drink," she said, shaking her head and brushing the hair from her eyes for the four hundredth time since yesterday. "I mean, I drink liquids. Not alcohol. I couldn't mix it with the pain pills. So who do we tell about the monsters?"

"Uh, what?"

"All this, everything we saw. Who do we talk to about this sort of thing?"

"I think the government has an eight hundred number but you just get one of those automated answering things. No. John and I are going to, uh, look into it. Today. Before they have a chance to come for you again."

I closed the refrigerator and faced her, then told her an abbreviated and less retarded version of John's story about the Drain Rooter site and the Mall of the Dead.

She said, "Why don't we just go? To another town, or state, or Canada. When's the last time you've heard of somebody exploding in Canada?"

I shook my head.

"Why not?"

Because we're under the eye, Amy.

"There are things you still don't know. The shadow people . . . they've spoken to me. They know my name. It's . . . personal somehow. With them. I think trying to get away from that by leaving—even climbing into a rocket ship and leaving the fuckin' planet—would be laughable. To them it'd be like watching a hamster trying to escape by running on his little wheel really fast. I picture the rest of my life, running scared, forever. No. I can't. I won't. We're gonna go in there, where they live. And we're gonna go armed."

"I wanna go."

"Amy—"

"No, don't even try. I want to see. I have a right to."

"Amy, we're going into that place with the intention of leaving it as a smoking hole in the ground."

Praise be to Allah!

"I know."

"No, you think this is cool, I can see it in your eyes. It's not cool. We do not have this thing under control. Let me tell you a story. When I was little we had our sewer line back up. Toilet overflowing and all that. So they had to come and root it out, and what they pulled out of the sewer line was a woodchuck. There was a break in the pipe somewhere, two joints that had pulled apart, and this thing had gotten in. Okay? I mean to a woodchuck, this had to be the adventure of a lifetime. Hidden tunnel, seeming to go on for miles. So he's crawling and exploring and waiting to see the hidden treasure at the end. And then, he gets drowned. *In our poo.*"

Amy nodded and said, "Well, that's sad."

"The saddest. John and I, we're the woodchuck. See, I can read it on you, that you think you're really a part of something now, that we're gonna do something really great today and change the world. Well Amy, understand what I'm about to say. There's something terribly wrong with us. John and me. Amy, there are days when I'm sure—sure—that I'm stone-cold raving batshit insane. That none of this is happening, that I'm raving about it from a padded room somewhere. And do you know how I respond to that, to that knowledge that I may be delusional and dangerous? I arm myself. With a gun."

"David, you're not—"

"Listen. The only reason I'm standing up to these guys now is because I'm in a corner. I don't have a choice. You do. And if you make the wrong choice, there is an excellent chance that these are your last hours on Earth. All the things you wanted to do with your life, they may not happen. All the things you like to do, all the things you thought you might like to do in the future, all gone. And it'll be because of me. Because I led you into my turd pipe."

She said, "Why do you, like, hate yourself?"

"If I knew me as somebody else, I would hate me just as much. Why have a double standard?"

"Well, that's just stupid."

I rubbed my eyes and sighed. I reached into my front pocket and pulled out the necklace and held it up.

"Here. It's good luck. Or something."

I went to Amy and reached around her neck, clasping the thin chain under her hair.

I glanced out of the window, saw the snow was coming down again.

Facing her, I said, "You deserved some kind of normal life, Amy. I can picture you, in college, a family back home. Maybe you're working part-time at a music store. Geeky guys coming in and flirting with you at the counter. And I could come in and make some kind of awkward conversation with you and you could keep making excuses not to go out with me and I would just keep coming back and back and then you would get a restraining order against me, and my dad would get it overturned. Finally you would agree and we could go to a picnic or bowling or whatever normal people do when they're together. What *do* normal people do when they're together?"

"I have no idea."

It's funny, pretending that it's normal to have a conversation with somebody standing three inches away.

She leaned in and—

IT LOOKED LIKE the world outside my window had lost its signal and gone to static. Snowing like hell, wind whipping it around. I leaned against my window, feeling the cold glass against my forehead, breaths fogging up a circular patch under my nose. There was a time when I would have found the idea of certain death a little comforting, like being on the last day of a job I hated. A weight lifted. Now, feeling the cold glass on my face and wet hair cooling my scalp and my mouth tasting vaguely like secondhand Altoids and knowing I would never see snow again, I felt a little like crying. But just a little.

I saw the grille of a car emerge like a ghost, headlights faint in the whiteout. The big car swung into my driveway, John's Caddie. Through the window I watched as John ducked out, wearing an Army-issue fatigue jacket. He circled around to his trunk, popped it and pulled out a canvas backpack. He slung it over his shoulder and then pulled out a large tool that was unmistakably a—

"Is that a medieval battle-ax?" Amy asked from behind me, rubbing a towel through her hair.

"With John, we'll be fortunate if it turns out to be nothing stupider than that."

The ax was a leftover from high school, when we used to be big into Dungeons and Dragons. I mean, um, bear hunting. John burst in the door at that moment, dusted with snow, shouting, "We are gonna fuck that place *up*."

He tossed down his load with a force that shook the floor, then bent over and hefted the ax that I believe was one of several props he stole from that medieval-themed restaurant he worked at for a while. He paused to let his eyes flick to mine and Amy's wet hair and presumably asked himself if our showers had overlapped in any way. He was too polite to ask.

Then he turned and stepped past me into the hallway. He studied the wall, then raised the ax and swung it into the wall with a *THOCK* that sent plaster dust flying.

He swung three more times, then thrust his hand into the hole he had created and pulled out a small object that fit in the palm of his hand. He glanced at it, wiped the dust on his shirt, then tossed it to me. I caught the small canister. Silver, the size of a pill bottle.

Amy saw it and asked, "What's that?"

"You've never seen it before?"

"Why would I?"

"Big Jim had it at one time. We don't know where he got it though."

I quickly relayed to her the story of the weather guy and the mall and how we came across the container.

"So," she said. "What's in it?"

CHAPTER 15

D-Day

"VERY SIMPLY," I said to Amy, "the reason we can see things that you can't is right there in that bottle. We don't know where it came from or what exactly it does. But in those first hours after you take it, your brain is tuned in like nothing you can imagine. Eyes like the Hubble telescope, sensing light that's not even on the spectrum. You might be able to read minds, make time stop, cook pasta that's exactly right every time. And you can see the shadowy things that share this world, the ones who are always present and always hidden. It'd be like if a doctor could walk around with microscopes strapped to his eyes all of the time, so he could just look and see the sickness crawling around inside us."

Amy pointed out, "Well, he'd still have to be able to see inside your blood vessels and lungs and all that. A microscope wouldn't—"

"These microscopes also have some kind of X-ray vision attachment."

She reached out and picked up the canister.

"Ugh. It's cold."

"The container is always cold," I said. "It refrigerates the contents twenty-four hours a day. And we don't know how. No batteries, no energy source. And it's been working for years. The sauce, it has to be kept cool or it becomes, uh, unstable."

Unstable, in the way that a swarm of killer bees is "unstable."

"And you're going to take it again?"

"I don't want to. But I think we have to. It'll level the playing field, get us on the same frequency as the bad guys. It's the reason we're alive."

Oh, and everybody else who has ever tried it has wound up dead. The irony.

I said, "When I ran across this bottle, it was empty, just like mine."

I opened the bottle and shook out the contents. Two capsules, black as licorice.

"I bet you're wondering where these two came from. We're always wondering the same thing. The stuff seems to show up when it wants to."

She said, "You're not going to let me take any, are you?"

"I wouldn't wish it on my worst enemy. But you're not supposed to take it. If you were, there would be three capsules in here."

John said, "We better swallow these before they attack us."

We did. We waited.

"Sooooo . . ." Amy asked, "how do you know when it's working?"

I said, "You just, uh, start noticing things. It's hard to explain. Like bits of radio signal coming in through the static."

With that, a thought passed through my head, a flash like a shooting star. Pro wrestling was *real*. But not real in the sense that we perceive reality. It was more real than reality. Then, I worked out pi to four

363

thousand decimal places and realized that if anyone ever drew a truly perfect circle it would actually look like a straight line to our eyes. I looked at the silver pill canister and realized it was more than four thousand years old. Or less than four seconds.

I said to John, "You know that if you walked around the world, your hat would travel thirty-one feet farther than your shoes?"

John said, "I dunno, Dave, but before we make a bomb I have to shave half the dog."

I nodded. He got up, called to Molly and herded her into my bathroom. I wondered when the soy sauce would take effect.

To kill some time, I got up and hunted around the closet in my laundry room until I found my squirt gun. This was one of those huge modern guns, green and with a logo that said BIG GUSHER on the side. It had a separate two-gallon tank with hooks for a belt. The commercials bragged it could spray a soaking, quarter-inch-wide stream of water for fifty feet and that was pretty much true. The gun was sticky from when John filled it with beer last summer.

I hunted around until I found a roll of duct tape and an extended disposable lighter, the kind people light grills with. I gathered three bottles of flammable chemicals that I would mix to form the fuel. I took my armload of items and dumped them on the table.

Amy said, "So, you're making a flamethrower?"

"Amy, we gotta be prepared. We don't know what we'll find in that place, but for all we know it could be the Devil himself."

"David, what possible good is that thing gonna do?"

"Oh, no, you didn't hear me. I said it's *a flamethrower*." Girls.

"But if something is from Hell why would you use a—"

Amy stopped, apparently deciding against pursuing that question and instead asked, "What am I taking? When we go? Is there a weapon or something for me?"

"Have you forgotten the woodchuck already?"

I went to work on the squirt gun. The sound of rustling and growling emerged from the bathroom. Under that I could detect the low hum of my beard trimmer.

Amy put her hand on mine, her other hand balled up in a fist on the table.

"There was a sheep," she said. "In Scotland, I think. And this sheep escaped from the ranch. And you know they shear sheep for their wool. Well, this thing stayed gone for seven years. Finally they found it, in a cave. And there was nobody to shear the sheep, so when they found it, its wool was gigantic. It was, like, a walking Afro. And it wound up back on the ranch, just another sheep, but for the rest of its life it knew that for a while, it was free. It had that and nobody could take it away. Do you understand? I'm like you; I want to face this thing. Whatever it is. We're like that sheep, taking our shot. If for no other reason than just to say we did."

"I do understand. Trust me, I do. And it takes a special kind of person to make up something so utterly bullshitty. You know their wool doesn't just keep growing like that."

"That's not even the point, David."

I went to take her other hand, saw my hand disappear into hers and realized that it was because she didn't have another hand. But there it was, thin fingers wrapped in a tight ball.

She looked down, curious, not sure what I was staring at. I said, "I think the sauce is working. Go put on the *Scooby* glasses. I want to try something."

She got up, found them on the counter, then sat down and I gestured to look at the spot where her hand shouldn't be.

"Now this time, really concentrate. I don't know if—"

No point in finishing the sentence. Her jaw hung open.

"Oh! I can see it! How is that possible?"

She tried it with and without the glasses, saw the hand appear and disappear. "Look! My fingernails! I had let them get long and I was meaning to cut them before I went in for the surgery. No wonder it hurts . . ."

Then she lifted the clenched fist off the table and, very slowly, uncurled the fingers. She laid the hand flat on the table.

"David. This is crazy."

"I'm pretty sure that's about the least crazy thing you're gonna see today."

The bathroom door burst open, and Molly came trotting out. The left half of her body had been shaved almost down to the skin. The right half was as shaggy as before. John emerged after her, brushing a layer of dog hair off his clothes.

John said, "Well, that's done."

Before I could stop her, Amy asked, "Why did you—"

"It was Molly's idea. She wants to look like two different dogs when she's coming and going. She thinks it will make it easier for her to steal food."

He turned to me.

"That's one complicated dog, Dave. Have you started on the bomb?"

"The what?"

SOCIETY IS DOOMED for one very simple reason: it takes dozens of men working months with millions of dollars in materials to build a building, but only one dumb-ass with a bomb to bring it down. John and I had scavenged the house for bomb-making materials. Neither of us knew how to make a bomb prior to today, but we improvised one by analyzing the molecular makeup of the ingredients. My head was taking on a fiery soreness, cooking like an engine run too long and too hard. I wondered, not for the first time, if using the soy sauce would shave years off my life and I realized that it probably didn't matter.

So, using a packet of Jell-O and the innards of two smoke detectors and a pack of shredded playing cards and the refrigerant from my truck's air conditioner and nine other ingredients, we fashioned a sticky explosive clay, mint green in color. We poured it into a tinfoil mold we made in the shape of a dog bone and stuck it in the freezer to solidify. The idea was to disguise it as something that would seem normal being in a dog owner's front pocket, should we get caught and searched.

I sat at the kitchen table, snapping brass bullets into the one spare magazine I had bought for the Smith.

"Here's what I think," said John. "That facility, they've got to have some kind of intercom system. We sneak our way to the office where the mic is, and put the boom box in front of it. We go right for the fucking jugular: 'November Rain,' on a loop. While they're all holdin' their ears and begging for forgiveness, we go find this Korrok fucker and shove this bomb right up his ass. Or get him to eat it, if it turns out he's a huge dog."

I nodded and stood. The real plan, the unspoken one that hid between John's words, was that we would die. But, we would die in the middle of what Korrok's people would remember as the single most retarded and baffling incident in their history. We would be their Guy Fawkes. They would create a holiday about us. If we were going to wind up in the belly of Korrok, might as well see if we could make him choke on the way down.

Me and John, I mean. Not Amy.

I let out a long breath and put on my coat. I dropped in the gun and the spare magazine. John threw on his Army jacket and leaned over, unzipped the backpack and pulled out a chainsaw. He had tied a length of bungee strap to it so he could carry it slung over his shoulder. He then picked up the homemade flamethrower, not questioning for a moment what it was or what it did. He flicked on the lighter and a delicate tongue of flame licked out in front of the barrel. He nodded in approval and blew it out, then grabbed the battle-ax off the floor and handed it to Amy. She managed to hold it aloft in her one hand for exactly two seconds before she let the head clang to the floor. She let go of the handle, then dug some ChapStick from her jacket and smeared it on her lips.

We were loading up the Bronco when John reminded me of the exploding dog bone. I ran inside, pulled it out of the aluminum-foil mold and walked into the yard with it in my hand.

I probably should have seen this next part coming. Molly ran over, half shaved and half shaggy, and snatched the bone from my fingers.

At John's request I'll skip over this next part, which involved us chasing the dog around the yard for a very long time and finally John tackling her, prying open her jaws and finding no remnant of exploding bone in there.

I began to walk away from the situation in disgust when a snow-covered John, still on the ground with Molly, said, "Look!"

He was holding up Molly's front paw. I saw nothing unusual about it, but then realized the pi-like symbol we had seen on the carcass of exploded Molly was missing from this dog's paw. Molly licked her nose and sneezed. John stood up; Molly flipped onto her feet and trotted away.

I said, "What do you think it means?"

"Hell, I don't know. We need the bone bomb back. Take the chainsaw and cut open the dog."

Amy objected to this and came up with what I thought was a far more disgusting plan of trying to flush the bone from the other end of Molly. She went inside and dug out two convenience-store burritos from my freezer and heated them in the microwave until they were lukewarm.

After feeding both burritos to Molly and seeing no immediate results, John said, "All right, let's go. We're gonna be late for our certain death."

WHITEOUT. THERE WAS more snow than air in the atmosphere. We went fifteen miles an hour through town, the whole place shut down under the storm. It was, I thought, an actual blizzard. I had never seen one. About halfway there, John squinted into his rearview mirror.

"What the hell?"

Red-and-blue lights swept across the frosted rear window. We all glanced at each other, figuring we could either pull over or plow through the snowstorm for the slowest police chase since O.J. I pulled over, two tires ramping up onto mounds of roadside snow. A blue, bear-like figure strode up to the driver's-side door. I rolled down the window and felt freezing bits of snow land on my cheek. A face leaned down. I saw it and felt myself tense, my hand going right to the butt of the Smith.

Oh, crap.

It was Drake. But it was not Drake. His wide face sat there inches from mine, an inhuman blankness in the expression, like that of an embalmed body at a funeral. His eyes were pure black, no whites, no irises. I blinked, and his eyes looked human again. Human, but as lifeless as a doll's.

Drake's mouth said, "OUT." He flung the word at me like a punch. I smelled a puff of breath that was chemically sweet, like a little kid after drinking too much Kool-Aid. Drake yanked open the door and grabbed my jacket, pulling me out. He clamped on my shoulders and spun me around and pushed me toward the truck. I heard the other door open and there was John, standing there, looking at Drake and knowing what I knew. Drake was gone.

The big cop pulled out a baton from a loop in his belt and smacked his palm with it.

"SO," he said, barking the sound so that it was barely an English word. "So. Big smart guy. Big guy. Dolls and jellyfish and the night comes to life and walks on Mulholland Drive."

He smacked his palm. His pudgy lips spread to reveal a shark's grin. I wanted to grab for my gun but a swing with that club could break the bones in my wrist in half a second. I don't know if I was poised to make my move or frozen in panic. At any second, the Drake thing could end this little adventure before it got started. I glanced at John, hoping he had some kind of plan. The look in his eyes said he was hoping the same from me. I looked back at Drake's squad car and saw he hadn't come alone. Riding with him was a muscular black cop who was climbing out of the passenger side of the car now, snow landing on his hat, grinning the grin of the freshly mad.

Drake stepped around to the grille of my truck. He said, "MUL-HOLLAND DRIVE! SMART GUY! THE BLUE BOX! THE BLUE KEY! THE BLUE EYE!" He swung the stick and a headlight exploded with a crash. Drake smiled again, then bent his knees and leapt six feet into the air. He landed on my hood with a *thud* that rocked the whole truck on its suspension. I saw Amy jump in the backseat, eyes bouncing back and forth between me and John. Molly barked, but made no other effort to help.

Drake looked down at me from his perch on my hood. He stuck the end of the baton into his pocket, unzipped his pants, and began pissing on my windshield. Urine splattered and yellowed the pile of snow bunched along my windshield wipers.

"HA! KORROK WAITS IN THE ALLEY, SMART GUY!"

Drake's partner was disrobing. The black cop was flinging clothing into the road, mumbling to himself. He finally yanked off a pair of boxers, put his hands on his naked hips and screamed something like "tubesteak" over and over again to the snowy sky.

Drake finished his pee, zipped up. He lifted one shoe, reached down and pulled it off. He peeled off his sock and raised the foot toward me.

He stood that way for a long moment, foot raised like a photo of a field-goal kicker caught in midkick. I glanced back and saw the other cop was packing handfuls of snow onto his groin.

I looked back at Drake and finally I saw what he was showing me. On his big toe was a tiny tattoo. The pi symbol, just like the old Molly had.

"THIS IS JUST A RECORDING, SMART GUY!"

He lowered his foot and pulled out his baton again. He held it up and pointed at me with his other hand.

"NOW BEND OVER! BEND OVER AND DROP YOUR PANTS, SMART GUY!"

Simultaneously, John and I ducked back inside the Bronco. I threw it into gear and slammed on the gas, Drake still standing on the hood.

The truck lurched forward and we barreled down the road, but Drake stayed planted, crouching like an oversized hood ornament. He bellowed at me over the wind, flinging aside his hat and tossing his hair.

"WHERE YOU GOING? HA HA HA! LET'S GO INTO THE ALLEY! HE'S WAITING, SMART GUY!"

He reared back with the baton, as if ready to smash the windshield. I slammed on the brakes, the truck spun out, Drake went flying.

He vanished behind the miniature mountain range of piled snow along the road. I heard a faint scream that twisted into a howl, a high-pitched sound that human vocal cords couldn't duplicate. I considered going to help him. The urge quickly passed. I threw the truck in reverse, stepped on the gas, threw it into gear and fishtailed down the road. I peered into my mirrors, looked nervously for him or his naked snow-crotched partner. Their car was nowhere to be seen. Molly stood and stared out the back window, shuddering and issuing a low, rumbling growl.

Amy was asking something, asking what was wrong with him, was he dead, should we go back. Neither I nor John answered. I just drove. *Gotta push on, don't even look back.*

Something moved in my rearview mirror, a dark shape against the snow. I looked, thought I saw something, something moving fast. Not a person. Or maybe I didn't see it.

WE FOUND THE inlet road in the snow, turned in and crept through the mall parking lot. We watched for other parked vehicles, saw none. Our light was fading fast.

We filed out and loaded up and marched across the lot, Molly in the lead, our heads on swivels. Visibility didn't even extend to the edge of the parking lot, where a white curtain of snow hid the rest of the world. I had the gun in my hand, didn't even remember pulling it out. A snowflake flew right up my nose. Just before we reached the door I saw John spin around, like he had seen something in the swirling mass of white. I squinted, could see nothing, and we both dismissed it as adrenaline. We should have known better.

We filed inside, using the same entrance John had used earlier that morning. Snow was pouring in through the skylight now, piling an inch high on the floor, drafts of chilled air flowing down from the gap. Once inside and out of the wind, John flicked the lighter that served as the pilot light for the toy flamethrower.

John said, "Drake's foot. What was the deal with that? I thought he was trying to kick your head and he just missed."

"He had that symbol, the little pi. Like Molly."

"What do you think, it's like a mark of some kind?"

"Of what?"

"Evil?"

Amy asked, "Wouldn't it make it harder to do evil if they had to carry around a mark?"

John shrugged. "Once they're barefoot and kicking you, it's already too late. Follow me."

We went into the maintenance room. To John and me, the big, decorative doorway stood in the center of the wall to our right, plain as day and as out of place as the face on Mars. Amy saw only a wall. Until, of course, she tried viewing it through the *Scooby* glasses. I let the little maintenance door close behind me. John looked at Amy and nodded his head toward the other door and said, "Ghost door."

I said, "Please don't call it that."

Molly trotted past me and went right to the door and sniffed at it. Interesting. John said, "I feel like we should look for a save point."

I saw a long, curved handle on the door. I let out a long breath and raised the gun. John raised the fire gusher. I reached out for the handle and watched as my hand passed right through.

"Shit," said John. "It's a ghost knob."

I sighed and looked at John, was about to suggest heading back home and curling up in front of the fireplace. But then Amy stepped forward, the wet and wrinkled cardboard glasses askew on her face.

She reached out with her left arm, the arm that, in reality, didn't have a hand. But with the hand that I could see, the ghost of a hand that was no longer there, she reached out and grabbed the door handle that was also not really there. The handle turned.

With a rumbling not unlike the sound in your head when you crunch ice, a vertical slit formed in the wall and then tore open, widening. John and I both crouched into a fighting stance and I felt my bladder loosen a little. The wall melted and peeled back like a curtain until there was a door-sized opening before us with a bunched seam around the edge, rolls of plaster and jutting splinters of wood. Beyond it was a tiny, round room that I somehow sensed was an elevator.

John stepped through the door and looked to his right. He pointed out a number on the wall, in black, that said "10." After a few seconds, it switched to "9."

I felt Molly brush past my legs and trot into the open doorway. I turned, put my hands on Amy's shoulders.

"Go."

"What? No."

"You've got money, from the insurance? When your parents—"

"Yeah, so—"

"Wait for us, wait someplace light. Give us an hour. Then if we're not back take my truck and—"

"David, I can't even drive."

I dug in my pocket and pressed my cell phone into her hand.

"Then call a cab. I'm dead serious. If we're not back in an hour, fly. Take the cab straight to the airport and fly away, get on a plane, go to Alaska. Stay far away from this place forever and ever and forget you ever knew me."

"Alaska? Why—"

"Because it's always daytime there."

"No it's not!"

"Actually, Dave," John said from behind me, "I think it's always nighttime there."

"It doesn't matter," squealed Amy, "because I'm not going anyw—"

"Amy, please. This is insane. When that door opened the only thought that went through my mind was that I would be damned for letting you die at the hands of whatever came through it. We've gone this far and you're still okay and I want to do this one good thing while I've got the chance. For no other reason than because when I die—and I'm pretty damned sure now that I will within the hour—I want to be able to say I did this one last thing, this one unselfish thing before I went."

I pulled the Smith & Wesson from my pocket and went to put it in her other hand, realized she didn't have another hand, then shoved it into her coat pocket instead. Amy started to say something, but was interrupted when the metal door exploded.

The little maintenance door flew across the room and bounced off the opposite wall. We all ducked, and in a cloud of dust I saw something the size of a man but shaped all wrong, backward joints jutting into the air, a tiny brainless head, skin of notched alligator hide. There was a second of brain paralysis when I couldn't register what I was seeing. But I had seen the thing before, in Jim's basement. Only this one was moving, crouching low like a predator, turning to look at us.

Amy was on her knees and had opened her mouth to say something, but before she could, a column of flame poured past her face.

"DOWN!" screamed John, about a half second later than I would have preferred. Orange fire licked the creature and the floor and the wall behind it. I thought I smelled my own hair burning. The beast writhed and thrashed about, but apparently its skin wasn't that flammable because when John let off there were only small tongues of flame licking at its shoulders.

It looked pissed.

John worked the shotgun-like pump on the squirt gun to build up the pressure and fire again. I flung my body aside and plunged my hand into my pocket to get the Smith—then remembered I had given it to Amy ten seconds ago. I pulled out my car keys instead and flung them at the beast; they bounced off its chest with a jingle.

The monster advanced on me, racing past Amy with quick, blurry little steps, moving like it was on fast-forward. I tried to stand but suddenly there were claws around my neck, and a second after that I was flying. A wall pounded my back and suddenly I was in the little round elevator looking up at John; the beast had thrown me like a child's toy. I scrambled to my feet and this thing was on me again, filling the doorway, blocking us into the little round room. Molly was standing there next to me, sniffing at the monster's foot and deciding it would be unpleasant to eat.

John was screaming something but then this thing had its claws in my shoulder, pain spilling down the whole side of my body. I leaned my head around the beast and screamed, "AAAAAMMMMMYYYYYY!!!!!! RUUUUUUUNNNNNN!!!!!!"

She stood there behind the beast, petrified for a long moment. The beast was doing something with its other hand, rearing back, probably half a second from ripping my face off. I felt John's hands clumsily prying at the monster's claws, trying to get them off me. The beast's face was two inches from mine, its little eyes twitching, and I could smell the thing and it smelled like Old Spice somehow. From the corner of my eye I saw that the number on the wall said, "2."

Amy turned to go and suddenly I had a new mission, to keep the beast here, to make it take as long as possible to eat us.

A second beast appeared.

In the ruins of the maintenance doorway, another monster just like this one. As it advanced on Amy I had the crazy thought that the thing had clumps of snow stuck to its crotch.

The number on the wall vanished. The ghost door closed.

Everything stopped. The wall had melted back into place as if it had always been as solid as a, uh, wall.

Suddenly I was looking at the head and shoulders and claws of the monster emerging from the solid wall, as if it were a mounted hunter's trophy. The ghost door had closed right on the bastard, half on this side and half on the other. After a second, the severed chunks clumped to the floor, leaving red stains behind on the wall. The clawed hand was still embedded in my shoulder, the severed arm hanging off and dripping red on the floor.

John muttered, "What the—I wonder how many employees they lose that way?"

"Amy!!" I screamed into the wall, tearing off the shorn limb and flinging it to the ground with disgust. The claws were still twitching on their own when it landed. Molly was at my feet, barking, yelping. I heard nothing from the other side. I pounded the wall with my palms, then felt the surface sliding under my fingers.

"AMY!!! AAAAMMMMYYYYY!!!"

I punched the wall and thought I broke my hand. I felt motion and knew that we were moving upward, which was impossible because the mall did not have a second floor. I cursed again, put my hands on my knees, realized that every life that touched mine ended in utter horror.

Molly whimpered at my feet. John said something, something about reaching the top and being ready and I got the idea. I stood upright and took the chainsaw from John, trembling all over. I looked over the chainsaw, figuring out how to work it. Could I have gotten caught in this situation with a dumber weapon?

I glanced around and realized the boom box hadn't made it into the elevator. Man, did any of it matter at this point?

Up and up and up we went. Was the elevator climbing in midair? John held the fire gusher at the ready. He was saying something about how there was nothing we could do and we just had to get in and out fast enough and that we had all the more reason to survive and blah, blah, blah. Whatever.

The trip up took twenty damned minutes. Hundreds of feet. Finally we jolted to a stop and an opening appeared in the wall. We were looking at a long corridor, rounded at the top and made seemingly of smooth stone, like marble or polished granite. It was lit with fluorescent lights and decorated with warning signs about contamination and ID badges.

I wrapped my fingers tight around the plastic handle of the chainsaw and stepped into the hall, Molly following a step behind. We went maybe the length of four or five city blocks, John with the little pilot flame dancing at the end of his flamethrowing toy, me wondering how much noise the chainsaw would make when I pulled the rope thing. Or if it even had gas in it.

We reached a door. Just a regular metal door with a knob. We readied ourselves. John flung it open and we ducked inside.

The floor turned into a metal grate and we realized we had emerged onto a catwalk. I looked over the rail and saw we were suspended over an expanse the size of an airplane hangar, but dimly lit. The floor was populated with people in white, bustling around like a marketplace, swarming around tables and equipment. It was noisy as hell. Machines and grinding and rustling of feet, people working in the dark.

We took a few steps forward and realized we weren't alone. A man, wearing a white jumpsuit with a hood and a glass faceplate that reminded me of the contamination-free "clean suits" you see people wearing in labs, stood on the catwalk about ten feet away. He had a Subway sandwich bag in one gloved hand and a pack of cigarettes in the other. He stared at us for a long moment, eyes bouncing from Molly to my chainsaw to the finger of flame dancing from a tool that the man probably couldn't help but think was a flamethrowing squirt gun.

John said, "We're from the fire department."

The man spun on his heels and sprinted the other direction, feet clanging on the grated metal floor. We gave chase. He passed through a doorway. We followed and found ourselves on a spiral stairwell going down, John shouting at the man all the way, asking to see his flammability permit.

The man hit bottom and threw himself out of another doorway. We followed and found ourselves at ground level on the factory floor, or whatever it was, surrounded by people in white jumpsuits who were doing an excellent job of ignoring us. These men did not wear the face masks and seemed, to a man, to be completely bald.

Dark, dark, dark. Little red lights here and there on pieces of machinery that I couldn't identify, but no overhead lights and no lamps and nothing but little glowing patches that cast upside-down shadows. The man we were chasing disappeared into the crowded darkness and we didn't follow.

To my left were blue plastic barrels, rows and rows of them, hundreds. At the edge were two without lids, full of a deep crimson fluid that indeed looked like transmission fluid. Two men were standing over one of the open barrels, dipping into it and collecting samples in vials. One of the men turned to face me, and I saw that he did not have a face.

Or, I should say he had half a face. The forehead curled down over where the eyes should be, joining the cheeks. The nostrils were wide and flat, African. He had a thin, lipless mouth and huge ears. The guy next to him was the same. The four guys down the row as well. Those guys were hefting huge translucent plastic bags, vacuum-packed and shrunk around what looked like sides of beef.

I gawked around like a little tourist kid. Along my left were long glass tanks as tall as houses, something you'd see at a city aquarium. The liquid inside was a cloudy pink. Floating inside were pale blurred shapes that might have been people and other things, smaller lumps that held the shape of small animals, dogs and things like squirrels. I walked down the row, dazed. I blinked, trying desperately to adjust to the semidarkness, trying to take everything in. I had the crazy thought that no wonder they didn't pay to light the place. Most of the people here didn't have eyes. No need to pay the extra electric bill.

No matter where you go, management is always a bunch of cheap bastards.

I heard John make a breathy sound behind me, shock or disgust or both. I followed his gaze and saw a wire cage twenty or so feet away, containing a thin, young boy. Maybe ten years old. He stood there, looking terrified, fingers hooked through the wire mesh, staring at me with wide blue eyes. There was a device next to the cage, round and maybe five feet tall. It had a red light glowing on the side. The light flipped to green, an electronic sound emitted. The boy screamed.

The boy's skin bubbled and wrinkled. One of his eyes deflated and ran down his cheek as a white goo, not unlike semen. Muscle liquefied and fell off his bones. He folded into the ground, left as a quivering lump. The lump bubbled and twitched and took on shape. Two stumpy feet emerged. A cloven hoof. Two more feet, a round body. I heard whimpering behind me, Molly watching along with me. In five seconds, I was looking through the cage at a pink, well-fed pig.

"Mother. Fucker."

That was John, behind me. The pig trotted calmly over to the wires of the cage, sniffing at me. It put its front hooves on the wire cage and I thought, but wasn't sure, I saw the same imprinted pi tattoo Molly once had and Drake had and—what the fuck did it all mean? I yanked the pull string on the chainsaw so hard I thought I'd rip it out. The saw roared to life.

John looked down at Molly and said, "You better poop that bomb because we're blowing this place to Hell."

378

"PUT IT DOWN!"

John and I spun to see a man in one of the "clean" suits, maybe thirty feet away, pointing an enormous rifle at us that seemed to have too many barrels. His voice was filtered through a small speaker on the side of the hood and he was shouldering his way past the white-suited workers.

John did not put the flamethrower down. What he did instead was point the flaming end of the thing at the man and say, "You put yours down, asshole."

I said, "I'd do it, sir. We're pissed."

"YOU HAVE ONE SECOND TO DROP THAT CHAINSAW AND THAT . . . THING."

At this point, John flung himself to the ground and screamed, "YOU SHOT ME! AAARRRRGHHH!"

Not a shot had been fired. I rushed to John's side. "You shot him! He has four kids! Or should I say, four *orphans*."

The man stepped over, the gun trained on John. The weapon seemed to be from the year 2050, smooth sides and a thin electronic sight that glowed green. There was a small barrel on the bottom and a cavernous one on top that looked like it fired cannon shells.

"YOU. STEP AWAY AND GET ON THE FLOOR OVER THERE."

I said, "You shot him, you son of a bitch!"

"DO IT AND DO IT NOW."

I stood and backed away. The man loomed over John and aimed the rifle right at his head.

"YOU'RE NOT SHOT. GET UP."

Two urges rushed through me at the same moment. There was the urge to surrender, to put an end to the tension and fear and accept my fate. And then there was the urge to do violence.

I don't remember making the choice. All I know is that my muscles caught fire with adrenaline and I suddenly felt the fear and rage that is the most intense high the human animal can feel. In that split second I knew I was overmatched but I also knew that if I was going to die, this was how I wanted to do it. I wanted to give this asshole a scar with an interesting story behind it.

I flung myself at the man, swinging the chainsaw like a baseball bat. I was aiming high, trying to chop his arm off at the shoulder. I missed by two feet and hit his hand.

It was the hand holding the grip of the rifle. The spinning chain bounced off the gun and the impact made me drop it. The chainsaw fell to the floor, rattling on the ground with the vibration of the motor. *Smooth*.

But the man screeched in pain and, to my horror, two of his fingers dropped to the ground in a red splatter. The rifle clattered down to the concrete. I dove for the gun and grabbed it by a handle that was slick with blood. I found the trigger to be where it is on most guns. I aimed it at the man's chest and climbed to my feet. John stood, looking at the man's fingerless stumps with disgust.

I said, "Sir, you need to get that looked at."

The man didn't move. My heart hammered. I realized I had crippled this man for the rest of his life. John said, "This is the part where you run away and find a first-aid kit, dipshit."

The man got to his feet and stumbled off. Around us, dozens or hundreds of the bald, faceless workers stood as still as the mannequins they resembled. Everything had come to a stop. Machines were being shut down.

I tried to catch my breath, felt like my bladder was going to let go. I said, "This is going well."

There was a *POCK* sound and suddenly one of the blue barrels next to me sprung a leak. John and I looked at it curiously for a moment before we noticed about a dozen men in clean suits racing toward us from just about every direction, each armed, dodging the worker mannequins and toppling equipment.

I raised the rifle, no idea what to do, heard pops of gunfire that seemed faint in the cavernous room. I turned, pointed at the massive tanks of pink fluid and who knows what else, and pulled the trigger.

The gun exploded. Or seemed to; instead of the crack of a rifle shot it let out a thunderous boom that punched the butt of the rifle into my shoulder. The tanks erupted in a spray of glass. Fluid and flailing

380

shapes poured out onto the floor, faceless workers sprinting off in every direction.

Madness ensued. Inhuman screams. Crashing glass, toppling tables. The things that spilled out of the tanks were writhing, thrashing limbs around, and I thought I saw a human face stuck on the body of a hairless baboon. But it was all a dark blur and John took off running. I followed.

We dodged people like running backs, the chaos passing around us. The scenery was a department-store hodgepodge of nonsense, something out of a dream. We ran past hundreds of the walking mannequins, past tables full of clothes and what looked like tailoring equipment and rolls of cloth. A shelf full of underwear. We ran past a section of men working on what looked like dentistry, drilling and crafting bridges and false teeth. We knocked over chairs and tables and filing cabinets. We saw a young woman strapped to a table, her legs missing. We saw racks of fat bags like we saw in Amy's bathroom, imprinted with numbers. I saw a man chained to a wall who seemed to have snakes for arms, each hand replaced by snapping jaws and venomous fangs.

I saw Molly as a low, running copper streak up ahead and realized with horror that John was following her. I heard more shots and saw two of the mannequin men fall, ragged holes in their backs. My guts turned to liquid and my hands tightened around the bulky rifle, feeling sweat and sticky blood on the trigger. We reached a wall and I saw wide stairs leading to a double door made of brushed steel, like a bank vault. A *closed* bank vault.

I heard shouts and clanging and saw people on the catwalk overhead, saw white suits circling around us in the crowd and heard orders shouted from every direction. A booming voice emerged from a public address system, announcing things in a throaty language that sounded like Hebrew. I suddenly knew how that woodchuck felt.

I pulled up the rifle, found a little switch next to the handle and flipped it, hoping it would make the other barrel work. I raised it to my shoulder.

So freaking dark . . .

I tried to get a fix through the glowing green sights. I felt hands on me. I squeezed the trigger and the gun roared, fire erupting, the barrel jumping like a jackhammer. I lost control of it almost immediately, the gun pushing my shoulder back until I was shooting straight up. In three seconds I was clicking an empty gun, night-blinded, smelling gunpowder. I heard a *thump-thump-thump* and realized it was bodies falling off the catwalk above.

Hands on me again, the worker clones or whatever they were, grabbing my jacket and pulling my hair. The gun was ripped from my hands and I heard a *whoosh*, a sound suspiciously like a gun being swung through the air. A bomb went off in my skull. Lights flared in front of my eyes and I went down hard. I heard barking and growling, felt Molly thrashing around near me. I almost went out. I heard John's voice, shouting in the bedlam.

"GENTLEMEN, I WOULD LIKE TO PROPOSE A *TOAST!*"

And then, the whole world was on fire.

Heat and light and horrible, inhuman shrieks. I got on my hands and knees and saw John hosing everything down, a fountain of orange light glaring in the darkness, a crowd of dark limbs flailing in a pool of flame. A hand grabbed me again from the crowd, its sleeve on fire—

A firearm!

—and I kicked at it, got free. From beside me, John frantically pumped the gun, and again flame poured forth with a sound like rushing wind. Suddenly I was being pulled up to my feet, pulled backward, pulled to the spot where the metal door had been. It was apparently open now because we kept going, into another space, a small area that felt like a corridor.

I heard the heavy *clang* of the door closing, and suddenly a light flickered on. It was John who had hold of me, a fist full of my jacket in his hand. He spun toward the door and we saw a thin man standing there, next to a metal box on the wall with a series of red buttons.

It was Robert North. He looked us over, then said, simply, "Incredible."

We were alone in a hallway, an orchestra of sounds from the other side of the steel door. Molly looked that direction and growled. North stepped away from us and strode down the corridor. We followed. I put my hand to my aching skull, pulled away bloody fingers. John took his hand off me and said, "Can you walk?"

"Yeah."

North led us through one doorway, then another. We finally emerged into an enormous round chamber with steps that led down to a platform, the place set up not unlike a basketball stadium. At the heart of the room where center court would be, there were maybe a dozen tall arches arranged in two concentric circles. It reminded me of Stonehenge. Around the room were beds and examination tables, but nobody was on them. On the floor, on a small platform, sat the fat bag, the exact one from Amy's bathroom ("44.42 kg" on the side), and not far from that sat the lifeless, copper-haired dummy I had seen appear on Amy's couch. North led us out of the Stonehenge room, barely glancing at it, and out another door. We went down another hall and into another large, domed room. This one had a cylinder of black glass in the center that rose all the way up to the ceiling.

North closed the door behind us, another sliding double door with metal a foot thick. I saw there were no other exits from the room and whatever comfort I had felt from escaping the mob had vanished. This was the end of the line.

North said, "I have a thousand questions to ask but no time to ask them."

I said, "We have to get back! To ground level, to the mall. Amy is . . ."

He turned, like he couldn't hear me, and walked toward the cylinder. I glanced around and saw that the walls, like all of the walls here, seemed to be made of glass-smooth stone. The door and the controls for the door all seemed to have been added later, the wiring in metal conduits on the exterior of the wall. I wondered again where exactly this place was. Were we still on Earth?

I ran up behind North, said, "Get us outta here. Get us out and tell us where would be the best place to put a bomb."

John said, "Yeah, the dog is rigged to blow."

John shook the pink plastic tank of flamethrower fuel on his hip, found it empty. He blew out the lighter at the barrel of the toy, then dropped it all to the floor. I noticed the barrel had partially melted.

North said, "I do not think you fully appreciate what this is."

I nodded toward North and said to John, "This is the guy, the one who I saw in my truck that night."

John said, "Okay. Can he explain what the fuck this place is? And what they're making out there?"

I waved my hand with impatience and said, "He can tell us all about that shit after we're outta here and after we've gotten to Amy. And after we blow this place to Hell. But before those assholes come rushing through that door."

North said, "I believe Amy is safe. And I assure you, the men outside cannot get in here. I know this facility very well."

"How do you know about Amy?" I asked. "You're a part of this? You work for these people?"

North said, "I was born here. And as for what they're doing out there, well, they're doing the same thing all thinking creatures do, from the moment they come to life. Trying to change the world as they see fit."

He looked at the black column.

"What do you think you're looking at there?"

John said, "You're gonna be looking at my fist, and then Dave's *dick*, if you don't—"

"Take a moment and try to understand what you've seen," North said. "You will not be angry once you understand. Your anger clouds you." North glanced around the room. "I was born here, as I said. *One month ago*. Do you understand?"

I was trying to think up a new threat of violence for North and then I saw John's eyes go wide. I turned on the black column and saw activity there in the darkness. Swirling shapes pouring through it. Streaks of light. Life.

North said, "Imagine a garment, woven from a single thread. And imagine that after forming that garment, that same continuing thread was used to weave another garment similar to the first. So you have a thread that is simultaneously part of two garments, but at some point the thread stops being part of one garment and becomes part of the other."

John waved his hand impatiently and said, "Who gives a shit?"

North gestured toward the column.

"This is the thread."

I said, "Good. John, pry the bomb from Molly's colon and blow this fucker."

North said, "The key to saving your friend, Amy, is through there."

I said, "You want us to go through? What's in there? Hell? Is that what happened, this thing opened up and a bunch of you monstrous fuckers came crawling in? That's why we've got so much weird shit in this town?"

"No man has traveled through this portal. Though they have tried it."

"Then what the fuck are you talking about?" I screamed.

John glanced at Molly and said, "Shit the bomb, Molly."

North said, "No, the only ones who can travel back and forth are the dark men."

John said, "Blacks? Is that why there aren't any in [Undisclosed]? They get sucked in?"

This threw North. He recovered and said, "No, the dark men are the ones who lived but have been torn from their bodies, through death and, well, other circumstances you would not understand. They come from all worlds with sentient thought. They are unrestricted by matter and as such, can exist in one dimension and then the next, in one time and then the next, and then, in none at all. They exist in numbers greater than you can imagine, a dark ocean that flows between worlds. And as more thinking beings are born and die, the ranks of the dark men swell like the waters of a flooding river."

"Okay!" said John. "Let's blow it up then." He leaned down and grabbed Molly by the shoulders. "We need you to shit the bomb, Molly. Shit it! Shit the bomb!"

She didn't even try.

John said, "Fuck it. Let's light the dog on fire."

North said, "You cannot destroy it. If you could, your universe would vanish into it."

I looked at him, then spun on Molly. "Shit it, Molly! NOW! SHIT IT!"

North seemed to be losing patience and he said, "Through that passage is the only way to save Amy Sullivan."

I turned on him. "Are you finally getting to the part where you tell us how to do that?"

"You must pass through."

"You just said—"

"There is a reason why you have drawn so much interest, Mr. Wong. The ones who run this facility, and others, have devoted more time and resources than you can imagine to developing an ability to pass from one side to the next. You and John here apparently can. And we do not know why."

I said, "I know why. But I'm sure not telling you."

North said, "If you do not go in, where will you go?"

He had a point. And we had come this far. I looked at the column and said, "Fine. How do we get in?"

"Just decide that you want to get in and you will."

I reached out a hand and touched the surface, like cut onyx. Close to it I thought I could see color in the blackness, blue with streaks of white. The column felt as solid as stone, but then suddenly I saw my fingers push into it, like it was made of warm wax. My hand vanished up to the wrist and then elbow and then I changed my mind, tried to pull back and realized I had no chance of doing it short of cutting off my arm. I turned to John to tell him to find something sharp, but at that moment blackness fell over my vision.

CHAPTER 16
Shit Narnia

THERE WAS A period not unlike the half-waking moments between snooze alarms. A timeless, restless void that could have been a second and could have been ten thousand years. I felt air on my face, a rushing wind that pummeled me. I could not see, realized my eyes were closed, and pried them open. My vision immediately went blurry, air blowing the fluids from my eyeballs. I felt like I was falling. I focused my eyes and saw the ground, way down there, hundreds of feet. Lush green grass and tiny pale shapes that could have been people, little dots that seemed to grow almost imperceptibly.

Wait a second. I AM falling. HOLY SHIT!

I started flailing my arms, hoping I somehow had the ability to fly in this world. It was no good. I fell and fell for what seemed like an irrationally long time and then, I wasn't falling. Instead I was tangled up in something soft and springy like cheesecloth, bouncing twice before landing once and for all.

I laid there for a moment in some kind of netting, dumbfounded, a split second before Molly's ass landed right on my face.

I struggled to sit up, saw that I was hanging in a piece of cloth the size of a house, suspended high in the air. Above me, a dozen wingless, flying creatures the size of people were keeping it suspended with ropes.

Angels, I thought. *I've gone to Heaven and I'm being carried on a tarp hefted by angels.*

This wasn't what I was taught to expect in Sunday School, but things are never the way you learn them in the classroom. The cloth convulsed and tossed me again into the air for a dizzying second. John had landed.

We were going lower, down and down. I peered through the translucent fabric, like looking through panty hose. I thought I saw a crowd down there, a flesh-colored sea with a space in the middle. I was half expecting to find gates of carved pearl and a judge waiting for me, half expecting the crowd down there to descend on me, douse me in drawn butter and eat me alive.

We went down and down and down, the air getting warmer and the wind getting calmer. We finally hit the ground with a jolt. I rolled and flailed in the netting, got on my feet, then fell back on my ass. I got a good look at the beasts carrying the tarp. They were a sort of humpbacked men, emitting a growling noise until the moment they landed. They were naked, with penises I worked hard not to notice, but they wore loose hoods that covered their heads and draped down over their chests.

One of the men walked near, penis flopping with each step; he extended a hand to help me up. I observed that he did not in fact have a humped back, but instead seemed to have some kind of apparatus that was riding on his back with straps made of hard, jointed plastic or something like it.

I let the naked man, hairy as Robin Williams, help me up, and then I withdrew my hand as quickly as possible. He stood back and joined the humpbacks who were forming a loose circle around me and John and the dog. Beyond them, I saw the crowd.

There were maybe a hundred people standing around, every one of them wearing hoods. Every one of them otherwise naked. I observed, with some dismay, that a large percentage of them were elderly. I noticed that one group of them were holding up a large, colorful banner but I could not make out what was on it.

I said to John, "Oooookay. So, you see Amy here?"

John said, "Dunno." He scanned the hooded nakedness around us and said, "You know what this is, right? We're in an alternate universe and this is *Eyes Wide Shut* world."

The crowd stared at us in silence. Molly sniffed the air. It was cool here, maybe in the high fifties, a mild winter. The grass around us was still green and soft and the landscape was made of the same low hills that Undisclosed was built on, spilling out around us like a wrinkled green rug. My head throbbed from getting clubbed earlier.

I said, "I wonder what they're expecting. Are we supposed to fight each other to the death?"

"In *Eyes Wide Shut* world, we'll be lucky if that's all it is."

From the crowd, a large man emerged, no hood, wearing a pin-stripe suit. Or should I say, he was wearing an imitation of a pinstripe suit. It was black with pinstripes that seemed to be about a quarter-inch wide, and a short, fat red tie that only hung down about six inches from his neck. He spread his arms.

"Gentlemen. Welcome."

His face was human, but *off*. A Michael Jackson sort of face. I had seen it on my television. The man wore no hood but he was wearing something like a latex mask, better than Halloween quality but still obvious it wasn't his real face. I could see the seams under his ear—the ear was part of the mask—and the hair was unmistakably a wig.

389

I said, "Where's the girl?"

The man hesitated, seemed confused. I said, "Red hair? She's missing a hand?"

"Ah," he said. "Amy Sullivan. She is very safe. Come."

The man gestured in one direction and the crowd stepped aside to make a clear path for us. One of the humpbacked men who had carried our net did something with his hands and the apparatus on his back jumped off on its own; it crawled around on the ground on six legs. It was a living creature, I realized, and it reminded me somewhat of a giant beetle. It munched on some grass and softly farted through slits in its hindquarters that I theorized had been supplying the propulsion used to keep it aloft.

The large man walked us through the path formed by the naked crowd. I saw the large banner again and this time could make out the image. It was a cartoonish painting of me, depicted as a muscular warrior with a gushing head wound, Molly at my feet, teeth bared, with the flesh of some slain enemy in her jaws. John was shown bearing a fistful of flame and with an enormously exaggerated crotch bulge.

The large man turned, said, "A select few interested parties were allowed to come and observe your arrival. We asked the ones who came to be considerate. Our style of dress here is quite different than what you are used to. We did not want to cause you stress, so we thought removing the garments would lessen your discomfort. I believe some of the styles would be quite unnerving for a person from your world."

We were led down the gauntlet of nudity, two walls of flaccid penises and graying pubic hair and bare legs webbed with blue veins. One tall man, I noticed, was awkwardly trying to hide a gigantic erection. Not even eyes, however, were visible behind the slits in the hoods that draped over their shoulders.

"Why the hoods?" asked John.

The large man didn't hear or didn't feel like replying.

We came upon a grassy hill, which I for some reason thought would have been the same hill the Sullivan house rested on back on the real Earth. The hill turned out to have a door in the side, a sort of underground building built into the hill. It occurred to me that all of their buildings may have been built this way, leaving the landscape itself uninterrupted.

The door slid to the side and as we passed through I saw that the door and the mechanism seemed to be made of carved stone, something dense and smooth. Maybe granite. I don't know my rocks. We were led down a hall lined with more hooded nudists. The overhead lights were cut into the ceiling and seemed to emit a perfectly natural sunlight that was somehow soothing. As we passed, the observers nodded and leaned to each other and gestured, noticing things and pointing them out to their neighbor. What was missing from this was any sound. No whispering, no grunting. They must have had specific instructions from the big guy not to speak and I thought maybe they spoke a foreign language when among themselves.

We entered a large, round ballroom-type chamber, and John and I stopped dead cold. In the center of the room was an enormous, flaming, golden statue. And I don't mean it was painted gold, either. It *was* gold, a twenty-foot-tall representation of the image on the banner outside. John and me and Molly, our backs to each other, ready for battle. A fountain of flame poured up from the center of the statue, so each of our backs were to it.

I said, "I think they were expecting us."

John nodded. "Look at that. It looks like the flame is shooting out of our asses."

We were led down a hall and into a small, round room with white walls that had a rough texture like stucco. The only furniture was two large, elaborately curved chairs that seemed to be made of uncut wood, as if the branches of a tree had grown into four legs and arms and a back, purely by chance. On the floor was a pillow, presumably for the dog.

The man gestured to the chairs and we sat, dog included. The man walked past me and stopped, observing the blood running down my neck.

"Your injury. Let us tend to it." He looked out through the open doorway and silently gestured to someone out there.

"Our world," he said, "is far more advanced than yours. For reasons you'll understand shortly."

A thin, bony naked woman entered the room, carrying two small, white kittens. She sat one of the fluffy cats in my lap and stuffed the other down my shirt. She turned and left.

"There," said the large man. "The kittens will make your sad go away."

The man looked back at the doorway we came through and, on its own, a door slid from the wall and clicked closed. The operation of the door was a whisper-quiet *SSSSssss-fump*. The inside of the door carried the same rough white texture, and the lines of the door disappeared once it was closed. I suddenly had the claustrophobia a bird fetus must feel at the moment before kicking its way out of the egg. The kitten scratched my chest and I opened my shirt to let it flop out onto my lap.

The man came around to the wall in front of us, an excited expression on his face that didn't translate through his mask that well.

"I suppose you are wondering where you are."

I raised my hand. "I'm going to say that we're in an alternate universe of some kind."

"That is correct. Do not think of it as a physical location. Think of it as another possible arrangement of the atoms in your universe to form something else. Today's cloud is tomorrow's puddle."

"Yes," I said. "That's much clearer."

Undaunted, the large man said, "But to perceive one world, and then the next, requires a point of connection or—"

"A wormhole?" said John, hoping to usher the guy along.

"I am unfamiliar with the term. Tell me, what was it like? Passing through?"

I shrugged and said, "I wasn't really paying attention."

John said, "Yeah, it wasn't that great."

The man waited for quite a long time for us to add something, but we did not. Finally he said, "We have been awaiting your coming, as you can see. We have worked for many years, suffered many tragic setbacks, in order to find and communicate with another plane such as yours. Some thought that travel from one to another was impossible, but here you are. Your world, you see, is a sort of twin to ours, an offspring born of the same litter."

The man turned and gestured to the wall and the letter "Y" appeared in black. Suddenly I realized that the texture on the walls was moving and twitching and that it was not stucco or plaster. They were insects, clustered together to cover the entire surface of the room. They were the size of dimes and seemed to have the chameleon's ability to change the color of their shells at will.

"Up until here," said the man, pointing to the place where the trunk of the "Y" split into two branches, "our histories were identical. This spot represents the year 1864, as you would call it, or Year Minus Sixty-two, as we would call it. There was a man named Adam Rooney from Tennessee. In your world and ours. In your world, he was killed at age seventeen during the Civil War, gored while trying to crossbreed a bull and a Clydesdale. In our world, the man survived."

The ranks of bugs on the wall changed colors again, turning shades of brown and tan and black, forming a rough portrait of an older man, smoking a pipe and looking out at the viewer through thick eyeglasses. He had a white Colonel Sanders beard. "Mr. Rooney," he continued, "was a genius. He went on to perform experiments with what he would call beastiology."

"Yes," John said. "People from our South are into that as well."

The large man skipped a beat and continued, "This is the art of transforming naturally occurring life into forms that can be used by man to better the world. By 1881 Rooney had a self-shearing sheep and a species of snake that could harvest corn. By 1890 his group had an insectile flying machine. In 1902, or Year Minus Twenty-four in our terms, he created a primitive thinking machine from the brain of a pig."

The image behind the man changed to a color depiction of several men standing over a vat of fluid. Inside it floated a twisted and deformed mass of what looked like brain tissue, about the size of a small dog. The men were wearing lab coats.

"I have studied your world for the last decade, your language, your history. It is astonishing to me that you went to such unending lengths to build computation machines from metal and silicon switches when you have much more efficient versions inside your own skulls. Did this not occur to your scientists? By your year 1922, we had self-feeding, self-healing, self-growing and self-modifying computers, organic ones, that were approximately ten times as powerful as what you are using now in your world."

The image shifted again, and this time a group of a dozen very proud-looking men were standing in front of a monster. The thing rose up behind them, no longer confined to a tank of fluid. It looked like a tree carved out of whale guts. It was a hideous twist of meat and fibers and strands that unspooled here and there like spiderweb. It stood as tall as a small tree, maybe twice as high as a man.

I got a dizzy spell, closed my eyes. A concussion? I clutched the kittens, one of them meowed. In just a few moments, I found I really did feel better.

"In 1926, or what we know as Year One, Mr. Rooney passed away. But something miraculous happened with the greatest of Mr. Rooney's creations, the computation machine that had aided him with all of his other creations. On the very day Mr. Rooney passed, his creation became sentient."

The large man gave a practiced pause in the middle of what I assumed was a prepared speech. This was where we were supposed to gasp in surprise, I guess. I nodded politely.

"It gave a name to itself," said the large man, "and expressed desires and emotions. This was an astonishing surprise. This creation carried on Rooney's work and conformed all of living nature to urge forth the advancement of mankind."

Suddenly our vision was flooded with a view of an open, muddy field. The entire room had switched to a full-motion image, a panoramic view that made me dizzy. The image zoomed in on a long trench, like those used in World War I. The trench extended off in both directions and standing along the lip of the trench were men and women and children, lined up shoulder to shoulder. Some of the children were crying. Everyone was wearing clothes that were streaked brown and white and seemed to be made entirely of thin strips wrapped around and around their bodies. I thought for a moment that they were all wrapped in bacon.

The people seemed to obey an unheard command and all stepped down into the muddy trench. The children had to be dragged down against their will. Suddenly, puffs of dirt burst up from the ground around their bare feet and then the trench was filling with a dark flood. A close-in shot revealed the flood to be thousands and thousands of spiders, sharp bodies and yellow stripes. Bred for war.

There was a chorus of screams. The spiders swarmed over the victims, burrowing into skin and through ragged holes in muscle. I saw a spider burst out of one man's eye, a half dozen tearing themselves out of holes in another man's back, emerging from his gut and carrying loops of intestine with them. Blood sprayed, limbs fell to the ground, bones were torn from legs and rib cages.

And then, the spiders were gone. The view lingered on the torn and bloodied victims and I realized that none had been killed. Instead, the spiders had left them in piles, hundreds and hundreds in a screaming, red, writhing mass, everyone missing limbs and baseball-sized chunks of flesh, men left blind and deaf and unable to move. No one came to their aid. The shot pulled back to reveal the trench stretched for miles in both directions, and the entire length now ran pink like a highway on a roadmap, the screams swelling up and up—

Then it was gone. The white room was back and the large man was standing before us, beaming with what I was pretty sure was pride. He said, "There are always those who resist progress."

My eyes bounced around the room and I again had that suffocating feeling. No door. Hell, I couldn't even point to the spot where the door had been. I looked over at John and he seemed to be trying to figure out if his chair could be used as a weapon. It looked rooted to the floor.

"Now," said the large man, "knowing your world, this part may be a difficulty for you. Let me give you an example. In your world, as in mine, is it not considered bad to take and use, without permission, an object that another man is currently using or depending on?"

"Yes, in our world we call this 'stealing,'" said John, with some impatience. "It is considered a greater crime, though, to unleash killer spiders on an unarmed crowd. We call that 'arachnicide.'"

"But what if the object that you stole would later have injured or killed the man? Then stealing it would be saving his life. Or what if he had intended to use it as a weapon later, against an innocent person? And what if that weapon would have killed the child who would later grow up to cure a terrible disease?"

John, who had settled right into this conversation, scratched his chin, shrugged and said, "Well, you don't know but you do the best you—"

"What if you *could* know," said the large man. "You already, in your world, have machines that can compute and forecast outcomes and scenarios, that can look at air temperatures and wind patterns and predict the weather ahead of time. What if there was a thinking machine, an entity so powerful that it could foresee the outcome of any action? In it you would have the ultimate morality, the true ability to know which path was the correct one."

I said, "Well, we have people in our world who believe in a . . ."

"I am not talking about a belief. What I am talking about exists here and now, in our world. It is something you can touch and see and smell. Something real."

The lower half of his mask twisted and I thought he was smiling. "Follow me."

Mercifully, the door opened. I had the urge to knock the guy down and make a run for it, but where would we go? It was impossible to be farther from home than we were. Our home, in fact, literally did not exist at that moment. The large man led us back into the hallway, now empty of people. He led us to another stone doorway and when the door slid back we were greeted with a shaft, about as wide as the shaft for a big service elevator. It led straight down, a row of lights vanishing into darkness hundreds of feet below.

Thin, black legs appeared over the edge, each as long as my body. I jumped back and heard a squeal as I stepped on a kitten, which was apparently following me. The large man put a calming hand on my shoulder.

The legs belonged to a spider.

A spider the size of a van.

It crawled up the opposite wall of the shaft, its mass neatly filling the entire space as if it were made for it. Its huge, bulbous back was facing us. A split formed in the spider's body and it opened, revealing a rather clean interior that was a milky white. A light even blinked on in the cavity.

The large man walked inside the spider, there was room to stand up in there. He welcomed us inside and I decided on the spot that I wasn't doing it, never, ever, ever. But John went in and then the dog and then the fluffy kittens, and at that point I didn't really have a choice. I got inside the thing and the cavity closed and sealed us in. After a moment the spider jolted and we were riding down.

"Are you thinking what I'm thinking?" asked John.

"That if Franz Kafka were here his head would explode?"

"Actually, yeah."

The large man, intent on continuing the tour, said, "We are on the verge of entering Year Seventy-seven of our new era, the era of guidance and enlightenment. We have made great strides. There is little that we need that we cannot extract from the very living energy that is the most powerful force the universe produces. Life is the energy that controls all other energies. Living man can split the atom and travel the stars and, soon, move from reality to reality. But it is life that is the engine at the center of all."

We rode for several more minutes then, much to my relief, the spider opened and let us out into a large, open room that had a dome shape like the last one and like the underground complex we had left in our world. John nudged me and pointed to a row of windows above

397

us, like the observation areas seen in some hospital operating rooms. Behind it were naked hooded figures, a crowd. I wondered if they had paid for tickets to this. Many people in the front row of the observation deck were pressed nakedly against the glass, producing a squished scrotum effect that I knew I would see in my nightmares. Just below the windows were clear vats, like man-sized Mason jars. They lined the walls and each were filled with deep red fluid. I was about to ask the man what the fluid was, but then he disappeared through another door and urged us to follow. We went through a hall, past another door, then the stench hit me.

Sulfur. A smell so strong it was a solid thing in my lungs. We went through and came out onto a catwalk, suspended in a dark space that seemed to go forever in each direction. I stepped out and stopped. I craned my neck, looking up and up and up, then looked down. I could see neither the top nor the bottom of the thing that grew before me.

Oh, dear Jesus . . .

"Gentlemen," said the large man. "You are seeing what only a select few have seen. You are looking at the ultimate manifestation of Mr. Rooney's creation, which now stands as the absolute wisdom and strength in all of existence. John, David, meet Korrok."

I hesitate in the telling of the story at this point. When I try to bring up an image of Korrok in my mind I see only the glob of stuff that collects in the kitchen drain, the mass of grease and hair washed by years of filthy dishwater. It was like someone collected all the drain slime in the world and knitted it into something the size of the Statue of Liberty, then brought it to life with the psychotic energy that fuels lynch mobs. There was so much to Korrok that it was impossible to see it, a jumbled mess of exposed organs and fibers and dangling, club-ended limbs, of dripping orifices and slimy orbs and dark, black bulbs with colors that moved on the surface like the rainbows in an oil slick. Every inch of it was moving. I stared and stared and stared, found my brain couldn't contain it all.

And then, in my head, I heard the high-pitched, cackling laughter of a child.

Welcome, said the alien voice in my head. It sounded like a toddler. *Your wiener is even smaller in person.*

It giggled. I thought, *Is this Korrok?*

With a tiny change in your brain chemistry, I could make you a child molester.

What do you want? I asked it, in my head.

Not big, black cocks. So we don't have that in common.

A long, loud laugh that rattled my bones. I glanced over and saw that John and the large man were talking to each other, oblivious to me.

I thought, *Get out of my head. You're not worth talking to.*

I AM KORROK. In the mountains of Uruguay, a goat gets its hoof caught in a posthole and the bone snaps like a twig. The splinter juts from its skin, blood spraying onto white fur. It is stuck like that for three days. Finally, a wolf mother comes along, carrying her pup in her jaws. She lets the pup feed off the goat, gnawing bits of fur and skin and tearing at muscle. The goat feels it and screams and there is pain and pain and neither the goat nor the wolf nor the pup understand their place in the machine. I stand above all, and call them fags. I AM KORROK.

Fuck off. You're just something they grew. A big, fucked-up mess. You look like you were made by a committee.

Long, loud, childish laugh.

David Wong, son of an insane prostitute and a mentally challenged Amway salesman. There are worlds and worlds and worlds, an infinity you cannot grasp. You could travel from one to another to another and find me in thousands upon thousands, spreading like stars in the sky from reality to reality. They invite me in. They give birth to me. And soon, yours will do the same, men are working tirelessly toward it. They bring me into their world because they always want what only I can give. In this place, seven billion men bear my mark. And of the limitless infinity of worlds, I rule over almost half of them.

And then I saw, for the first time, the way the darkness in the chamber moved. The black shapes, the shadow men, the little slips of nothing swirled in this place, covering Korrok like smoke from an oil fire. They moved over and through him, in and out of every orifice and fold of skin. His dark disciples. I heard a sound and realized I was being talked to from the outside. I turned to face the large man.

". . . the greatest good for the greatest people," he was finishing. "So you understand. When Korrok judges, there is no question. All of the human minds who have ever lived in history, all of your thinkers and writers and philosophers and teachers, could not equal even one node of Korrok's neural web. We have learned this the hard way."

I looked down at Molly, then sort of nudged her belly with my foot. Try to loosen that shit up in there.

The large man said, "Twenty years ago, Korrok foretold your coming. Korrok showed us the way to your world, opened lines of communication. We could not cross to your plane ourselves. We tried. Oh, did we. You see, when a man is transferred to the other plane, the body arrives. But only the body, walking aimless like a cow. The person becomes . . . detached in the transition. But nonetheless, we worked tirelessly to create in your world what we have here, in preparation for the glorious day when we could overcome these obstacles and set our own feet on the land and see your sun with our own eyes."

The large man put a hand on my shoulder. I shuddered.

"Your friend, the girl, Amy Sullivan. She is known because she was the first step. She was successfully transported from one location to another in your world, without passing anywhere in between and without harm. Your people did this. Korrok showed them the way. With that, we knew we were close, could see the faint glow of the sun signaling a new dawn. Gentlemen, with your arrival, that dawn has come. What one man can do, other men can do, and you will show us the way to pass from world to world. It is the ultimate good. And it is impossible for it to be otherwise. Korrok told us you would be honored, and well you should be."

The man craned his neck, looking up in the darkness. He said, "You cannot begin to calculate the wisdom, the continued melding of a billion geniuses. You see, in our world, whenever a man is born with special wisdom and intelligence, he shares his wisdom with Korrok so that Korrok may be greater. Watch."

A thin structure emerged from the wall about two stories above us. It tilted down and seemed to have no steps, as if it were a chute of some kind. An orifice that seemed to have something like a beak opened on Korrok at the end of the chute. A fat man came tumbling down the slide, his limbs flailing. He wore the same brown strips of clothing I saw in the video of the bug room. Korrok snatched the man into the beak, crunching his bones in a wet, red spray.

I heard a high-pitched laugh in my head.

Mmmmmm! Bacon!

In front of me a slit formed in Korrok and opened wide. An electric blue eye the size of a movie screen was peering out at me. A thin, black, vertical pupil.

I ran.

I sprinted back through the door, off the catwalk, back through the other doors and down the hall and back into the round room with the naked viewing gallery. People were still up there, rustling and gesturing now, excited to see the crazy happenings with the strange visitor. The door out of the round room slid shut before I got to it and I slapped at it ineffectively with my palms. The large man called out from behind me and I spun, breathing hard. He held out his hands in a calming gesture.

"We understand. I assure you, we do. I have observed you. You know I have. And you have seen some of our work. We are advancing into your world with astonishing speed. Our workers prepare day and night. There are legions on our side there. And soon all of your turmoil and unrest and confusion will vanish under the soft hand of Korrok."

A kitten put its paw on my foot. I punted it across the room.

"Just watch," said the large man. "We can perform what in your world would be a miracle. Observe."

The floor under my feet vanished. Or, I should say, it turned transparent, like glass. Under me were dozens of terrified upturned faces. They were uncovered and they looked just like people from my world. And right then, somehow I knew that under the large man's mask I would find something quite different than the wide eyes and unshaven

401

faces I saw now below me. I was looking down at what was a sort of prison chamber on the floor below, each person down there trapped in a hexagonal glass section not much wider than their shoulders, a massive crystalline beehive. The floor wasn't quite soundproof, because I could faintly hear their screams. I saw John step through the door and stop in revulsion.

The large man motioned with his hand and one hexagon rose silently up from the floor. Inside was a man in his thirties with curly black hair, held there in the glass booth like a museum exhibit. I heard the hiss of the same mechanism raising other pods, and soon we were surrounded by six of the hexagonal glass booths. The large man said, "We command the cell itself, at will. We can turn muscle to bone and back, skin to carapace, fingers into claws. And we can do it in any way we choose. Watch."

The curly-haired man stared at us in terror, his palms flat against the glass. Then he screamed. It wasn't immediately apparent what was wrong with him, but then I saw one of his knees bend backward, splitting the flesh. The other one did the same, his legs extending upward, jutting as high as his shoulders. His skin melted from his face and hardened into a small, insectile head and skin that became gray and notched like alligator hide. Molly whined and trotted off into a corner. I wasn't sure if she was terrified or if the burritos were finally getting to her.

I pivoted around the room and was now looking at a half dozen of the beasts that had chased us here, the beasts from Jim's basement. Beastments. The glass walls lowered and the creatures were standing open in the room now, facing us in a circle.

"And once the bodies have been changed," said the large man, "the brains have changed. Memories are only arrangements of neural connections and once altered they can no more resist our commands than a twig can resist the flame." He studied me from behind his rubbery face, said, "As you know."

I moved toward the large man, intending to take him hostage and negotiate an exit from this place. I reached for the gun in my pocket, realized I didn't have it and pulled out the spare magazine instead. I threw it at the large man and he flinched as it bounced off his chest. I lunged.

They moved so *fast*. In a blur I had a bundle of talons clamped around my neck and arms and legs. Two of the monsters were on me, holding me still as a Ken doll. The large man looked downcast, I suppose. The mask sagged a little. He said, "What we have for you to do is so important. Korrok has seen the outcome. It will happen if you resist or if you do not resist. All that will change is your personal well-being. It is for the greater good. Do you not see that?"

He almost sounded on the verge of tears, crushed by my tragic inability to grasp the obvious. Two of the monsters carried me from the room, dragging me backward down the hall. The other four descended upon John and I heard him cursing loudly. The large man followed me and the door sealed over the sound of John screaming that he was having a seizure and that they should let him go. I screamed, "Light the dog! John! Light the dog!" but I assumed the doors were just as sound-proof from the inside as out. I was hauled into yet another small, round room, accompanied by the large man. The door swept shut behind us and the two creatures turned me loose. I saw we were not alone, that there was a small figure huddled against the far wall. Red hair.

"Amy!"

I ran toward her, and was smacked in the face by nothing. I fell to the ground and realized I had run into a glass or otherwise transparent barrier that separated the room.

Amy looked up at me in dull surprise. She looked to be beyond shock. Largeman said, "Our representatives are all over your world. We have been planning this for years and all of the pieces are in place. It is just a matter of clearing the way, of wiping your world clean. Two glasses. Yours with water, ours with wine. To fill the other with wine, the water must first be spilled. Do you not see that the wine is better?"

A door opened on Amy's side of the room, and two men came in. They were not naked, far from it. They were dressed in what looked like layers of leather half a foot thick, shoulders bulging with some kind of hard padding. They looked like members of a bomb squad. Between them they carried a container the size of a fifty-five-gallon drum. It was red and stamped with an enormous yellow warning label captioned in a foreign language that used lettering like Elvish. They sat the container on the floor and activated a latch. They then turned and ran from the room.

Amy stood and pressed herself against the far wall. The top of the container opened and slid aside. I held my breath, eyes bouncing from Amy to the container, waiting to see what would emerge from the dark opening. I ran up and pressed my palms against the glass, screamed her name. I noticed she didn't have a left hand.

A single, tiny white insect zipped out of the container. Thin and wingless but flying nonetheless, it streaked through the air and moved toward Amy. She backed away from it, following it with her eyes as it swirled overhead.

"It is a miraculous being," said Largeman. "It has the mind and instincts and urges of a man, only without limbs or nerves or sense organs. It knows only to fly and to breed, and once it finds its host it will produce twenty thousand offspring in a matter of minutes. They grow quickly in the soft tissue of the host and then they burst forth, each to find new hosts. And so on."

I knew that already. The insect buzzed around and around and around. Then it landed on her shoulder and Amy swatted it like a mosquito. I screamed at her again, she couldn't hear me. Then it was Amy's turn to scream. She was pulling her hand back and looking at it like it had just been impaled on a tack. She shook the hand and rubbed it on the wall and did everything she could to try to dislodge the insect, but it was useless. It had burrowed into her.

I banged on the glass with my hands, looking in, helpless. Amy looked at her hand and at me, baffled, not even sure what any of this meant. I spun on Largeman, said, "Undo it. Give her an antidote, insecticide, whatever kills those things."

"Any such solution would kill her as well. No, this can end only one way. Korrok has seen it."

I turned back and saw Amy had slid down and was sitting on the floor again, looking hopeless. Looking like she expected to wake up at any moment, find herself back in bed.

"The future is what it is," said Largeman. "Your people have been poisoned with the myths of lone men turning the tide, improbable tales of heroes outrunning explosions with their feet. Such tales are forbidden here. Events are laid forth and they cannot be turned. There are no heroes, Mr. Wong. Korrok has computed it down to the atom and we have left nothing to chance."

At that moment, the door swung open. A slimy spray of brown flew across the room in a wide arc.

JOHN HAD A plan.

If he is to be believed, while I was being hauled into the room with Amy, the four Beastments holding John tried to keep him still as he proclaimed seizure and thrashed his limbs about.

"SEIZURE! I'M SEIZURING HERE!"

This caused a commotion up in the observation deck, with the observers not sure what to do with Largeman gone and the Transdimensional Visitor Festival spinning quickly out of control. Molly began whining in earnest at that moment, quivering all over. John knew that both of General Valdez's Mexillent Microwave Burritos were about to make a reappearance.

A door opened and an emergency crew rushed in, four hooded women each carrying a kitten in each hand. More people filed into the room behind them, and John figured they were from the observation deck and were using this as an excuse to get a closer look. These people seemed to have some authority, and with a gesture of their hands the four inhuman guards let go of John's arms. He fell to the floor and immediately the girls piled their kittens on his body and fussed over him.

"I must have my medicine!!" John shouted to a small, pale man who he guessed was Asian. Neither the man nor anyone else seemed to know what John was saying. "My seizure medicine!"

405

John reached into his pocket and several of the onlookers jumped back. John pulled out his tobacco and cigarette papers and held them up to show they were not weapons. The group stood and watched in fascination as John sat and brushed the kittens aside. He gathered all of his concentration and went about rolling the one, perfect cigarette that could save our universe.

He spread the tobacco, rolled, wound up with a cone-shaped tobacco horn that had John cursing in frustration. He tried a second time, almost got it, and then finally a third. Perfect.

He glanced at Molly and nodded. Then, with a squeal and a sound like a hard rainfall, Molly let go. A spray of shit ejected from her hindquarters, and in it was a lump that John instantly recognized as half a dog bone that went undigested since it was an unstable, ultra–high explosive compound instead of the antlers and fermented cow fur that actual dog biscuits are made of. John lit his perfect cigarette, took a puff and nodded his thanks to the group.

John leapt to his feet. He held out his hands to the group of humans and the four monstrosities in the room. He said, "Everybody stand back!" He went to the puddle of feces, grimaced as he fished out the soggy chunk of explosive dog biscuit. He used his pinky finger to dig out a small dent in the half bone, then lodged the unlit end of the cigarette into it. He set the smoking apparatus onto a dry piece of floor, stood, checked his watch, then looked over at the thin yellow-brown stream that was leaking from the dog.

"Molly, it's time to go bye-bye."

John picked up the shitting dog, holding her across his chest with both arms, her paws dangling. He sprinted out of the room, screaming "Get out! Everyone get out! It's gonna blow!"

John hefted the dog down the hall, came to the first closed door he could find. He saw no handle on the door and no buttons or controls. He screamed, "Open, you fuck!" and the door slid obediently open.

John saw Largeman and saw a room imprisoning Amy and saw me looking outraged and decided it was best to turn Molly's ass toward Largeman and hope she shat on him. She did.

I threw my hand in front of my face as warm shit splattered in a wide stream across the room, the dog letting out an agonized yelp. Largeman was surprised by this turn of events and threw himself to the ground. John let Molly go, pulled his Zippo from his pocket, lit it and flung it at one of the Beastments. The lighter smacked it in the head with a flare of yellow and blue, the thing letting out a howl. John then ran over and administered a hard kick to Largeman's ribs. In a blur the two Beastments were on him, Largeman telling them not to kill him, everything was under control.

As if to specifically contradict this assertion, I noticed a lump of fairly solid feces on the floor from which emerged another, cracked piece of our dog biscuit bomb. I grabbed it in my hand, ran and dove and snatched John's lighter from the floor. I saw the group from the hall pushing in through the door now, including four of the Beastments that were tossing naked people aside and imposing themselves into the room. I held up the dog turd and flicked the lighter, the flame dancing an inch away from the explosive excrement.

"There's enough explosive in this poo to collapse this whole cave. Now back the fuck off."

Whatever basic English these people knew apparently didn't include those two phrases. Nobody moved for a long time, the only sound the wet, farty mechanism of Molly's digestive system.

"NOW!"

Largeman understood perfectly. He stumbled to his feet and nodded to the Beastments in the door. It occurred to me for the first time that the people here communicated with a sort of telepathy. I would have to make some time later to be fascinated by that. At his inaudible instructions the room was cleared and the door was shut. Only John and I and Molly were left, along with Largey Largeman. I turned to Amy, who was looking at us with eyes squinted in a sort of disgusted, accident-scene curiosity.

I said, "Get back! Back against the wall!"

John and I didn't need to discuss the plan. We got on the floor, dug out the hunk of dog bone from the poo—we had maybe a quarter of the bone—and we used John's car keys to chip off a tiny hunk the size of a grain of rice. We used some of the dog poo to stick the shard to the glass, about two inches off the floor. John lit the Zippo, leaned it against the glass so that the flame licked the smear of feces.

We threw ourselves to the far end of the room and covered our heads. The sound was massive, a sharp *PAKK!* that was like nails in the eardrums. There was no sound of shattering glass and I was afraid it had failed. I rose and saw in the clearing smoke that a large, puckered hole had formed in the clear wall, like a hole punched in taffy. Amy ran out and I threw my arms around her.

She said, "Where are we? I don't know how—"

"Later." I turned to Largeman. "If you can't cure her then you get us outta here, get us back to our world. We'll find a way."

"Gladly. We haven't long before she . . . hatches."

I said, "And let me guess. If she dies, these things come out of her right away, right?"

He didn't reply, but I knew I was right.

"Okay, so you got some serious motivation to keep her safe, right? Now get us the fuck out of here."

John said, "You better hurry, too."

TWO ROOMS AWAY, an inch of ash fell from a rolled cigarette crammed into a poo-smeared dog biscuit. A faint ember of orange light smoldered away at the remaining two inches.

JOHN SAID TO me, "We have"—he thought for a moment—"five minutes, thirteen seconds before biscuit time."

I set my watch. I couldn't find the countdown feature, managed to change the date and the time zone both before I got it set, then had to adjust for the time lost.

4:48.

We burst out of the door, me with my arm around Largeman's neck, holding the lighter to his cheek.

"Nobody move, or I'll light his fucking face on fire!" I meant it, too.

Either they took this threat seriously or Largeman was giving them instructions to back off. We pushed him down the hall and he pointed us to an elevator.

4:12.

We climbed inside another giant spider, much to Amy's horror, and took an agonizingly long, slow ride down. Amy was having trouble standing, squeezing her eyes shut and wrapping her arms around her gut.

Something's growing in there. Oh, shit, shit, shit.

Down and down and down. These people built their skyscrapers upside down.

1:32.

Finally, it stopped. We emerged in a round, tube-like hallway. We passed through one thick, round door after another.

:58.

We entered an enormous chamber. Organic machines and clear tubes and huge, egg-shaped pods that thrummed with power. I barely noticed any of it. What caught my attention was an enormous creature in the center of the room, shaped something like a huge, elephant-sized toad. It squatted in the center of the room and at the soundless command of Largeman, it opened its enormous mouth wide.

Blackness. Inside this creature was the same swirling darkness we saw in the dark column in the mall complex. I squinted and with concentration I could see light, shapes, a room. A moving figure . . .

:36.

Largeman stepped aside and pointed us toward the mouth.

"Go. Now."

I said, "Where does it go? I mean, specifically, where will we come out?"

"Theoretically? You should not emerge far from where you went in. But it is difficult to predict."

"Amy survived going through. She'll survive going back?"

No answer. I stepped up to the dark portal and as I got closer I realized I could see faintly through it. There did seem to be a small room on the other side, barely visible. I held my breath and stepped into the mouth of the beast, felt again that disconnected, time-lost feeling of an unexpected nap. I was pitched forward and landed on a hardwood floor. I looked up and saw I was in a hallway, turned and saw an open doorway with a VNV Nation poster on it.

I stood and realized I was looking through the Irish elevator door in the Sullivan house, only instead of open air I was looking into the toad room I had just come from. The door stood open next to me, as if it had been flung open when I fell in.

:22.

Molly leapt through and trotted past me. John pushed Amy through and she tumbled onto the floor and instantly went into a fetal position, face twisted in pain. There was a commotion in the other room now. I could see a dozen of the Beastments in there, wreaking havoc. There was a crowd of naked humanity as word seemed to have spread that things were about to go terribly wrong.

Largeman had ahold of John as they had apparently either changed their mind or had decided to keep him as a souvenir. There was a struggle of flailing arms and kicking feet and John grabbed Largeman's face and came away with a leathery bundle—the man's mask.

John froze. The man's back was to me so I couldn't see what John saw, but the look in John's eyes was a sort of sudden blankness. He didn't scream or puke or react at all; it was like his brain suddenly crashed like Windows.

I heard footsteps in the hall of the Sullivan house. I spun and saw Robert North jogging toward me from the stairwell, wearing a long, tan woman's overcoat and an enormous feathery hat.

"Hey!" I shouted. "We made it! She's sick, she has—look, get me some, uh . . . a cross or some holy water or . . . oh, get the Jesus picture! We'll rub it on her."

:11.

I turned and saw that the man had snatched the mask from John's hand and was sticking it back on his face. I opened my mouth to scream to John, then wondered if sound would even travel through the rift. Then that question was answered when—

:00.

—a deep, heavy *THOOMPH* like a sonic boom hammered the world on the other side of the door. The crowd in the room flew into a frenzy. John kicked his way to his feet and ran in my direction. He threw himself through, fell into the hallway. I went to close the door, but North calmly strode over. He reached out a hand, stopped the door, and looked in at Largeman. The two stared at each other across worlds and the man on the other side mouthed something that seemed like a bitter insult. Though I couldn't hear it and I knew neither of these men, the meaning was clear. *I should have known you were behind this.*

Amy's skin was bulging and swelling in places. I grabbed her hand and wrapped an arm around her neck and pulled her close, whispered that it was going to be okay, that we would get her fixed right up, that—

BANG!

There was suddenly warm blood all over me and a ragged hole appeared in Amy's temple. She went limp in my arms.

Standing a few feet away, was North.

He was holding a little silver gun.

A woman's gun.

A thread of smoke drifting up from the barrel.

EVERYTHING INSIDE MY head turned black as deep space. I just sat there, shirt and arms flecked with red, just looking at her, at her slack face, her mouth hanging half open. And suddenly her body was being pulled from my arms and North was pulling her, dragging Amy by her feet like a rag doll. John just stood there, he just fucking stood there while all this happened and I found I had no strength to stand.

North wrestled with Amy's body and threw the legs into the doorway,

411

then came around and lifted the shoulders and pushed them through. The crowd in the other world, in the toad room, seemed completely confused by this, a dead body forcing its own way through the portal. But Largeman got it and he screamed. He screamed so loud I could hear it on the other side and soon the people around him understood it and bedlam ensued.

It was too late. Amy's body ruptured, spilling out a cloud of the swirling white insects. The flying parasites saw a room full of hosts and poured forth into the naked crowd. A stampede ensued. The rest of Amy's body exploded, bits of blood and bone flying back into the hallway. I heard a metallic tinkling sound like a coin hitting the floor, just as North slammed the door shut. He opened it again and saw only the Undisclosed night sky and a downpour of snow.

I started to stand but North spun and put the pistol on me.

"I know what you are thinking," he said.

"And you are wrong."

He started to say something else but at that moment John came up behind him and punched him in the kidneys. North arched his back and suddenly I saw the metallic object I had heard hit the floor. It was a shiny, curved bit of steel, flecked with red. Something a surgeon would use to brace a broken spine.

I picked up the piece of metal and jabbed it into the wrist of North's gun hand. I felt it go in, punching through skin and popping between the two bones of his forearm. North shrieked and the gun clattered to the floor.

I grabbed the gun, pointed it at North's heart, and watched him melt. Literally. He fell into a puddle of goo and, from it, emerged a creature not unlike a jellyfish.

A man-o'-war, actually . . .

It floated up, just as we had seen it do a couple of days ago. I squeezed the trigger and sent shot after shot at the thing, chips of wood flecking off the walls. The jellyfish barely noticed. It floated downstairs and Molly ran barking after it.

We never saw it again.

There was a puddle of marbled goo on the floor that seemed to be steaming, dissolving. North's leftovers.

I took a step forward and yanked open the door, just as North had. A blast of cold air and a dusting of snow blew in; the Sullivans' backyard lay ten feet below. I was amazed that there was still light outside. The whole thing had only taken an hour or so. I sat down on the hardwood floor, sticky dots of blood drying on my face, snowflakes melting on my knees. I couldn't think of a single reason to ever stand up again.

WE WENT OUT to my truck, then remembered that my truck was not at this house but was at the mall about a mile away. I also had lost my keys at some point but couldn't remember when. We set out wading through the storm, not sure if a person could walk that far in ankle-deep snow without getting frostbite. We didn't care. We plowed through it, not talking. The afternoon was fast fading to evening and what would happen after darkness fell and the shadows grew, we didn't know. A few minutes into our trip, during which we made depressingly little progress and lost feeling in all twenty of our toes, a pickup came grinding up behind us, pulling over just ahead. The driver leaned out, a young guy with a red baseball cap.

"Yo!" he said, looking over the dusting of snow on our coats. "What's up? Want a ride?"

We did.

The guy had bucket seats so John climbed into the bed and rode it out back there. I asked the guy if he was going by the old mall, he said he wasn't, I asked him if he was going south close to my neighborhood, he said he was. I looked around for Molly, saw she hadn't followed us, and climbed in. We drove.

"This be some snowy shit, yo!" he said. He had a little triangle of hair under his bottom lip. A soul patch, they call it. I said, "Yep."

"It's been hella slick drivin' in this shit. I'm swervin' and gettin' stuck here and there. All the other drivers be hatin' on me."

I stared at the man.

"Are you *Fred Durst*? Of the band *Limp Bizkit*?"

He smirked and concentrated on the road.

Eventually he said, "Gettin' hella dark out here. I'm thinkin' you two don't wanna be around when it gets fully dark, yo. Things be movin' and suckin' and hatin' on everything. But you know that, am I right?"

I said, "And you're saying that you're not one of them?" I glanced in the rearview mirror at John, huddled against the wind in the truck bed. I gauged whether or not I could get the wheel away from this guy and shove him out if he should try to eat me or whatever.

Fred Durst said, "Well, I ain't Fred Durst. You'll see what you wanna see. If John were in here, he'd see somebody else. But the point is there's darkness, yeah, but there's light and it all balances out. Like them yin and yang fishes, forever bitin' each other's tails. You know how it be."

I studied his blue eyes, said, "Why don't you tell me who you really are before I punch you in the face?"

"Yo, I told you. You just didn't listen. But I'm on your side. I been watching you. In fact, you could say that I've been 'dogging' you the whole time."

"I have no clue what you're talking about and I'm in no mood to be riddled. Talk straight or shut the fuck up. Are you the good witch? Some kind of angel? Are you Jesus, Fred Durst?"

"It don't matter. You had a job to do and you did it, even if you didn't know you had a job to do or that you were doin' it. The blade that cuts out the colon cancer's got an ugly job, right? I guess it's gotta have faith in the surgeon to get it through while its head's bein' sliced through blood and impacted shit."

"You know what? Fuck you. All this, this whole thing, is bullshit from top to bottom. I don't even know what I believe but I know we killed some ugliness back there. And Amy's dead because of it and she never hurt anybody. She's born and she gets shit on for twenty years and then she dies for no reason and I'm still alive and I should have been killed a long time ago. Hell, *I've* considered killing me several times, as a favor to the world."

Fred Durst said, "Yo, I know it's hard. You know there was that boxer, back in the nineties, Evander Holyfield. You know he got to be champion and then he had that heart disease. Ended his career, was gonna end his life. He goes to this televangelist, one of those hairspray-and-polyester dudes. Dude prays and dances over him and Evander goes back to the doctor. Doctor says he didn't have heart disease no more. Holyfield says it's a miracle but it turned out they had diagnosed him wrong."

"That could not have anything less to do with this conversation. You know what you people are like, Fred? You're like the genie from the bottle in those stories. You get a wish and you wish for a million dollars and then it turns out the million is from an insurance settlement because your best friend died."

"Yep," said Fred, as if I hadn't spoken at all. "He neeeever had the heart problem. Ain't that somethin'? Turned out it was a smudge on his X-rays or some shit. Do you wish you had died instead of Amy? Like, if you could do it over again?"

"Fuck off."

"I'm asking the question, yo. Would you do it?"

"Yes."

"Seriously?"

"Yes. Of course."

"You'd trade your life for hers? So tomorrow David Wong is dead, Amy Sullivan is alive?"

"Stop asking me, Fred. You're making my head hurt."

"Okay."

"I mean, what are you gonna do, shoot me? Shoot me and resurrect Amy? Or tell me that I've been dead the whole time like in that shitty Bruce Willis movie?"

"Dude, how would you have gone to work every day if you were—"

"Shut up, Fred. We're here."

We rolled to a stop and I saw my little house, all the edges rounded under snow. Fred said, "You know what, don't be too afraid of the dark, yo. You got a watch on your back now. Okay, dude?"

415

I had nothing else to say to Fred so I jumped out and trudged to the sidewalk. I heard the truck pull away and John came up behind me. I got halfway to my door and stopped. Footprints. Fresh prints, leading from the front door around back. The back being where the toolshed was.

I had, incredibly, forgotten all about the toolshed and the body within. I went around, following the tracks and finding myself walking slower and slower, shuffling like a man on his way to death row.

I go around that corner, and everything will change. Everything.

I had put it off long enough, though. I should have done this two nights ago. I rounded the corner and saw the toolshed and was unsurprised to see the door was standing wide open. The lock was hanging there, unhooked, and that was no surprise, either. I had put the key back on the nail by the kitchen door and any cop with a warrant could have gotten it. I went to the door, swung it open and saw two things that could not register in my mind.

The first was Amy.

She was standing there, alive, arms wrapped around her parka. She was looking down at the corpse on the floor, seeming totally lost, like something absolutely did not compute. I could sympathize with her. She heard me, looked, had an expression of shock that was almost comical. She looked at me, then at the floor, then back at me.

I said, "It's me, Amy."

She didn't respond. I moved toward her, wanting to squeeze her and take her inside and never let her out of my sight again. She backed away from me, bumping into the shelf full of glass jars. She looked like she was planning her escape. I understood that, too. And that was the second thing:

The body on the floor was me.

I know my own face pretty well, even blue and frozen like a meatsicle as this one was, nestled among the wrinkled tarp that Amy had thrown open. There was a big, bloody hole right in my heart. John stepped in behind me and looked down at the body and then over at Amy, going through the same tangled path of thought I had just tread.

John said to Amy, "Can I see your feet?"

Amy didn't answer.

John said, "I know you don't understand this, but you gotta realize that Dave and I saw you get killed not twenty minutes ago. So we got some confusion to sort through."

Amy nodded and spoke for the first time, saying, "Okay."

She left the shed and sat on the steps at my back door. With the snow pouring down on her she pulled off her little leather boot and her sock. I watched as John picked up her foot, examined it, then had her do the same with the other one.

He turned to me and said, "They're clean."

And with that, everything snapped into place for me. All the pieces of the puzzle. If you figured it out before now, well, go win a Nobel Prize, Mr. Genius.

I said, "They're stocking the world with their own people, with replacements. Things that can bridge the world between the spiritual and physical, Korrok extending the shadows into our world like fingers, controlling his meat puppets. That's what they were doing in there, making things that look like people. Monsters, under their control. *His* control. Like with Drake. So what happened to the real Drake? Dead?"

Amy looked up, eyes wide, understanding where this was going.

John said, "Dunno. Maybe they got him and all the other people locked away somewhere. But I doubt it. You know, these replacements, the copies, they gotta have all the memories of the real people. So who knows how they use the originals."

I said, "That mark, then, on the foot. That's their mark. And if we had looked on the other Amy—"

"We'd have seen a mark like the symbol for pi. It's probably a brand logo."

"So they made an Amy," I said. "Probably when they took her. They made a new Amy and infected her—"

"Because they knew if we thought it was her, we would try to bring her back here," we finished together.

417

John said, "And that would have been the end. We would have gotten infected when she, uh, hatched, then whoever was nearby when, you know, we hatched . . ."

"So North knew what he was doing," I said. "When he shot her, he knew it was the right thing. Because that wasn't Amy."

I stood up, took a step toward the toolshed and was stopped. I had a redhead squeezing me. Amy was clamped on with all of her strength, her arms around my ribs, her face buried in my shirt. She was crying, saying she was sorry but I couldn't figure out for what. I ran my hand through her hair and whispered in her ear that it was almost over, that it really was going to be okay this time and I just had to take care of this one last thing.

John put a hand on her shoulder and pulled her back toward him. A strange gesture, almost protective. But I was free from her and I stepped toward the shed.

I heard Amy behind me, saying through choking sobs that she had lost the gun, that she had shot the monster at the mall and ran and ran and lost the thing in the snow. And she called a cab and—

John shushed her and she went quiet. I moved toward the toolshed, my heart pounding, suddenly feeling lighter than air, a weight lifted from my shoulders. I looked up at the snow pouring down from the night sky and suddenly everything seemed all right. I said, "North knew what he was doing, and I knew what I was doing the other night. When I shot this thing in my toolshed."

I reached the little building. John didn't follow, but apparently already knew what I would find. I threw aside the tarp wrapped around the corpse's feet and began tearing at frozen laces on a pair of black leather hiking boots, just like mine. Even a scuff along the toe, like mine. The body snatchers were insane about their detail. They had to be.

I said, "I came home and I found this thing in my yard, this thing that looked just like me, and I ran in and got the gun and I popped him. He probably would've tried to kill me if—"

I stopped. I had pulled off the shoe and peeled off the frozen sock, but saw absolutely no mark on the dead foot. I chuckled, out loud for some reason. I dropped the foot and grabbed for the other one, started to pull apart the laces, lost the grip in my numbing fingers and threw the foot aside, realizing that I was fooling myself.

I stood there, laughing softly, steam puffing into the darkness. Then finally did what I should have done first. I went and sat on the step Amy had vacated. As I passed, John pulled Amy back behind him, backing off from me. Giving me lots of space. I started to take off my right shoe, thought, then went for the left instead. I yanked off the boot and the sock and looked at my big toe. Then I started laughing, laughing so hard I could barely breathe.

John looked at me with no expression because he already knew, looked like he had known for some time. Amy hung back, behind him, looking nervously between us. I brought up the foot and rubbed at the pi symbol on my toe, as if I could make it come off. I knew, of course, that it never, ever would.

Epilogue

"AND, WELL, THAT'S my story," I said. "I'm sorry that it's so, you know. Retarded."

There is no word in the English language for the feeling someone gets when they suddenly realize they're standing next to an unholy monster impersonating a human. Monstralization, maybe? I suppose it doesn't matter because the reporter I was talking to wasn't experiencing that emotion right now.

Arnie Blondestone of *American Lifestyle* magazine (or was it *American Living*? It was too bland to remember) had neither a tape recorder nor a notebook visible. Arnie and

I had been walking as we talked, me relaying my story in the moldy halls of the defunct Undisclosed Shopping Centre. I stopped in front of a narrow, closed maintenance door and faced him. I said, "There it is. The door. *The* door."

He glanced at it and said dramatically, "The door to another world!"

"Well, uh, it was. Through there and then in the little room behind it. But it wasn't a real door, like I said. It was a ghost door." I was going to add that John had named the other world "Shit Narnia" but I decided not to lower Arnie's opinion of us any more than I already had.

"Well," Arnie said, rubbing his hands together excitedly. "Let's go."

"Have you been listening? Even if we could, you really think they'd let us escape again? And I'm not even sure that world is habitable now anyway."

"Come on, let's give it a shot. Just let me poke my head through. I mean, don't get me wrong, I completely believe your story. I just wanna confirm that one detail. The one about the ghost door that leads to the world of the bug herders."

I suspected he might be patronizing me. I shook my head and said, "We can't. Even if we wanted to. The door is gone. The other door, I mean. We've been back here several times but the wall where the ghost door was is just a wall now. But I know you're not asking because you think it's there. You're asking because you think I'm nuts."

That's not true, though. If he thought I was dangerous, would he really have let himself get stuck in this abandoned place with me? I could have a cache of guns in here for all he knows. And if he thinks I'm bullshitting him, couldn't he have easily excused himself by now? So what was it? Morbid curiosity? What's your game, Arnie?

Arnie reached out and turned the rusting silver knob on the maintenance door. It swung open with a labored creak. He glanced inside the room and then back at me. He gestured at the door as if to say, "See?"

I said, "What?"

"This is the door you said got blown off its hinges when that thing, the monster came through it?"

Hmmm. That was an interesting point. I walked up to the maintenance door and ran my hand over it.

"They must have fixed it, I guess. But look at the opposite wall. You can kind of see marks in the plaster where the door bounced off it. See those scuff marks at the top there?"

Arnie shrugged, unimpressed. I tried to imagine this article in *Life in the USA* magazine, complete with a big full-color photo of the wall with the caption, "These are the actual scuff marks that prove an unholy demon-engineered beast burst through a nearby door in order to prevent David Wong from passing through an invisible portal to a gargantuan secret complex with a path to an alternate reality inhabited by a race of half human beastmasters." I mean, *I* would read that article but I would probably be the only one.

But why was he still here? Hell, why had he come in the first place? No matter what he said, I still got this vibe from him that he wanted to believe me and that I was letting him down. He had been listening patiently to my story for six hours straight. I wouldn't have done that if the roles were reversed. I would have politely said, "Well, I think I got all I need!" and then sprinted the other direction, laughing maniacally.

But Arnie looked like he had come here expecting answers and would now leave empty-handed. I had seen that look before, on the faces of tourists visiting the Texas Book Depository in Dallas where Lee Harvey Oswald took the shots at JFK. I took that tour and met some conspiracy buffs, all of us standing at the gunman's window and looking down to the spot where the motorcade passed. It's right there below the window, an easy shot at a slow-moving car. No mystery, just a kid and a rifle and a tragedy. They came looking for dark and terrible revelations and instead found out something even more dark and terrible: that their lives were trite and boring.

I had a thought and said to Arnie, "The cop, John's uncle Drake. He really did disappear, you can look that up, along with everything else. And that's two cops who've gone missing and in both cases I was the last to talk to them before they did. They've questioned me and I have a lawyer and everything."

"And you told the cops he was sucked into another dimension, killed and replaced by a monster?"

"Basically, only without the words 'another dimension' or 'replaced' or 'monster.' We told them he pulled us over and acted all crazy. His partner, the black guy? The one who was piling snow on his crotch? He went back to work that next day, like nothing happened. That's the one Amy shot, you know."

"Can I talk to him? Because he's also secretly a monster, right?"

"I dunno. His name is Murphy I think. I bet he doesn't remember that day, though."

Arnie eyed me carefully. He couldn't ask me the big question, couldn't point out the elephant in the room. *How do I know you haven't killed all these people, Mr. Wong? The cops, Fred, Big Jim? How do I know I'm not talking to a bona fide serial killer right now?*

Instead he said, "Look at this from my point of view, Wong—"

"No, stop. Stop that reporter bullshit, that act where you change your personality according to what you think'll get the most information. Acting like the skeptic one second and my best friend the next and my interrogator after that, whatever it takes to coax the 'real' story outta me. I've been honest with you, Arnie." *Mostly.* "Now be honest with me. Can you do that? Do you have a real personality in there or is everything an interview technique with you?"

He threw out his arms to his sides, his "what the hell do you want from me" gesture, but said nothing.

"I want to know what you're doing here, Arnie. I mean, you picked this story, right? You probably got people feedin' you ideas all day and you get to decide which one gets written up, right? But you drove down to the ass middle of nowhere from, uh—"

"Chicago."

"—from Chicago and used up a whole day out of your schedule to hear this. And you came prepared, notes and shit, you read all the Web sites about us. So you got another day of preparation in this thing on top of that. Tell me, Arnie, what did you think you were gonna find?"

He shrugged again. Hesitant. "I don't know."

I had another thought and said, "You're down here on your own time, aren't you?"

He didn't answer, but his expression answered for him.

I stuffed my hands into my pockets and felt the little metal canister. Cold. I let out a long breath. I nodded toward the floor, which had never been tiled. Just bare, unfinished plywood, graying with age.

"You see that part of the floor over there, Arnie, the section of plywood next to the wall? See how it's all scratched around the edges, like it's been pried up?"

He didn't answer, but he was looking at it.

"Help me pull it up. You gotta see this."

Doubt crept into Arnie's face. Maybe a little fear. Maybe afraid of what was under there, maybe just not wanting to mess up his suit.

I got down on my knees and started without him. The board had warped and I knew it would come right up. John and I had never replaced the nails when we pulled it up months ago because by that point in the project we had both been pretty drunk. I pulled up the sheet of plywood, probably three by five feet in size, and leaned it against the wall. Under it there was a framework of metal rails holding up the floor. And under that, a body. More of a skeleton by now, to be accurate.

I stepped back from the square hole in the floor and gestured for Arnie to see for himself. He gave me a cautious look, stepped forward, and froze in place. A look of—

Monstralization?

—cold recognition hit his face. He didn't know exactly who or what I was, couldn't know, but he did know at that moment that I had killed.

Trying to sound casual, he said, "And who is that?"

"Me."

Arnie took two steps back and here it was, the big moment. The moment at which Arnie would turn on his heels and run away, or plunge fully into the dark madness of Wongworld.

Arnie really looked like he would run. I turned and sat calmly down on the floor, my back against the wall, looking up at him. If he ran, I would let him go.

Would you?

He hesitated, ran a hand over his mouth. The bones below him were long rid of any muscle or skin, now a dried-up, ash-colored framework covered in crumbling clothes. I thought of the squirming masses of beetles and worms and spiders and maggots that had feasted on "my" body down there, building writhing nests where my mouth had been. I gave a shudder.

I said, "We were gonna shove it through the portal, but by the time we got here it was gone. No ghost door. So we debated for about half an hour, had a dozen beers, then finally decided to cram it under the floor and go back home."

Arnie stood silent for a long moment, then said, "What, you didn't worry about somebody finding it? Like the cops?"

"What crime would they charge me with? Suicide?"

Arnie actually barked a dry laugh. He turned away from the corpse under the floor, surely wishing he could rewind his life to a time before he had seen it. He walked to the opposite side of the room and sat.

He said, "This doesn't change anything. Fine, there's a body. But that don't make the rest of your story true."

I sighed and said, "Arnie, come on. I know what you're saying but, really, what did you think you were gonna find here? Talk to me, buddy."

He shook his head. "I don't know. I don't—it's a hobby of mine. That's all. The paranormal, all that."

He stopped talking. I waited. He said, "And the thing with the shadows, I guess, kind of caught my eye. In your story. There's a lot of that going around now, on the Net, elsewhere, stories of the shadow people. I think Dean Koontz wrote a novel about them, but you have to ask, did his book come first or did the stories come first? But all of a sudden, everyone's talking about them. Everyone and no one. Do you know what I mean?"

Oh, I know, Arnie. Trust me, I know.

He continued, "And I would think back to what I saw, in my basement that day. The shadow. And after that, every now and then, maybe I saw them but maybe I didn't, you know? It's like once you see a

425

mouse in your kitchen you start seeing it everywhere. But there's something else, too. At certain times, mostly when I'm really sleepy—and this is gonna sound crazy as shit but considering what you've said I think I might as well let it out—at those times I think I see a cat. Just glimpses, out the corner of my eye. A cat slipping around a corner or running past my chair. And I think, okay, that's Fluffy. That's my cat, Fluffy. But I've never owned a cat. And then I think I can remember that maybe I did own a cat. Or maybe I didn't. And I swear I can remember a life with it and one without it, and then I heard your story—"

"With Todd?" I said. "You heard about the thing with Todd and thought maybe it was the same thing? That maybe the shadow people took your cat?"

He shook his head, but not in disagreement. It was a gesture of resignation. He said, "I'll never say the phrase 'the shadow people took my cat' out loud or agree to it when you say it out loud. I got a life to live, you know. But yeah, in my drunker moments I think that somehow I had a cat and that the cat was stolen from me, both in the present and the past. And then I heard bits of your story and I think, here's somebody who's been down the same road. If nothin' else, maybe he's got the same psychological disorder or maybe we did the same drugs in college and maybe I can get to the bottom of it. So that's why I'm here. The short version, anyway."

And that's true, Arnie. I believe you. But that isn't the whole truth, is it? Why do you keep stopping short of the whole story?

I said, "There's more, isn't there?"

He looked over at the open grave in the floor and said, "You say John helped you move the body?"

"Sure. I couldn't have done it alone. It's hard enough hauling my own fat ass around without having to double the load."

"So after he knew about, you know. After he knew the truth, you're saying he stuck around?"

I shrugged. "Well—"

"Because you guys killed a cop when you found out he was one of these things. Why would it be different?"

426

"Well, that was only after he actually turned into the monster—"

"And what about Amy? Can I talk to her?"

"Uh, no."

"Is she still—"

alive

"—around?"

I didn't answer. Arnie sat up straight, energized to be back in reporter mode, ready to dig again. "There's more, isn't there? What is it? Does it have to do with the girl? With Amy? What happened to her?"

I rubbed my eyes and said . . .

IF YOU HAD asked me then, as I sat there in the snow and biting cold of my backyard, I would have said it was the worst moment of my life. And that would have been a ridiculous thing to say, since technically my "life" had only been a couple of days long at that point.

I don't know how long I sat there looking at my bare foot and the symbol on my toe, with Amy standing a few feet away in a horrified paralysis. I saw John sit on a tree stump and pull out his cigarette-rolling kit, watched him carefully roll one before patting around his pockets for a lighter and realizing he had left it in another universe. He threw the cigarette aside with a curse. That's when Amy began crying, like a switch had been thrown. Softly at first, her head in her hand, her fingers clawing handfuls of copper hair. She leaned against the toolshed and then she was crying hard, a wretched, coughing sound as her body convulsed with sobs. Little kid–type crying. Jerking, unrestrained and terrible, terrible, terrible.

"Let's, uh, all go inside . . ." John began, weakly. "Amy, come on."

She didn't hear him, her whole body spasming with sobs, a sound like her lungs were having a fistfight. It was truly awful. I closed my eyes and would have plugged my ears, too, but not even that would block it because the very air stank from the sheer awfulness of it all.

John looked long at Amy, then at me. Finally he nodded to himself as if coming to some conclusion and said, "Okay." He stabbed a finger at Amy.

"Amy," he said in a voice that was strong and abrupt. "Stand up straight." She didn't.

"*Hey*. Amy." He strode over and grabbed the shoulder of her jacket, shaking her. "Man up. The night's work ain't done. You ready to man up?"

She wiped her face and looked at him.

"Okay," John said, "you still got the gold cross? The one Dave gave you?"

She nodded. I noticed a snowflake landed on the lashes of one of her eyes.

"Okay," John said. "Take the cross and touch Monster Dave with it. If he's evil, he'll explode."

I pulled on my sock and shoe and said, almost too quiet to hear, "Leave her alone, John."

"Human Dave wouldn't have said that!" John shouted, loud enough for my neighbors to hear. "Now sit still while she touches you with the cross." He turned to Amy and pulled on her arm. "Come on. Man up."

He pulled her to her feet—roughly, I thought—and she mumbled something to him so I couldn't hear. John answered with, "Don't worry. I'll take care of it." She pulled her arm from him and he said, "Amy, I'm not asking you. This needs to be done."

She dug into her shirt for the cross necklace and wrapped the thin chain around her fist. She glanced doubtfully at John, who urged her on with a gesture.

Holding the cross between thumb and finger like a key, she took a few cautious steps toward me, her face showing caution bordering on naked fear. I heard myself say, "Amy . . ."

"SHUT UP!" John screamed. "Don't listen to his lies, Amy, for that is a crafty one there."

She drew closer, holding the cross at arm's length. I looked down at the powdering of snow on my pants. I looked up suddenly, the cross an

428

inch away from my face. This movement seemed to startle Amy and she lunged forward with the necklace. The cross jabbed me right in the eye.

"OH, SON OF A BITCH!" I threw myself to my feet, clasping my stinging eye. "You jabbed that thing right in my—"

"I KNEW IT!" screamed John, his face a picture of indignant monstralization. "AMY, BACK AWAY."

John tore off his coat and flung it into the snow. Then he pulled his shirt over his head and stood there, bare-chested, snow landing on his naked shoulders like dandruff. I blinked my injured eye and was relieved to see I wasn't blinded. I said, "John, don't be a—"

"SHUT UP. I hope you likes Chinese, Monster Dave." John threw up his fists. "Because today the menu is Kung Fu Chicken. And it's ALL YOU CAN EAT, BABY."

John flung himself into a pseudo-karate stance, one hand poised behind him and one in front, posed like a cartoon cactus. I thought for an odd moment he had moved his limbs so fast they had made that *whoosh* sound through the air but then I realized John was making that sound with his mouth.

"WAIT!" This was Amy. She ran over between us. "I got him in the eye with it! Don't. John, don't. Calm down."

John let her stop him, of course. He reached around her and jabbed a finger at me.

"She just saved your life, my friend. I'd have been wearin' you like a pair of pants."

I sighed and said, "I'm going inside."

I turned and walked toward my door. After a moment, John dropped his hands by his sides and said, "Yeah." He picked his jacket and shirt from the snow and bundled them up in his hand. We strode in casually, like we were coming in after a tiring game of basketball. Amy stayed behind, standing there in the angry swarm of snowflakes. John turned to her, said, "Come in where it's warm, Amy. We'll hammer this out over a nice can of Leinenkugel's."

She looked at him and then at me, not quite sure what had just transpired. John went back to her and leaned down, whispering harshly but out of my hearing. Almost like he was scolding her. She said something back, casting nervous glances at me. They continued this covert argument for a few minutes, with me already inside and watching from my kitchen. I wasn't completely sure what it was about and I still don't know. Finally John stomped away from her, toward the house. He turned back to her one last time and said, just loud enough for me to hear, "You know fucking well what I mean. I mean you literally never knew him. When we showed up at your house that was Monster Dave and it was Monster Dave thereafter. And I'll tell you what, whatever you think, he's a lot nicer now than he was before. But you wouldn't know."

He stormed away from her, looking pissed, and brushed past me as he entered the kitchen. I said to his back, "John, we gotta move that body."

"It can wait. You'll still be dead tomorrow."

I took one last look at Amy outside, snow gathering on her like a lawn ornament. I said, "You coming?"

She made no move and I waited at the door for a bit before finally turning and heading inside. I went to the living room and sat in my leather recliner. I stared into the cold, dead fireplace on the far wall. It was one of those gas fireplaces that would burn real logs so that it looked authentic, a modern heating source dressed up to look like an old-fashioned one. It was an idea I had always found ridiculous, wondering if in the future they wouldn't have some kind of laser fireplace dressed up to look like a mere gas fireplace, with fake gas lines running from it.

I heard the kitchen door click open and I knew Amy had decided to come in. That shouldn't have surprised me. Where else could she have gone? I thought for a moment and glanced at the notepad next to my phone, the one I used to leave myself messages ("GET MILK" it said in my hurried scrawl); I wondered if I drew up a quick Last Will and Testament would it be legally binding. John is a notary. I could write it up in a few sentences, leaving the house to Amy so she would have somewhere to live, sign it and then shoot myself in the temple. But then I felt my pockets and once more remembered I had lost the Smith hours ago. I ditched the plan for the time being.

430

John popped out of the bathroom, fully clothed now, and turned to intercept Amy in the kitchen. They talked some more in those same low, rough tones before both of them entered the living room. Amy sat stiffly on the couch, her arms wrapped around her midsection as I had seen her do so often before. It suddenly occurred to me that when she sat that way the stump of her left wrist was hidden behind her right upper arm. To a passerby, it wouldn't immediately be apparent she was missing a hand so there would be no reason to do the double take that Amy had grown to dread. Seeing her like that, they'd just think she was cold. John took a spot on the floor between us, sitting cross-legged. "Okay," he said, as if he were the moderator of this panel. "How much do you remember, Monster Dave? What memories did they give you?"

I shrugged and said, "Everything, I guess. There's that missing bit from when I first showed up here—"

"When you came here and shot the real Dave?"

"Yeah. It happened out in the yard, I guess. There were tracks all over. But otherwise it's the same as before. Or, you know. As far as I know."

"But you don't know anything of the real stuff? Like where you came from or why you're here?"

I said, "Did you remember those things at the time of your birth?"

"But you remember your—I mean Dave's—childhood and all that. School and your parents and friends?"

I waved a dismissive hand. "Yeah, yeah. You and I met in computer class. Mr. Gertz. You did the ASCII vagina, got kicked out, and so on."

"And you know you got to be at work tomorrow? And you know where?"

"Video store. Wally's. Sucks. Coworkers are retarded. Yeah, yeah."

"And the five hundred dollars you borrowed from me last month."

"Fuck you."

John nodded in satisfaction. "Okay, then. I'm goin' home. I gotta sleep in my own bed tonight because I got work tomorrow. And if I don't leave right now, I'm gonna get snowed in here. Amy is going to stay here tonight."

He raised a hand to silence my objection.

"I don't wanna hear it," he said. "She's gonna stay here and watch you. Now we don't know what exactly you morph into, but if it's like those things we saw before, we know one weakness is fire. Amy, if you see Dave turn into any kind of monster, set him on fire. Dave, show Amy where the flammables are in this house. Get her a lighter and one of those huge cans of hairspray that old ladies use, if you have any. Got it?"

John climbed to his feet, Amy looking at him with an incredulous, squinted look, like he had broken some new bounds of human idiocy that she previously had not thought possible. John said to her, "Remember what we talked about." And with that, he pulled open the front door and vanished into the white swirl of the storm.

On the David Wong Social Awkwardness Scale, with "1" being going to the "Pickup" instead of "Order" counter at a restaurant and "10" being a guy getting caught on national TV having sex with a dead baboon, I'd have to say that the following minutes alone with Amy rated about a 9.6. A while into this wordless meeting, ten minutes or an hour, I don't know, the phone rang. We both jumped out of our skin. I picked up, glancing out of my window to see sheets of ice bits raining down in the night.

"Hello?"

"It's me. I made it home. Slick as hell, did a three-sixty going around a corner at Lex and Main. Have you turned into a monster yet?"

"No, John."

"Get this. Molly is here."

"At your place? John, how does she even know where you live?"

"It's even better than that. She wasn't standing outside the building when I got here. She was *in my apartment*."

"She *broke in?*"

"Don't know. She's eating a package of hot dogs right now."

I sensed Amy walking past behind me and a moment later my bathroom door closed. I said, "You gave her the whole pack?"

"Yeah, they're expired. She'll stop eating when she gets full, won't she? Hey, is your power out?"

"No, lights are still on."

And with that, the lights went out.

"Fuck. They're out now, John."

"Yeah, mine were off when I got in. I thought it was the bad guys maybe, making their move. But I turned on the radio and it's down in several parts of town. I guess they're working on it. They got the storm on every station, talking like it's a natural disaster. The ice is knocking down trees and power lines and they said at the state prison the snow drifted up against the fences so high that inmates were able to just walk over it. The guards couldn't shoot 'em because they were afraid of the ACLU."

It hadn't occurred to me that the winter storm had been a huge event for practically every person in town except for the three of us, who had bigger fish to fry. I got off the phone with John, blinked as my eyes adjusted to the darkness and then dug around my cabinets for candles. Amy emerged from the bathroom, her purse slung over her shoulder, and she pawed around the wall to find her way. She put her glasses on, as if they would help her see in the dark. She asked, "Will your heat go off with the power out?"

"Oh, I'm sure it won't."

I wasn't sure, though. Can people really just freeze to death in their homes in times like this? I hunted around for a book of matches, found none in the kitchen and tried the bathroom as the only other likely place. I pulled open the drawer on the vanity and found my matches. I opened the medicine cabinet—

Someone had been here. I normally have three prescription bottles of medication and all of it was gone. Hell, even the aspirin was gone. All of it had been here after we came home to find the house ransacked. I had checked.

I shuffled around in the drawers to see if anything else was missing and I saw my scissors were gone, too. I could have just misplaced them, though. I suddenly flashed on Amy leaving the bathroom, her purse with her, and figured out what a smarter person would have figured out the minute John told Amy to stay with me.

It turned out I was wrong about the furnace. The house started losing heat rapidly the moment the lights went down. I guess the gas stays on but the electric fans that blow the heat around don't operate without electricity. An hour later, Amy and I were huddled in front of my fake fireplace, sitting on the floor and wrapped in blankets like Bugs Bunny Indians. I got the fireplace lit and turned up as high as it would go. There were no logs in it but they were just for visual effect anyway, the blue flames licking the air and putting out their own heat. We sat there like that, a flickering pool of amber light around us, with no sound but the hiss of the gas and the creak of the wind leaning on exterior walls. The silence was driving me nuts.

"You have my medication in your purse?" I finally asked.

She didn't answer.

I said, "So I'm on suicide watch? Do you have my scissors, too?"

She said, "I'm sorry that I freaked out before, in the yard. That wasn't fair. You have to accept people for what they are—"

"No, no. Amy, you were right. You were right then, when you freaked out. You're wrong now, that you're calmed down and telling yourself everything's gonna be okay. It's not."

"You did fine today. Yesterday, too."

"That's not the point. Whatever happens, whenever it happens, we know one thing—that I won't be able to control it. Amy, you have to get out of town. Away from this place."

"We all do. Let's all move away. Bring John if you want."

Bring John, she says. Like he's my pet . . .

I said, "Amy, I told you before—"

"No. We tried it your way. Let's get far away from here and if the bad guys follow, we'll deal with it then. But let's at least try."

"Okay, but it'll take time for us, John and me. We got jobs, we got to get things in order. John's got family here. But you, you can go now and I say we do it tomorrow. Is there anywhere you can go? You got friends far away? Anywhere? Somebody with a couch you can crash on?"

"I don't know. I guess. I know a girl on the Internet; she lives in Utah with another girl. They're lesbians."

"Good. That's good. You'll call them or send them something on your computer and ask if you can crash there. We'll buy a plane ticket and fly your ass to Utah."

She said nothing. She scooted over and leaned her head on my shoulder, ribbons of firelight dancing on the lenses of her glasses. Eventually she said, "And then I'll never, ever see you again."

I couldn't think of a way to answer that without telling an outright lie, so I just mumbled something that sounded reassuring. She said, "I'll go, but I'll call when I'm out there. And you have to take my calls. If you don't I'll just come right back. If I don't get an answer from you I'll be on a flight the next day."

"Okay. Um, sure."

She rearranged herself so that she was lying down, her head on my lap. Her breathing slowed and softened as she drifted off. She mumbled, "It's, like, so cool that it's snowing out there but not in here. It can't snow on us. That's so cool . . ."

She started snoring softly.

And that was that. I formulated a plan that if she got out there and away from the Hell that is this town, got a job and went to bars with her lesbian roommates, she'd settle in. Forget all about this, all about me. Out there the guys would figure out how hot she was, even without both hands, and she'd meet somebody and she'd stop calling and then all the loose ends would be tied up. I could shoot myself or take a bunch of pills and that would clean up the situation once and for all. I could do a real will, even have a lawyer draw it up, complete with a stipulation that John had to deliver my eulogy in the form of a seventeen-minute-long guitar solo, performed with a dual-necked guitar shaped like a naked woman. As for the property, I could sign it over to—

I saw a light to my left. I slowly turned my head to see that, with power still out all over the city, the television had clicked on.

Hands. That's what I saw, a pair of hands, palms pressed against the screen. Then another pair, fingers clawing at the glass as if trying to escape. For a moment I thought it was snowing in the background but then my mind registered the worms, the white flying worms that poured through the air behind them. I thought I heard a scream, or felt it somehow, and a spray of red splattered the hands on the screen. A pair of hands fell away and just two were left, grabbing at the glass in desperation. One hand formed a fist and smashed against the glass, as if trying to break it. It pounded again and again, and I thought I could see blooms of blood opening on the knuckles. The fist reared way back this time and swung and—

Thump

—the TV shook. I almost pissed my pants. The fist pulled back, blood trickling down between the fingers now, and smashed against the screen once more. Again, the TV rattled on the shelf of my entertainment center, the whole set edging forward an inch with the impact. The fist drew back one last time—the set clicked off. Blackness.

Those transmissions, the ones from Shit Narnia, never returned. It took me four hours to fall asleep.

IT ACTUALLY WASN'T for another couple of days that we were able to get Amy on a plane. The storm broke that next day but the weather had still messed up the flight schedules. It took a day to hear back from her lesbians. They were thrilled to the point of giddiness to have her, though, and after an hour-long, giggly phone conversation they made arrangements to meet her at the airport in Salt Lake City. The two girls lived in Millcreek, which I guess was just outside of the city.

We kept busy during those two days before Amy left for presumably forever and I successfully avoided any real conversation with her. I had lots of snow to clear off the sidewalk and even made paths around the side of the house for Molly. We took Amy shopping and she bought luggage and a bunch of sweaters because we couldn't convince her that Utah wasn't a frozen, mountainous wasteland year-round. I went back to Wally's and finished a long-delayed project of placing anti-theft stickers on all of our DVDs. It was the kind of tedious, dreaded task that I wouldn't want to dump in someone else's lap after I committed suicide.

On Wednesday Amy packed up and I drove her the three hours to Undisclosed International Airport in my Bronco. I had begged John to come along to act as a buffer against the awkwardness but he had work, his crew fixing a wall on a local diner that had collapsed under the weight of a fallen tree. Several times during the drive Amy would ask me if I was okay and I would say, "Sure!" and turn up the radio.

I almost made it. I carried her bags in and we waded through the airport bullshit that seemed to take forever. She picked up her boarding pass and we checked her bags and there the security guys made it clear that only the one with a boarding pass could go any farther. I said good-bye and wished her a pleasant flight. And that's where Amy lost it. She threw her arms around my neck and started crying into my shirt, telling me I had saved her life and she didn't know what she would do if something happened to me and a whole lot of other ridiculous things. Then she made me promise that I would take care of myself. I did, before I could catch it.

She stepped back and wiped her eyes and said, "You promise?"

"Yeah."

"Remember that. Remember you promised."

I pointed at her and said, "Hey, say what you want about me but I keep my promises."

"And you guys will come see me out in Utah? I'm serious about this now. I'm gonna be mad if you don't."

"Sure, Amy. You and me can share a room, John can sleep with the lesb—"

"And you'll look after Molly? And take care of my house?"

By "take care of" she meant "destroy." We had talked about that, decided to burn the place down. Our only point of disagreement is I wanted to make it look like an accident to collect the insurance money. She wanted to do the opposite, let the insurance lapse and just blatantly torch the place.

We kissed and said some gooey things to each other that would sound silly if you weren't there. I stood around and waited for her to board, passing through security and letting them check her shoes and

all that shit, watched her walk away and kept watching out of a termi-
nal window as her plane climbed and turned into a speck in the sky. I
didn't cry. And if you think I did, good luck proving it, asshole.

I started to wander back toward the exits when I noticed a little girl
following me. She couldn't have been more than five years old, chubby,
blond hair down to her waist. I walked, she kept up, I stopped, she
stopped. Her eyes never left mine. I finally turned and was about to ask
if she was lost, when she got down on her hands and knees and then
lay flat on her stomach.

Confused, I considered just walking away when she started slithering along the floor like a snake, legs clasped together and swishing
back and forth behind her like a tail. She slithered across the floor
like this all the way to the nearest wall, pushing her way into the
men's restroom, opening the swinging door with the crown of her
head.

Of course, I followed. I stepped into the room and saw the little girl
melt into a puddle of black oil. The blackness rose and took shape and
I began to consider that I had made a mistake.

I started to back out of the room, realizing the two guys pissing at
the urinals nearby didn't even acknowledge any of this. Suddenly the
black shape sprung at me and for a second, all I could see was darkness.

THE AIR STANK. My ankles were submerged in cold liquid that sloshed
when I moved my feet. I blinked and could almost see I was in a doorless room. I reached out and touched a metal wall. I could see only by
two small spots of orange light and I realized with horror that it was
the shadow creature's eyes. There was a steady rumbling sound from
all around us and I had to brace myself as the floor seemed to shift and
tilt under me. The black thing stood at the end of the room and stared.

"Where are we?" I asked, to see if it would respond more than anything else.

The answer did not come in the form of an audible voice, but a picture. In a blink I had a perfect, mental image of an airliner and of a spot

438

under the passenger compartment where a large center fuel tank was housed. I was standing inside the center fuel tank of a passenger jet. The liquid at my feet was jet fuel. I also knew with some certainty that this was Amy's plane, that I was standing just a few feet under the spot where she was sitting and likely striking up a conversation with whoever she was seated with.

Strangely, the first thought that came to me—even before "Am I really here?"—was that they had forgotten to fill up this tank. Then the answer came to me that they often leave it empty depending on the distance and load of the flight. Then I realized how creepy it was that I was having this telepathic conversation with this thing and I made an effort to close my mind to it.

The shadow thing moved. It drifted like a puff of smoke in a mild breeze, stopping near a bulky apparatus that emerged from the ceiling and dangled to the floor, probably an instrument for measuring how much fuel was left. The fumes were burning my eyes and nose and lungs. It was making me light-headed. The black thing drifted to the apparatus, swirled a black appendage over and around a conduit, a jointed line that probably housed an electrical wire. The black thing caressed the line, almost sensually. Sparks flew from the conduit.

I screamed.

I TURNED TO Arnie and said, "There was light and heat and noise. A sound like a junkyard falling down a mountain."

I concentrated, tried to bring back the memory. That very real feeling of my flesh burning to vapor in a millisecond, my bones cooking to black charcoal. But I couldn't, not really. The memory was hazy and unreal, like the memories of the hamster we owned when I was five, the one that escaped and then got eaten by a snapping turtle. I can't picture it, but I know it was there. And that it wasn't very fast.

"And then," I said, "everything was back the way it was. I was standing there again, in the dark, shoes and socks soaked in that stinking, ice-cold liquid. To say it was a weird feeling doesn't do it justice, because

439

at that moment I had a distinct memory of the explosion happening and an equally clear memory of it not happening."

This seemed to confuse Arnie, understandably enough. He said, "So, did the plane go down or not?"

"No." I paused for a moment and said, "It didn't. Not yet."

This confused Arnie further, but he waited patiently for me to explain. A good reporter, down to the last.

I said, "And as I was standing there, in the stench and the darkness, a thought came into my head, perfect and clear. The voice of that thing, the shadow man. 'This moment,' it said, 'is forever.' And I understood right then that all moments are forever and that they can go back there to that spot at any time, in the wet, stinking belly of that plane. They can go back and short that wire or jam open some valve and blow Amy out of the air along with two hundred other people. But that ain't so strange, is it? You drive to the doctor's office to hear the results of your X-ray and you pray that it isn't cancer. Isn't that what you're praying for, that God will reach back in the past? Back before the X-ray was taken, before you even saw the doctor. Months before, so He can stop that tumor from forming in the first place?"

Arnie nodded and said, "Only this was the opposite, right? A threat. They were tellin' you they can go back and make bad things happen, take your girl out of the equation. Anytime they want. So you wake up someday and see empty bed beside you and say, 'Gosh, it's a pity Amy died in that plane crash all those years ago.' And you look and see all the headlines have changed and all those lives are lost and history is tweaked. Changed to suit their needs."

I said, "You do catch on, Arnie. It takes a little time, but you do catch on."

"And the message," he continued, "was that you need to back off. 'Cause why else make the threat? They were saying you need to stop interfering with whatever plans they got, because if not they'll go back and cut Amy out of the timeline."

I started to speak, couldn't, then swallowed and finally said, "You see, I screwed it up. I had it just right in the beginning, I had no con-

440

nections. No family, no money, no career, no nothin'. What could they do to me? What could they take from me? But all that changed with Amy. Now they've got me, now they've got a hold on me. And I see her and she'd look up at me with those green eyes and I think, hey, saving the world, that's Hollywood bullshit. The best I can do is save this little bit of the world, this little corner that me and this girl stand in. And every time I think that, somewhere I can hear laughter. Them laughing. Like the game is over, check and mate."

Arnie said, "And you never ate her?"

"What?"

"You never turned into a monster and ate her?"

"No. I've never turned into a monster at all." I thought for a moment and said, "As far as I know."

"But you're going to?"

I shrugged. Arnie let out a breath, then stood up off the floor and brushed off his pants with his hands. He said, "I don't know what this'll mean to ya, in light of what you just said. But I think you should hear it."

"Are you going to tell me everything this time, Arnie? The real reason you're here? Because I'm gonna tell you now, if you do decide to write all this up as a feature article it's gonna suck."

"For the purposes of what I'm gonna say," Arnie began, "we're gonna start with the premise that the shadow people are real, okay? Not that I'm convinced, but just for the purpose of what I'm about to say."

"Yeah, yeah."

"And that time don't mean the same thing to them as it means to you and me. And, like you said, they can reach backward and pull you right out of the past and present and everything and nobody is the wiser."

"Right, right." I motioned impatiently for him to go on.

"So how far back do you think they could go? Could they go back and vanish the guy who cured polio?"

"Oh. I don't—I don't think so."

"But say they worked it like links in a chain, they touch the guy who pulled Bill Gates out of a car wreck thirty years ago. Make it so that guy was never born, so he could never save Gates. Gates dies as a child and tomorrow we wake up in a world where everybody is using Macs?"

I shivered. "Oh. I don't know, Arnie. Do you?"

"You mentioned earlier that you got a box on your TV that you play games on? The games where you wander around and shoot people?"

"Well, John's does. He's got six of them, if you count the ones in his closet. A PlayStation and an Xbox and whatever else they sell."

Arnie nodded. "Those names mean nothin' to me. Tell me, you don't find anything weird about it? Don't get a funny feeling when you play on those things?"

I shrugged. "I dunno. Not really."

Arnie, said, "The first time I saw one of those game machines was a month ago. And then, everybody had one."

He waited, but I didn't reply.

"I got a nephew," continued Arnie. "Eleven years old. He's all about comics and his remote-controlled cars and Rob Schneider movies. But a few weeks ago I come home and I see him sittin' on the couch, leaning forward like he's entranced. I mean, I never saw concentration like that on a kid's face. Never. And he's got this plastic thing in his hands with buttons on it and he's just hammering away. And I turn to the television and I almost get sick. There's just a gun barrel on the screen, at the bottom, muzzle flash shootin' out the end and people getting ripped to shreds. Sprays of blood everywhere. And I realize, with a feeling like I ate something rotten, that he's controlling the gun. He's sitting there operating a damned murder simulator and his mom comes in and tells him to say hi, that his uncle Arnie is visiting and she glances at the TV like it's nothin', like it's perfectly normal for a kid to do somethin' that used to make new recruits puke back in the war. To look at a human shape—and the people on the screen looked like they were real as you and me—to look at a human shape and pull that trigger and watch it go down and not even flinch, to not feel that instinctual twinge at causing a death . . ."

Arnie wiped sweat off his brow.

He said, "I served next to some coldhearted bastards in the war, guys who had that stare, you know, kids from the streets, kids who got beat before bed every night growin' up. And even those guys, those hard characters, they would freeze up the first time they had to pull a trigger with a living thing at the other end."

I said, "Well, they're pretty violent but they're just games—"

"Open your ears, Wong. I'm not tellin' you these games have been around and I'm such an old geezer that I never noticed them. These games, the devices that play them, they didn't exist before last month. And now they're everywhere, on every TV set and, hey, ask around and people say they've been common for years and years. I'm a journalist, I travel, I got kids in the family, I know the world. And they didn't sell these game boxes before, I know they didn't because it's insane that they do at all. But I start seeing the shadows move and I get up one day and suddenly every kid is glued to a box that's *training* him. Tell me it ain't. Millions of them, all over the country, all over the world, millions of kids spending hours and hours getting quicker and quicker on the trigger, getting truer and truer aim and colder and colder inside. That's training. That's conditioning if I ever saw it. And in your world, in this world, this version of reality that played out, nobody finds this strange? Really?"

"Well . . ."

There was nothing to say. The thought that the bad guys had that kind of power just sank me, left me numb. The bad thing was I couldn't even write off Arnie as crazy, since he had already wasted most of his day on me and that really wouldn't be fair.

"And the thing is," said Arnie, "as time goes on I can feel it fading. Like a dream. I get used to the idea, I think, 'Yeah, sure, they've always been there, these games. It's me, it's the stress, it's age, it's the drugs I did back in the day comin' back.' But then I flip around on the news and I see other little differences, things I know ain't right. Like the pope. Pope John Paul the second, still out there popin' and lookin' one hundred years old. I remember that guy getting shot and killed, way back in the early nineties. He got replaced by a guy named Pope Leo the something. And I squint and I can almost picture that other pope's face. A black guy. Younger, in his fifties. But no. No, he's nowhere to be found now and here's yet another little thing that's been tweaked. And it's impossible and it's so big, the idea of it, that thinkin' about it makes me feel like a worm stuck in the treads of a tire on an eighteen-wheeler. You know what I'm saying?"

I nodded, slowly. "Yes. Yes, Arnie, I do."

"So what do we do? If this is really what's goin' on, what do we do?"

"I'm going to suggest 'nothing.' "

He turned to me. "Because you're afraid they'll take Amy. Look, if we entertain the idea that these things are real and that this thing, this 'Korrok' is really tampering with the world, and I assume it's not for the purpose of making it better, then surely there's something we can—"

"Oh, there is, Arnie. I know there is. It's called being willing to sacrifice everyone around me for the cause. And why not? All of the great men do it. The pyramids were built with tens of thousands of nobodies who were worked to death so that the big thing could be achieved. That's the name of the game, that's how you defeat the bad guys. Just be willing to spend your friends like pennies, that's all. You asked me earlier if I was a sociopath. Well, you'd better hope I am because the world was built by sociopaths, men willing to send a million innocent boys into battle to be chopped to screaming giblets, all so a banner can be raised over another piece of land with houses and markets and roads soon after."

I was talking faster and faster. I bit back my next sentence, made myself calm down. Got to focus. Freaking ADD.

I said, "That psychologist back in school, she gave me the PCL-R, that's a test where they rate you from zero to forty based on personality traits of sociopaths. Glibness, inflated ego, violence, juvenile delinquency, all that serial killer shit. Anything above a score of thirty gets you a diagnosis of sociopathy. I got a twenty-nine. And the irony is that I had to steal the file from the cabinet to find out that score. Do you think that's worth the extra point?"

He shook his head slowly. "I'm not following you."

"Which would prove I'm a monster, Arnie? Sacrificing the people I love for the fight? Or walking away from the fight to save the people I love?"

Arnie didn't want to get sucked into a debate on that subject and instead said, "Just hear me out. Say we just go public with it, with your story. My story, too."

"Why, Arnie? What good is that gonna do?"

"You get other people to come forward, other people like us who sense what's goin' on. Strength in numbers. Hell, people believe in angels and UFOs and every other thing. They'll listen. The bad guys can't make us all disappear, can they? They got to have limits to what they can do. They got to."

"Why?"

Arnie again threw out his hands, like an NBA player acting baffled by a referee's call.

"This is all I got, Wong. I have no faith to speak of and no skill but what you see. The truth, the power of knowledge in the hands of the people, all that journalism school song and dance, that's what I believe in. It's all I believe in. I got nothin' else. I got nothin' else to fight with. But I know this, too. You took my calls for a reason. So that makes me think you had the same idea."

I said, "It was Amy's idea. Meeting you."

Arnie asked, "She's still in Utah?"

"Who?"

"Amy."

"Just checking. Yeah, she's still there with the lesbians. There's been some incidents since she left. A big monstrous guy came after me and I killed him. Twice. Had to cut off his head. I found a big slug thing in my kitchen. We fought a monster made of meat. They take their shots. I didn't want Amy to be a part of that, I wanted something better for her. I tried to sort of cut her off, get her to start a new life. Her own life. But she calls me. All the time. Ever since she left, she calls and calls. I wound up with a four-hundred-dollar phone bill one month. I told her about you wantin' to meet me and she told me I should do it, that she had a feeling."

"See? She knows. She knows, and you know, that we got to shine light on these cockroaches. The shadows hate the light, let's shine *my* light on these bastards. Let people know what's happening to their world."

I said, "Just telling our stories, that won't do shit. Testimony of two nutjobs, that'll just get us lumped in with the Roswell guys, a minority of nerds pleading a ridiculous case, supported by e-mails from equally crazy and lonely people."

"Then what do you want to—"

"We show them this."

I pulled the silver canister from my pocket.

"This is real, Arnie. A physical piece of evidence. That's what Amy thought, that if you could get this in the hands of somebody, a lab or something. I don't know. And there's gotta be more soy sauce out there. We already got two canisters. Or maybe it'll come back in this bottle, the way it did before. Maybe the bottle manufactures it. But you got to know people, at a university, somebody with an electron microscope. Because I'm thinkin' that whoever takes the first close look at the soy sauce is gonna have a brown stain down the bottom of his lab coat a second later." I thought for a moment and said, "Just make sure they keep it cold."

Arnie nodded. "Yeah. Yeah. Make that the story. Hell, let 'em see the effects themselves, feed the shit to a lab rat and watch the fun begin, see the thing start levitating and speaking French."

And just like that, I felt an intoxicating rush of hope. I tried to crush it, to push it down, to expose it to reality and kill it off. But I couldn't. It was a sunrise, a kid's sight of snowfall on a school morning. Hope. That all this can turn out okay, that somehow a tide this big and black can be turned back. Hope like a wildfire, thoughts of presents under a Christmas tree and a smell of cookies coming from a kitchen and a certain look in a girl's eyes that lights you up inside. That beautiful border between nightmare and morning when you realize that all of the monsters menacing you have evaporated like smoke,

446

leaving behind only the warm blankets and the pale sunlight of a Saturday dawn.

Amy Sullivan. Her name is Amy Sullivan. Her plane landed in Salt Lake City and she called me just two days ago and we talked for four hours and she had bought a new album and made me listen to the whole thing over the phone. Amy Sullivan. She's still there. Amy—

I said, "And you're willing to risk everything? Your life, your family? I mean, best-case scenario, your career as a journalist is gonna be over because from now on this is all you're gonna be known for. And don't forget that there may be people, real people, who don't want this out. The people who ransacked my apartment, the people from the factory or the CIA or NSA or *Men in Black,* whoever it was—they don't want this stuff known. Are you ready for all that, Arnie?"

"Shit. I been around, Wong. My first year out of journalism school I got knocked cold at a segregation protest. That was 1964. I wake up with my camera busted on the pavement and blood runnin' down my shirt. This fat guy steps over me and says, 'Stay down, nigger.' I think back then I knew what I was doin' this job for. But in the years since—"

Arnie saw the look on my face and stopped talking.

"What?"

I didn't answer. I couldn't answer.

"What? Wong?"

"They—they called you 'nigger'? Even though you're white?"

"Is that some kind of joke? What are you . . . hey! What are you laughing at?"

I couldn't answer. This time it was because laughter was choking off my air. Arnie was infuriated.

"What? Asshole, answer me!"

I couldn't. It was the kind of laughter that's so hard it doesn't make sound, a spasm in the lungs. And the brain. I was bent with it. Arnie stomped over and grabbed my shirt, pushing me against the wall.

"What?"

I choked out, "Describe yourself to me, Arnie. Physically, tell me what you look like."

Arnie stepped back. Horror blew all expression off his face. He knew exactly what I was asking.

He muttered, "No, no . . . You're fucking with me."

"Come on, Arnie. I got places to be."

"No . . ."

"Because to me you're not black, Arnie. To me you're a chubby white guy with a gray mustache. A big, fat necktie tied in a huge Windsor knot."

Arnie's eyes went wide, then narrowed in disgust. He threw me against the wall one last time, then backed away.

"My first thought when I saw you, Arnie, was that you looked just like I imagined you. I actually said that to myself. I should have known. And now I've wasted my whole day."

He sprayed something nasty under his breath, turned on his heels and stormed from the room. I sat there, seizures of suppressed laughter trembling through my gut. Gotta cut that out. Inappropriate laughter is the universal first sign of madness. I took a series of long breaths. My whole afternoon. Wasted. Slowly the ridiculousness of the situation suddenly stopped being funny and started pissing me off. If Arnie left in his car, I didn't have a ride back. I climbed to my feet and followed the echoes of his footsteps through the mall.

I caught up to Arnie in the dark of the parking lot. He had his keys in his hand and was walking toward the rental car, then stopped. He was staring at the car, at a spot toward the rear. The trunk.

I walked up slowly, not sure what he would do next. You never know how people will react in this situation. The way he was looking at the trunk, he knew something. What would he do when he figured out the truth? What would you do in his shoes?

I stepped up, about ten feet behind him. I said, "You think there's somethin' in there, Arnie?"

He didn't answer. He was studying his car keys.

"Come on Arnie. Open it. The sooner you do, the sooner we can move on."

With shaking fingers, Arnie twisted the keys in the lock. He lifted the trunk lid, stared wordlessly at what was below him for probably a full minute. His keys fell from his hand and hit the gravel with a *chink* and for a moment, I was sure Arnie would faint. Was that even possible for somebody who was already dead? An interesting question.

I strode up behind Arnie. In the trunk was a thin, black man, probably in his early sixties. A graying afro that grew in a pattern-baldness horseshoe around a head that was splattered with blood.

The head was not attached to the body. It had been neatly sliced off, a job so quick and efficient that the bloodstained bow tie around the severed neck was still tied and straight. The man in the trunk could not have looked more different than the Arnie Blondestone I had known. But he was undoubtedly the real one.

I said, "I'm sorry, Arnie. I really am. I think I'm one of the few people in the world who can truly sympathize with you."

Arnie wheeled on me like I was the Devil. He pointed a finger gun at me and said, "You did this! You killed me, you son of a bitch!"

"Look at your body, Arnie. The one in the trunk, I mean. Look at the dried blood. You've been dead for days. No, I think somebody got wind that you had contacted me and so they took you out. I'm really sorry about that. It's sorta my fault, I guess."

"*I'm not a fuckin' ghost!* This is bullshit! Bullshit! I drove you all around town! I can touch you!"

He reached out and grabbed my shirt to demonstrate. "What kind of trick are you playing, asshole? Is this some game you play, the way you made me see that thing in your truck? Did you drug me?"

I reached up and easily pulled Arnie's hand off my shirt. I then reached out, put my hands under his armpits and lifted him into the air. He was about as heavy as a department store mannequin. I doubt you've ever lifted one of those but you can probably guess that they're not very heavy.

Arnie's eyes grew wide once again and I set him gently back down.

I said, "You're an astral body. Do you know what that means, Arnie?"

Arnie didn't hear. He clutched at his chest, looking at the world around him as if suddenly every stone and blade of grass held some new terror behind it. I said, "It's a stage of manifestation between the physical and spiritual. A body that's half there."

Arnie ran. He sprinted to the driver's side of the sedan and yanked open the door. He threw himself into the seat and went to get his car keys, realized he didn't have them. He put his hands on his face and leaned over the steering wheel, eyes closed.

I walked up to his door and said through the window, "This is my fault, Arnie. Not just you gettin' killed, but this, this half life you've got. I did this, I projected you. It's the soy sauce, it's one thing it lets me do. I'm thinkin' you got killed right after we talked on the phone. You know how you talk to somebody and you imagine what they look like based on their voice? Well, when you got killed you immediately assumed the shape of—"

"This can't be. It can't. I don't accept that. I—I got grandkids. I got a vacation comin' this June, I'm goin' to Atlantic City. I got tickets."

"Yeah, you're in the denial stage right now, Arnie. This is all normal. I gotta go, okay? I have to go call Amy and tell her she owes me five bucks."

"Shut the fuck up, Wong. Right now. I refuse to believe that I'm only here because I popped outta your imagina—"

Arnie vanished. I said to the empty car, "I'm sorry, Arnie. I really am."

I went around to the trunk of the car and almost closed it, but thought that maybe I shouldn't have my fingerprints on a trunk containing a corpse. This also eliminated the idea of driving the car back to the restaurant. I looked up into the starless, overcast sky and hoped the rain would hold off until I got back to my truck.

I WALKED INTO the night. I passed a weedy vacant lot, a Burger King, a church operating out of a building that used to be a bowling alley. I passed a rail-thin guy who looked homeless, and did a double take because he was wearing a stained white T-shirt that seemed to have my name on it. It had a yellow caricature of a bucktoothed Asian man that said MR. WONG under it. I thought I had seen that character before somewhere, and dismissed it.

450

Half a block later I saw two kids who looked maybe thirteen, smoking cigarettes and looking at me suspiciously. The kid on the left had a black concert shirt with a picture of some glam-rock band on it. Below that it said, THE DARKNESS. The other kid had on a flannel shirt, unbuttoned. Most of the T-shirt underneath was obscured, but between the flannel the words, IS HUNGRY peeked out.

I thought I could see a sentence forming there, which wouldn't be all that strange in the context of my life. I passed an old lady coming out of a storefront craft store; her blouse didn't say anything. I saw a busty girl with an olive T-shirt that said STAY OUT OF IRAQ and I thought that might apply.

I stepped onto the blacktop of the They China Food! parking lot and saw a white T-shirt approach. I squinted and saw it said in bold, black letters, BALLS: IT'S WHAT'S FOR DINNER. I looked up and saw it was John wearing the shirt.

"Where'd you go?" he asked. "I saw your Bronco but the lady at the counter was closing up. Said you left a long time ago. Did you meet the guy?"

I asked, "Did the waitress remember me being with a guy?"

"She said she couldn't remember. The question seemed to confuse her a little. Did he show? I came so he could get my picture."

I waved my hand dismissively toward the horizon. "Eh, it didn't work out. Turned out he was dead the whole time. He didn't even know it. He was a semi-solid astral body."

"I hate it when they do that."

"Yeah, I had to break the news to him. He was drivin' around a rental car with his own corpse in the trunk. I'm lookin' at this old white guy who looks like a door-to-door salesman, and that's not even what he really looked like at all."

"Well he's black, right? Dave, his picture was at the top of all those articles I printed out for you. Got the bow tie? Kind of bald? Didn't you read any of them?"

"I don't know. I got busy."

"So I guess he's not gonna do the article?"

I gave John a scowl that told him I wasn't going to dignify that question. I said, "I gotta go back out to the mall. I left that floorboard pulled up. I was showin' Arnie the body."

"I'll put it down. I was gonna go out there anyway."

"You go out there by yourself? Why?"

He shrugged. "Hey, Amy called, lookin' for you."

"Big surprise there."

"She said call her cell phone as soon as you get in. Hey, didn't you bet her five bucks the thing with the reporter would turn out to be a clusterfuck?"

I WALKED IN my front door and threw the silver canister on the end table with my car keys and spare change. I found my TV remote between sofa cushions and clicked on the TV. It was some show about a family that builds custom motorcycles while they scream at each other. About a half hour later the phone rang. I glanced at the caller ID, picked up and said, "You owe me five bucks."

Amy said, "Hi! It's me! What did you say?"

"Nothing. I don't think that thing with the reporter is gonna happen."

"Can you hear me? Go to your door."

"What did you say? Amy? Hello?"

Somebody could get rich by inventing just one cell phone that actually works.

"Go to your door."

This all seemed very strange. I tensed up, went to my front door and peered out of the little window at the top. Nothing. Cautiously I opened the door and stepped onto the porch. I turned to my right and saw Amy sitting in one of my plastic chairs, her cell phone in her hand. She was wearing a white-and-yellow sundress and sandals. Her hair was longer than I had last seen it, actually touching her shoulders a little now. That was about as long as it would grow. In a timid voice she said, "Surprise!"

"Are you—are you really here?"

452

"Yep! I flew in this afternoon. For your birthday. John knew all about it, blame him. He didn't really go to work today so he could pick me up instead. He wanted it to be a surprise."

I *was* surprised, if for no reason other than the sudden realization that my birthday was just two days away.

"So you're here? Now?"

"Yep! Hey, check this out. This is awesome."

Amy leapt to her feet, raised one leg and planted her foot on the railing of the porch. This caused her dress to fall back on her thigh and my heart skipped a beat, like I had never seen that particular naked patch of skin on a woman before. Amy was pointing out something on her ankle and she was putting her leg back down before I took my eyes off her thigh long enough to notice it. She had gotten a small tattoo on her ankle, of a Chinese character.

"It's, uh, nice," I said. "What does it mean?"

"Ankle."

She laughed, then closed the distance between us and clamped a hug around me that knocked the wind out of my lungs. She said, "Do you like it? I told Crystal you wouldn't like it."

"What difference does that make? If you like it, then that's that. If I don't like it I can screw myself."

"So you're saying you don't like it."

"It's fine, Amy. You, uh, just got the one, right?"

She pulled away from me and gave me the most sly and devious expression her face could manage.

"Maybe. You won't know *unless you check me*."

I laughed. She giggled. We both fell silent. We left a trail of clothing from the front door to the sofa.

A CERTAIN AMOUNT of time later, Amy and I lay on the couch under an American flag afghan that John had bought me from a garage sale years ago. The TV was still on, we were both watching it absently. I asked, "So, how long are you in town?"

Amy didn't answer at first, then said, "These guys get all worked up about building these motorcycles, don't they?"

"You're still working at that craft shop, right? When do you have to be back at work?"

She shrugged.

"Amy?"

"I quit."

"Oh. So when are you going back?"

"I wanted to talk to you about that."

"Amy, no. No. You can't stay here."

"Why? You have another girlfriend?"

"You know what I'm talking about."

"I can't go back there, David. It's awful. Crystal and Tonya, they're always, like, having naked pillow fights and stuff. I can't be around that."

"Really?"

"No. They told me to tell you that." She laughed.

"Amy, don't make me go through all that again, explaining why it's not safe. I shouldn't have to."

She twisted around to face me.

"No, see, I worked it all out. I think that right there, that's proof you're not, like, evil or whatever. You're looking out for my safety even though you're lonely and depressed every minute I'm away. If you were truly bad you'd only care about yourself. You'd tell me you wanted me to stay around, knowing it was dangerous for me but doing it anyway."

I thought about this for a moment, then said, "You're wrong."

"How?"

"I *do* want you to stay."

"Good," she said brightly. "I will then."

She kissed me on the cheek and rolled over again. I tried to figure out exactly at what point I had lost control of the discussion. She said, "Now, I really don't have a place to stay here in town . . ."

"Well . . ."

"But John said I could stay with him until I found something."

"Over his dead body."

She laughed, said, "He told me to tell you that. He also wanted me to tell you he has a king-sized bed so there's plenty of room for me. And that he sleeps naked."

"You can stay here. For now. But Amy, you're not *living* with me. You understand me? I mean, you'll be living here, but not 'they'll be getting married next' living here. It'll be 'she doesn't have a place to stay' living here. Okay?"

"Sure. Everything's worked out then. You know, it's good to be back. One thing I can say about [Undisclosed], you know it's gonna be more interesting than Utah."

NOTHING INTERESTING HAPPENED for the next four months.

ON A BLISTERING late-August day, John and I hauled Amy and about a dozen cardboard boxes of her possessions down an exit ramp, my Bronco passing a green HOME OF [OMITTED] UNIVERSITY sign.

The school was a little more than two hours from Undisclosed, which I had figured was a safe distance should a pit open under the town and swallow it into Hell once and for all, and yet close enough that Amy would agree to go. It had taken about twelve arguments and one crying fit to come to that compromise. In the end I convinced her that she would have to get some kind of education and actually continue her life at some point. See the world, broaden her horizons. Get off my couch and stop typing on that damned laptop. She was a sheltered kid. She had a shitty time in high school and had barely been outside city limits since. You don't realize how terrifying the world can be for someone like that, someone who would rather stay in a familiar hole than an unfamiliar mansion.

Which is why you haven't exactly jumped at the chance to move away, either . . .

But we finally looked into the college thing, did the research and found that her SAT scores were actually good enough to get her a partial scholarship. That and some future-crippling student loans were all it took to get her in the door. There was lots of paperwork and Amy turned into a nervous wreck for the last three weeks before move-in day at the dorms. But here we were.

And that, I thought, *will be that. The Utah thing was poorly thought out but now she'll have classes and meet fascinating people and she'll love it. She'll call every day, then every week. And then she'll mention a guy. A friend, she'll say. And then she'll call once a month, only visit twice a semester and then you'll get the call and she'll say she's sorry, she's met someone, he's an English major and plays lacrosse or some shit. And she will have grown up. She'll get some job right out of school in some other city and she'll never, ever come back here.*

And that's how it should be. She'll be out of my orbit, out of my sphere of concern, a poor target for anyone or anything that wants to get to me. She'll be safe. This time.

When a man plans, a woman laughs.

We unloaded boxes and waded through the lobby of the dorms. We wound up waiting in line for elevators along with crowds of skinny girls and well-dressed parents, chubby boys that looked far too young for college and a surprising number of Asian kids. Some guy came along and was handing out packets of forms, dorm rules and shit, and struck up a conversation with Amy. She got along so easily with people, so laid back. She had a light jacket draped over her arm on this ninety-four-degree day. It concealed her missing hand perfectly. They talked and she giggled and he moved on, handing out his packets.

I said, "That guy seemed nice."

She said, "Uh-huh."

"Did you get his name?"

"James or Jack or something."

I said, "Well-dressed guy. Probably gonna be a doctor or something."

John looked at me, then at Amy then at me again. He said, "He, uh, had a nice ass, too."

Amy turned, rolled her eyes and we piled into the elevator. We rode up and moved her stuff to her tiny dorm room. And so, for the second time, I said good-bye to Amy and for the second time was sure it was going to be forever. We hugged and I wished her good fortune about a dozen times. Finally I broke off and headed for the hall, sure that I had succeeded, thinking that if you love someone you do have to set them free and that I had done just that, for the good of all. And *juuuuust* as I was almost out of grabbing range Amy snagged the back of my shirt with a fist and turned me around. She said, "Uh, thank you for helping me move."

"You said that already. No problem." She looked like she had something else to say. Quite a bit else, in fact.

John said, "Yeah, it's not a big deal for me to lift heavy objects. I'm sort of used to it, *if you know what I mean*."

I held up a hand to silence him. "John—"

"Of course I'm talking about my penis."

I said to Amy, "Ignore him. His penis is just like everybody else's."

Amy said, "I was just gonna ask you if—"

"*You've never seen my penis!*" bellowed John. "I'd show it right now, to everybody here. If we had time."

I turned on him. "If we had time? What?"

"Because, well, if you want to look at my penis, you'd better have a whole afternoon, buddy! You best have five or six hours to take it all in, lest its majesty escape you!"

Before I could stop her, Amy said, "That doesn't make any sense."

"It would make sense if you could see it!" shouted John, plainly agitated. "It would be making loooooong sense, honey!"

"John, just calm down, okay." I gestured down the hall. "Go wait by the elevator."

He didn't move. From behind me, I heard Amy say, "Do you want to get engaged?"

And there it was. I had a sinking feeling, visualized a moth flapping toward a blowtorch. I tried to think of the best, most soothing way to turn her down and said, "Sure."

John looked at his watch. "Well, congratulations. Now we gotta roll. If we leave now there'll still be enough light to get in some basketball."

THE DAY WAS so hot it stank. Asphalt baked under our shoes, bodies rustled against one another dancing to the irregular *PAP PAP PAP* beat of a basketball smacking the pavement. I backed toward the hoop, about where the free-throw line would be if we had played on an actual court rather than this giant cracked piece of playground sandpaper. I spun, jumped, threw up a shot that was doomed the moment it left my fingers.

John snatched the rebound, spun, jumped, slammed. He pumped his fist in victory. "Ring it up! Two hundred seventy-four to one thirty-seven!" In John's game, each shot is worth one hundred and thirty-seven points. "If I had a dime for every basket I made today, you'd still suck!"

I tracked down the loose ball and handed it to John. In this game, like life, scoring means you get to keep the ball. He dribbled twice, glanced up over my shoulder, and froze. I saw the expression on his face and turned. John squinted and asked, "Was that there before?"

It was a black sphere, floating just over the weeds at courtside. It was gleaming and about three feet wide, looking like a giant hovering eight ball. John strode over to it and I heard him say, "You can sort of see into it. I think I see people."

He bent over and picked up a broken chunk of concrete. He lobbed it at the sphere, which swallowed it noiselessly. John looked over his shoulder at me and said, "Hole to another dimension, I bet. Wanna go through?"

"After this point."

John got the ball and dribbled behind the cracks and bundles of weeds we called the three-point line. I knew from the look in his eyes that he was going to take the shot. As soon as the ball left his hands I was bounding toward the rim, that subconscious gauge in the back of

458

my mind already telling me it was a miss off the backboard. It clanged, I leapt. I scooped the rebound from the air one-handed and before John could recover into defense I turned and hooked a shot that ripped prettily through the net.

"Like a drop in the bucket, baby," I said. "Splash!"

"Damn." John said, hands on his hips, chest heaving. "Your game be *chubby* today." He said this in such a way so that "chubby" rhymed with "today." "Tied at two seventy-four, Monster Dave."

He retrieved the ball from the grass, then heaved a chest pass at me that missed badly. I turned to watch the ball go and, sure enough, saw it hit the black sphere and disappear just like the piece of concrete had.

"Whoops," said John. "I tossed our ball into another universe."

"You wanna go home?"

"Yeah, just let me get my ball."

He walked over to the sphere and peered into it. He lifted a leg and stuck it through, then ducked in and soon it was just his left leg sticking out of this floating ball. He pulled it through and he was gone. I sighed, looked at my watch and wandered toward the spherical portal. I knew he wasn't coming back until I at least poked my head through, so I bent over and pushed my way in.

The air on the other side was at least thirty degrees cooler. I stepped out, realizing as I did that I was emerging from a white sphere on this side, brilliant as sunlit snow. I stepped out onto a basketball court that itself was not terribly different than the one we had left. But the world was changed nonetheless. The sun was gone. The overcast sky was an unnatural ceiling of tar-flavored cotton candy and the air had a vague farty smell.

I scanned the landscape and saw other small differences. The park in Undisclosed had been in a polished neighborhood, Victorian houses and carpet lawns. Here the houses looked empty and forgotten, windows smashed, weeds overgrowing, rusting mailboxes. The yellowing white house nearest to us had a single nonsense word spray-painted across the front:

BLOODWORMS.

A dry wind blew, bringing with it that vague sulfur stench once again. I saw John standing nearby, looking up at the rim of one of the half dozen goals that bordered the court.

He said, "Where you been? I've been walking around for two hours."

"Time must move differently here. I came right after you."

"That's always your excuse."

I said, "At least it's cooler here."

"No nets here, though." He was right, the naked rims stood silently over us like very tall, thin and largely ineffective sentries. He said, "This one's regulation but a couple of those other goals are bent on the rims. Must be a lot of dunking in this world."

There was a tinkling sound from behind us. Glass breaking. We both turned. A bone-thin woman dressed in rags stumbled toward us. She had feebly hurled a glass jar at us that crashed twenty feet short on the pavement. Her eyes were swollen in amazement, a bony finger aimed right at us.

"Y-y-y-you!!" she screeched. "Unstained! Unstained! How!?!?" Her left arm was missing, ending just above her elbow in a jagged stump, as if it had simply rotted off. Her screaming was suddenly cut short when four beings I can only describe as some kind of flying baboons descended on her, beating her savagely with clubs. They hauled her unconscious body into the sky. We watched them fly away, saw they weren't coming back for us. We exchanged a look, then shot free throws to see who would start with the ball.

John won. We played for a bit but the game wasn't that much fun. It was the wind. That steady, rotten wind that blew constantly from the south and brought with it faint sounds of screaming and an insectile shrieking noise; it drove every outside shot off the mark by a couple of inches. Soon we both abandoned three-point shots, which brought the game under the hoop. That was John's domain. His three-inch height advantage gave him a series of rebounds and easy layups, quickly giving him a 548-point lead. Sweat stung my eyes as I drove under the hoop once more, trying a little running hook under the baseline. John's hands were quick, swatting the shot away. The ball went bouncing off the court.

"Hey!" John shouted after it. "Toss it back!"

I turned to see who he was shouting at. There, by the ball, was hovering what looked vaguely like one of those wet/dry Shopvacs they sell at Sears. It made no sound. I could only presume it was some kind of droid common to this world, though it lacked any kind of eyes or robotic facial features we add to our movie robots to give them personality. What it did have was a bristling array of probes in front of it that were aimed at the two of us, sensors of some kind.

I said, "That thing doesn't have any kind of ball-handling appendages. You're going to have to go after it."

John turned on me, indignant. "I got it last time."

After five solid minutes of debate we decided to go get it together. At the ball site we noticed the droid was still there, taking its silent measurements or whatever. To our surprise, it spoke.

"Identification please."

John smiled. "Assey Cocklord."

It turned to me, repeated the question.

"Felipe Enormowang."

"Identification not on database. Please state your habitation sector."

John: "Your Ass."

Me: "The suburbs west of Your Ass."

"Sector not on database. Please report to your nearest quarantine facility. Failure to report within thirty minutes will result in—"

We walked away and left the thing chattering back there. It was my ball and I managed to score two quick baskets to get myself back into the game.

Suddenly, from the sky rose a wobbly, mechanical thumping sound, like a car running on a flat tire. I looked up at it and John took the opportunity to steal the ball from my sweat-coated hands. He stepped and hopped and again utilized his genetic ability to dunk a basketball.

461

"Booyah!" he said, arms in the air. "Dunk off a steal! I done dominated you in two universes, bitch!"

I was sick of basketball. My game had gone as sour as the ominous wind that blew and I longed for the courts of my own universe. Also, that distracting pulsing sound grew louder. I grabbed the ball and sat down on it, using it as a stool.

John said, "Come on. Let's get in another game before we have to go back to Hot World. I bet it's not even seventy out here."

"Nah," I said. I noticed an old, time-browned newspaper on the ground, headline in three-inch-tall letters: "PHENOMENON CONTINUES AROUND SOUTH POLE, PRESIDENT URGES CALM."

That thrumming, pulsing sound grew louder. Suddenly there was a sharp CRACK and we both spun around. Where the Shopvac droid had been there was now only a charred spot on the ground and bits of twisted debris.

Above and behind it were five human figures flying slowly toward us on little booths that looked like lecterns. They descended, landing in front of us, undulating clouds of bright blue plasma cushioning the machines as they touched down. All five were adult males, clean, wearing sleek black uniforms that looked military. It occurred to me that they had probably been nearby for some time now but had been hidden by some kind of futurey cloaking device like those ships on *Star Trek*.

They stepped off their flying machines and approached us. One guy took the lead, a handsome officer in his thirties, a neatly trimmed beard.

"Good afternoon," he said. "I am Sergeant Vance McElroy of the Human Liberation Army. Your appearance here must be quite a surprise to you, but not to us. Prophecy has foretold the coming of strangers from another world since the day of the Great Corruption. It is an honor to meet you. I confess that I do not know from where you came, but I can tell by looking at you that you have not been infected with the . . ."

He talked for what seemed like forever. The wind kicked up again and I wondered if there were any indoor courts here. I couldn't find a pause long enough to ask the guy. I looked over and saw John giving the man a series of his fake "I'm listening thoughtfully" nods.

". . . and if you cannot defeat him then all hope for mankind is lost. Gentlemen, the winds of destiny have blown us together. A bright dawn is about to grace this lost and broken world."

We hung in awkward silence for a moment, but then I had an idea. "Question," I said. "That flying Shopvac earlier mentioned a quarantine. I presume they used old public buildings for this, such as hospitals and schools, right? So my question is, do any of these converted quarantines still have their gymnasiums intact? Or at least the part that had the basketball goals?"

"No, I'm afraid all of the educational institutions were razed with the first siege, right before the mass book burnings. Human ignorance has been their greatest weapon. But that is not the worst the dark ones have done. Often the . . ."

He droned on and on, and I instantly regretted asking the question. I looked at my watch, saw that it displayed 66:69 as the time. I began to accumulate a list of all of the ways this universe sucked.

". . . therefore, only with your unique otherworldly genetic makeup can you resist the infection of the—"

"Yes, that's very interesting," said John. "But to perform this task you request we'll need a number of items from our world. You must allow us to return there and come back to begin our quest."

The man nodded. "It is good, then. We shall await your return."

We picked up our ball and ducked back through the dimensional rift. We stepped from the black sphere and were glad to see the sunlight and netted goals. We weren't so happy with the return of the oppressive heat, but decided to deal with it rather than return to that other crappy, dysfunctional universe.

We decided on one more game. Before we could inbound the ball, a gang of four strong-looking, attractive, twentysomethings walked up. Two boys, one black, one white. Two girls, one Asian, one a pretty blonde. They oozed curiosity upon seeing the portal and exchanged what sounded from a distance like witty comments. The white boy and girl seemed to dislike each other and bickered good-naturedly as they stepped through the portal, a sense of adventure in the air.

John rolled his eyes. We had an argument over who had the ball last, but John finally admitted he was wrong and gave it to me. We played for a bit, but fatigue had set in and we exchanged two missed shots each.

Then, suddenly, all four of the twentysomethings were ejected from the black sphere. They were covered in dirt and bruises and minor cuts.

"Look!" gushed the Asian girl. "It's the same moment when we left! None of that time passed here!"

"She's right!" said the black kid. "Yo, am I glad to see that sun! We saved the whole damn world, man!"

The white boy and girl kissed, apparently having fallen in love during their quest. The boy disengaged and looked at us with excited eyes. "Dude, you guys won't believe what just happened to us!"

John turned to him.

"You bored a stranger with your stupid-ass story, and he pulled out his cock and whipped you with it like a stagecoach driver?"

The kid shut up, baffled. John picked up the ball and bounced a pass to me.

"Your ball."

was the last survivor of the plague.

As the team made its way through the abandoned village, the priest described the outbreak that had taken every single member of the tribe but him. Painful sores, blindness, madness, limbs that in the course of minutes seemed to rot and split like bad fruit. Horrors an old man should not have to see in his declining years (the priest had lived to the ripe old age of thirty-seven).

The priest believed he had been spared by Koddock only to relay the tale to me, to warn me off. He bid me farewell, saying he intended to strike out into the jungle, to walk west until he touched the sun or until the land reclaimed him. I didn't tell him that walking that direction meant he *might* wind up as part of a tour group out of Iquitos. I shook his hand and left Peru for good.

A week later I was back in New York, relaxing with Sharon after Dr. Haleine's memorial service, enjoying cups of coffee laced with a great deal of brandy.

We stood on the balcony, looking over the city through clouds of my pipe smoke.

Sharon said, "Those poor people. Why did they have to die?"

I snorted a laugh around my pipe. "We all have to, dear."

She didn't smile. "You know what I mean. The way they died, sick and blind and screaming for their gods to save them, with no answer in return."

She turned her eyes to me.

"The gods are cruel, aren't they, Albie?"

I drew a deep breath and replied, "Every living being has but one need: power. Power over other living things. You need it to grow, to eat, to reproduce. And cruelty is the ultimate expression of power. To impose needless, extreme suffering and humiliation on another. It is the purest demonstration of strength. Toddlers learn it in the nursery.

"Therefore every organism, from the microbe up, wears its cruelty as a badge to mark its upward progress. Prey must be subdued, competition must be starved, enemies must be wiped out. One would thus assume that we find the same among the gods, only more so. That at each level of the heavens we find higher and higher levels of greed, brutality and mindless spite. How else could they have become gods?"

Sharon shivered, though it was not cold on the balcony.

In a barely audible voice she asked, "But is that really the way it is? The work you do—you would know better than anyone."

I set my pipe aside and turned, to let her look into my eyes. I said,

Afterword

If you want to know when the next edition in the John and Dave series will appear on bookshelves or when the film adaptation will hit theaters, go to my permanent home on the Web at JohnDiesattheEnd.com. There you can keep up with the latest news and further explore the *John Dies at the End* universe. You can also find me at comedy megasite *Cracked.com*, where I serve as the editor and, as such, have somehow gained full-time employment writing poop jokes. Yes, it is a ridiculous universe we live in.

Speaking of which, it should be pointed out that the story behind this story, the tale of how *John Dies at the End* wound up in print at all, should be an inspiration to anyone who works in a cubicle and/or is really easily inspired.

Back in 2001 I was living a double life. During the day I was just a guy doing data entry at a law office, for single digits an hour. But at night, I would change out of those khakis and assume another identity: Guy Doing Data

Entry at an Insurance Company. Fortunately the 75 hours a week I spent filling in columns of numbers on computer screens didn't leave much time for the crushing depression.

Around Halloween of 2001, during the few hours of personal time between cubicles, I took to the Internet and shared a tale of me and my friend and a monster made of meat. On the first day, only six people read the story. The next day, the number grew to eight. Then ten. I had clearly stumbled onto a word-of-mouth phenomenon and after one year, the story had been read by nearly seventeen people.

Riding this buzz, I sat down again and relayed more of the tale and would do the same the following year. By 2005 the chronicles of our adventures had grown to 150,000 words. E-mails poured in from readers, fans telling me they stayed up all night reading the story, then called in sick to work the next morning to finish it. People were printing the whole tale, eating up a ream of paper and three ink cartridges in the process, then binding it with rubber bands and loaning it to friends.

I believed for the first time that I had tapped into something, and that something was the fact that lots of people are crazy and/or have lots of spare time on their hands.

At this point I was contacted by independent horror publisher Permuted Press, who asked me about doing a print run of the story as a trade paperback. I told them no, that no one would ever actually pay money to read it. Then the transmission went out on my car and I decided I couldn't turn my nose up on whatever meager amount of money would come in. The resulting book, written by a data entry clerk with no previous publishing experience and not even an English degree to boast of, sold about five thousand copies through sheer word of mouth. When the print run ended, rare copies were selling on eBay for up to $120.

Next I got an e-mail from horror writer/director/producer Don Coscarelli (who made two of my favorite horror movies of all time, *Phantasm* and *Bubba Ho-Tep*), which I immediately deleted, assuming it was a hoax. But he was persistent and after convincing me on the phone that it wasn't all an elaborate prank to get me up on a stage so he could pour a bucket of pig's blood on me, we made the deal to turn *John Dies at the End* into a movie. After the ink was dry, more than half a dozen other offers for film rights would come in.

At that point it was pretty clear that the entire world was just fucking with me. Keep in mind I was still working at the insurance company, still sitting in a cubicle every day, eating those awful diagonally sliced sandwiches from the vending machine, and reading memos about the dress code.

Word of mouth. That's all it was. No one "discovered" me, I didn't get some big break out of the blue. It was a slow advance of strangers from around the world, passing around the link and loaning out those sad homemade copies. These are the zealots who would later buy copies, loan them to friends, then buy more copies when those never came back. Hundreds of passionate strangers whom I've still never met—they're responsible for the edition you hold in your hands. I wish I could thank all of them by name. So, let me do that now. (Please turn the page.)

The *John Dies at the End* Memorial Wall of Dedicated —and in Some Cases, Clearly Insane— Fans

Amy Brown
Brandon Sharp
Michael T. Hawkins
Curtis Jeffs
Jennifer Liang
Nate Bailey
Chuck Sebian-Lander
Tomas Fitzgerald
Stuart Layt
Ira Jacobs
Sean Gray
Shane Peter Davis
Anthony Clark
James A Russell
Andrew Gordon
Alex Lysick
Steve Clark
Joshua Daum
Jess and Brett Ferricher
Jason Phebus
Owen Sprod
Ira Porter
Matt Nolan
Jakob Beacham
Adam Quigley
Evan Lewis
Isaac Rowntree
James Goede
Ben Schuplin
Eoghan C.
Robert Lawson
Ryan Salyers
Joshua Madden
Sean Hyslop
Stewart Dawson
Ryan Aston
Nikki Barajas
Angela Soper
Daniel Andrew

Laura Taylor
Tim Richardson
Ville Nousiainen
Matt Garner
Charles Cooper
Tamir Hadary
Lucas de Carvalho Martinez
Alex Augustine
Tyrone Cameron
Bob Clark
Vincent Simone
Dave Henry
Thomas Buttrick
Kevin Murray
Craig Taylor
Joshua Heimendinger
Tom Cherry
John Walton
Robert Hight
Steffanie Hirsack
Joel Benge-Abbot
Lee Smith
Daniel Sloane
Michael Cornett
Will Timson
Larry Coffey
Nicholas Charlton
Samuel Raab
Rich Beischer
Anthony Nguyen
Erica Bercegeay
Jonathan Edwards
Alex Ennis
Damien Unger
Brian Wesley Schwartz
Joshua Lucero
Peter Christensen
Joel Thompson
Devin Pentecost

Lee Beckman
Ross Wiseman
Nick Mathews
Josh Yagley
Jim Mahar
Ryan King
Rianna Turner
David Scully
Victoria Liakhova
Alex Zechiel
Katters Smao
Scott Holcomb
Eric Holodnak
Christopher Wells
Drew Dexter
Nadine Hearity
Lance Johnson
Nathan Cleary
Michael Schmidt
Ed Gardiner
Nikola Pilipovic
Popovici Alexandru
Jesse Hayen
Heather Holl
Kevin Smith
  (not the famous one)
Nicholas Seitz
Benjamin Ashley
Michael Scheahan
Jim Ribby
Nathan West
Ben Driscoll
Jenn Tharp
Zac Wiggy
Christopher Petterson
Joel Vandale
Jonny Ashley
Beau Ferreira
Matt Overstreet

Jadon Grayson
Andrew Patterson
Matthew Waller
Kristina Himmelsjö
Cassie Hillyuck
Nicholas Russell
Ben Moore
Alex Mathews
Lee Banford
Katie Roe
Zachary Harper
Scott Bailey
Michael Freel
Asaf Läckgren
Brad Schoonover
SPC Nicholas Young
David Morris
Magnus Eek Olsen
Michael Hartley
Josh Rickert
Dustin Quam
Jeff Pallagi
Brian Tolman
Matt Cowger
Spenser Stefaniuk
Paul Harris
Isaac Davidson
Colin Newby
Luke McCarthy
Ian Douglas
Z. Sheldon
Mark Gomer
Alex Winfield
B. I. Flight
Daniel Griffin
Brandi Couch
Justin Dunsing
Jack Talbot
Todd Aquino-Michaels
Henry Copestake
Eric Bates
Alexander Corwin
Philip Howard
Kevin Smart
Janet Mysliwiec
J. Molloy
Peter Armstrong
Alex Hirzel

Justin Davis
Ben Wolfe
Jonathan Kimak
Sam Mackey
Walker Reynolds
Brendan Reilly
Stewart Hills
Melissa Black
Robert Roboi Parras
Brandon Robinson
Kenneth Cross
Kitty Butchko
Juan Cabrera
Phil Loring
Courtney Shelton
Kevin Kuchta
Mark Cawdrey
Alex Huss
Carrie Rivard
Jeremy Stevens
Josh Cohen
Jason Glass
Jordan Dillman
David Binford
Jon McCullough
Paul Calhoun
Allin Cook
Garrett Hille
Joel Paine
Fabio Zaccagnini
Courtney Olivecrona
Nick Stolk
David Piniella
Joe Vandale
Matt Picioccio
Eric Pelchat
Hunter Tammaro
Loren Cress
Adam Woodyard
Zachary Helming
Michael Purdy
David Nelson
Scott Clark
Bo Söderlund
Ashley Monroy
Reid A. Dawson
Tyler Calvert
Rutger Schreuders

Ethan John Davies
Alex Pascarelli
Conor Burnell
Brian Lemak
Jeremy Root
Christopher Brown
David Bulger
Aaron W. Mosley II
Stacy Farina
Austin Pettyjohn
Jamie Lachance
Jason Domanowski
Josh Hendren
Brandon Dixson-Jack
Isaac Westerhoff
Simon Thelwell
Brandon Spoelstra
Ian Breakey
Kim McMillan
Steven Irvine
Megan Schnitz
Mikki Cioffi
Petter Vilberg
Chris Heilman
Eric Main
Laura McDowell
Tom Andry
Nikolai Gloeckler
Dawn Morrow
Michael Dubya
Cole Goater
Steven Gordon
Matthew Porreca
Matthew Parker
Sean Levesque
Ike Wassom
Teddy Lee
Rowan Chapman Hill
Dan Heerdt
Karen Nickerson
Marie Petty
John Diebold
David Scott
J. "Buck" Caldwell
Kyle Nelson
John Plandowski
Miia Lempinen
Jack Clarkson

Dean Perkins
Joe Bautista
Nathaniel Lichfield
Jess Jeffery
Brian Malik
Frank Looney
Kenny Heard
Kyle Hellkamp
Robert Parsons
Connor Bishop
Rhett Stafford
Ellen Boring
Benjamin Deason
Sean Tessena
Chris Jensen
Jeremy Harvey
Russell Monett
Jeff Ward
Jonathan Barone
Thomas Gorney
Devin McGinty
Ross Cochran
Dustin J. Shifflett
Dan Bromley
Amanda Mack
Brian Mack
Brandon Crawford
Julian Smith
Andrew Briggs
Jefferson Nieto
Mick Weaver
John O'Connor
Hector Wakefield
Doug Tammany
John Honey
Stephanie Wagar
Aaron Jones
Jonathan Björklund
Garii Pearce
Mike Brenner
James Rodriquez

Philip Zaslavchik
Matt Best
Jimmy Bean
Louie Klein
Aaron Macke
Josh Palmer
Jude Taylor
Jake Brown
Jay Locke
Michael Keen
Walter Sojda
Ben Pearson
Casper Van Gemert
David Costelloe
KYTE
Don Shilney
J. D. Beideman
Sean Emery
Dave Eng
Brian Durbin
Jeff Lengyel
Damian Holter
Manie du Preez
Andy Melat
Teemu Nordlund
Cress Fox
Tommy Scala
Richard Kreski
Salvatore Ciano
Laura Engelman
Clae Wilson
Tim Young
David Saulmon
Joshua Svendsen
Breno Nakao
Brooks Cary
Joseph Zebrowski
Kyle Sechrest
Reid Sheldon
Alan Thompson
James Robson

Matias Ignacio
Lara Koenig
Steve Wetherell
Greg Pfaff
Jarad Geer
Rebecca Johnson
Lyz King
Denny Wright
Joe Defilippis
Aaron Kinney
Jeff Devine
Casey Harris
Tarik Ghabra
Nathaniel MacDonald
Tom Heafey
Azrael Macool
Mark Ulissi
Simon Clair
Ben Ireland
Brian Lemmon
Marc Williams
Christana Waterstreet
Cory Batts
David Starr
Kaitlyn Werner
Jason Elledge
Luke Norman
John Miller
Courtney Childs
Anthony Sgromo
Greg Ulfik
Rich Larden
Nate Arnold
Brent Donoughe
Ben Heidorn
Gerald Rice
Oliver Grünewald
Ben Heidorn
and
Mark Chun-Ting
"Chuwy" Chu

**This is by no means an inclusive list, and I hope those who
were left off will forgive me. Thank you, all of you.
Hopefully you will still be alive when I get the sequel written.**

Until then, you know where to find me:

JohnDiesattheEnd.com   Cracked.com

—DW

DON'T MISS THE SEQUEL TO
JOHN DIES AT THE END

Hilarious, terrifying, engaging and wrenching, *This Book Is Full of Spiders*, the next thrilling installment, takes us for a wild ride with two slackers from the midwest who really have better things to do with their time than prevent the apocalypse.

AVAILABLE OCTOBER 2012 WHEREVER BOOKS ARE SOLD